Jono Pech is an award-winning writer and former journalist with a background in daily newspapers. He now works as a marketing and communications adviser in Geelong, Victoria, on Australia's south-east coast, after spending a year as a media officer for a Member of Parliament. Jono's work has been published in *The Age*, *Sydney Morning Herald* and *Geelong Advertiser*. He also hosts a weekly podcast called *Puttin' In Work* between binges of video games, NBA, and Netflix sessions with his wife Hannah. *The Spy and the Maven* is Jono's first novel.

Follow the author
Twitter.com/jonohimself

~∞~

Facebook.com/thespyandthemaven
Twitter.com/spyandthemaven

THE SPY AND THE MAVEN

A NOVEL

JONO PECH

For Hannah and my amazing family.

Acknowledgements

From the bottom of my heart, I thank my Publishizer supporters and producers Andrew Hurrell, Sarah Saunders, Matt Trestrail, Ross Kinney, Dianne and Andrew Holman, Rowan Gordon, Steve and Debbie Trestrail, Aaron Lane, Alissa Millard, Dan and Naomi Pech, Dylan Tickell, Bernie and Shirley Murnane, Buddy Watson, Patrick Searles, Dan Rizzo, Emily Jemmeson, Yvonne Hurrell, Steve and Narelle Nimmo, Allen and Jan Jones, Ian and Julie Pech, Maree Whitehead, Malcolm and Lynette Pech, Michael and Lyndell Tucker, Tim Smock, Gary Hughes, Josh Cole, Chris and Liz Walters, and a guy named Matt Neal.

Without each of you, the book you're holding would just be a digital file sitting inside my wife's $489 laptop.

An epic thank you to Andrew Goldfarb (BEYOND), Colin Moriarty, Erin Bovenzi, and the Kinda Funny community.

Special shout-outs go to Jesse Cusworth, my parents Ian and Julie Pech, Trey Zink, Matt Neal (again), Hannah, and the Publishizer crew for your contributions – whether large or small, they all helped incredibly.

And finally, thank you Jesus Christ for being my irreducible minimum and the bread of life that nourishes my soul.

The Spy and the Maven

~∞~

Investigative Espionage Adventure

Chapter 1

Interrogation

Study Scarpino.

These two words were the spark that started a fierce fire. I had no idea what this email subject line referred to, but it came as a sharp jab in the ribs, catching my interest like an attractive woman in a comic book shop. It was intriguing in its simplicity, yet vague enough to demand my attention.

More than a decade of journalism experience had taught me how to tell a meaningful subject title from a total time waster. As an investigative reporter with a strong online following, my tip-offs typically range from incomprehensible babble to over-informative jargon. But just often enough, my inbox sprouts a flower amongst the weeds. Most of the subject lines are self-explanatory and some are altogether arbitrary, but even a blank heading can be enticing.

The second I read "Study Scarpino", I sensed I was about to lose myself in this story. Little did I know, in a matter of weeks it would almost literally drag me here - and I haven't got a clue where *here* is.

Long Island has been my home for about three years, but I've never been inside this building. It appears to be either a doctor's surgery or a veterinary clinic. Tonight its original function is irrelevant. I can't shake the feeling that it's merely the closest available venue for a morally-questionable interrogation.

If I sound vague, it's because I honestly don't understand what's going on. I was at home, minding my own business after a long day of digging into other people's business. Almost every night I watch Netflix alone in my oversized apartment. Cheesy dialogue fills the empty stillness of the silence on the fourth floor. I was searching the fridge for a missing avocado when a hard knock on the door took me by surprise. It startled me, but I tend to startle easily. I may or may not have shrieked – there's no way to prove it either way. Even though I hadn't buzzed anyone up from the street, I overlooked the fact that my apartment door had a peephole installed for unexpected and possibly unwanted late night visitors such as this.

At 10.12 on a Thursday night, I hoped to find my flirtatious Eurasian landlord at my apartment's entrance, perhaps coming to me with her computer troubles. Instead, I opened the door to two very scary men in black suits. They flashed some kind of government credentials, then hit me with a good deal of double-talk and agency jargon. To be honest, I was too bewildered to process anything other than what they said. They suggested I go with them and there was definitely a strong implication of violence if I didn't co-operate. It hurts to admit this, but I was naïve enough to think a government agency would play by the rules.

So here I wait, alone in this room with no answers and more questions than an over-zealous housewife who's returned to college after two dozen years of child-rearing.

The suits dumped me in this wooden chair and left me alone with my competing thoughts to just look around, marvelling at the nothingness of this room. A single fluorescent light illuminates the blank white walls. The grey linoleum floor is bare, aside from the single cheap desk in front of me. Its spotless laminate top hosts only a black porcelain mug in the corner, filled with coffee that appears to have sat untouched for hours.

I don't like unsolved mysteries, which made journalism a great career choice. Now this cold beverage is taunting me with its inert strangeness. I scratch my chin and bite my lip, pondering all the secrets of the cold coffee and what it can tell me about this scenario.

Why is it here?

Why didn't anyone drink it?

Why haven't *I* been offered a latte?

I'm convinced this coffee is not here by accident. It's a total power move and it's working better than I want to admit. Nerves like this haven't taken over since the days of waiting for a reprimand in the school principal's office. Something tells me I'll be lucky to leave this place with just a sternly written note to my mother.

A solid ten minutes passes without anyone arriving to offer a drink. Chai lattes are my beverage of choice, but even an instant blend coffee would satisfy me at this point. Yet, here I sit. Slightly parched. If the circumstances weren't so weird and messed up, I would've fallen asleep at this desk by now.

The second I consider slipping away to catch an Uber ride home, the door flies open and two more individuals in black suits approach me with the personal warmth of an Arctic breeze.

A thin, brown-skinned balding chap trails an older woman with a ponytail pulled back so tight that it nearly irons out her forehead wrinkles. Their outfits are stereotypical secret service, but that's not saying a lot. By day, they could pass for funeral parlour staff. It's the imposing body language, not to mention the whole kidnapping thing, that suggests this is something far more sinister.

"Andrew Maven." The bald agent flashes an unconvincing smile, like an overfed wolf in sheep's clothing. "Thank you for taking the time to meet with us."

"Well, I suppose you're welcome," I say. "But I don't really feel as if I had much of choice, to be honest." My directness doesn't seem to be appreciated, judging by the bald man's scowl, but I continue to ask if my captors are going to introduce themselves.

3

"I'm sorry, it doesn't work that way," Mr Bald replies.

If I'm being honest, he doesn't appear to be very sorry at all.

"All I can tell you is that we're part of a special operations agency and you have some very important information, which we'd like to discuss with you."

"Right. So you're depriving me of vital information, while asking me to share my own."

Mr Bald's vacant stare confirms this summary is correct.

"I'm sorry. If you can't even tell me who you are – what makes you think I'm going to be an open book?"

"You love this country, don't you?" Mr Bald begins pacing the room, hands behind his back as he appeals to my patriotic side. I bet he doesn't know I considered moving to Canada in the middle of last year's presidential election. "You want to... keep it safe? Protect it from harm?"

"Look, Captain America. I don't mean to be rude... but I'm going to need some identification or something before we continue."

I might come across as confident and even brash, but I assure you it's a front. Since high school, any face-to-face confrontation has made my heart race like it's taking on Usain Bolt.

I keep looking over to Ms Ponytail for some female empathy, but her silent penetrating stare only makes me even more nervous.

"Mr Maven," Mr Bald says, leaning forward into an intimidating pose. I find myself staring into his bare scalp, searching for my own reflection. It's surely the shiniest head I've ever seen up this close. "You're not in a position to be demanding anything. You have some very... sensitive information. The very fact we know this should suggest to you we're in a position of *authority* and you need to co-operate."

Of course, I have a valid retort but he doesn't give me time to do more than purse my lips.

"You've been contacted by a rogue agent, most likely going by the codename 'Mars'. The contact took place in the past few weeks and you've been investigating him ever since. Please, stop me if I'm wrong."

I'm shocked by what he knows, but I have to retaliate. I'm going to do what I always do when I'm nervous: crack wise.

"You're not wrong. You're one hundred per cent correct. I'm dazzled by your insight. You know so much about me, yet I know *nothing* about you. And that really doesn't seem fair. Can we start with a name?" I push the plastic frames up on my nose, trying almost too hard to look casual. "A Twitter handle, maybe? What's your golf handicap? Do you two co-ordinate your outfits or was it an awkward moment when you turned up in the same suit this morning?"

"This may be funny to you, but I assure you, Mr Maven... we're very serious."

"I get it – you're in character. Look. Don't take this to heart. I'm a big *Men in Black* fan. But your costumes could use some work. Get some dark Ray Bans and you're *just* about there. One accessory would make all the difference. You know what I mean?"

Ms Ponytail has had enough and curses at me, proving a) she's not the nice one, and b) she isn't a mute.

"The sooner you help us, the sooner you can leave. It's that simple." There's no denying her firmness, but she underestimates my willingness to protect my sources – not to mention my outrage at the thought of having my emails hacked.

"Maybe a coffee would sweeten the deal. I know you've got an espresso machine," I say, gesturing to the cold mug beside me. "A bite to eat would be even better. I've been craving Taco Bell lately and I wanted to fight it off, but what's the point of life if you can't enjoy a good burrito once in a while?"

"Mr Maven..."

"I'm sorry, I'm sorry. It's OK. I'm done." I hold up my hands in surrender and clear my throat, preparing to give my answer. "Now ask me what you really want to ask me. You're getting the band back together and you want me to play alto sax. Am I right? Which one is Jake and which one's Elwood?"

Ms Ponytail murmurs a resentful grunt and grabs Mr Bald for an abrupt aside near the room's entrance, only a few feet away from me. I don't even care that they're ignoring me. I've rattled their rhythm. They can't know they're intimidating me.

I should be recording this – I'm sure the whole thing is very illegal. Then again, it's not worth the trouble of having my phone confiscated and destroyed. I haven't backed up my data to the cloud for a couple of months and I don't want to lose an adorable video of Tiger Woods playing with an empty milk carton. That's my chubby Siamese cat. The real Tiger is half-Thai and named after a feline, so it seemed like the perfect name for my cat, until the sex scandals and fallout relegated his highlights from *Sports-Center* to *TMZ*.

Their conversation isn't meant for my ears, but the woman in black has made little attempt to lower her voice. I can make out a word here and there, particularly the term "jackass". Mr Bald huffs a stern response and the bass in his voice carries it a lot further than hers.

"We know Mars *trusts* him. He's got clout. Scarpino has been thorough... We have confirmation from the top."

"It just doesn't line up with his file," Ms Ponytail says in frustration.

"What's in my file?"

My new friends shoot me a synchronised glare, as if I must possess superhuman hearing to follow their conversation.

"There can't be much in my file that I haven't tweeted or mentioned on my podcast. Is the podcast in my file? Did you know we had eighty-three thousand downloads last week?"

"That's enough, Mr Maven. You need—"

"Hey, does my file happen to say—"

"Mr Maven—"

"...when my golf club membership is due? I have a feeling it's coming up soon, but I've lost the paperwork."

"Drop the act!" Mr Bald abruptly steps up to me and turns his head sideways like a drill sergeant preparing to chew out an army cadet. "We know Agent Mars has contacted you. Do you get many emails from rogue spies?"

"Hey, whatever you heard—"

"Enough!" Mr Bald pounds his fist on the table, sending tiny ripples across the surface of the cold coffee. The gesture draws my eyes to his hand and I notice his silver wristwatch is shimmering more than any I've ever seen - even shinier than his bald dome. With no real expertise or even basic knowledge about watches, the shininess of the timepiece is all I have to judge its value. In any case, this looks like a very expensive watch colliding with the table's laminate surface.

"This isn't *America's Got Talent*," Mr Bald says. I don't understand the reference, but I allow him to continue. "Quit *dancing* around the question and tell us what you know."

Oh, there it is. He made a joke. But he's not laughing. I'm confused. This endless cycle is wearing my nerves thin. For all I know, the email could've been from a criminal or terrorist and these two are just doing their jobs. I slump back in my chair, let out an exaggerated breath and promise to divulge everything I know - to be honest, it's not much. You can't betray a source you can't identify.

"I've never spoken to him, I've never seen him, he's never answered a single question of mine," I admit. "But, I can tell you what I *do* know if you'll indulge my curiosity. Who's Scarpino?"

Now he's really mad. "Scarpino!" he shouts, saliva flying in my direction. "- is the one who convinced us not to arrest you for treason. Now you're going to answer our questions, Mr Maven."

"*Treason?*"

I've never even had a parking ticket. This can't be happening. I'm smart enough to recognise this statement as a scare tactic, but it would be naïve to assume I'll get out of this without repercussions.

"Look, I... I need a lawyer. This is all so illegal. And I won't say a thing until I have some legal counsel up in here."

"I assure you. It's all perfectly legal."

"Mr Maven, this isn't about you," Ms Ponytail interjects, finally bringing a calm tone to the room. "We're presenting you with an opportunity here. You can be on the right side of history or you can go down as having aided and abetted a wanted criminal, a terrorist and an enemy of the state. How does that sound?"

My mouth gets drier with every accusation. I haven't done anything wrong, but sometimes that doesn't matter in this post-9/11 world of ours. "It sounds like something I want to avoid."

"Good," she says, grinning with the self-satisfaction of a Best Buy salesman who's convinced a customer to purchase an extended warranty. "Now, Mr Maven. Please, share what you know about the rogue agent Mars."

I wince with regret over my predicament and suck air through gritted teeth. Revealing sources is not how I've built on years of success, earning the freedom to work freelance and dictate my own terms. But technically, the little information I do have makes Mars less of a source and more of a mystery. I start explaining about the "Study Scarpino" email.

"The context was really bare. You know? It was almost cryptic. He was – assuming it's a he – avoiding certain words, clearly for fear of monitoring or censorship. And I have to say, whoever Mars is, he was probably justified. Did you hack my emails?"

"We'll tell you everything when you give us what we need," Ms Ponytail says.

I definitely don't believe her, but in this room, I feel the only choice is to play along. This is their home turf and I'm so out of my depth that I'd need the coast guard to bring me back.

Chapter 2

Position

If I'm being perfectly honest, my Long Island apartment is too big for my simple lifestyle. A good example is the fact that one room is almost empty, occupied only by "nostalgia boxes" I've never unpacked. Each of them is overflowing with junk that my younger self would never believe could one day gather dust. Cherished photos, old magazines, college relics, old concert tickets – even CDs and DVDs made redundant by the convenience of the internet. My open-plan kitchen and lounge room are entirely black and white, except for the framed movie posters and newspaper clippings covering the walls.

It's a little sad really – I have literally everything I need, but there's a certain missing factor that I can't explain. This apartment has become an appropriate metaphor for my recent success: it's more than I need and it's somewhat empty because there's no one to share it with. I'd never admit this to Tiger Woods because he's so very easily offended. The first time I kicked him off the couch he refused to look at me for two days. When it comes down to it, cats are jerks. I've always been a dog person at heart, but an unfortunate allergy has stopped me from living out my dream of becoming the heroic comic book news reporter Tintin, going on adventures with a wire-haired fox terrier. I'm sure no hero ever took their cat along for a wild escapade and didn't regret it.

The path that led me here was a road rarely travelled. The short version of the story is that my newspaper wouldn't support my effort to launch a full-scale investigation into corruption at New York City Hall. I understood their reasoning. There just weren't enough resources. Newsrooms are shrinking. Media convergence means print journalists are doing more with less, as people choose to read their news online and even on social media, often while using the bathroom. But I knew the people of New York wanted this investigation. I felt they deserved it. So I thought outside the box and launched a campaign to crowdfund the effort. I was always drawn hardest to the fact-finding and research side of journalism. As a teenager I was set on becoming a cop, but it turned out I wasn't made for police work. My grandfather was a cop, my uncle is still a detective in Grand Rapids, and I grew up obsessed with criminal investigation. Journalism and writing only became the focus when I realised I hated gun violence and I always defaulted to decisions that avoided any form of physical confrontation. Bravery in the face of violence really isn't my thing. I guess some people would consider things I've done courageous, but it's more of a "pen is mightier than the sword" type of bravery. Anyway – that's how I quit my job and began working from home.

It was the hardest decision I've ever made. But it paid off. Taking that risk became a way to blaze my own trail. Traditional news media didn't like it at all. They watched me become a cultural icon in the online world – like some kind of Robin Hood of journalism, ditching the system to truly serve the people. That definitely wasn't my intention or even the way I would describe what happened, but it became the dominant narrative and it spread like a Facebook meme. Out of nowhere, I had access to people who wouldn't even take my calls. I had so many "off-the-record" interviews that I needed a separate notepad just to keep track.

It's almost as if it was meant to be. My surname "Maven" is Hebrew for "one who understands". A Maven has become an expert through accumulating knowledge and I'm pleased to have lived up to the family name as a leader in my field.

My college buddy Tresy once told me there are two kinds of writers: the people who want to break news so they can control the narrative; and the people who respond to the news and try to contradict it the next day. It was this insight that made me realise the journalist in me not only wants to be the first person to say something, but in many instances I want to be the last person to say something.

When you're "internet famous", it's easy to get stuck inside an echo chamber of positive feedback until you start believing your own hype. The alternative is to give oxygen to the barrage of hate and cyber bullying you get from anonymous strangers by trying to please everyone. But you can't take one without the other. You either have to refuse all unsolicited criticism, good and bad, or you have to take in an equal amount of love and hate to maintain a sense of perspective on your work and identity.

When I sit back and try to evaluate all of this, I've honestly hit the career jackpot. News reporters generally don't make a lot of money, but I'd guess I'm in the top half of a per cent and most would kill for the clout I've attained. I know I landed in this position because a higher power looked favourably on me. There were too many factors involved for it to just fall together with such perfect timing. Crowdfunding that breakout investigation was the right idea, but pulling it off was only possible because I was in the right place at the right time. The right people saw it and shared it with the right audience, and the findings of my investigation were the exact result needed to attract national media attention.

The second factor in the success is that I actually *did* it. I took the chance. A lot of people have great ideas, but not many are willing to take risks to see them through. That was the catalyst to finding an audience as an individual – deciding not to be another cog in the larger machine of daily news. But with every additional ten thousand Twitter followers and every magazine cover story I see on the news stand, I can feel success pulling me away from the people who keep me grounded – childhood friends, college roommates... even my family. It's reached the point where I look at these units of success – my influence, finances, critical praise – as a burden instead of the stepladder to self-fulfilment I always sought to climb.

The crazy thing is that I always feel as though this discontent could disappear and everything could fit into place with just one or two meaningful relationships or purposeful accomplishments. This thought has become a trap I've fallen deeper into over time and I fear now that I'm too settled in the process to ever go back. No one ever goes back. I'm addicted to my own discontent. I've heard the cliché that "money is not the answer" a thousand times over the years, in church sermons, in autobiographies, and from almost anyone who has struggled with purpose after success. But I never took it as gospel. I always learn better from life experience. Disposable income won't change this feeling. As punk rocker Fat Mike once pointed out, happiness is not the by-product of precious metal-mine extracts.

"You're leaving *The Times* to freelance?"

My news editor's jaw hung open for four entire seconds when I resigned three years ago.

"I wish I could convince you to stay," she said. "But at the same time, I'm actually a bit jealous. It's a brave thing you're doing, Andrew."

The vote of confidence filled me with pride, especially coming from a close mentor and veteran of print journalism. I knew it was a risk, but I also knew it was time to break free. To this day, her next words have bounced around my head like a pinball, both motivating me and bringing me to disillusion, depending on my mood.

"One way or another, Maven – you're going to sink or you're going to soar."

Is it possible to do both? That's what I've wondered on many occasions since that day. In the past couple years, a handful of huge stories have justified my move, but I've otherwise been criticised for resting on my laurels. Guest columns and podcast advertising have paid the bills, but that kind of work wasn't why I left one of the country's largest media publications. If I try to analyse my output, it's possible the success has made me too focused on my own profile. Regardless, I need to find my next big yarn and I need it soon. My aforementioned college room-mate Tresy was kind enough to highlight this fact over the phone several weeks ago, as I frothed some milk for a chai latte.

"I keep going to your website thinking you're holding out on me, but it hasn't been updated for like a month."

"Yeah," I said, glancing at my TV, which had been paused since Tresy phoned. "I'm sort of between big stories. You got something for me?"

"How 'bout this – ask President Trump if $22.4 trillion is enough debt, or should my kids expect to pay taxes for the air they breathe?"

"Good question, but I don't know Trump. Where did you get that number from?"

"I bet you can find the White House email. You've got contacts. You knew Obama."

"I knew Obama's *chef*. There's a big difference."

"That's one degree of separation though. Ask and it will be given to you. Seek and you will find."

"That's your opinion, Tresy."

"I'm sure that's in the Bible."

I sipped my drink and tuned out to Tresy's droning diatribe on how to address the national debt ceiling. It was easy to lose focus as I faced the framed front-page articles adorning my apartment's feature wall. This collection of my favourite newspaper articles in recent years includes the council scandal, the drug ring I exposed, and my feature on federal government corruption. I've done my best work from home as a freelancer, but I do miss the newsroom. I miss the camaraderie, the thrill of the deadline, the arguments and discussion. Even the bad coffee, the fluorescent lighting, the constant sound of ringing phones, and the ridiculous feedback from our angry but passionate readers. I wish I knew back then, as the editorial department shrank and jobs moved offshore, that one day I'd be nostalgic for the daily cycle of chaos. Workplace banter has been replaced with Twitter notifications and YouTube comments.

"I've got this idea for a light-hearted piece – finding people with the same names as giant celebrities," I told Tresy.

"That could be kinda funny. Doesn't sound very hard-hitting, though."

"It's not. But it'll be fun. Think about it. There's a reasonable chance that somewhere in America lives a middle-aged man, perhaps a janitor, a taxi driver, maybe even a cop, named Justin Bieber."

"Oh yeah."

"For thirty or forty years, this name fit him like a glove. And now he's been superseded by a punk kid with an amazing voice, a lot of luck and too much money. Now Justin Bieber the janitor wants to be Bobby Baxter or Steve Smith or Johnny Gooch. But he can't let the pop star win. He just can't. So instead, he drinks and he tries to forget."

"You're a strange unit, Maven."

"I mean, I would read that article."

"While we're pitching stuff, I had the best idea for greeting cards. It really is a great idea. I mean, I could make money off this, somehow, I just know. It hasn't been done."

"Well, what is it?" I'm yet to hear a good idea from Tresy, but greeting cards? I was intrigued.

"OK. So it's somebody's birthday, or maybe a bon voyage party, their anniversary – whatever. You get them a card. And you never know what to write."

"I don't?"

"Well, people who aren't writers."

"Isn't that why they make the cards with messages written inside already?"

"Exactly. But it's always some bullcrap thing like 'All the best, hope it's a special day, and yada yada yada'. No one wants anyone to think they can't write their own message. So my idea is that you get the card and it comes with a bit of paper, a little inspirational message. You with me?"

"I think so."

"You take the personal and the poetic message and scribble it out in your own handwriting. Cha-ching."

"That is... actually a good idea, Tresy."

"I know, right?"

"But it raises some ethical questions – it's like plagiarising song lyrics for a love letter. If they aren't your own words, do they carry any meaning at all? Will people pay money to knowingly mislead their loved ones? D'ya know what I mean?"

"Yeah, I get you. But that's a problem for the marketing department to deal with."

"Spoken like a true ethicist."

As I said goodbye, I found myself unable to move on from Tresy's earlier statements. It hurts to say, but he was right on the money. Not about the greeting cards. If that could've worked, it would've been done by now. But I'm afraid he was right about my lack of recent productivity. His tone alone told me he thought my story idea was lame. I just needed something hard-hitting – a real home run. I sat down at my laptop to sort through my inbox and saw an email that had been sitting there for about twenty minutes, unopened, waiting patiently like a Pandora's box ready to change my life forever.

Study Scarpino.

Chapter 3

Proposition

Who is Scarpino? A Bond villain, maybe? The first lines of the email only amplified my instant intrigue:

I heard your interview with the senator. Everything you think you know about this country is fumes and reflections, designed to medicate and mislead.

Do you want to be right or do you just want to know the truth?

Pull the thread and a Metric ton will come undone.

Study Scarpino. We'll meet soon

Psycho-babble or a guarded tip-off? My inbox has seen everything on the spectrum between conspiracy nonsense and legitimate news tips, but I've never had to decode a message this cryptic. It's almost as if they're taunting me, trying to lure me into an investigation. If it wasn't for referencing the podcast I record in my spare bedroom, I'd have written this off as a spam message because the email address itself was complete gibberish. The general vagueness fascinated me more than anything, so I responded, simply asking who the sender was and what he was talking about. To my surprise, a response came back in less than ten minutes.

Uncle Sam has an itchy palm and you're the one to put him in cuffs.

I can tell you everything you need to know but first you have to study Scarpino. The trail begins and ends in Manhattan.

Join the club, Maven. Stay the night. Find the one-winged angel, find life on Mars.

And that was two or three weeks ago. Since then, on and off, I've been trying to figure out what the heck it all meant. On a wild hunch, I filed some Freedom of Information Act applications, but nothing fruitful came back to my desk. There's been no more response from Mars and I've found not a single lead – at least until those two fellas in suits brought me to this room for a pop quiz.

~∞~

Now I've told Ms Ponytail and Mr Bald everything I know, which admittedly isn't much. I look up at the duo hovering over me, feeling the anticipation of a game show contestant waiting to hear whether my response is acceptable and I get to go home with a new car or a kick in the pants. I get the sense that Ms Ponytail hasn't broken eye contact this whole time.

"You're sure that's how it happened? Your first contact was that day?"

"Yeah, that's what I said. I remember it vividly. You know, most people my age only call their friends on the phone when something terrible has happened. So when Tresy called, I thought maybe there was a car accident or something."

"What specifics were mentioned? In the email."

"I've told you word for word the entire thing. Manhattan was the only detail and it doesn't really help."

She looks disappointed by my response. I suppose this means they didn't hack my account. That's a relief. Some combination of the email's words in my search history must have set off alarm bells and led them to me, which is an outrage in itself, but right now I don't have time to debate the finer details of the USA Freedom Act's citizen surveillance.

The duo of suits huddles again, this time further in the corner of the room where I can't hear their hushed conversation. I've been very co-operative and a little validation would really put me at ease. Perhaps these guys aren't so bad after all. Maybe I'll get a medal for this.

Yeah, right. If anything I do contributes to stopping this terrorist, I just know I'll be left standing to the side like Chewbacca at the end of *Star Wars*, wailing as Han and Luke take all the credit for destroying the Death Star.

I wonder how long I'll have to wait before I write or talk about this whole experience without getting audited to hell. As her male counterpart leaves the room, Ms Ponytail approaches me with a real-life smile stretched across her face.

"Mr Maven, we thank you for your co-operation. It's been... well, interesting."

"It's been something, all right."

"There's more. We don't just want your information. We want to send you into the field to make contact."

"Uh... huh." My wide eyes and gaping jaw must give away my true feelings because she goes on to address the lingering question.

"I won't lie. It will be dangerous. But you'll be compensated. And we can make sure you have a certain level of clearance access to information that will aid your ongoing research."

The overwhelming sense that this could be my life's best or worst decision consumes my entire body. Oxygen fills my lungs after a brief moment of shock, shifting my attention to my weak knees and the fact that I have nowhere to run, even if I could.

"On a scale from one to ten, exactly how dangerous is this going to be?"

"One to ten?"

"Yeah. Is it dangerous like reheating a chicken burrito after a week in the fridge? Or are we talking dangerous like being a Republican in San Francisco?"

"Somewhere in the middle."

Wow, not even a chuckle. But now I have real questions.

"Are you really sure I'm capable? I mean, guys with glasses are never good in fights. I have no combat experience, no weapons training. I did a triathlon one time... But these days, you know, my back does this crazy pulsing thing when I try to—"

Ms Ponytail cuts me off, more out of impatience than anything else. "You'll be under direct supervision from one of the finest and most experienced agents we've ever had. He is extremely motivated and has a strong incentive to locate the runaway target, whether he's here in New York or somewhere abroad. You'll find him together. Then I'm sure you'll come up with a scoop that'll sell more than a few newspapers."

It's more about the clicks and "time on page" these days, but I take her point. I run my shaking hand through my hair, then crack my knuckles on the back of my cranium as I consider my options.

They've given me a choice, although the decision feels like it was made long ago. In my view, which is admittedly shrouded under this immense pressure, I can pick from the following scenarios:

1. Throw my chair against the wall, run for the hills, and hope to God that I'm not gunned down. I go on to live in constant fear that someone cuts my car's brake lines, or beats me to death with a phone book as I sleep.

2. Lie. I could make up some story about agoraphobia, how I can't leave the house for more than twenty minutes without freaking out. Unfortunately, that would place me about forty-five minutes overdue for a tantrum or nervous breakdown. This would also be unethical and against my upbringing. Should it turn out I could have helped prevent a national disaster, the guilt would be overburdening and my mother would be very disappointed in me. She wouldn't tell me this, but I would know it.

3. Do as I'm told, accept the mission and hope it works out for the best. This has the broadest spectrum of win/lose potential.

The worst-case scenario would see me killed by a rebel spy called Mars, who I can only assume is named after the Greek god of war. The best-case scenario? I'm instrumental in a plot to halt a psychotic terrorist and I get to both write and participate in the story of the year. My news sense tells me this case will make for a ripping-good yarn. Could I possibly forgive myself for passing that up? This could be my very own *Serial* or *S-Town*, handed over on a silver platter. Then I get to write a tell-all novel of the whole experience, and there would be documentaries, maybe even a movie about me. I'd be played by someone far more attractive – like James Franco's little brother, or maybe Ben Affleck's little brother.

"Sign me up," I say, lightly pounding the table with my fist. "But on one condition. While I'm gone, you have to promise me that someone will feed my cat."

Chapter 4

Destination

It's another overcast morning on Long Island, but the vanilla sky does nothing to taper my excitement. Here I am, outside my home, bag packed, not knowing if I'll be gone for a day or a month. I must admit, as frightening as it sounds, being invited to be part of this operation is a true thrill. I've always shared that somewhat universal feeling that my life held a greater purpose, that I was meant for more than this.

Don't get me wrong – my work is important. I've made a lot of people mad by telling the truth. I've cost bad people a lot of money and I've saved innocent people from being ripped off and even hurt. But this here, this is a chance to be responsible for saving lives. This newfound direction could be just what I've needed. This is James Bond sidekick material. I could be the next Q!

My daydreaming ends abruptly as Mr Bald, who is far less imposing in the light of day, introduces me to my very own 007. The word "experienced" echoes in my ear, as I evaluate whether or not Agent Rust looks qualified to be my protector. He very well could have been bred for action. If my personal safety has to rest in the hands of a stranger, something tells me this is the guy I want in my corner.

I reach out for a handshake, but immediately regret it. The cartilage of my fingers screams for life inside Rust's calloused coal miner's grip. His plain black polo shirt struggles to cover his biceps, which push the cotton's elasticity to its limit. His flexing forearm reminds me of a Christmas ham. As he shakes my hand, I look down and notice his veins protruding like a blood bank nurse's dream. This is an overly detailed description, I know, but it's not every day you meet a secret agent.

"Andrew Maven," I manage to wheeze, realising I've been holding my breath as my hand suffocates inside his vice grip.

"Rust," he grunts back. "If you're ready..."

Hopefully speaking in half sentences isn't one of his habits, but for now I can take the hint. I throw my bag on the back seat of his black Cadillac Escalade and ignore every childhood safety warning about riding in cars with strangers.

"So, 'Rust'. Is that a first name, last name?"

"Codename."

"Oh. Cool."

I wait a minute or two for Rust to initiate conversation, but he doesn't so much as breathe in my direction.

"See this guy in the hat?" I point to a man crossing the street as we wait at a red light. "That's my barber. He calls me 'Tommy' every time I see him. I've been going there for four years."

"Hm."

"But my name's Andrew, you see. So it's... yeah. Anyway."

My attempts to engage in banter, or even to fill the silence, are fruitless. No music, Rust tells me. No radio either. The ride into Manhattan should take a little under an hour today, but it will feel a lot longer if we're not going to speak.

Our destination is the island's newest high-rise hotel, where our objective is to search for any traces of Agent Mars. I've never been anywhere near the Commonwealth Manhattan Club Hotel, but this agency has acquired a media pass for today's official open-ing. This feels like a tenuous lead to me, based on Mars' email telling me to "join the club." I thought a rogue spy would be a little more cryptic than this, but I'm not privy to the inside intelligence Rust's agency holds. The hotel's owner Kenton Moriarty is notorious for his shifty operations. They must think housing a wanted criminal is right in his wheelhouse.

Moriarty made his fortune the same way every property owner in New York did – he inherited it. His father was a powerful political figure in American labour unions. As a Chicago native, he invested in Manhattan real estate during the early '90s, right before New York turned from the cesspool of America into the greatest city on earth. My uncle Leo worked in east coast construction management for a good while and any time the news mentioned the unions he'd say the same thing: "Never trust a Moriarty." I never knew any Moriartys, so I'd just nod and go back to playing with my G.I. Joes.

"Nervous?" Rust breaks fifteen minutes of awkward silence with this word that makes my stomach turn. I don't know if it's the quiet or my pale complexion that helps him deduct that my discomfort level is turned up to eleven.

"A little." I pride myself on my honesty, but this confession is an embarrassing one. It's a total understatement. "I mean, I'm just doing what I've always done. I'm going to a public event to ask famous people a few questions."

"This isn't your typical soiree. You'll be extracting classified information, transmitting audio, wearing a vest, and carrying a piece."

"A gun?" I gasp, hoping Rust can sense the horror in my voice. "I'm not shooting anyone. Wait, am I going to be shot?"

"Relax, kid." Rust almost sounds disgusted by my response, speaking through gritted teeth as though every statement is a reluctant compromise. "It's self-defence."

"From what?"

"We're up against a rebel agent here. I understand you're a civilian, but whether or not you trust him, there's no intel on the company he's keeping or what he's trying to accomplish, other than bringing everyone down with him."

"You're telling the story. I honestly don't know what he's threatening to do, but you guys are taking it very seriously. It kind of freaks me out."

Rust speaks with a low, gruff timbre, which I can only ima-gine formed over many years smoking cigarettes with a diet of gravel soup.

"You don't need to know what's at stake to know this has the potential to be life and death."

"I get that, but I'm not exactly comfortable walking into a party with a handgun in the middle of New York City – you know what I mean?"

"Fine," he grunts. "Have it your way. It's your safety at risk."

"Where are you in all this? Aren't you supposed to be the brawn?"

"I'll be listening from inside the building, giving you instruc-tions to gain the intelligence."

"So you're the brains and the brawn. What am I?"

"You're the bait. But if you need me, I'll be there."

"That's comforting." This comes across sarcastic, but I genu-inely feel like I can put my trust in this guy. I've read about hyper-sensitive disorders and Rust fits the bill. I imagine he'd have an intense inner monologue, constantly processing his surroundings. If he's the rule and not the exception, it's safe to assume the cha-rismatic image of a martini-sipping, poker-playing undercover spy is a mere Hollywood fantasy. I suspect his tactical approach is to remain unseen and unheard altogether. Appearance doesn't seem to concern Rust either. His salt and peppered hair is shaved down to a single inch and a clear lack of medical treatment has left almost half his left eyebrow scarred and hairless. Another scar, thin but long, marks the upper corner of his forehead, only an inch below his hairline. His rugged jaw is carved like a Baldwin brother, despite the decades of outdoor activity that have marked his weathered face. I imagine his nose has been broken several times over, but it's always possible he was just born that way.

"Quit staring at me," Rust barks, revealing an unmatched peripheral vision as he negotiates the New York traffic.

"Sorry."

The yellow cabs fly by like stars past the Millenium Falcon as we enter the Queens Midtown Tunnel into Manhattan. Rust drives as one with the road, the traffic bending to his will. I need to see if I can get into the same driver-training course. I wonder what else agents learn in spy school. Do they teach you high-stakes poker? Jet ski classes? Is there a seduction school?

As I daydream about Rust's education, I recall the vagueness of my briefing from Ms Ponytail, which failed to clarify exactly who was giving me these orders. Her explanation was either too complicated to comprehend fully or deliberately encoded with jargon and confusing double-talk. It was like struggling to understand lyrics that don't seem to make any sense, so you can only assume you've misheard them. I really should've asked for it in writing, for my news reporting if nothing else. Keeping these details more or less classified must be a strategic policy for working with civilians.

"So do you really think this Mars guy is as bad as they say?" I ask Rust. I have no real reason to doubt Mr Bald and Ms Ponytail, but I'd like to hear his perspective.

"He's a traitor. That's all that matters."

"But in and of itself, going AWOL doesn't make someone a traitor. Even that's no reason to go full hog, right? There must be an imminent threat."

"That's the thing about rogues. They're capable of so much, but you never know what they're willing to do. They get disgruntled with the system, the process, they get all kinds of ideas. Maybe they start to sympathise with the people we're up against. They know enough to attract a following and then you've got a real mess on your hands."

"So is it, like, terrorism, insurgence, other kinds of havoc?"

"Potentially all of the above. But we don't know. For the sake of your co-operation, just know that it could be even worse. The boy's a time bomb."

"Right. Are we talking *The Anarchist's Cookbook* here?"

"Not quite. It's more about what he's capable of... considering his training and the ideas he has."

"Which are...?"

"That everyone is out to get him. That everyone is in on it. We're the bad guys."

"Based on what?"

"That's what I don't understand."

"Maybe I can find out."

"It doesn't matter. Once we bring him in, I'll be able to talk some sense into him."

"You two have a relationship?"

"You could say that."

After meeting and interviewing so many people with varied backgrounds and experiences, I feel I can accurately judge particular qualities in a person. Rust speaks as if he has no time to be anything but direct. No pleases and no thank yous. There's no room for pleasantries on the battlefield. His quiet demeanour, his curmudgeon act and the years of harsh experiences I read in his face tell me he's carrying the weight of several terrible tragedies. His tired eyes bear the pain of betrayal, or perhaps I'm just seeing the burden of a chaotic life spent as a typical secret agent assassin spy. Both possibilities are intriguing. I want – no, I *need* to find out more about him.

"So, how long have you been doing this?"

"Driving?"

"No, the... tactical espionage."

"This is more of a clandestine operation," Rust corrects me, eyes locked on the road. "We want to get in and out without anyone even knowing about it."

"Right. So, the bald guy and ponytail lady said I could report on this. That means I need to take notes. You OK with that?"

"If I say it, you can report it."

This response surprises me. It's a little alarming because it suggests he has very little to say. I pull a pen and notepad out from my satchel and make note of the date.

"I think they said you're their most experienced agent?"

"Must be. I've probably been working as long as you've been alive." This is hard to believe, based on his appearance, but I guess he's older than he looks. I'm thirty-three, which puts him at least in his early or mid-fifties.

"You know, I've always wondered: What's the career progression for someone like you? Armed forces, CIA case officer, field operative, then... whatever this is now? Special ops? Secret spy service?"

"Something like that." This appears to be his final answer, even as I patiently wait for more. "It's classified."

"Sure. I get that. But, you know, they didn't tell me a thing. And I think you've gotta trust me enough to tell me who I'm working for. If I'm going to be your co-pilot on this mission..."

"Co-pilot? Really?"

Rust scowls and I regret the phrasing instantly. I'm too experienced to let him intimidate me or make me feel sheepish.

"Look, you probably know everything about me. Can I at least get the basics? Who I'm working for. Their general purpose?"

"That's fair."

"It is?" His concession catches me off-guard.

"I know what it's like to be left in the dark, so I'll tell you this in plain English. But you can't use this for material. No questions and none of this gets out."

I nod, flip my notebook closed and let him continue.

"Metric started as a special black ops offshoot of the CIA's Special Activities Division. It's now become wholly independent, taking on only the most dangerous and classified operations on US soil and abroad."

"So there's an even more secretive version of America's most secretive government agency?"

"Correct."

That explains why Mars' email capitalised the word 'Metric'. It's a small detail, but when you're as obsessive about grammar as I am, you notice these things. I wonder what other clues he hid in there.

"It's relatively small," Rust continues. "There's only a dozen or so field operatives we call agents. This means focused operations, interagency intelligence access and no paper trails. No questions asked. No logo. No website. No Facebook, chat snaps or

Twitter-grams."

"Got it," I nod, ignoring Rust's accidentally made-up social media networks.

"And that's all you need to know."

"So Metric is kinda like *Marvel's Agents of S.H.I.E.L.D.*"

"Hm." The lack of response indicates Rust doesn't get the reference, which is a relief because I realise now that S.H.I.E.L.D. bears no resemblance to his description of Metric. I'd have to revoke one of my nerd cards if I were caught out on this.

"I think I've heard about these units," I say, as I trawl my memory. "The Special Operations Division had a handful of agency officers in, like, a team unit they called 'the Shop'. Lock pickers, hackers, safecrackers, tech heads and all of that. Like an *Ocean's Eleven* of secret agents."

"I can't confirm or deny that," Rust mumbles, most likely missing the reference again. "But the difference is, you've heard about the Shop. I know you've never heard of Metric. It's not a team – it's a division, each agent working independently with orders from the top. Half of us don't even know each other."

"Yeah, I've never read or heard *a thing* about Metric."

"The people who know Metric know you don't talk about Metric."

"So it's like *Fight Club*."

"Hm. Never heard of *that*."

That's zero out of three. This confirms Rust doesn't read books and comics, or watch TV and movies. He's like a machine. I'd compare him to the Terminator but it would be a waste of my time.

~∞~

We pull into the parking garage of the Commonwealth Manhattan Club Hotel, bypassing the valet service out front. I've done this before to avoid an unnecessary tip, but Rust has far too much precious equipment stored here to allow civilians near his unusual luggage. It's quite funny seeing him interact with the hotel staff – there must be five separate bell boys offering to carry his bags as we make our way to the eighth floor. Each of them leaves disappointed by his growls and monosyllabic refusal.

Our hotel room is immaculate but ordinary for such an expensive building. There's nothing wrong with it, but I expected more. I wanted velvet carpet or a chandelier or something.

"There's only one bed," I state, fishing for an explanation. I haven't shared a bed with a grown man since this one college party with my buddy Tresy, and even then, we slept head to foot to avoid accidental spooning.

"We're not staying, kid." Rust drops his bags on the bed with the same sense of purpose that guides his every action. He turns the dials on his locked black briefcase until it pops open, revealing a plethora of gadgets and small containers. "My guess is we won't be welcome by the time we're done here."

"That's what I was afraid of."

Rust unzips a black pouch and tips it over into his hand. Turning to me, he holds up its contents – two tiny objects that could be halves of a small plastic cashew.

"This is our in-ear comms device. It's called the Nano GEAR."

"Nano GEAR..."

"Guarded Ear."

"Nanocommunications. Now we're talking."

Rust installs the device into his ear, explaining that it becomes virtually invisible to the naked eye. "Inductive digital audio, noise cancellation, one hundred decibel range of sensitivity. The Nano GEAR is waterproof, shatterproof, idiot proof. It has a built-in GPS tracker, microphone and AI system."

"Wow. Is that all?"

"You shouldn't need it, but it will automatically translate up to seventeen languages close to real-time, converting the audio into digital data."

I tuck it in, mimicking Rust's instructions, deep inside my ear. I'm surprised how well it clings to my ear, due to its detailed exterior design. I don't even want to know how much these things are worth. Knowing my luck, mine will fall out and roll down a drain or something.

"What's the range on this bad boy?"

"Limitless. It's a digital transmission, but there's also a local comms radius of twelve miles."

"Meaning?"

"Anyone with the same tech is automatically wired into our open audio channel. You can hear me, I can hear you – no frequency tuning necessary." Rust returns to his bag of goodies as he preps me for the rest of the mission. "In the unlikely event that we get separated beyond that distance, my private channel is 140.85. You're gonna be on 89.7. Just say 'Nano GEAR channel' as a voice command to activate the tuning feature – got that?"

"Let me write that down. Should I take your phone number too, just in case?"

Rust doesn't scoff but I can tell he wants to. "We don't use cell phones. Too susceptible to security breach. You're in the news. You know about the hacks."

"OK... I thought you'd have some high-tech smartphone, maybe a wristwatch. Like Dick Tracy."

"Not for me. Intel is always available via the built-in AI."

"I hope your artificial intelligence can beat Siri, 'cause she's getting pretty smart these days."

"You won't need to use it."

"Right. So it's true?" I'm hoping the flow of the conversation will trick Rust into revealing something he probably shouldn't. "The CIA, NSA are always listening? You know, they can activate the microphones on our cell phones and all that jazz?"

"No comment."

I walk over to the mirror to check out my Nano GEAR and I'm taken aback by how inconspicuous it is. I also notice that I neglected to consider the importance of stealth when I dressed this morning. I'm definitely more of a hoodie and sweatshirt guy, but about four years ago I bought this salmon knitted sweater and almost immediately regretted it. It only gets worn out of obligation – I just can't bear to admit that I've paid for something that will go to waste, even though I've grown to detest it. Every time I wear it I hope it gets ruined. Salmon. What was I thinking?

"What does he look like?" I ask, still marvelling at the Nano

GEAR. "Agent Mars."

In the mirror's reflection I see Rust staring out the window across the city, deep in thought. There's a fair chance he's systematically conjuring up his plan of attack for the afternoon.

"He looks like me. But younger. Twenty-eight years old. Fit... But he'll see you before you see him."

"Well, what's the plan if he isn't there? Or if Kent Moriarty won't tell us anything?"

"That's when I get involved. Moriarty's likely familiar with you, which will allow me to get close without raising suspicion. And I can be very convincing."

"What, are you going to dangle him from the top floor window?"

Rust pouts and raises an eyebrow, impressed with the suggestion, despite my sarcastic tone. "That works."

"Oh boy." I'm starting to feel nauseous. I'm not ready for this, not at all, and I'll need to psyche myself up for the possibility of violence. "Can you promise me something, in this little caper?"

Rust turns to me as if he can't wait to shoot down my request.

"It's the gun."

"What about it?" The pros and cons of gun control aren't topics we should be discussing, but I need to bring this up.

"To be honest, and I know this is your thing, but I'm uncomfortable with it. I mean, there's so much that could go wrong. I bet you're good enough to get the job done without guns. Can't you use tranquilliser darts or something non-lethal?"

"A tranq gun?" Rust smirks, as if I suggested using a marshmallow launcher. "Anaesthetists study for years to administer the precise level of immobilising agents required to knock a patient out safely. If you're shooting that junk into someone's neck with a gun, they'll either shake it off or they'll die from an overdose."

"OK. What about tasers?"

"A taser is one shot, short-range – not exactly ideal for my line of work."

"Right. Then at least, with your gun, just... *please* don't use it unless you absolutely have to. I know you're experienced. You seem like a total badass. Is that a fair assessment?"

"That's a very fair assessment."

"And I'm guessing you know how to handle yourself without shooting up the place. Just consider it a challenge – you know what I mean? Like when Larry Bird played a whole basketball game left-handed."

Rust squints slightly, throwing the idea around until he nods with acceptance. Yes. I believe I've successfully manipulated him into attempting non-lethal violence.

"I can do that," he says. "But I'm here to protect you and get the job done. If there's ever any real danger, the guns are out and your escapade comes to an end."

"Really? Thank you. I appreciate it. Honestly."

"Just tell me," Rust examines my outfit, finally revealing a semblance of curiosity. "What's with the pink sweater? Is this considered fashion nowadays?"

Did I mention I hate this sweater?

"It's not pink," I protest. "It's salmon."

"Salmon?"

"Salmon. Like the fish."

Rust scrunches up his face. He clearly doesn't believe in salmon. He rejects salmon as a colour.

"It's pink, kid."

"I'm noticing this 'kid' thing is popping up a lot. Is that one of your things? Aren't I a bit old for that?" Rust gives a smirk of disinterest and I continue my objection. "I feel like I'm almost old enough to call a young adult 'kid' – you know what I mean? I've got a lot of grey hairs starting to come through."

Rust ignores my question altogether, which I'll chalk up as a loss. "Kid", it is. I accept the condescending nickname and peer out the same wide window that occupied Rust's attention moments ago. There's an exhaustion that comes from simply living and working in New York City, but the same hustle and bustle always makes Manhattan a sight to behold. It really is the city that never sleeps. The buildings, the people... There's always something new to observe. Our eighth-storey view is low enough that pedestrians still look like people, but it's high enough that you have to imagine their expressions, their motivations, their moods.

It reminds me of when I was young and we'd go camping at Lake Michigan. There was a United Methodist camp site with plenty to do, but when the other kids went off to play, I'd stay behind and just enjoy the quiet. I'd look across to other lakeside camp sites in the distance and I'd imagine what people were saying to each other and what was happening in their lives. It was so serene. I'd wander off and find quiet places where I could play alone. It sounds weird, but I remember sitting by a stream and feeling like the woods were whispering to me, telling me secrets. Manhattan, though... This city is constantly yelling. At the very least, it's grumbling like a disgruntled foodie trying to send a steak back to the kitchen. It can be alienating sometimes. I've lived in either Queens or Long Island for seven years and even I feel like a tourist in Manhattan. But right now from this height, behind the glass, everything is quiet below. I draw a long breath and take in this peaceful moment, predicting it could be my last for some time.

"A penny for your thoughts?" Rust asks, stirring me out of my daze.

"A lot of things."

"Hm. If you really want to wear pink, it's OK. I'm more open-minded than I look."

"It's salmon."

Rust shakes his head, unable to accept my stance on the matter. In his world of black and white, with no shades of grey, it's no wonder he sees no distinction between pink and salmon.

Chapter 5

Investigation

At eighty-two storeys and nine hundred and twenty feet, the Commonwealth Manhattan Club Hotel is now the twelfth tallest building in New York and certainly the tallest hotel. It's become the crown jewel of Kenton Moriarty's real estate empire and his first foray into tourism and hospitality. Just like his old man, Moriarty is an opportunist. He was wise to invest in New York while it was down, believing it would bounce back in good time. In the first three years after 9/11, Moriarty bought real estate anywhere he could. Prices were low – especially space at the top of buildings downtown where businesses were reluctant to invest. It seems ridiculous now, but there were legitimate fears that the economy would never recover. Within ten years those rational fears were shown to be unjustified, as Lower Manhattan's population almost doubled, along with Moriarty's portfolio and net worth.

"I heard Obama's coming today."

"*He's not,*" Rust's voice rings in my earpiece.

It's time to join the party downstairs. I'm alone in the elevator, testing out my new communication toy. The audio is crystal clear, as if Rust has shrivelled down, *Honey, I Shrunk The Kids*-style, and set up camp inside my eardrum. He'll stay in our hotel room, providing support and direction as I work the party. I don't need any old dudes cramping my style. I can do that all on my own. Plus, if I really need him, he can join me as my "photographer".

"What about Trump, keeping tabs on his real estate rival?"

"No presidents, past or present. Stay focused, kid."

"I'm sorry," I mutter. "I'm just nervous. Can we talk about our plan? I'd be more relaxed if we could talk over the plan. I want it to... I want to be prepared – you know what I mean?"

The elevator stops at the ground floor and I step out into the vast lobby. I wander around until I realise I've travelled too far – the function room is up a floor, accessible via a dark marble spiral staircase, rising above the centre of the lobby.

"The plan is to find Agent Mars. Find Moriarty, you find Mars."

"How though?"

"You'll question him, find out what he knows and take any clues that lead to Mars."

"Right. I have to say, it's not much of a plan. I'm a journo, not a detective. I can investigate, but I usually have some research to back me up."

It's curious that no one finds it odd to see a grown man seemingly talking to himself in public. Everyone is so accustomed to Bluetooth headsets and hands-free phones that I'm just another inconsiderate lout with no shame and no sense of personal space.

"I've seen your file, kid. You're capable."

"What's in my file?"

"A lot things."

"What is there that you can tell me? Anything that I wouldn't just freely admit?"

"Not really. You come from a good family. You work hard. You're a good person. You understand God and all of that."

"Most of the time."

"Plus, this right here is all we have right now. If we have to, we'll improvise."

"Right. I'll improv like the late and great Robin Williams."

"If you need me to come down, you can choose an expression or code word."

"Oh yeah. That sounds fun." I struggle up the final stairs with the stomp of a Clydesdale, exposing my current level of fitness. "How about 'These pretzels are making me thirsty'? That'll work."

"*Sure.*"

"It's a *Seinfeld* thing. But hey, then if there are pretzels, and they do make me thirsty..."

"*Just... try to keep a low profile. And try not to screw this up.*"

"Low pro. Don't screw up. Got it."

I step through a wide set of doors leading into the function room. Its grandiose layout blows my mind. Clearly this feature was the focus of the hotel's architects, making the elaborate lobby design modest by comparison. A crystal chandelier the size of my living room towers from the high ceiling. If I look over my glasses, in my blurred vision it resembles a hovering UFO ready to take party-goers back to the mother ship. At centre stage a smooth jazz band is in full swing, with a backdrop of Moriarty's smug mug on a giant banner. The "old money" billionaire's unmistakable face must be fifteen feet high for everyone to see. Violent people might describe Moriarty as "punchable". His permanent look of self-satisfaction punctuates a think-lipped smile, underlining horn-rimmed glasses and a thin, pointed nose.

I hesitate to throw around the word "punchable" because I know how it feels to be described that way. I try not to read the comments sections online, but my buddy Tresy tells me it started when Buzzfeed ran a feature on me with the headline "Andrew Maven is pretty much famous on the internet". The trolls have badmouthed me in blog posts and tweets for a couple of years, but I can't help that my regular smile is sometimes interpreted as smug. The difference between Moriarty and me is that he's always had a reason to be smug, but I've looked this way long before I had any semblance of professional triumph.

"Your name, sir?" A perky young woman sits at the room's entry station, ready to scan her alphabetical sheet of invitees.

"Andrew Maven. I have a press pass." I fumble my pockets for the media lanyard Metric was able to secure.

"OK, let me just..."

"That's a lot of guests," I say as she turns the pages.

"Yeah, it's a big day for us. OK, here it is, sir."

She hands me a name tag and flashes a polite cheesy smile, pointing me further inside the room as a queue starts to form behind me. Instinctively, I grin back at her, until I step away and see my listed credentials.

ANDREW MAVEN
The Times

I haven't worked at *The Times* in years, but I suppose "Freelance/podcaster" doesn't have the same ring to it. Instead of pinning the name tag to my chest, I drop it into the depths of my pocket. It's probably best to stay incognito as much as possible. I run my eyes across the room. The royal blue carpet beneath my feet is barely visible through the thick crowd and dispersed tables of hors d'oeuvres, champagne, Pinot noir and other French-sounding culinary delights. I watch the wait staff buzz around busier than bees, serving groups of New York's elite. Brimming with positive vibes and shining eyes, they offer trays of delicate treats and individual dipping sauces. I always feel bad turning them away, even if it's an appetiser I can't stand. I just can't shake the feeling that they'll take it personally.

There's a different vibe here today, compared to the classy events I've attended in the past. Everyone is dressed to impress, but of course, no one wants to admit they are actually impressed. There are senators, socialites, CEOs, councillors, and board directors from hospitals, tourism groups, colleges and a whole bunch of service authorities – the type of people who can afford to attend a party at 2.30pm on a Friday, drink champagne and not have to worry about going back to work until Monday morning. Then there are the journos, making the most of the free food. You can always count on a reporter to find something for free, whether it's a Biro or a plate of scones. Given the growing nature of citizen journalism and accessibility of online content, free stuff is one of the few remaining perks for reporters attending live news events.

Speaking of journalists, I need to prepare questions in my head so I can extract what I want from Moriarty. These situations are akin to capturing a creature intelligent enough to disable any man-made snares. I need to outsmart someone who's smart enough to know I'm trying to outsmart him. The toughest interviews take a "trial and error" approach, ignoring social instincts in favour of disciplined questioning. It's often hit or miss until you stumble across a query that catches the subject off-guard. Once they reveal something they didn't want you to hear, they'll try too hard to substantiate or to clarify. That's when you've got them. My method works almost every time – as long as I can keep them long enough to reach this point. The more elusive the subject, the harder it is – especially these days when politicians and executives are taught to run circles around journalists.

"*Having fun, Maven?*" Rust is as grumpy as Harrison Ford on a talk show.

"Are you watching the security cameras as well, now?"

"*Just get to work.*"

As I scan the room for Moriarty, I wonder if Rust can hear me munching on these delicious golden arancini balls. The deep-fried snacks are rolled with rice, mozzarella and a rich pasta sauce, stuffed into bread crumbs of happiness. I hear someone nearby refer to them as a "pleasure explosion" and it's hard to disagree. I could probably eat half a dozen if the crowd nearby wasn't starting to murmur and turn the same direction, like ducks in a pond at feeding time.

Moriarty is in the building.

I catch a glimpse through the moving cluster of guests before he disappears. Planning ahead, I search the room for familiar faces he could be trying to find. There's a few I recognise from my days at *The Times* and plenty I know from TV or newspapers. There are even some people I met at a recent celebrity golf tournament out at the Ferry Point club. I use the term "celebrity" *very* loosely. The organisers heard about my 7.2 handicap and obviously couldn't get Bill Murray to return their calls. I played well, despite being a little wayward on the fairways.

I make my way through the crowd until Moriarty is within spitting distance. I watch him, studying his mannerisms and inter-actions with guests. I chuckle at the way he listens during conver-sation, as though he's merely waiting for people to finish talking so he can be the centre of attention again.

If he looked across he'd see me peering through my glasses, trying to catch his eye, but he's just too busy gushing about the hotel to anyone who will listen. Right now it's one of New York's university vice-chancellors, Evelyn Adamalski. She's surprisingly young for a vice-chancellor, but she's as affable as they come. A former newspaper colleague often referred to her as "Evelyn Adamalski – the vice-chancellor of my heart". This could be the opening I need.

I stand to their side, waiting for a moment to interject without seeming too brazen. Moriarty turns to me, smiles, and walks away. This is my tenth grade dance all over again.

"Hi Andrew," Evelyn says with genuine excitement, oblivious to my disappointment.

"Ms Adamalski, it's nice to see you." I make eye contact in between tracking Moriarty's movement.

"I love your sweater. Salmon suits you."

"Thank you." I turn my head away and cover my mouth, pre-tending to cough. "Did you hear that, Rust?"

"Still pink."

"What was that?" Evelyn asks, rightfully confused by my muttering.

"Sorry, I was just trying to remember the last time I saw you. It's been some time, I think."

"Maven. Get back to Moriarty. This isn't an ice cream social."

"Yes! You're not at *The Times* anymore." I'm surprised Evelyn has remembered this much, given we've only had a handful of conversations in the past. She doesn't strike me as my typical readership, but I guess that's the transcendent beauty of the inter-net.

Moriarty is approaching the side of the stage as the jazz band packs up for a break in play. I'm going to have to sit through some speeches, it seems.

"I went freelance a few years ago," I tell Evelyn. "But it's going well. How are things at the university?"

"Yes, fantastic!" she gushes. "We're going through a process of restructuring courses at the moment, just making sure they are digitally leveraged for the tech-savvy world. You know, the new media environment. Of course *you* know. It's really fantastic."

"Oh yeah." I can hear the passion in Evelyn's voice and I can feel how little I truly care, but my disinterest doesn't slow her at all. She's in full "public relations" mode, probably hoping I'm fascinated enough to provide some coverage.

"One of the exciting parts of our three-year plan is that we're revitalising each campus to make it easier for students to connect with each other and with their college. It's really exciting."

"That's what you've got to do these days, it seems." I'm a maestro when it comes to pretending I'm paying attention.

"Totally! Lifelong learning is so important to me. I feel like we need to provide students with real choices about how, when and where they can learn in a way that suits their needs. It's so important to me."

"Yeah, that's it. That's what you want."

The room hushes and I excuse myself from Evelyn as the master of ceremonies interrupts her spiel about the university's strong industry partnerships.

"*Thank goodness,*" Rust mutters. "*Is she three sheets to the wind or is she always that talkative?*"

"I'm proud to admit that I have no idea what that means, Rust."

The MC's brief welcome and shout-outs to the most dignified guests lead into an introduction for Moriarty's official hotel opening address. The audience applauds and he flashes that Cheshire Cat grin for the cameras before giving his greetings and salutations.

"It's a pleasure to welcome you all today, finally, to our grand opening. We've been up and running about six months now and we're already deep in the weeds planning our next development.

Needless to say, today's event has been incubating and marinating for quite some time, but as always, we must bend to the schedule of our local senators, our guests of honour and, of course, the mayor of this fine city."

Moriarty gestures to a section of the room to his left, where I can only assume our city councillors are smiling and nodding along.

"Again, thank you for making your way out. It's always an honour to throw an event worthy of so many dignitaries and celebrated figures. Can I make a suggestion? Or not even a suggestion – a demand, really. Make sure you try the arancini balls. There's enough for everyone. Except you, Mr Giuliani. I'm sorry – but I heard about your cholesterol and I can't be held responsible for any mishaps. I just can't."

When the fake laughs die down, Moriarty begins talking about the facility, its staff, its customers, how much the building project cost and finally the investments contributed by council, federal and state governments. I'd wager he won't mention New York's $9 billion in debt off the state books, the limitless dark money passing hands in elections, the widening disparity between rich and poor, or the slow inevitable death of small business. That would be an unpopular move. That's something I would do. That's another reason I'm not wearing my name badge.

"In today's economy, a sharp mind and a willingness to work hard are the most valuable assets you can possess. Some of us learn this the hard way, but our own history is the greatest teacher of all. It just *is*. There are myriad examples in my own life of failures that spurred on my greatest successes. And with that, I'm pleased to say The Moriarty Corporation is well-positioned to grow and meet the needs of this city, this country, and even our burgeoning markets in Japan and China. I'm sure our shareholders would tell you their returns are more than satisfactory. Personally, I'd say we're making money hand over fist, and that's only going to continue for a long time."

I don't think that was a joke, but there's more fake laughter as Moriarty pauses, stroking his parted hair into perfect position.

"I'm on the record stating that this hotel is our first step towards partnerships that foster international expansion, diversification and things of this nature... but I'll leave the business talk for our annual meeting in a couple of months. I hope many of you plan to attend, but that's your prerogative. For now, let me take you for a walk."

Yada yada yada – please hurry up and say something about a rogue spy. Moriarty lowers his head, his back arched and his arms stretched forward, leaning on the lectern as he gathers his thoughts.

"My family has been watching over this city for decades, with an influence that's ubiquitous from Battery Park to the top of Manhattan. Through everything, the glorious highs, and the incredible lows. Even in the darkest depths, this community has battled, fought, scraped, endured, and now – now we see our glorious city is back on top. Back where it belongs. Our community has given the world a master class in perseverance. From the bodegas to the skyscrapers, you can't help fall in love with this city. Am I right?"

The audience applauds as if Moriarty has landed a golf ball three feet from the hole in the US PGA Tour. Right when I start thinking he'll talk until his vocabulary runs dry, he goes on to thank "the community" of New York City. When a public presentation in this city begins focusing on unabashed praise for the community, you know it's wrapping up. I move closer to the front of the room in hopes of catching him as soon as he's done.

"The Moriarty Corporation is one that sees the forest through the trees. I have no doubt that one day we'll look back and see that this building and this company will capture the industry zeitgeist of the Trump era, for lack of a better term. My goal now – and I really hope this is the most salient point today – is that my company can continue to do what I've always aspired to do, and that's work hard for this city, work to bring jobs, to bring tourism, to bring economic stimulus and most of all to see New York prosper as, frankly, the greatest city on the entire planet. I want to thank you again for coming here today. Please enjoy your afternoon and take care."

The audience eats up every morsel of Moriarty's speech, the same way I'm consuming arancini balls like an antidote to anxiety. Uncle Leo used to say "Never trust a Moriarty", but Kenton wasn't lying about these appetisers.

I try to catch his attention amid the cheers and adulation accompanying him down from the centre platform, but it's not going to be easy. A crowd of yes-men and gold diggers is swarming around him faster than a pit crew on a Formula One race car. This could be difficult, especially if he doesn't recognise me. He shakes hands with a group of senior guests, who seem in competition to see who can go the longest without admitting their combovers do nothing to hide their retreating hairlines. I call out and excuse myself as I make an introduction to Moriarty. To my surprise, he turns his head sideways at the mention of my name, as if I'm not how he'd pictured me.

"Andrew Maven," he repeats. "I've heard of you. Call me Kent. It's a pleasure."

"Thank you. This is really something," I tell him, gesturing around the room.

"No, thank *you*. So, are you *investigating* me for corruption or inviting me to do a podcast? I have to say, I don't like your chances either way."

I laugh out of politeness, despite the high probability that he's serious, and I try to ignore the question. "Do you have a couple minutes for an interview?"

"There's actually a media statement for the opening, a fact sheet and some quotes from yours truly." Moriarty is elusive, as any New York billionaire would be when asked to sacrifice their schmooze time. "Just find my publicist and she'll shoot through a copy – she's the one in the ridiculous red dress over there."

"Actually, I have a couple of questions not included in the release. Do you have a minute?"

"I'm sorry." He starts to turn away. "There are just too many people here to make exceptions for media. I just can't. Take care."

"*Think fast, Maven*," Rust's voice cuts through the party commotion. *"You're losing him."*

As much as I've planned ahead, Moriarty is too savvy to give in to my badgering. I have to resort to dirty tricks. How do you get someone to engage against their will? Think of the internet trolls. My only choice is to infuriate him.

"It's *really* a cool place," I blurt out. "Almost as nice as The Plaza."

Moriarty stops dead and turns half way back so I'm creeping inside his peripheral vision. He's been triggered.

"What did you say?"

"I was just saying how I enjoy this place. It's spiffy. I bet you get basketball teams staying and everything."

"Spiffy? It's $800 a night," he states as a matter of fact. "So, yeah."

Appealing to Moriarty's sense of pride through condescension is my best hope at engaging a reaction. I'm not a great liar but knowing that Rust is listening spurs me on.

"$800? Wow. OK. That's interesting. How do you come to that rate? Do you adjust it based on feedback?"

"Look, Andrew. I don't need to justify—"

"I'm sorry," I interrupt, shocking Moriarty even more. "This place is awesome, but I've heard some *stories* about security."

"Stories?"

"Stories. Yeah. A few stories."

This is weird. I've developed a facade where I'm acting but playing my normal self as a character. If you've ever crossed the street in a country that drives on the opposite side of the road, you'd know that a small tweak to something you've done a million times can make it feel confusing and borderline dangerous.

"Tell me if this is wrong," I begin to posit. "But I've heard celebrities won't, like, stay here anymore because it always leaks out to the media or whatever."

"You're joking." Moriarty is incredulous. A passing trio of flirtatious women wave hello to the billionaire and he politely chuckles, directing them to the bar. They fade away out of view, along with the smile on Moriarty's face when he realises he's left with a smarmy journalist disrespecting his business.

"This is ridiculous. We have politicians, Hollywood stars, athletes, ambassadors, high-class business people from all over the world. These accusations are unfounded and, frankly, preposterous. I can't hear this right now. I just can't."

Moriarty is firm, not harsh, but I can tell underneath he's boiling and waiting to erupt. The populated room is the only thing keeping him from exploding at me. He reminds me of a furious big city lawyer forced to hold back their emotion in front of a stereotypical "no nonsense" judge.

"Kent, the questions have to be asked. People take security very seriously. Confidentiality and privacy – you know what I mean?"

"*That's good, Maven. Keep that going.*"

I swallow, trying to dampen my dry mouth. "Is it possible for a guest to stay here and no one knows about it? If I was looking for someone here, could I find them?"

Moriarty bites his lip and stares at me. Is he hiding something or just plain furious? It's as though he's aware of my ulterior motive, or maybe he can hear Rust talking in my ear.

"I tell you what, Andrew. I don't really know what you're getting at, but whatever it is, my publicist can fill you in. She'll tell you all about the security features of the hotel. Enjoy your afternoon."

Moriarty disappears into the crowd, leaving me with no leads – nothing but a craving for more arancini balls.

I can't help feeling that I blew my chance, even though there's a strong possibility that Mars was never here. Now and then, a journalist is forced to pursue a story they don't believe in. I used to feel a sense of relief when a source would shut down those stories, but just like my persistent editors, Rust and Metric won't rest until we've explored every option.

It's a good thing I came here with a back-up plan.

"Rust." I place a finger to my ear. The inherent coolness of such a gesture isn't lost on me at all. "I think I'm gonna need a professional in here. These pretzels are making me thirsty."

The click of what could only be a magazine round sliding into a handgun sends a shiver through my tingling vertebrae.

"I thought you'd never ask. Give me four minutes."

"I'll give you five or even six, if you like."

"Four's good."

Chapter 6

Confrontation

Anxiety is oozing out my pores. I wipe my perspiring forehead, hoping to hide my fear and avoid looking like a crackhead. This isn't a problem I ever expected to face. No one has mistaken me for a drug addict since I walked into my college dorm resembling a young Bob Dylan – afro, aviators and 311 band T-shirt. I imagine Dylan would've been into rap rock if he went to college in the early 2000s.

Our new unfamiliar surroundings are the source of my uncontrollable sweating. Once Rust arrived at the party, he scanned the room like a hawk with a vendetta. For the next twenty-five minutes he paced about, watching security guard movements and noting surveillance camera black spots. The process would've been a lot faster if he wasn't posing as a photographer. It seemed as if every ambitious yuppie and tipsy hipster was attracted to him, each asking to have their photo taken. I'm sure they never met a shooter with such a curmudgeonly approach to photography. They really had no idea Rust would prefer to shoot an AK47 than a Canon EOS 1200D.

Moriarty eventually disappeared from the room and Rust trailed close behind. He instructed me to "stand by" and that's exactly what I did. I "stood by" the snack table until Rust returned, somehow knowing exactly where Moriarty had gone – the penthouse. I knew better than to question the source of his information. When I asked how we could get there, Rust discretely flashed a card attached to a lanyard.

"This card key will take us straight to the top. Full security clearance, from the basement to the roof."

So here we are, standing in an elevator, trespassing to investigate Agent Mars. I don't know if Rust will threaten Moriarty, I don't know if he'll pull a gun on him, and I don't know if the billionaire's entourage will be ready to open fire right back at anything we have to throw. I stare at the floor for so long that my glasses almost slip off my face. The peaceful elevator music is a stark contrast from what I feel mounting inside.

"Relax."

"Hm?" I look up at Rust and adjust my sliding spectacles.

"You need to relax, kid. I've got your back. I'm not going to let anything happen to you."

Thirty-two. Thirty-three. Thirty-four. We're almost halfway.

"Plus, remember you're wearing a bulletproof vest underneath that pink monstrosity."

"It's not so much me that I'm worried about, as much as... the situation," I explain. "In general. I don't want anyone to get hurt. I've got a bad feeling about this."

"Hm. I told you to relax."

"And I told you already, this sweater isn't pink. But that doesn't change how you feel."

"Yeah, yeah. It's *salmon*. I get it."

After what feels like minutes, the elevator reaches the eighty-second floor, the doors open and reveal a small lobby area. We should not be here. This is restricted access. The pounding inside my chest creates a sensation I haven't experienced since feeling the boom of Lars Ulrich's bass drum at my first Metallica show. I thought I could be having a heart attack at the time. A cardiac arrest is probably the worst way to be saved by the bell, but hey. Right now, I'm under enough stress that I'd just about take any reason not to be here.

Rust is more emotionally perceptive than I give him credit for. He tells me to be brave before leading me into the unknown.

One large open space with panoramic views takes up most of the hotel's top floor penthouse. The glass windows extend from the ceiling right to the hardwood floor. There's no sight like Manhattan from the sky. Just breathtaking.

"Whoa," I whisper to myself, taking in the five-star surroundings as Rust soldiers on without me. The massive room appears designed for leisure – warm, well-lit and filled with expensive furniture and entertainment equipment. It's like a rec room in Richie Rich's mansion. Pool table, ping pong, treadmill, bench press, pinball, guitar amps, and an incredible theatre set-up. The rest of the top floor seems to consist of compartmented office spaces, sectioned off from the leisure area. Shelves, books, antiques, tribal instruments and artefacts line each wall. Either Moriarty is a collector, or he's got a second job as a globetrotting tomb raider.

Moriarty stands alone across the room, his $3000 designer-label jacket hanging on a chair and his shirt sleeves rolled back. He's facing away from us, coolly hitting golf balls into a netted indoor driving range. A projected image shows a lush virtual golf course and an LED screen above his head flashes numbers and letters after each swing.

"*219 yards,*" it reads in bright-yellow.

Decent.

"You're not supposed to be here, Mr Maven," Moriarty calls out across the space. "Speak with my publicist like normal. Like I told you already."

222 yards.

"This isn't a normal request, Kent."

"You're as tenacious as that sweater is ugly. This is meant to be my private lounge. That means I come here to relax in privacy, not get harassed by *The Times*. How did you even get here?"

231 yards.

Moriarty has an impressive golf swing, but he needs to move through the shot more and he should face his head down to keep the ball from drifting left. I know what you're thinking – I don't seem like a typical golfer. Whether it's work or hobbies, I find it's a lot easier to enjoy something when you're naturally good at it. I had a year or two of lessons, but I developed most of my golfing prowess in college. My buddy Tresy always thought he could beat me and I made a lot of money by making sure he never did. Team sports were never my thing, but on the golf course I felt in control. That's one of the things you need to remember in golf. Control, patience, timing. But now isn't the time to offer tips to Moriarty.

"I'm not with *The Times* anymore. I'm a freelance."

"A freelance?" Moriarty points his golf club towards the elevator, without even a hint of geniality. "Get the hell out of my hotel. And no photos up here, please." Moriarty goes back to sizing up his swing, shaking his head and muttering. "I can't believe I'm being harassed by the guy from Weezer."

233 yards.

I turn to Rust, surrendering the situation to him. He grunts in total indifference and hands me the camera by its strap. In a clear act of defiance, he steps up to Moriarty and folds his arms.

"We're looking for someone named Mars. Might've been through here. Sound familiar?"

"Do I *look* like the concierge? You think I follow the day-to-day minutia of the hotel? I'm the owner, you moron. You want to find someone, do it the old-fashioned way."

"This is serious."

"My custom-made Rolex is *seriously* telling me it's time for you to leave."

"Please."

"You're dismissed."

237 yards.

Rust takes a step forward, unsatisfied with the prospect of leaving empty-handed and miffed at Moriarty's general air of arrogance. To be fair, our request isn't exactly reasonable, nor are we entitled to be up here. I'm far too reasonable and impartial for espionage.

"We're not leaving. We don't want trouble. Only information.

And you're going to give it to us."

Moriarty finally stops hitting golf balls, perplexed by the sudden dynamic shift as Rust refuses to show trepidation. His eyes run over the veteran agent as though the bigger picture is crystallising in his mind.

"You're no photographer... Special ops, perhaps?" Moriarty suggests, seemingly proud of his summation. "With a news reporter, of all people. You must be desperate."

"How do you know I'm not special ops?" I ask in offence, my voice cracking and demonstrating exactly why I'm not spy material. Even with his back to me, I can feel Rust glaring as Moriarty continues to ramble.

"Look – I could tell you exactly what you want to know. You could leave here happy and it would cost me nothing to tell you. But I don't need to do that. Because this is America." He places the golf club on the floor, resting his hands on the handle like a royal sceptre. "We're a country of five hundred billionaires."

"Their vote is worth the same as mine," I say.

"You think so? This is not a democracy, Mr Maven. Just look at last year's presidential election. Let's not kid ourselves. This is a corporate plutocracy and the rich rule. Everyone else bows down on bended knee. That's been ubiquitous throughout our history, but now more than ever. I'm sorry. Even Aristotle knew that."

Moriarty rests the golf club against the wall and walks over to a nearby liquor cabinet, lined with expensive bottles of bourbon. He begins to pour himself a drink, placing a single large ice cube into his clear crystal tumbler.

"Look what happened when the UK gave in to populism last year and allowed everyday morons to vote on leaving the European Union. Economic disaster."

"Why are you talking about politics, Kent? We just want to find this guy and we'll go."

Moriarty takes a deep sip and savours the smooth taste before ignoring me and continuing his rant.

"The problem with the media is they think they're in control. The reality is, the more people like me are in control, the better off this country will be. You can quote me on *that*. You're in *my* world now, and that makes me God. I really thought your people understood commerce, Maven."

My people? It seems Moriarty has made the false assumption that I'm Jewish. It happens a lot with a Hebrew surname. Mom's family is fully Dutch and Dad's mother is as Anglo-Saxon as they get, making me about as Jewish as Christmas. Although I'm sometimes neurotic, and technically one sixteenth Hebrew, it's not enough for me to identify as an ethnic minority.

"As offensive as that is, we're just here to talk. We're actually trying to stop what could be an act of terrorism."

"Oh, I bet you are," Moriarty says, laced with sarcasm. "No, that's one too many qualifiers for me to care. I've seen no semblance of salient evidence that this affects me in any way. Unless there's a bomb going off in my hotel, I frankly don't give a damn. In fact, you want to talk about terrorism? 9/11 was probably the best thing that happened to me. Those tumbling Twin Towers were like manna from heaven, as your people would say. I've been making money hand over fist ever since."

For only half a second, Moriarty looks flustered, as if he's allowed himself to reveal more than he intended.

"That's all completely off the record, by the way. Try publishing any of this and I'll sue you for what little you have."

"I do OK."

"Please. Take your freelance money and secret service buddy out on the street. You want information? You need to break in here and steal it like you people always do."

Moriarty removes his spectacles and meticulously wipes them with a microfibre cloth from his chest pocket. I suspect he's still on edge, but he's at least presenting the illusion that he's disinterested in our existence.

"I was raised with manners, so I'll politely tell you one last time: *please* get the hell out of my hotel before I break your damn necks. It's not hard. It's a Hobson's choice, really. And you can forget about calling my publicist."

"Moriarty," Rust steps up again, closing the gap between the two. "You're going to tell us what we want to hear or you're going to find out just how much you like the view from the eighty-second floor."

"*Enough.*" Moriarty flips his golf club, catching it by the head. He points the handle towards an intercom unit on the nearby wall, pressing and holding in a flat button. "Greg? I need an immediate removal in the penthouse."

"*Yes, sir.*"

"Stomp on up here and bring that big guy. The Peruvian."

I feel this is the time to save Moriarty from unnecessary violence with a very stern warning. "I can't tell you who this is, Kent. But he'll probably kick your teeth out the window if you don't help."

"You don't *threaten* a man like me," he snaps back. "I've heard it all before. I'm still standing."

"If it's a fight you want," Rust says, "now is a good time to reconsider. I don't lose."

Moriarty laughs, proving he's either crazy or ignorant. He briefly places the golf club against a nearby chair, but only so he can throw his suit jacket around his shoulders like Martin Sheen in *The West Wing.*

"Look here. I know you're Metric. No one else has the balls to ask these questions. But you're old. And your people have done enough. Twice in a month? Please. You're pushing your luck."

"Twice?" I repeat.

"Maybe they don't tell you everything – your guy was in here like a shadow in the night. He's taken my list and vanished."

"That's Mars," Rust mutters, perhaps for my benefit. "What did he take?"

"He didn't leave an inventory. It was like he was invisible. We could barely prove that he was here." Moriarty pauses, as if hearing these words come out of his own mouth have triggered something in his head. "Are you telling me he *wasn't* Metric?"

"Let's go," I tell Rust, growing nervous at the thought of security's impending arrival.

"Oh, you're not going anywhere." Moriarty waves his golf

club like a magic wand. "I need to know, if he wasn't Metric, then just what the hell happened here two weeks ago? You've got me vacillating between curious and furious."

The elevator behind us sounds its alerting ding and Rust twirls around, whipping out a handgun from his waist as if it's an extension of his own body.

"Whoa! Rust! Is that necessary?"

Ignoring me, he focuses his gun on the elevator doors, where a pair of bruisers step out with their own pistols raised at us.

"OK. I-I'm gonna die," I stammer under my breath.

"You're not going to die." Rust's general sense of calm is disturbing.

"It's two on one."

"That's why I told you to bring a weapon."

The one Moriarty calls Greg has a real babyface on top of his burly frame, like a software developer who took up mountain climbing to get ripped because he was sick of girls rejecting him. The Peruvian is far bigger. He could easily pass for a dopey bouncer working under a South American drug lord. It's not their imposing size that frightens me, so much as the handguns pointed at us.

Moriarty's voice bellows across the room, bypassing us as he commands his armed cronies.

"Greg, make sure at least one of these two survives. I have questions."

"God."

I say a quick prayer in my head, but all I can think of is "Don't let me die". I'm learning now, as a man of many words, that a legitimate fear of death has an amazing crippling effect on the ability to think clearly. Rust tries to calm me, explaining, "Don't move. Don't say a word." I take this instruction as literally as possible and stop breathing until my body tells me I require oxygen to live. The security guards' arrivals have given Rust the look of a wild ram about to butt heads – teeth gritted and eyes focused.

The lead henchmen, the one they call Greg, is fixing his pistol and his eyes on Rust. The Peruvian giant focuses on me. Even without a gun, this mountain of a man could destroy me with ease. I have visions of being crushed like an ant underneath his gargantuan frame. If it weren't for Rust's warning, I would try to explain that I'm unarmed and no danger to them whatsoever.

Rust places his gun on the hardwood floor in surrender and slides it to Greg. It falls a few feet short, just as Rust intended. As the security officer bends down to pick up the pistol, he makes what I can only presume is a rookie mistake – he takes his eyes off the target. Faster than a John Wayne quick draw, Rust pulls a second pistol from inside his jacket and fires a single bullet into a fire extinguisher near Greg and the Peruvian. The pressurised canister explodes with a billow of white mist, shooting a constant hazy stream to the roof. A surrounding vicinity of fifteen to twenty feet quickly becomes thick with the fog-like effect.

"What did you *do*?" Moriarty screams through the chaos.

Rust acts fast, with the henchmen still off-guard and blinded. He launches forward and disappears into the white cloud, the way Batman preys on a room of goons clouded by smoke bombs.

Let's get nuts.

Chapter 7

Confliction

I can't see a thing, but the audible cue of two thuds tell me Rust has clotheslined both security guards to the ground.

"Holy smokes. Are you OK?"

I turn back to Moriarty and find him in shock with his jaw hanging in fear, until he notices me watching.

"Step back, Maven." With a menacing grimace, he holds his golf club towards me like a sabre, ready to swing at any movement.

"I don't want anyone to get hurt," I tell him, raising my hands to decrease the tension. "We just needed to know about this guy, Mars, and we're leaving."

"You can't leave without telling me what's going on. Metric's into some shady—"

A crash behind me startles Moriarty, as the three grown men roll around inside the stream of mist, tearing up his expensive furnishings. The fire extinguisher's cloud is dissipating, revealing the struggle taking place inside. Both Greg and the Peruvian are taking wild swings, doing everything in their power to fight Rust in a fit of coughing and spluttering through the mist.

"Greg! Shoot him, already!"

With blood dripping from his nose and his shirt torn right

through the middle, Greg throws a frantic fist, but he misses completely as Rust ducks. He parries a second blow before thrusting a punch into Greg's kidney.

I can't believe what I'm seeing. All I can do is cringe as I try to follow everything unfolding before me.

With Rust unable to keep both brawlers in control at once, the Peruvian grabs him from behind and locks in a choke hold. This gives Greg the freedom to fumble around for his dropped gun.

"Shoot! Him!" Moriarty commands.

Before I can even feel concerned for Rust's safety, he turns the tables with shocking speed. Hitting the Peruvian with a *Matrix* move, Rust furnishes his chest and midsection with a wave of fast elbows. This knocks the wind right out of him and slackens his grip just long enough for Rust to overpower Greg, right as he tries to draw his weapon. Rust wrenches Greg's wrist and whips the pistol into his face, then turns his focus to delivering more hits than the Beatles in the late '60s.

Greg's gun spins across the floor and disappears in a pile of white foam, away from trigger-happy hands. The recovering Peruvian slips across the wet floor in an almost comical fashion as Rust whips Greg into a bookshelf against the wall. Down but not out, Greg picks himself up, brandishing a set of wireless surround-sound speakers. With gritted teeth, he pegs one of the boxes like a shot put at Rust's face. The first one misses, knocking over a water cooler and spreading even more mess across the hard floors. The second speaker box hurtles towards Rust's face and he's only just able to protect himself from its sharp corners. He stumbles, right into the charging Peruvian, raising an elbow in time to drop the giant faster than a three hundred pound sack of potatoes.

"Get him." I mutter to myself, visualising Rust's next move as if I have telepathic control over the brawl. Gritting his teeth in a Neanderthal rage, Greg winds up for another punch. Rust ducks fast and counters the strike by grabbing his misplaced arm and twisting it around in a sickening angle. Locking one foot in front of Greg's ankle, Rust throws him forward, slamming the goon's face into the hardwood flooring.

I can't see him getting up from that one.

Moriarty barks across the room: "Take that old bastard down, Coello, or you're out of a job!"

I can't tell if the Peruvian even heard the command, but he responds by ramming his knee into Rust's spine. The crunch that sounds across the room is a chiropractor's worst nightmare. Out of breath, Rust swings a hard punch, but it lands with a soft thud on the Peruvian's soaking wet leather jacket, which absorbs the force like a tennis ball against a tin shed. The Peruvian glares and shoves Rust, sending him staggering back into a glass coffee table that can only shatter underneath his weight.

"Rust!"

"Leave him, Maven," Moriarty takes a threatening step closer with his golf club extended. "Let's see how this plays out." He presses the intercom again and starts to beckon up yet another helper. "Is that Daniel?"

"No, sir."

"Sorry. Smalls? Yeah, get up here. I need you to bring in the water man. And call a janitor too. We've got a real mess."

The water man? I don't like the sound of that. This could get out of hand. I want to help, but I've always been afraid of being punched in the face. Maybe a lifetime of wearing glasses has helped me avoid that type of violence. Right now I feel about as useful as a white crayon, standing here, watching Rust throw his body around the room. The camera he handed me is useless as a weapon. I look nearby for a projectile of my own, but the only object in reach is a rolled up poster tube. You can't throw a poster tube and expect results.

The Peruvian checks on his ally briefly, but Greg is too groggy to be of any assistance. As he forages through the carpet of foam for a fallen pistol, Rust has enough time to shake off the cobwebs and get to his feet. The broken coffee table was holding a remote control and a set of bongos, so I'm just waiting for Rust to craft a deadly weapon out of glass shards, plastic and cowhide. It turns out a nearby shelf, covered in oriental antiques and artefacts, is the only ammunition he needs.

Rust hurls an ornate decorative plate like a frisbee towards the unprepared Peruvian. It shatters on the wall behind him. Up next, a priceless vase lands square in his face, knocking him down and breaking into a hundred pieces.

"Oh, come on," Moriarty whines. "That was late 14th-century Ming dynasty."

The Peruvian gives up his search for a gun, instead opting to charge towards Rust. He wraps his arms around Rust's waist in a spear tackle, lifting him in the air and ramming him into the big-screen TV mounted on the wall.

Still locked in the Peruvian's grip, Rust throws punch after punch into the side of his head, wearing him down with each strike. As the hold loosens, Rust is able to free himself and daze his opponent with a backhanded chop across the face. He tears the destroyed eighty-four-inch television from its wall mounting with brute force, creating a small puff of drywall dust that disappears into the air. With an awkward momentum, he slams the TV downward across the Peruvian's head, treating his neck like a spring-loaded rod.

Unknown to Rust, Greg is now on his feet and has almost found his bearings. In his foggy stupor, all he can manage is to charge at Rust with reckless abandon and ruthless aggression. I yell out a warning, but whether or not he hears me is unclear. Rust crouches at the last instant and flips Greg up and over, landing squarely on top of the TV and the Peruvian beneath it. They lie there motionless, tangled in cables and sandwiched by fallen sound systems, media devices and video game cables.

"Glad that's not my console," I say. "Game over, Greggy."

The sound of more footsteps interrupts my victorious quip and draws attention to the elevator entrance. Moriarty's back-up has arrived. Judging by his drawn pistol, he's not the janitor. Could he be the Water Man? Who *is* the Water Man? How many people did Moriarty call up? I'm confused.

"What the hell happened here? Are you OK, sir?"

"He's over there!"

The room's incredible state of disorder distracts the Water

Man enough to leave him completely unprepared for Rust's stealth attack. At the last second, the Water Man reacts and turns his weapon in panic. His jerky movement is so quick that his feet slide along the slippery surface and he loses balance. One hard punch to the face sends him to the ground.

Oh, he's not the Water Man. I've figured it out. He's just a regular security guard. The Water Man has to be the water-cooler maintenance guy, en route to replace the destroyed container. Moriarty is so arrogant that he's more concerned with restocking his water supply than ensuring the outcome of the fight. I'm sure by now he regrets underestimating Rust's physical prowess.

"I think that's enough violence for now, wouldn't you say, Kent?"

I look over to Moriarty, expecting to see him munching on some good old humble pie. Instead, he's reaching for the intercom again, probably to call on a whole army of security. With Rust too far away to act, I have no choice but to take action. I'm ready to throw down and take a swing if I have to, but when he sees me coming it's his golf club that's swinging. I duck his horizontal stroke but the returning hit connects hard with my hip. Even though it hurts like hell, it's not enough to knock me over. I cover my head, anticipating a second strike that never comes.

I look up to find Moriarty creeping backwards with caution in his eyes. Rust has locked onto him, looking as relentless as a starved zombie. I've noticed throughout the encounter his face has been unchanged, with gritted teeth and a furrowed brow. This facial quirk acts as a chilling battle mask.

"Just leave, already," Moriarty shouts across the twenty-yard gap between us. "No more questions."

Despite my suggestion that we quit while we're ahead, Rust is adamant there's still more to learn. White foam coats his clothes and drips from his bleeding face, like he's dived in and out of a bubble bath. And somehow he's still menacing.

I have to insist he rests after what he's been through. If we're sticking around, it's my turn to chip in.

This is my moment.

I lean across to Moriarty's set of golf clubs and pull out a 3-wood.

"Kent, there's just a few more things." I start to place a ball on the tee and line it up with the cowering billionaire. "If you're ready to sit down and talk, it's going to be a *lot* easier."

"Hold up, Andrew. You can't do this. I'm a respected figure in this city and I could end your career."

I prepare to swing, setting my feet and enjoying the familiar grip in my hand.

"Don't confuse power with respect. If people knew what you really were..."

"If people knew? People crave elitism. They want to be told what's best for them because they're not capable of even knowing what they want in their own narrow world. Now, put that golf club down. Or get ready to—"

Nope.

I relax my right elbow, raise the club, swivelling my head in time to turn my body in textbook motion. The titanium head connects with power. My perfect follow-through sends the golf ball hurtling like a missile towards Moriarty, embedding into the wall two feet above his head.

260 yards.

"What are you, nuts? You crazy son of a bitch!" Moriarty flips out on the floor in a foetal position. It's about time he showed some respect for the threat of violence. Rust seems slightly amused but maintains his solemn disposition.

"It's been a while since I've been to the driving range. I think I could go all day. Do you think people can't see through your act, Kent?"

"People don't care about ethics," he spits back, covering his face in fear. His angst is outweighed only by his pride. "It's a dog and pony show. No one wants to see how the sausage gets made."

"Enough games," Rust says, ready to tag team back into the interrogation. "There are two ways to deal with these kinds of crooks. Only one of them works."

He's right. Simply by approaching Moriarty and raising a fist,

Rust is able to break the billionaire's stubborn policy on sharing information.

"OK, OK! It's cool! Just, cool it!"

With two firm hands, Rust picks Moriarty up by the scruff of his shirt, almost lifting him off the ground. The juxtaposition amuses me – a property tycoon in a $5000 suit cowers in fear at the hands of a secret agent wearing a cheap polo shirt and blue jeans, covered in foam, sweat, plasterboard and several people's blood.

It's time to spill the beans.

"This guy, you're calling him Agent Mars... he was here a fortnight ago. First we thought it was just an act of vandalism. My statue got messed up, beyond repair."

"Statue?"

"There was a statue of me... in the lobby."

"Of you?" Rust asks with judgement in his voice.

"What can I say? I have an ego. But he smashed the damn arm off. What am I gonna do with a one-armed marble sculpture?"

"Hm... One-armed."

"That mean something?" I ask.

"So we checked the cameras the next day. Can you please put me down, already?"

"Keep talking," Rust insists, lifting him even higher off the ground.

"We checked the cameras after we saw my file room was compromised. We found one good glimpse where we could actually see something."

Moriarty's speech is accelerating to resemble a race-track announcer, in his attempt to get the information out as soon as possible.

"He was dressed head to toe in some kind of aromatic polyamide. Military grade. Stealth tech. Damn near invisible, the way he moved – it was a Spectral Suit. *Had* to be."

"Hm. Metric outfit," Rust mumbles.

"Exactly."

"You sure?"

"It's burrowed into my mind. You know how much those suits would sell for on the black market?"

Moriarty drops to the floor in a flailing heap and winces in pain as Rust turns back to me.

"One-armed statue," he repeats to himself, as if it means something.

My email from Mars said "Find the one-winged angel". That's got to be something. Rust certainly has some thoughts about it.

"You're happy then?"

"Pleased as punch. Let's clear out, kid."

Now that Rust has what he needs, he's taken on the urgency of a college kid snapping shut his text book and bounding for the door at the end of class. I want to leave too, but there's something still nagging at me.

"Kent, you mentioned a list before."

"Just a list of names. Can't say more than that."

"You're gonna have to."

It could be that Rust is a few steps away, but the mention of the list has given Moriarty a new sense of defiance and fatigue.

"Look, Maven, you've drained me already. There are some things you're going to have to just find out on your own. Find your guy and I'm sure he'll fill you in. Enough, already."

"OK," I concede. "*You're* dismissed, Moriarty."

As I hustle back to catch up with Rust, I get my first chance to assess the overall carnage. An exploded fire extinguisher, shards of a priceless vase spread across the dewy floor, a roof dripping white liquid on half the room, and a shattered glass coffee table.

"Nano GEAR channel 182.05," Rust says, activating a private channel connection via his earpiece. "HQ, this is Agent Rust. Currently vacating a scene of physical engagement. Need assistance to collect gear and vehicle. Room 809. I'm supervising civilian assistant Andrew Maven. Will spend the night at registered safehouse number two. Full report to follow."

We pass the eighty-four-inch LED television sandwiched by what's left of Greg and the Peruvian. I suspect each of them could be waking up about now, but their sense of self-preservation is telling them they're better off playing dead. What a mess.

"This would've been a lot cleaner if you'd let me shoot them," Rust says, as if he read my mind.

"Probably a bit easier on your body too," I admit. "But thanks. I'd prefer to keep a clean conscience for as long as possible."

While we wait for the elevator to arrive, still in earshot of Moriarty, I hear one final quip across the room.

"I can't believe I got hustled by a guy in a pink sweater."

I can only sigh. It's *salmon*. And I hate it more than ever.

I glance at Rust and notice he's quietly grinning at Moriarty's parting words. It's the first time I've really seen him smile, bringing out lines of wrinkles like tiger stripes around his tired eyes.

The elevator dings and we step inside. I mash the "close" button as if it's a PlayStation controller. The doors meet, closing the curtain on Rust's battle scene.

We're safe.

I exhale a deep, long breath. I'm not used to this type of insanity. I want to crawl up in a ball on my couch, eat Skittles and watch the Knicks lose again. Instead, I can only guess what Rust has planned for tomorrow.

"I *told* you it was pink."

Chapter 8

Progression

I slept surprisingly well last night. My pure exhaustion out-weighed the anxiety and stress of yesterday's events. Now that we're in daylight again, those pressures have come back to haunt me like a high school football injury. Don't get me wrong – there is an element of relief. It's easy to forget that Mars' cryptic email barely pointed us in the right direction. The result wasn't what we expected. We didn't find Mars, but it was undeniably the place to look.

"How do you deal with all this?" I ask Rust. He looks up from the bundle of papers spread across our breakfast table.

It's early. The morning tilts through the city skyscrapers, sunlight poking through the gaps between buildings. The safe-house turned out to be something resembling an Airbnb. It was a fairly empty apartment stocked with a surprising amount of gauze and antiseptic. I spent the night taking notes, trying to recall the events of the afternoon, while Rust held private conversations behind a closed door.

We've found a quiet cafe nearby, out on the streets of Hell's Kitchen – Manhattan's gritty mid-town west neighbourhood. I try not to spend too much time here, but I know I'm safe with Rust at my side. This must be how Kanye West feels, stepping out with his entourage and fearing no consequence as he acts like the centre of the universe.

"What do you mean?" Rust responds. Today an unzipped black hooded sweatshirt is wrapped over his matching polo, shielding the typical New York spring chill. For the past few minutes he's been focused on the papers in front of him. Some are photos, some appear to be crib notes and others are text-heavy documents. Now he's flicking through the files with the urgency of a wealthy bachelor searching his address book for a last-minute date to his cousin's wedding.

"That *tension*. Yesterday... That was... My heart rate is still kind of crazy thinking about it."

Rust doesn't react. I've seen him bleed now – a small bandage covers the bottom of his battered chin – so I know he's not a robot. He's just immune to panic and fear.

"If I tried to do what you did, I'd be limping like a grandma in church. On a scale from one to ten, what did yesterday rank for you, in terms of craziness?"

"I don't know. Usually that's nothing. Zero?" Rust boasts. "Without shooting anyone... that probably made it a four."

"Come on."

"It was a walk in the park. Like a simulation run. But I get it. That's not normal. In this line of work, you learn to keep your cool. Panicking only leads to rash decisions. Rash decisions get you killed. You just have to slow down and breathe. Think carefully, but trust your instincts."

I appreciate Rust actually taking the time to explain this. There'd be a lot to learn from his experience and skills, if he was only willing to teach.

In college I did a lot of research into prescription drugs and anxiety disorders. I never took any medications, but I had this fantasy that I'd discover I was living with some mild disability that drugs would balance out. This would immediately increase my intelligence and productivity, like Bradley Cooper's pills in *Limitless*. It would unlock parts of my brain I'd never even used and I'd become a superhuman. I could accomplish what I saw Rust do yesterday, on a cerebral and physical level. That was my fantasy. I clearly had too much spare time in college.

"Those were some total Batman, Jason Bourne moves. You are hardcore. The things you do, the way you move. Is that something you can teach?"

"That depends." Rust takes a bite from his toast, spread with thick butter and crushed raspberries. "Some of it is taught. Some of it is experience. Some of it's how you were born."

I push my oatmeal to the side to make room for my notepad, sensing this conversation could become a key feature of my big article.

"So there's, like, an action gene. A stealth gene?"

"Heh." Rust is amused by the choice of words. "You'd be surprised."

I pause to sip my chai latte and consider another question. Feature articles with celebrities seemingly always go into excruciating details about their lunch or breakfast orders, as if there's some level of insight to be gained from how they take their eggs or coffee, or the way they use their utensils. The reality is there's little else to observe, leaving the reporter extrapolating every morsel of information in hope of painting a complete picture. All I'm learning from Rust's breakfast is that he enjoys raspberries.

"It was just... so incredible. The way you reacted, in the moment – you know what I mean?" I'm trying to sound more like a play-by-play announcer than a fanboy, but I'm aware that I'm coming across flustered instead. "I'm sorry I couldn't do anything to help. It's just, you know... I just stood there."

"It's fine."

"I mean, I'm a pacifist, but I should've done something. I left you hanging... like a pair of Dunlop Volleys on a ghetto power line. I just, I froze up. Didn't want to get in your way – you know what I mean?"

"I know what you mean."

I look up from my latte-stained notepad, expecting to see Rust with a vexed look of frustration on account of my rambling. Instead, he's holding eye contact, for the first time making me feel that he wants to engage.

"You handled yourself fine. You're a civilian. And that golf trick was... entertaining. I didn't take you for a golfer."

"Not many people do. I'm just glad I didn't hit him. I'm still in shock. You're, like, an action hero."

"A hero?" Rust's disdain is clear. He doesn't seem to relish the title at all. "No... A hero is celebrated. Revered." A pregnant pause gives way to his first deep reflection. "Here's a quote for you, kid... I used to dream of becoming a hero. But I realised fast that anyone who survives through this world knows you only stay alive by staying under the radar. Infamy only puts a target on your back. That's the best way to end up on the wrong end of a bullet."

Rust looks back to his papers, turning them over until he reaches a black-and-white image of a woman I don't recognise.

"There are no heroes in my world. No living legends. Just old dogs with a lot of scars... and a pocket full of stories no one would ever believe."

I glance up from my shorthand notes to see Rust's eyes focusing on a document line by line, signalling the end of his musing. It doesn't seem to bother him that half the text has been redacted.

"After what I've seen this week, I think I'd believe anything," I say.

This doesn't elicit any follow-up comments, but that wasn't my intention. It's just the truth.

As we sit and finish breakfast, I watch the passing freak show of interesting individuals who inhabit this fair city. If you can make it here, according to Frank Sinatra, you can make it anywhere. I don't believe that for a second. There are thousands, if not millions, of people in this city who are so ingrained in the New York way of life that they wouldn't be able to handle anything less than the hustle-bustle and chaos of Manhattan. As unpopular as Donald Trump is in New York, I doubt his pre-political antics would have yielded the same success if he had been launched into a neighbouring city.

As I look around, I can see a handful of people with the weird and wonderful flavours of New York flowing through their veins.

A middle-aged woman is less than fifteen feet away, staring into a parking meter and using her hands to shield the sunlight hitting the display screen. At first, I think she is trying to read the LED information, but it becomes apparent she's searching for her own reflection, as she brushes stray locks of hairs around her ears and even applies foundation make-up to her white cheeks.

New York is the most photographed city in the world and the people are as interesting as the architecture. I think weirdos are naturally drawn to New York because they feel normal here. This dog's breakfast of immigration and criminal activity somehow became a major centre of the world's entertainment industry, home to planet Earth's most expensive real estate markets and two of the biggest running international stock exchanges. Such an amazing history has made New York a natural hub of unique characters. Take, for example, the homeless man I used to pass on the way to my old office. Instead of a sob story about losing his children or house, his cardboard plea for spare change promised life advice for any donations over a dollar. I'm sure it was at least partly ironic, but his charismatic demeanour helped him become somewhat of a local celebrity. Lately he's even become a social media sensation. Hipsters and tourists love to pose with him, film clips of his hilarious advice and post them online. I'm sure he'll pop up on a morning talk show quite soon. It's a fantastic story – one that would've excited me at some stage in my career – but I've got no time for simply "fantastic" stories anymore. I'm a world-changer now. At least, that's what I've been led to believe in my moments of confidence.

"Rust, for future reference, would you prefer to be referred to as 'tough as an ox', or 'tougher than a $2 steak'?"

He responds by taking my pen away, either to gain my attention or to shut me up. He then places all but one document inside a worn manila folder, which he packs into a briefcase.

"Heard of the Hell's Kitchen Flea Market?"

The triad of markets at the Chelsea Antiques Garage has been open every weekend for more than twenty years. Rust slides across the black and white photo I noticed earlier – a headshot of a straight-faced woman in formal military uniform. Caucasian, blonde, early thirties. No outstanding features.

"This is our target. Goes by Queen. Photo's some years old now."

"Who is she? How's she going to help us find Mars?"

"The only person a rogue spy can trust is another rogue spy."

"So, she's Metric?"

"Former Metric. Informant. According to these files, she worked her way up as an analyst for the Australian Security Intelligence Organisation. From there, we recruited her for signals intelligence as back-up support for Metric operations."

"SIGINT?"

"That's it."

"And what makes you think she knows anything about Mars?"

"She got caught up in one of my field operations the last time I saw her. She wasn't meant to get involved. There were complications." Rust drops this last word with a heavy emphasis, indicating complications in his line of work have far greater consequences than anywhere else. "She had to get a steel plate in her head. And her arm amputated."

"For real?" The fact that she wasn't even a field agent is a terrifying reminder of the mess I could get myself into with Metric.

"At the elbow. Just like the Moriarty statue."

"One-winged angel... How 'bout that?" The conversation breaks while a waitress collects our empty breakfast dishes. "So... How was I meant to figure that out without you?"

Rust shrugs, unsure of the answer but content with the result. "Either way, it means we're ahead of schedule. If my intel is right, Queen's working the market today."

Rust hands his briefcase off to a man sitting inside the cafe, presumably a friend of Metric. It's only a few city blocks to the flea market so we pass the time by going over the new plan. I ask Rust why Metric hasn't gone after Queen, the same way we're chasing down Mars. I can't imagine they would be cool with a former analyst running around New York City.

"She's not dangerous," Rust insists. "The incident... Her mind is damaged. Diagnosed psychogenic amnesia."

"Actual amnesia?"

"I mentioned the metal plate. Seems she's conveniently forgotten anything that would make her a threat to Metric and no one would believe a thing she said, anyway. She still knows what happens to people who try to talk about Metric."

"That's... dark."

"Probably helps that she's not a legal citizen. She isn't qualified to work in US intelligence. Makes her even less believable."

Rust has a fast pace to his stride and I have to hustle just to keep up. I feel like I could lose a few pounds by spending a week with him.

"What's the connection to Mars? Just the fact they're both rogues?"

"He's the one who tracked her down a couple years back. Used her for street level intel, the kind you don't find in dossiers. That keeps the NYPD satisfied and keeps Metric at a distance. Until now, anyway."

"Will she want to see you?"

"Doubt it. You need to approach her, in case she's expecting you. Find out if Mars is with her. Just be ready."

As we wait for traffic to pass, I watch two men on the opposite street doing the same. One is dressed in a sharp suit, the other in skinny jeans and a faded leather jacket. He looks nervous and scattered, bothered by the very presence of the businessman beside him. To me, Mr Wall Street couldn't be any less intimidating. He's just standing there staring, oblivious, and shifting his jaw around as if he has popcorn wedged in his gums. Like so many New Yorkers, he's up early and off to work on a Saturday. I'm not sure how the anti-social survive in this city. There are too many people. It would be so exhausting. New York is a place where no one is polite but everyone is capable of great kindness to those in need. I've seen this time and time again, from the way the city has pulled together after disasters to the willingness of someone on the street giving directions to lost tourists. This is a city where it's perfectly legal to walk around topless, but flirting in public can carry a $25 fine. Like all rules in NYC, these have become more of a suggestion than enforced law.

"Do I need a disguise?" I ask Rust, as we begin walking again.

"You're not *that* famous," he scoffs. "This is Hell's Kitchen... not the Twitter."

"I just meant, from the bad guys. Like, a cover."

"We actually want Mars to recognise you. Plus, we still don't know he's actually there."

"I guess so."

Despite having just eaten, wafting odours are tempting me from cafes and street vendors on every corner. The delicious scent of fresh bread and hot soup cuts straight through the general stink of the metropolitan outdoors – a fusion of hot concrete, trash and petrol fumes.

"Backtracking a little, to your comment," I say, drawing a confused expression from Rust. "You said 'This is Hell's Kitchen, not Twitter.' But Twitter and New York have a lot in common. They're both filled with a combination of crazies, psychos, scam artists, celebrities, business people, foreigners and news media."

"That's great. Very perceptive."

Sarcasm fits Rust like a six-fingered glove. So close to comfortable, but still very out of place. I suppose he's not in the mood for my analogies.

It's not surprising Mr Bald and Ms Ponytail found a disparity between my case file and my real-life persona. People reading my most well-known writing often assume I'm a humourless news hound, while those who know my podcast or follow me on Twitter are often surprised I would investigate anything deeper than the "Paul is dead" Beatles conspiracy theory. This is both pleasing and indicative of the divide between my professional and personal interests. Just because I write with a passion for political, judicial and municipal analysis doesn't mean I can't also have a favourite Teenage Mutant Ninja Turtle.

It's Michelangelo, by the way. I'm not ashamed.

Inside a dimly-lit indoor parking garage, Rust and I face down the crowded flea market, filled with the hundreds of vendors across the floor. As we bypass the chattering crowd filling the entryway, we're met by the first of many rows of stalls selling antiques, crafts, wares and knick knacks you'd struggle to find anywhere else in the city.

"You got that photo?"

"She's the one with a missing arm."

Rust goes on ahead while I take the photograph and circle to the opposite side. I roam along my aisle and stop only to inspect the clerks working at each stall. Are they a woman? No? Keep walking. Yes? Does she have two arms? Yes. Keep walking. This is easier said than done, the way the stallholders are pimping their products and trying to weasel their way into conversation.

"What's goin' on? Raining outside?"

I shake my head and try to keep walking.

"Yeah, there's nothing good happening out there today."

I know he's talking about the weather, but he could just as easily be referring to Hell's Kitchen in general. A lot of development has taken place to change the neighbourhood's identify from a bastion of poor and working-class Irish Americans to a gentrified community, hit hard by the nearby disaster of 9/11. Developers have even tried to shake the devilish moniker and rename it "Clinton", but Hell's Kitchen's reputation as Manhattan's Wild West still bears scars of the past due to overpopulation, homelessness and above-average levels of crime – depending on who you ask.

There's a lot of positivity in the community too. Children's laughter blends with the chatter of multiple dialects to form a unique but comforting soundtrack. These blissful tones bounce off the concrete ceiling and walls, reminding me of this neighbourhood's diversity and vibrancy in the face of harsh times. There's always some sunshine to find among the shadows.

But back to my search.

Are they a woman? Yes. Does she have two arms? No.

I stop walking. It doesn't look like the photo, but it has to be her. Tending to a stall of soy candles, soaps and summer dresses,

Queen looks the way I think the kids would describe a hipster these days. Or maybe it's punk? No, she's a hippie. I don't know. It's getting too hard to follow the labels.

Short-bleached dreadlocks fall from one half of her otherwise shaved head. Her faded grey jeans are so baggy that they must have been custom-made. As she raises her single arm to point a customer towards her stock, the cuff of her loose-fitting shirt falls down to reveal a sleeve of tattoos in scribbled cursive graffiti.

"Rust," I say through my Nano GEAR. "I've found her."

"Do you have a visual?"

"I'm looking at a woman with one arm. How's that for a visual?"

"It matches the photo?"

"Not really. But it's her. Can you see the hippie stall next to the second-hand books? Right there, talking to a customer."

"You sure?"

"Pretty sure. She's changed her look, but she's one arm short of... Well, it's one arm."

"I'll keep my distance for now. Make contact and I'll respond as required."

I hold up the black and white photo again for comparison. She is *completely* different, almost unrecognisable from her days with Metric. There's no better reason to undergo a total makeover than being an enemy of the state.

I approach Queen and pretend I'm interested in what she's selling. Cherry soap. Fascinating. Honey soap. How bohemian.

"You right, mate? Need a hand with anythin'?" Queen's thick Australian accent is so out of place that it takes a few seconds just to understand her.

"Yeah, I'm... I'm good. Just looking."

"Rightio, give us a shout if you need anythin'. It's all organic. All local stuff."

"Uhuh." I pick up and inspect the honey soap, apparently a top seller. It smells just like honey. Shocking.

"So, do you have anything... from Mars?"

Queen smiles in response, out of curiosity as much as politeness. "Like, the planet? We've got some red crystals. That's sorta... alien-lookin', yeah?"

Bless her – she's trying to be helpful even though she thinks I'm asking about extra terrestrials.

"Just, anything to do with Mars," I say, raising a suggestive eyebrow.

"I don't think I can help you, mate." Queen grimaces and scratches her forehead with her long green and gold painted nails. Perhaps a more direct approach is required.

"*Agent* Mars?" Now she clearly knows what I'm getting at, but doesn't look any more pleased about it.

"I reckon maybe you should keep on walkin', mate."

"It's OK," I assure her, checking that no one is close by. "I know about Metric. Mars sent us after you."

This must be a poor choice of words because a look of pure horror has crossed Queen's face. I can see the wheels turning as she considers who I could be and what I could know.

In a flash, she vaults over the stall, one arm and all. Her Timberland boots miss me by mere inches as her legs hurtle past and she begins to flee.

"Rust! She's running!"

Chapter 9

Information

My eyes race to track the sequence of events as Queen hauls through the crowd. I don't want to witness another brawl, especially not here. There's no Water Man to clean up this mess. I spot Rust, ready to step in front of a sprinting Queen. He spreads his arms wide open, catching her attention and stopping her dead in her tracks.

"Queen! I'm the only agent here."

I can faintly make out her response through the Nano GEAR. She's certainly surprised to see him and isn't shy about making her feelings clear. She points at the side of Rust's face and a second later the Nano GEAR signal drops out. This must be Rust's way of proving there's no listening ears and their conversation is private.

From a distance, there's little I can make out. The discussion gets more and more heated as neither of them seem prepared to back down. I'm not the greatest lip reader, but I can tell Queen's not describing a sunset or a newborn puppy, based on the number of F-bombs she's dropping. I don't want her to catch me staring, given our strange encounter earlier. If she gets startled and doesn't believe Rust, she could bolt and we'll never see her again.

In an attempt to appear casual, I stroll along to the next stall and look through its wares. Wood-carved coasters, etched lithographs, school calculators. There's some really random junk here. I spin a hanging mobile of homemade jewellery until something shiny catches my eye. A sterling silver ring sparkles with engraved cursive text. Is it the one ring to rule them all?

"German," the clerk tells me, with a thick dialect. I hold it up to the light.

"Wahrheit... um jeden Preis?" My accent could use a lot of work but I think I've got that right. I look back to Rust and he's still deep in conversation.

"Yes," the German clerk says. "This is a shorter version of German saying: '*Friede wenn möglich, aber die Wahrheit um jeden Preis.*' Meaning 'Peace if possible, but truth at any cost.' An old saying. A good saying."

"Martin Luther."

The clerk nods, smiling with a familiar look you get when you meet someone with the same obscure musical tastes. In this country, Martin Luther King is a hero, an icon, and a cultural symbol of the fight for human rights and equality. His namesake, a German 16th-century renegade in his own right, doesn't quite carry the same sense of historic wonder here, despite having an equal impact on the culture of his time. The residential halls at my college campus were named after great theologians throughout history. Martin Luther, John Calvin, John Wesley. I took a special interest in Luther and read a few essays on the impact of the *Ninety-five Theses* – his list of public declarations that shook up the Catholic Church by exposing its corruption and abusive failures.

I tell the German clerk I'll buy the ring on a chain, but he lacks the change to break a $50 bill. After he throws in a laser pointer and wooden keyring at a discount, I look back to Rust, who's now leading Queen towards me. I swallow hard, trying to wet my drying throat.

"Hey," she says, hand in her pocket.

"Hi there."

My smile fades when it's not reciprocated. Instead of responding, she stares. She examines my face, reading into my soul. I've been wired to feel good when a woman gazes at my face, but this is simply uncomfortable. There's no joy in her eyes, just a guarded reservation.

"Is everything... all right?"

"Yeah." She nods, smiling for only a nanosecond. "This way."

~∞~

Queen leads us to a dive bar just a minute's walk from the market. According to the sign on the window, The Naughty Dog is an "intercontinental tavern and liquor store". I follow Queen inside and pass under the hanging bunting stretched across the roof, made up of national flags from around the world. Different parts of the bar are decorated in paraphernalia and merchandise from each continent.

"All beers, from everywhere," Queen says, gesturing to the long fridge backing up the bar. "Aussie beers, German beers... That's really all you need. And Irish beers."

Of all the snacks that could be displayed on the bar, there's a plate of cold watermelon. No peanuts, no pretzels. The Naughty Dog is serving free watermelon, sliced into juicy green and pink triangles.

"Come on, someone get that boy an Oettinger!" An early-twenties loudmouth at the booth behind us butchers his pronunciation of the German beer, sounding as ignorantly American as possible. His annoying group of frat boys are intoxicated with glee and ignorance, despite the fact it's a Saturday morning.

"What are you lads drinkin'?" Queen asks us, without a drop of irony. "My shout."

Usually I'd make a joke about the type of people who consume alcohol at 9am, but after the week I've had, I could do with a little something just to take off the edge. Rust orders a whiskey dry. I ask for a Fosters beer, hoping to impress Queen with a nod towards her homeland. My pride turns to embarrassment when she responds with raucous laughter and berates the credibility of the brand. If I was flexible enough, I'd kick myself.

"If you want an actual real Aussie beer, we'll get two James Boags." I'm no dialectologist but I sense very little American influence in her accent. She's as Australian as Vegemite, her homeland's foul black breakfast spread.

Once the barman busts open our bottles and leaves us with some breathing room, Queen starts to lay down the law. "This goes without saying, but no nanos, fellas. Get those earpieces out."

The way Aussies talk and abbreviate everything, "no nanos" could quite easily be her way of telling us "no grandmothers".

Rust uses a voice command to disconnect his Nano GEAR. I mimic him, and place mine on the bar next to my drink, just to be sure.

"All right. Basically, I haven't seen Mars in yonks. Probably a year."

Rust isn't impressed. "You mean—"

"Hold up. Calm down, Charlie Brown. I have something that'll help."

"Talk fast."

"I'll tell you everything. But I'm gonna need somethin'. You lads were sent here to help me. I could try to put you in touch with Mars, but he wouldn't have a bar of it – pardon the pun."

"You're saying..."

"I'm saying I need a hand with somethin'."

"Absolutely not. We're on a mission here."

"It's important, Rusty. You owe me."

"How do you figure?" Rust asks, curious with disbelief. "Scarpino let you leave Metric without consequence. I don't know another soul who could say that."

Holding her beer with a firm grip, Queen points to her lack of a second arm. It's an irrefutable argument. "You call *this* without consequence?"

"Look, you're playing everyday citizen down here, while there are people rotting in Guantanamo Bay who've done less than you. The fact that you don't 'remember' half of what you saw is the only thing keeping you alive."

I have to think if she'd done anything more sinister than going AWOL from Metric she wouldn't be sitting in front of us.

"Mate, I paid my dues for this country. I sacrificed everything'. I lost my mind for Metric. I lost my arm for *you*."

"For Pete's sake. You don't even remember that."

"I *know* what happened. Don't even act like you had nothin' to do with it."

"You're playing that card?" Rust is trying to sound incredulous, but it seems he was expecting and dreading this conversation.

"Yeah, I'm playin' that card. I'm playin' the 'I've lost my bloody arm' card. I'm also playin' the 'you'd be dogmeat right now if it weren't for me' card."

A frustrated sigh slips from Rust, admitting an element of debt to Queen. Maybe someone like Mars gave her the missing details or maybe she just did the math to figure it all out.

"You're still sore about that."

"I've got a whole bloody stack of cards to play here, Rusty. And I'm not bluffin'. You want Mars, you need to—"

"Queen. Just..." Rust groans and gives into Queen's demand, the way an old woman succumbs to her natural hair colour. "What is it? What do you need?"

"OK. Good." She suddenly has nothing to say. I guess she wasn't expecting co-operation without compromise. Pondering her next statement, she drags the plate of watermelon closer and picks up a single dripping slice.

"Well. How do you feel about doing some good in the world?"

"Hooray. Get to the point." Ice cubes clink inside Rust's glass as he lowers it to the counter. The comforting sound takes me back to that sweet spot between college and moving to New York. It was a brief era when I could afford the time and the money to sit around with my friends and throw back a couple of quiet drinks without worrying about too many calories or too few brain cells.

"I've got a mate. Cassandra. Rough as guts with a heart of gold."

"If you think I'm flying to Melbourne or Sydney to find some no-hope, dope-fiend floozy..."

"Mate, she grew up in Hell's Kitchen. She used to work in the markets here. She's fine, she knows how to take care of herself. But she fell in with the wrong crowd. Got herself a debt she couldn't pay back."

"Junkie?"

"Nah, clean. I'm fairly sure," Queen replies through munches of watermelon. "But she's in deep trouble."

"With who?"

Adding nothing to the conversation, I sit and listen, peeling at the label of my beer bottle.

"One of the Irish families."

"If you say Moriarty..."

"No way. I forget exactly, but it's somethin' real Irish sounding. Let's just say *O'Brien*." Queen drops the watermelon rind back on the plate and picks up another slice. "It really doesn't matter what his name is. He's a tosser."

"I'm sure."

"So this O'Brien guy is small time, but he's got ties back to The Westies. For the sake of clarity, he's like the idiot cousin. It's like I always say, there's one in every Irish family."

"Hey now," I interject, against my better judgement. "Let's not perpetuate any negative stereotypes?"

"There's stereotypes and there's reality. Fair dinkum, you don't roll around with these fellas unless you have to. Cass was in way too deep, all right, so her little *sister* offered to help out."

"Her actual sister?" I ask.

"Yeah, kid's a *genius*. Hustled her way into college, studyin' biochemical engineering or somethin' equally nerdy. So she does the only thing she can do to help a cruddy situation. She's a chemist. So she makes drugs."

"Great." Rust takes a short sip from his whiskey. "Explain why this isn't a case for our friends at the NYPD."

"I don't think Cass wants her sister to throw her whole life away."

"Sounds like that's already happened."

"No way!" Queen flashes an optimistic smile. "It's like I always say, there's a path out, a new life just waitin' for her – we gotta open the door!"

"Right. You're clearly the expert on making a new life. So

what are we talking – meth? Coke?"

"I dunno. Doesn't matter. Lucinda – that's the sister's name – she's repaid the debt twice over and they still won't let her out. They're doing too well out of it. She's makin' top shop product and no one's willing to help out to set her loose."

Rust swishes the ice around in his glass, intentionally clinking it against the crystal edge. "And you?"

"Yeah, why can't you do it?"

Queen chugs the last quarter of her beer and gestures to the bartender for another.

"One-armed Aussie hipster? Not exactly the scariest way to put the fear in a drug kingpin."

Hipster. I knew she was a hipster.

"But you, Rusty? I've seen what you can do." Queen punches the air with a fast hook. "You're scary as all heck. You can put the pound on 'em, the old knuckle sandwich and scare 'em straight."

Even with one arm, Queen looks as though she'd beat me to a pulp just for looking at her sideways. But she's right. Rust at the age of fifty-something is fitter than I've ever been. A sound escapes his mouth that can only be described as his body uttering "I'm getting too old for this."

Our meeting with Queen can't be going how he expected. She assures him it'll all be clean, that simply taking O'Brien out would send waves right up to the so-called "Westies" and draw more attention to Lucinda's talent. But O'Brien is, in Queen's words, a wuss. If Rust can scare him into releasing Lucinda, he'd be too embarrassed to tell anyone and too timid to go after her.

The conclusion seems inevitable so I'm just trying to push it along as fast as possible. Maybe a stroke to Rust's ego will push him over the edge.

"C'mon. You could do this without breaking a sweat. A couple punks? You've handled worse – is that safe to say?"

"That's very safe to say."

"So let's get this show on the road.

"Hmm." Rust groans in acceptance. "I have a lot of questions. You've put me between the devil and the deep blue sea here. You don't want to know what Scarpino would suggest if I took this back to Metric." Queen nods knowingly as Rust pushes his chair back, squeaking harshly across the sticky wooden floor. He walks deeper into the venue, but stops to leave us with one last comment before disappearing down a hallway. "We'll be keeping this between us."

"Sure... I get that." Queen raises her beer along with her volume as Rust gets closer to the bathroom. "And I thank you for it!"

A few moments of silence pass and I have no idea what to say. I usually relish the opportunity to talk to people who look like Queen. They almost always have a twisted and fascinating worldview. Something about Queen scares me, though. I try to tell myself it's not the whole one-arm thing... but I feel like it probably is the one-arm thing. I know enough about psychology to understand people fear that which is different and unknown. I just need to break the silence. What do I say? Perhaps I should appeal to her interests.

"What's the deal with seedless watermelon? We can grow this stuff without seeds, but we can't make chewing gum with flavour that lasts more than five minutes?"

Queen doesn't react. She looks deep into her beer, as if it's a nebulous andromeda of answers to life's mysteries.

"Is that Jerry Seinfeld or somethin'?"

"Um... No. I think that's an Andrew Maven original. But I have been known to subconsciously steal jokes."

"Right. I bet Rusty loves those jokes."

"I don't think he even realises when I'm joking. He just thinks I'm weird."

Queen smirks, which tells me she's shared this experience in one way or another. "I dunno how much you know about him, but I never met anyone who's more of a Captain America. 'Hail to the chief,' and all that."

"Yeah, he's hardcore."

"That's an understatement. I mean, I'm shocked he's keepin' this off the books. Actually, the most shockin' part is that he's not running Metric by now."

"How did *you* get wrapped up with them? Are you like an Australian correspondent, a mole, or something?"

"Nope. Joined the international relations team as an analyst. Informant. Never expected to see any action."

Even for an Aussie, she's rough around the edges. It could just be part of her cover, but I can't imagine her sitting at a desk and working the phone. Come to think of it, I don't even know what informants do. Maybe she was out on the street undercover gathering intelligence the old-fashioned way.

"So you went from foreign affairs to... field ops?"

"I'm not part of your feature article, mate. It's not gonna help you any for me to spill my life story."

"It's interesting."

"Yeah," she admits. "I bet. One-armed runaway spy with a convenient case of partial-amnesia."

"Exactly. I didn't realise that even happens."

"Believe me. It does. But I remember enough to know Rusty is gonna help on this one. He's got a soft spot for scientists."

"You don't say?"

"Let me warn you though, before he gets back from takin' a slash. Be careful. You can't trust anyone."

"Sound advice, I'm sure." I nod in thoughtful agreement, wondering if I can ask her to be more specific with her advice. "Unfortunately, I don't feel like I have much of a choice."

I finish my drink and slide my empty bottle across the sticky bar. Regardless of my stress levels, there's just something dirty about drinking this early in the day.

"There is... *something* though." I swivel on my chair to face Queen, who's chugging her beer as if it is the first bottle of an entire carton that's about to reach its expiration date. "It's something Rust doesn't seem to care about, but I think it's totally relevant."

"What's that?" she asks, wiping her lips.

I look across to the bathroom door to make sure Rust isn't coming back yet. He still scares me, but the coast is clear. The bartender is counting cash and the loud frat boys in the corner are arguing about which of them is more of a "consummate stickman", whatever that means.

"Mars stole a *list* from Kenton Moriarty at the Manhattan Club Commonwealth Hotel," I say with a lowered voice. "He broke in there just for this list. That's all. A couple weeks ago. I want to know what it was. Rust... I think he only wants to find Mars - you know what I mean?"

"I'm sure he does."

"But is that unusual? I think there's got to be something to it."

Queen breaks eye contact. She looks slightly amused as she adjusts the shoulder of her shirt and indicates a coy reluctance to go into detail.

"You've got a lot to learn about the Foxes."

"What are the Foxes?"

Her smile vanishes. "Nothing. Forget it." She reaches over and places her hand firm on the bar in front of me. "Do me a favour and don't mention any of this conversation to Rusty, Metric or anyone, OK?"

I nod, not wanting to cause any trouble. Plus, Queen still scares me.

"You look smart enough, and scared enough, to know that even with one arm, I could probably kick your arse."

"Mm. Thanks for the brutal honesty."

"Sorry. I'm just sayin'. What's your name again?"

Everyone else gets to have these cool one-word titles. Why not me?

"It's Maven. You can call me Maven."

Queen chugs at her third beer for a moment before placing the bottle on the wooden counter. "So what's a Maven?"

"I am."

"Rightio."

"It's actually a Hebrew word. It's a person who's an expert. Like, a guru."

"Ah yeah. I reckon I've heard it in a Kanye song."

"You probably did."

As Queen and the approaching barman exchange familiar pleasantries, I swivel on my stool and examine the rest of the mostly empty pub.

The international décor is tacky at face value, but here it comes across as quaint. At The Naughty Dog, all the nations of the world coexist in harmony. Have a Heineken, drink some Japanese sake, sip on a Thai Singha, maybe even uncork some Manische-witz. The Naughty Dog has it figured out, but outside these doors we're still divided by racial animosity and disagreement.

I have this theory that the only way nations of the world will ever stop fighting is if we go to war with another planet. I don't believe in intelligent extra terrestrial life, which makes it a theory without application, but I find it curious how we extend the boundaries of our geographic allegiances based on the greatest present threat. We learnt this from the President's speech before the climax of *Independence Day*.

High school sports are the best example. First we compete with classmates at recess and in team try-outs. Then we make the squad and "fight" against other schools. They're our new mortal enemies until we get chosen to qualify for a regional team, and then if you're good enough you make the state team. Each time you advance to a higher level, your former enemies and opponents become teammates and allies. Eventually you're good enough for the national team so you "go to war" with other countries. But instead of three-pointers we're usually dropping bombs. The only way we can theoretically achieve world peace is if our existence as a planet is threatened by something that makes every diplomatic dispute and international feud completely and utterly irrelevant. It's a fitting irony that the threat of total annihilation is the only event with potential to bring us all together.

"Bads, you should've been there!" The loud frat boys are get-ting excited as their latest arrival recites an encounter from the previous night out. "Me and Gribble were on the dance floor next to Birdman and Stevo, and it was packed. So the guy who was there last week, he came past and I was just throwing these low punches – bam, bam, bam! Then when the bouncers came past I just made it look like it was part of a dance move."

"Yeah, not bad, Huzz. I'll pay that."

"So I'm laying in the punches, then dancing away like it's all good."

Rust returns to interrupt my eavesdropping, taking up the stool between Queen and me. He doesn't want to walk into anything without being prepared, but after half a dozen questions Queen is fed up with the interrogation.

"Look. Rusty. There's some ripper intel up for grabs here, if you just do me this one favour. Honest. It doesn't have to be a big thing. Let's get it over with."

"This better be solid. The intel."

"Rock solid. Like Ayer's Rock, mate. Don't you worry." Queen drops a handful of cash on the bar. "We can head over right now, take care of business and be done this arvo in time for a late lunch."

"And this O'Brien. He'll be there?"

"Never leaves. He just cracks the whip and makes sure Cass's sister works non-stop."

"You know this how?"

"Security is chilled. Honestly, these people are about as thick as a tree stump. You wouldn't believe it. They work out of a warehouse in West Harlem. You can see straight through from the roof opposite the road."

"In the middle of Harlem?" Rust asks, rightfully baffled.

"I never said they were smart."

Rust grunts, repeating what's fast becoming his signature catchphrase in the character bio written in my head. "If I'm gonna shake down a drug den, on a Saturday afternoon, I'm gonna need at least one more of these whiskeys. Better make it a double."

"That's the spirit," Queen says excitedly. "A man's not a camel. But I had the last shout, so maybe the next round's on the US government?"

Our taxes at work. This is definitely going in my article.

Chapter 10

Operation

Selfie sticks used to really bother me. You can't ask a passer-by to take that photo? But hey. Whatever. Just like a lot of things that used to bother me – pop music, rom-coms, e-cigarettes, vegans, people who don't like *Breaking Bad* – I find myself not caring anymore. Live and let live.

Since I farewelled my early twenties, I've become far more tolerant. Perhaps I'm simply more apathetic to things that don't affect me. Either way, I find my eyes transfixed on this delirious Asian couple outside our car, struggling to take a selfie in front of a Bank of America. They're trying and failing to fit the Bank of America sign in the background of their photo. It must be four tries before they're happy. I don't get it. There's literally a bank on almost every corner of this island.

Seriously.

There are almost three thousand in New York City and the Bank of America beside the Asian couple is one of two hundred and eighteen. Is this particular branch famous? Was it featured in an episode of *Sex and the City*? I'll never know.

"Maven, c'mon."

Queen and Rust are waiting outside the car, growing increasingly impatient. Before I got distracted by the Bank of America fans, I was trying to read the signs along the street.

"Can we park here?" I'm not used to riding in a private car in New York. It's always taxis, subways and Uber. I wouldn't even consider driving here. I don't know how anyone manages the stress.

"I haven't been this side of Central Park in ages," Queen says to no one in particular.

Rust pays no attention to my concerns. I bet he has a "get out of parking fines" card in his wallet, right next to his licence to kill.

"I don't really go south much either though," Queen continues. "I've kinda got a little square, from Hell's Kitchen down to the village. What's that movie, *Wall Street Wolves*?"

"*The Wolf of Wall Street.*" I slam the car door and check that it's locked.

"Yeah, that one. When it came out, that was the last time I went south. Wanted to see how it all worked."

"So, Lucinda. How will I recognise her?" Rust says, clearly wanting to get in and out as soon as possible.

"Don't think there'll be many black women in there... or women, full stop."

"Right. Black woman. Young. Probably in a lab."

Harlem is rough. It almost feels like a different city compared to how I've come to know downtown Manhattan. A man on the street beside us is fashioning a wire hanger into a single long wire, blatantly attempting to break into what I will assume is his own vehicle.

"Well, she could be anywhere, really. They barely let her leave."

"What about the parents? The rest of the family?" I ask. "They haven't tried to do anything before now?"

Queen leads us past a post-pubescent teenager dressed as the Statue of Liberty, handing out fliers for a business we don't care about. We continue walking down the street towards our target, which looks like a cheap housing complex.

"Her folks are from Nairobi. Think they moved to Modesto or

something. I doubt they understand what's happening. Cassie's kept them in the dark."

"A Kenyan scientist... She really has done well in this country."

"Until now," Rust says.

"That's what I mean," Queen says. "We can't let the story end like this."

We follow Queen into the belly of the old building and up its stairs – three storeys in all. It's not pretty. Aside from its favourable position near the warehouse, this seems like a place where we could get away with murder. There are fist-sized holes in the wall, while laundry and trash bags litter the hallways. I think back to Tiger Woods, home alone in my apartment. I really hope Metric is feeding the poor thing. We've only been away for about twenty-four hours, but I usually have time to arrange a neighbour or friend to help out. He's probably destroyed my living room out of boredom by now. As I've mentioned before, cats are jerks.

Sunlight streams into the dusty hallway as Queen forces open a heavy door on the top floor.

"Welcome to the roof."

As the exit swings open, a flock of startled pigeons scatters in a panic, as if we're cops breaking up their underage kegger. There's very little up here – some potted plants, a carpet of bird droppings and a single table setting, littered with overflowing ash trays. From this height we can see the rooftops of several nearby buildings. A graffiti artist going by "Prince Plakapong" seems to have claimed the area as his own, with street tags everywhere I look. The view isn't much to speak of, but sure enough, we can see straight through the neighbouring warehouse. The top skylight windows are clear enough to make out some people and furniture inside.

Queen came prepared. She's gazing through a pair of cheap binoculars, likely bought somewhere at the Hell's Kitchen Flea Market.

"What did I tell you? Lacklustre security at best. Looks like two blokes... three blokes. There's O'Brien. Wearin' that haggard-arse baseball cap."

"Let me see." Rust reaches for the binoculars.

"He's the old one," she explains, handing them over. "Sorry. *Older.* I know you old people get sensitive about that word."

"This... This is a serious operation, Queen. Not small-time, by any stretch. Look at that equipment."

"I said the *security* was small-time."

"It looks like... Hm. Can't see."

"There's, like, boilers and all that filtration stuff."

"Which side is the entrance?"

I take a seat at the cigarette-covered table, feeling left out. This is the first time since arriving to Manhattan that I'm calm enough to check all my phone messages. There are twenty-two emails, five texts, three missed calls and far too many Twitter notifications to read.

I'm grateful to have a legion of fans and supporters who are so passionate that they get upset at me for not producing enough content. At the same time, there seems to be a smaller but louder group of Americans who get out of bed just to shout at me and tell me I suck. That hurts, sometimes. Not always. But sometimes.

I'll admit that I've Googled myself more than anyone should. My criticism seems to alternate from over-the-top praise to pathological abuse. I've been called so many names by anonymous trolls that most of them don't land anymore. The important thing is to find a way to keep in touch with your own sense of identity and understanding of who you are and what motivates you.

I'm often criticised using polar-opposite terms that contradict any conclusion towards what I really am. The response to a single article can see me labelled "too liberal" *and* "too conservative." Can I possibly be a "manchild" *and* an "old fart"? "Superficial" *and* "over-analytic"? In a similar vein, I've been praised for being a trail blazer, but also as a throwback to old-school journalism.

One critique negates the other, so which is it?

Do you shut out the pessimistic and believe your own hype, or do you try to stay grounded and address your faults?

For your sanity's sake, you either have to listen to all the noise or none of it. A lot of the criticisms can't co-exist. The only conclusion is that I am to these people whatever they want me to be. Truth is objective and it isn't for me to decide what I am. If someone tells you you're offensive, you don't get to disagree. But that doesn't mean you've done anything wrong – it just means you can't control the context and reaction to anything you create for other people to consume.

"I've never done a stake out," Queen says. "It's fun. Maven, you played that *Grand Theft Auto*?"

"Yeah, of course," I scoff. "I'm actually a pretty big gamer."

"Yeah, you look like a big gamer."

"Come on, kid," Rust scolds me, even though it was Queen who started the conversation. "We're not here to talk computers and gadgets. I'm making my way down."

"Do... Do you want back-up?" I ask, hoping the answer is a resounding "no".

"From you? I'll manage just fine." Rust tries not to laugh. That was a little more resounding than I wanted. I must look offended because Rust offers an explanation. "You're about as physically intimidating as a kindergarten teacher."

"Well. You haven't seen *Kindergarten Cop*, have you?"

My ego is bruised, but at least my body won't be. I'll chill and keep watch. The Nano GEAR will ensure I don't miss anything. Rust brushes past me and disappears through the door we used earlier. The pigeons scatter again, growing weary of the increased roof traffic.

I finally get my turn with the binoculars and I'm surprised how little can be seen through the warehouse windows. There's a large open space, like all warehouses, with one separate room at the entry point. There's a lot of equipment but I can't tell if I'm looking at barrels of methylamine or kegs of beer.

Queen's clearly been through more than I'll ever know – apparently more than she even remembers – but she's maintained a confidence and attitude that many would envy. There's no one I admire more than people who overcome disability to live an uncompromised lifestyle. I'd struggle to function with an ingrown toenail, let alone the loss of a sense or limb.

"There was a guy at my college who had a hook arm. You ever thought about getting a hook arm?"

"Do I look like a pirate?" Queen barks back, without lowering the binoculars.

"I'm sorry. I just—"

"It's OK." She looks up, chuckling to herself. "I'm just messin' with you."

"Oh."

"I've actually got one at home. I don't wear it to the market 'cause it scares people. Hence this loose-flowing top."

"Yeah."

"You don't need to be scared, mate." Queen leans back on the ledge, looking up at me with friendly eyes. "I'm not some hot shot maverick spy on the run like Mars. I was an analyst with Metric. I sat at a computer all day."

"Right. But you don't remember?"

"I don't remember the work, but I remember it was ninety-five per cent in an office."

"And the other five per cent?"

She points to the sleeve where her arm used to be, now just a hidden stump. "You're lookin' at it."

"It's funny – well, not funny. But I find it interesting. You don't seem the type. The computer hacker, the code breaker – you know what I mean?"

"Yeah, well." Queen returns to her surveillance duties. "You don't exactly come across like a secret agent's sidekick yourself."

"Touché."

"It's like they say. Life comes at you fast. One day you're an IT whiz workin' for an overseas government... the next day you've got a plate in your head, you're livin' on the street, wearin' a hook arm, and hopin' no one asks for a social security number."

"Hopefully... Well, I think I'll be OK."

"I told you. Be careful what you get into, Maven."

Queen's words cast a doubt over me that I can't ignore, but

for now, I'll try my best to heed her advice. Rust strolls out of our building's front exit over to the warehouse entrance.

"Go, you good thing," Queen says, spurring Rust on from afar. "Go in hard."

He approaches the mysterious drug lab with the familiarity of a mailman on his routine delivery route. Compared to stealing codes from nuclear disposal facilities, breaking into Soviet army bases and freeing soldiers from Middle Eastern compounds, Rust must find a Harlem drug lab infiltration totally mundane.

"Gimme those binos." Queen reaches her arm out, ending my turn as the team spotter. "You've got the Nano. I'll be the eyes, you be the ears."

It dawns on me that Rust has probably been listening to my entire conversation with Queen. This surveillance thing is tricky to get used to. It seems he's taken a direct approach, knocking on the front door instead of penetrating the warehouse's security weaknesses.

"Can't see Rusty, but I can see this thug answering the door," Queen commentates. "And... he's got him in a hammer lock. He's down on the ground. That was quick."

"Way to go."

"Now he's... inside. Sussing it out. Just lookin' around. Now he's gone."

"*Maven,*" Rust whispers to me. "*How many in the next room?*"

I relay the question to Queen and she informs me there are two, but both have been cautioned by the noise.

"Rust is waiting," she says. "With his gun out."

"Crap."

"He's knockin' on the wall... They're comin' to inves– Oh! Damn!"

"What is it?"

"Rust just pistol whipped one bloke... and now he's choked out the other one!"

"That sounds about right. You doing OK in there, Rust?"

"*Maintain radio silence.*"

"Uh... affirmative?" I pull the Nano GEAR out and cup my

hands around it, hoping it will dampen the sound. "He wants me to shut up."

Queen explains the voice commands that will mute my end of the device and switch the incoming audio to a loud speaker. With the security guards disposed, Rust appears to have a clear path for now.

"He's waiting at the door."

"Still armed?" I ask.

"Obviously."

Queen describes the series of events as Rust advances to the next room, holding O'Brien at gunpoint amid a lot of screaming and colourful language.

"He's got him on his knees. That bastard is down!"

As soon as O'Brien stops protesting, we can hear Rust run through his list of demands.

"You've got a young girl working for you. Not anymore. She's a free woman. You're going to let her go, no questions asked, and you're never going to see her again. You won't talk to her. You won't look at her. You won't think about her. Do you understand me?"

"Yeah, yeah!" From this distance I can only make out the figure of O'Brien. His face is covered by a blue cap, but I gather he's close to tears.

"Where is she?"

"I'm right here." The distant female voice comes from someone we can't see through the windows. *"But I'm not leaving."*

"What the...?" Queen can't hide her shock, seeing Lucinda emerge from the basement or a room hidden from our view.

"We need to leave - now," Rust asserts.

"I told you, I'm staying. And you're gonna put your gun down - now."

"Lady, I don't have time for this. You don't have to come with me, but you don't need to stay here anymore. Just lower your gun before you do something stupid."

"A gun?" I gasp in horror. You'd never know Lucinda had a weapon from the tone in Rust's voice. He's unaffected by the tension. Cool as a cucumber. In a millisecond he could perform an ocular pat down – a visual threat assessment to determine the chances of Lucinda actually putting a bullet through his head.

"*I wanna stay,*" she tells him. "*I need to stay. I'm working.*"

"What is she saying?" Queen is as confused as any of us, but it's clear Cassie's sister is breaking bad.

"*Look. I don't know what they've done to you, but we're outta here right now. Just be calm and don't escalate this.*"

"*I got your escalation right here.*"

I audibly gasp at the ringing sound of a single gunshot. It echoes through the warehouse with a sick resonance.

"Rust!"

"He's OK."

"What the heck is going on?" I shriek at Queen, talking over Lucinda's bizarre threats. A warning shot is *still* a gunshot. There are thirty-five thousand police officers in the New York Police Department. There's a decent to good chance that one of them is on their way here now.

"Should we help?"

"Nah, nah. Rust can handle this," Queen says unconvincingly.

"She doesn't know what she's doing down there! You can't predict a crazy person."

"Well, what are we 'sposed to do?" Queen asks, her mounting stress beginning to show.

"I've got an idea. Give me those binoculars, please."

I fumble through my pockets until I find the laser pointer I just bought at the flea market. I disable the mute setting of my Nano GEAR and scramble to explain my plan to Rust, hoping he can hear me over the escalating conversation. I don't blame them for wondering what the heck is happening.

"Rust – tell Lucinda there's a marksman with a sniper rifle on the next building." I crouch down, peering through a gap in the brick ledge, and shine the laser pointer through the window onto Lucinda's chest.

"*I'm happy to talk this out,*" Rust tells his hosts. "*But you need to lower your gun. I've got a sniper on the next roof and I'd hate to lose this bet.*"

"A bet? This isn't a game, grandpa." She looks young. Scared. She seems so out of place, dressed in lab gear and black jeans, but she is certainly gripping that pistol with intent.

"He bet me that he could knock the baseball cap off this Irish mobster with his first shot." Following Rust's prompt, I move the laser pointer from Lucinda over to O'Brien. *"You don't want to know where the second one's going."*

Lucinda's face is now hidden from view but her boss looks like he's about to wet his pants.

"You little beauty, Maven!"

I'm too focused on steadying the laser to respond to Queen, but I'm relieved that I've been able to help stabilise a hostile situation. Now all we have to do is wait for Rust, Lucinda and O'Brien to talk this out so we can get get out of here.

Before I can try to piece together the evolving conversation in the warehouse, the approaching blare of a police siren takes Queen and the Nano GEAR further along the rooftop, out of earshot.

"Bloody coppers," I hear her mumble. "We need to take care of this."

"Meaning what?"

"We can't let them get to that warehouse. We don't want Rust to have to call in any favours from Metric, remember? This one's on the down-low."

The panic starts to set in. Rust seems above reproach, given his government job, but if this back-fires on O'Brien and Lucinda, there's a chance Queen will hold back her information on Mars. And that won't end well for anyone.

We rush downstairs and Queen explains her improvised plan to distract and discard the police. It's a bit crazy – but as they say, it might be crazy enough to work.

At the bottom floor, the two officers approaching the warehouse change their path when they notice us hustling towards them. They almost look too young to wear the iconic dark blue NYPD uniforms. I'm more comfortable hanging back as Queen rushes ahead, showing no fear of invading their personal space.

"Thank goodness." She slaps her thigh and flashes a mischievous smile. "I was just about to ring the cops."

Despite her opening line, the officers show no sign of familiarity towards us.

"Please don't move, ma'am." Without making eye contact, the taller officer guides her to hold still. "Sir, do you know these people?"

Before I can answer, an old man creeps out of the building with a gut resembling a weather balloon. There's a fear in his eyes, but he's bold enough to stand in front of us to make his accusation.

"This is the people! They're not from here, officers."

Bless his soul, he's called the cops on us. We may have deserved it, snooping around the building and loitering on the rooftop. Queen does well to ignore his vague assertion.

"What are the chances though?" she says, still referring to the cops' arrival. "Crazy timing."

"Ma'am, we had a 9-1-1 call about a *gun* firing nearby. Do you know anything about that?"

"I heard it!" the old man shouts. "They were up on the roof doing the spray paint graffiti."

"Nah, mate," Queen shakes her head, turning back to the cops. "Plenty of noise down on the street. You know there's a lot of old cars in this neighbourhood? Low-socio economic demographic."

"Meaning?"

"Well, officer, when an internal combustion engine has a moment of external combustion..."

"Back-fire," the shorter officer says to his partner. "That's what I was talkin' about before, Corey."

"But this isn't your apartment building?" Officer Corey asks Queen. The second cop seems to be deferring to him, or maybe he's just speechless due to Queen's foreign accent, strange appearance and missing arm.

"Truth told, I'm here lookin' for my cousin," she lies without a hint of fear. "I'm actually real stoked you're here. It's perfect timing."

"And you?" Officer Corey points to me.

"I'm the *landlord*," I respond with more confidence than I expected to hear from my own lips.

"Landlord? For this building?"

"Her building." I nod towards Queen, who looks slightly impressed with my deception.

"Why are you two here if it's not your building? It's not a good idea to just wander into other people's buildings."

Now the old man looks as curious as the officers. He's lingering in the doorway, arms crossed as he tries to figure out if he's done the right thing.

"Well, it's my cousin, y'know... I dunno if I should tell you this," Queen says, looking down with a bashful shame. "He's goin' through withdrawal from all sorts of drugs so he's not meant to be out of the house, even. It's my bad. I was lookin' after him. Thought I could take a nap, but he's bolted. He's gotta be nearby, I reckon." She peers up to the building behind us with an expression of disappointment. "His mates used to live here so I thought he might've wandered in, you know? Old habits, and all. So far, no luck. But we'll keep lookin'. He always turns up."

"And you?" The cop repeats the same question as before, gesturing towards me again. I still can't tell if he's buying our story.

"I'm just here to help. The, uh... The front door lock is busted and I didn't get round to fixing it yet. So I'm feeling partly responsible."

"Right." He looks cautious, but not altogether sceptical. "And the gunshot?"

"That, I don't know. I haven't heard anything. But it wouldn't surprise me, officer. We *really* need to clean up these streets. I'm thinking about joining the neighbourhood watch group."

"Since you're here, officers," Queen interrupts. "You might've seen my cousin – bloke in his twenties? He's nearby, for sure. He doesn't move so fast since he broke his arm and he's throwin' up every ten minutes."

Officer Corey tells us he wants to follow us to our non-existent building, but Queen puts him off the idea by overwhelming him with information about her neighbour's burglaries and a whole lot of paperwork.

"Right. Ugh." Officer Corey looks distracted, almost bored. "Trevor, these guys are just looking for their cousin. You happy to call this in? I'm OK with calling it in as a false alarm and a missing person."

Officer Trevor nods and uses the radio attached to his utility belt to report back to his colleagues. "Two-eight-six Carrol. We've got a false alarm on the ten-ten. No shots fired, no suspicious persons."

"Ten-four, thank you. Return to patrol," a female voice responds.

"Ten-four. Lemme put out an APB for a missing male on foot in the Harlem district. Aged early-twenties, British, possible EDP, arm in a sling. Drug affected. May have thrown up on himself."

"Almost definitely," Queen adds, ignoring the assumption that she's from the UK.

The cops waste no time returning to their vehicle, barely pausing to tip their caps. I can't believe that worked.

In 2001, Manhattan locals The Strokes released their debut LP *Is This It?*, which became a seminal album in the post-punk/garage rock revival of the 21st-century. This helped pave the way for mainstream success from bands like The White Stripes, The Hives, The Vines, and probably a dozen other groups starting with "The". But there was one song on *Is This It?* that didn't go down so well. A track titled *New York City Cops* was removed from the album just a few months after its release, due to its harsh criticism of the NYPD. You see, a valiant response to the 9/11 terrorist attack forced everyone to stand up and applaud the city's fire department and police force as heroes.

Truth be told, the tragedy of 9/11 was arguably the best thing that could happen for the NYPD's reputation. The city of five boroughs was a cesspool in the 1970s and '80s, but Mayor Rudy Giuliani cleaned up the streets through a tough approach to crime, even for minor criminals like graffiti artists and people jumping turnstiles at the subway. This shift, along with an aggressive pursuit to end organised crime, more or less cleaned up the streets. The side-effect of such a hard-nosed approach was that an overzealous police force produced aggressive officers responsible for unwarranted brutality, including the shooting of several unarmed suspects. Long after Mayor Giuliani's reign and approach to crime had passed, the NYPD was left with a bad reputation – that is, until 9/11 brought the city together, led by the brave efforts of the police and fire departments. Still, I can't help remembering this song's chorus after our encounter with young officers Corey and Trevor. These New York City cops ain't too smart.

"You all right, mate?" Queen asks me, turning her head sideways. "You look about as comfortable as a bloody emu on a tightrope."

"I'm not used to lying. What do we do now?" I'm unsure if we should check on Rust or sneak past the old guy's prying eyes to return to the rooftop.

"I'm done," Rust's voice responds through the Nano GEAR. *"Let's get the hell out of here."*

A few seconds later he bursts out of the warehouse, gun holstered and eyes burning with rage.

"What the hell is wrong with you?" Rust storms past us towards his car, waiting for an explanation from the Aussie.

"I'm as surprised as you, mate."

"Somehow I doubt that."

"I'm sure this is all a big misunderstanding," I interject in an attempt to keep the peace. "Let's go somewhere and figure it out."

Rust falls silent and climbs into the driver's seat, ignoring Queen's barrage of questions until the message gets through.

After we've passed just a few blocks, Rust turns into a street that leads to a place I've only read about – the Crack is Wack Playground. This basketball and handball court is home to one of New York's most famous murals, given its position adjacent to Harlem River Drive across the Grand Central Parkway.

Unfortunately, we aren't here to play three-on-three. Rust

turns the car off and throws his attention to Queen in the passenger seat, finally breaking his silence.

"I'm done with this. I've jumped through your hoops. Tell me what you know about Mars."

"C'mon, Rust, can you at least tell me what happened with Lucinda? I have to tell Cassie *somethin'* about her sister."

"My patience is worn out. I held up my part of the bargain."

Rust's tone makes me feel like a kid again, listening to Dad scold my older brother for breaking a window at school. I can only sit in the back seat and choke on the tension.

"I did what you asked," he snarls through gritted teeth. "Now start talking or I'll do this the Metric way."

"OK! Geeze," Queen submits with a dejected slump. "Don't shout, Sherlock. You'll get your pound of flesh."

"That's Shylock. *The Merchant of Venice.*" I can't help correct her slip of the tongue. Queen glares at me, as if I asked the teacher to assign weekend homework, then continues.

"First off, Rusty, I'm sorry for whatever went down. You know I wouldn't set you up for anythin' dodgy. I've got nothin' to gain from that."

"Enough. Get to Mars."

"Rightio." Queen looks ahead, focusing on the kids playing at the park as she explains that she received a handwritten note from Mars about two weeks ago.

"I woke up after a big night and it was right there under the front doormat. No joke. I didn't see him, I didn't talk to him."

"What did it say?"

"I've got it right here."

Queen reaches into her baggy pants and pulls out a leather wallet. She opens it to produce a folded piece of paper, similar to what I've been using to take notes for the past couple days. Rust snatches and unwraps it like the birthday present he always wanted. There can't be much to read because a few seconds later he's staring a hole through Queen again.

"What's it mean? Where is that?"

"Hold on," Queen says. "You've got the note. We can talk

about it. But please, tell me what happened at the warehouse."

Rust frowns and explains his conversation with Lucinda. It starts off just as Queen explained. She offered to repay Cassie's debt and used her knowledge of biochemistry to make some street level drugs. Somewhere in the process she learnt about O'Brien's sick wife who was taking part in an experimental medical drug trial. O'Brien wanted to know if she'd been given the placebo or the real drugs. Her health was bad enough that they didn't want to waste any time with a dead-end treatment. Lucinda offered her services to retrosynthesise the drug and determine its chemical properties. It turned out to be the real deal and she realised she could theoretically reverse engineer it and start up a charitable black market hospital. Like some kind of Robin Hood-Walter White hybrid, she's been making truckloads of cash and helping sick people in the process.

That's as far as Rust got before he stormed out of the warehouse in a rage. It was clearly a symbiotic relationship and he didn't want to stick around any longer to question the ethics or the motivation behind such an exercise. I'm sure Queen wishes he'd asked why Lucinda hadn't been in touch with her sister, since that would've saved us a lot of time and effort, but here we are. No more mystery, no damsel in distress. Just a disappointing anti-climax that leads us to our next clue.

Rust steers the conversation back to the ticking time bomb, leaving Queen no time to vent her frustration.

"This note says 'Manhattan Hill'. What's that mean?"

I reach forward and take the scrap of paper.

Send the Maven to Manhattan Hill. I'll be waiting over the rainbow.

Thanks for everything.

Mars

"Where?" I ask, with an inflexion that comes out far more whiny than I intend.

Queen gives the world's most aggressive shrug and lets her arm fall, smacking against her lap. With nothing more to contribute, she unbuckles her seatbelt and pushes open her car door.

"That's what it says. That's all I got. I've lived in New York five years now – I never heard of Manhattan Hill."

"You're leaving?"

"I'll take the subway. Let you two figure this out. I'm clearly not meant for this crap anymore."

"I'd like to say 'thanks'," Rust tells her. "But you haven't been much help."

This is a bit harsh, in my opinion. I feel like Queen's done as much as she could to help. Saying goodbye on such a down note leaves me feeling empty, knowing there's so much more to her story that I'll never learn. The journo in me has dozens of questions about her past, present and her future. Even what I've learnt in a few hours is enough to write a book on: She's a secret government analyst who made it from Australia to America, lost her memories, lost her arm. Despite everything, she's making a life of it on the streets of Hell's Kitchen until her luck runs out and she's either arrested or deported. As Queen put it, she's not cut out for this anymore. Whatever happened to her before she left Metric, it's turned her from a top analyst in espionage into a street gossiper who can't even get the right details for a Harlem drug operation.

"Sorry I asked for your help. Everything's gone that way for me since I left Metric."

"Maybe it's just you," Rust says with bitter resentment, still refusing to look her in the eye.

"Yeah, maybe that's true. My life's just been a garbage truck on fire rollin' down the street, but it started with this."

She points to her missing arm, hoping one last time to engage some sympathy from Rust, or at least a glimmer of repentance over whatever transpired in their shared past.

"But... clearly you don't give a toss. I hope you fellas find what you're lookin' for," she says with just the right blend of optimism and disappointment to sound genuine. "Keep rockin', Maven. Say g'day to Mars for me."

"It was good meeting you," is all I can come up with as Queen slams the door shut and skips away. I want nothing more than to sit her down and be the counsel that she obviously needs right now, but there's no time. Even if there was, I'm not sure she would volunteer for anything like that. For all her evident issues, she seems comfortable in her own skin and at peace with her role in this world. That's more than I can say for most people. I look over at Rust for the hint of regret he denied while Queen was here, but he couldn't appear to care less about her departure.

"Manhattan Hill..." he says to himself. Saying it aloud makes no difference. "I'm going to call this through to HQ."

"We can figure this out," I insist. "Let's at least try. Sometimes if you stare at a crossword for long enough, the puzzle will solve itself."

"We don't have that much time. There's not much to work with. Manhattan Hill. Over the rainbow. What do we know?"

"Well," I say, scratching my chin stubble. "We know that there's no Manhattan Hills in New York City. The whole island was levelled out. It's flat as a pancake."

"There's a Manhattan Hill in Hong Kong," Rust recalls. "High rise complex, five buildings. Seems appropriate. China may as well be on the other side of a rainbow. How's your Cantonese, kid?"

"Non-existent."

Rust starts the Escalade's engine. "Well, I hope you like Chinese food."

"I'm allergic to MSG."

"Hm. You're out of luck." Rust just grunted at my allergy as if such biological imperfections are beneath him. There's something still bothering me. As much as I love getting stamps in my passport, I'd rather not travel overseas unless I absolutely have no other option.

"Do you really think Mars would hide out in Hong Kong if he wanted *me* to find him? Me, who speaks no second language, with no knowledge of Chinese culture and no espionage abilities."

"I suppose not." Rust turns the engine off again, dejected by the metaphorical road block.

"Ordinarily, this is the point of an investigation where I would give up or press pause. Taking such a major leap of faith is just not worth my time, especially if I don't know the full story, which Mars can only expect is the case here."

"What are you saying?"

"Maybe it's something more simple – you know what I mean? We're overthinking it. Give me a second."

I pull out my phone and punch "Manhattan Hill USA" into Google.

"Let me ask the Nano," Rust says, putting his finger to his ear.

"It's OK, I got this. Look, there are at least six Manhattans in the US. There's one in Illinois. Looks small, but it's home to a major contractor in petrochemicals."

Rust screws up his face with doubt. "Doesn't add up."

"Well, take your pick." I scroll through the names displayed on my phone. "Manhattan Beach, California? Manhattan in Nevada. Maybe he's hitting the blackjack table."

"I doubt it."

The solution hits me like a wet fish to the face.

"*Kansas!* Rust, that's totally it! He's waiting *over the rainbow*."

"Kansas, huh..."

"Don't tell me you haven't seen *The Wizard of Oz*. It's so obvious. It's not even cryptic."

Rust bears his teeth and grinds them hard before dropping his body into a disappointed slump. I sense both relief and annoyance for reasons he's not in a rush to make clear. "Why didn't I think of that... You can't use this for material. This is top secret."

"Sure, just for something different," I say sarcastically.

"Metric HQ is based out of Kansas."

"Of course it is." Nothing surprises me anymore. The CIA's got Virginia. The NSA has Maryland. Metric's got Kansas.

"Wichita? Topeka?"

"It doesn't matter where."

"But the point is, he's hiding in plain sight."

"Almost."

Rust turns the ignition with a hint of a smirk as the engine roars. "Pack your bags and tap your shoes, Dorothy. We're on the next flight to Kansas."

Chapter 11

Transition

Rust wasn't kidding. We didn't even wait a day to catch a plane out of New York. From the driver's seat of the Escalade, he conveyed a message to HQ and used the Nano AI to access directions to LaGuardia Airport in Queens for the next available flight. A tornado watch in Kansas had us rushing to arrive before flights were grounded. Usually this would be reason enough to stay away from the area altogether, but there's a job to do.

Kansas is part of an area they call Tornado Alley, along with Oklahoma, Illinois, Colorado, Minnesota, Texas and half a dozen other states. Tornado watches are issued frequently in middle America – it's the tornado *warning* you need to look out for. A tornado *emergency* basically means you either hide underground or start preparing your will.

We'll fly into Wichita and drive to Manhattan, a college city where there was coincidentally a major twister back in 2008. I had a friend at Kansas State University and he told me it completely levelled parts of the campus. The EF4 tornado destroyed thirty-one homes and a bunch of businesses, leaving about $20 million in damage and annihilating the university's Wind Erosion Laboratory garage. Yes, that actually happened. It was a lot worse in other parts of Kansas and neighbouring states. That week about one hundred and ninety tornadoes killed seven people, not including the body count from lightning, flooding and straight-line winds.

How do I know all this? I just read it on Wikipedia. We're all instant experts with this factually questionable encyclopaedia in our pockets.

In the past few hours alone, I've discovered Metric has failed to feed my cat, Rust's ID gets us straight through security, and he's really not a fan of Mexican food. I assumed there would be plenty of opportunities to satisfy my Taco Bell cravings this week, but Rust insists we eat on the move. He's all about efficiency – hence the grunting – but you don't eat Taco Bell on the move. You sit down and you enjoy it. You owe yourself that much. You owe Taco Bell that much.

Even in our short layover at the Minneapolis airport, Rust is flexing his Metric muscles to get us around the limits of security. People sometimes talk about going back in time to take out Hitler. My next pit stop while traversing time and space would be to sort out Richard Reid – not the Fantastic Four guy, but the shoe bomber. Reid was the radical Islamic terrorist from Florida who tried to blow up a plane with an explosive inside his boot – only two months after 9/11. As a result, the TSA started randomly searching the shoes of travellers. Five years later, they started forcing passengers to remove every shoe for inspection. Airports are the worst, but they're a lot more bearable with Rust's golden ticket. It seems to work like the fast pass at Disneyland – no lines. I can't think of a better perk. Since siding with Metric, I've received a last-minute invitation to a hotel opening, restricted access to its penthouse, a direct line to interview a former government rogue analyst, and now a free pass to skip through airport security. Journalism is a lot easier when you're working for a secret service.

With Rust busy making calls back to Metric HQ, I've been left alone with my thoughts for the first time in a couple days. I keep checking my phone for news, expecting to read some kind of revelation about Moriarty's business interests, something about a dust up at his hotel opening, or a police report about a middle-aged bruiser and his nerdy sidekick with a vitamin D deficiency. I can't help thinking the trail we're leaving behind will catch someone's attention. Rust is far too good at covering his tracks and leaving no reliable witnesses. The whole fight at Moriarty's would be sitting there on security footage, sure, but he's got way more to lose by revealing that embarrassment to anyone. He'd never live it down.

~∞~

"You're a Gemini, right? You've got Gemini written all over you."

"I'm not, actually."

Since boarding this plane for Wichita, I've been stuck next to an elderly new-age over-sharer. I'm a spiritual person, but I certainly don't believe in looking to the stars to find my future. I also don't believe in talking in great length to total strangers on public transport. I generally keep to myself, but this is serving as a decent distraction from everything that's been happening.

"Aries?" she asks.

"Nope."

"Oh, you're a classic Leo."

She looks confused as I keep shaking my head.

"Well, what are you?"

"I'm a journalist." Now she looks at me like I'm stupid. I reveal I was born in October, which draws a smile as she starts thinking about all the ways I'm a classic Libra. I can't hold my tongue any longer.

"To be honest, I think astrology is a bunch of crap. I had a magic eight-ball when I was a kid. It was more accurate than any horoscope I've ever read."

The old woman's jaw hangs as if she's never met someone who didn't share her kooky beliefs. I can't tell if she's mad or just shocked by my frankness.

"You don't even know what astrology is," she stammers, blinking almost constantly. "You are not just *one* zodiac sign. In actual astrology you take into account the sun, moon and every planet in the solar system. You also have to take into account the angular aspects that the planets are making to each other and apply rules of *geometry* to the primary angles in order to see how planets interact to one another in a certain geometrical relationship. That sounds complicated, but it's *not*."

"It does sound complicated."

"Look, I'm not young..."

I can tell that.

"...and I can't answer every question about the universe..."

Shocker.

"...but there's only one way I've been able to make sense of this wacky world, and that's by looking to the stars."

The only thing that stops me making fun of her is my own faith and spirituality. Sure, I think what she believes is total garbage. There's no credence in astrology. But she's at least recognising that there is a greater power out there and that we aren't just floating around this world by random chance. People act as if tolerance is about having no beliefs – it's more about how your beliefs lead you to treat people who disagree with you.

I don't care what anyone says – everyone puts their faith in something. Even atheists understand the world through theories of science that can't be proven. Believing that this giant universe is expanding and we all ended up here by accident because of some random event billions of years ago – that takes just as much faith. Instead of an ancient text, these people put their trust in someone way smarter than them, believing that their interpretation of fragile data based on assumptions is accurate enough to draw a conclusion about the age of our planet and the way it came to be. Every observation put forward as scientific evidence has an alternate explanation. We all live in the same world, but we all come to different conclusions. Objective truth is pretty darn impossible to find.

I mean, some of us can't even agree about the colour of a sweater.

~∞~

It's only two hours to Manhattan so we'll have almost the entire day tomorrow to find Mars. As we pass through the Wichita air-port exit, a sign on the window informs travellers they're forbidden from taking guns inside. I've never owned a weapon, but I would pray that anyone who thinks it's OK to walk around with a gun in public would be wise enough not to walk into an airport packing heat. Rust is the exception to the rule.

"I forgot my toothbrush. Do you have any gum?"

"I don't."

"Well, can we stop somewhere for gum before the motel?"

"Why not just buy a toothbrush?"

"You're a thinker, Rust."

"I'm an adult."

Much to Rust's chagrin, the only rental car available at this hour is a white Toyota Corolla. Seems like that's a fine vehicle to me, but Rust seemed to have something blacker and more manly in mind – something American.

"You don't even have one of those German cars?" he asks. "The Golf? An Audi?"

"Come on, Mr Grumpy Pants. The Corolla's incognito. And white's the safest colour on the road. You know what I mean?"

Rust shoots me that patented icy stare as the cashier hands him the keys. As we trudge into the dim parking lot to check out our new wheels, I stare out at the city lights, breathe in the fresh Kansan air, and hope to God we have the right location.

Chapter 12

Generation

I always wanted to take a road trip adventure through the American heartland. I never thought it would happen like this. There won't be any stops at the quirky landmarks along the way. I'll sigh as we drive straight past the Kansas Underground Salt Museum, the micro breweries and other roadside attractions. With Rust's connections and a slight detour, I bet we could've even scored access to the Prairie Dunes Country Club golf course right outside Hutchinson. But that just won't happen today, even if it is one of America's finest private golf clubs.

Life is unfair. No time for fun, Mr Maven.

I've already been awake for an hour or so, on account of the morning sun creeping through the motel's cheap, thin curtains. The one-hour time difference means we'll make the most of the daylight. After a much-needed shower, I'm hoping the motel's instant coffee can energise me.

It's certainly no chai latte.

An impatient Rust watches me stir the sad drink. I attempt to strike up a conversation, asking Rust for his thoughts on the old astrologist on the plane.

"No opinion. I try not to pass judgement about the people I'm risking my neck to protect. It makes it harder to do this job."

"It does?"

"The dumber they are, the less aware they are. Most people don't know or care, and they don't care to know."

"Do you think they're happier that way?"

"Maybe."

"Interesting." I take a sip of the coffee, regretting my milk-to-water ratio. "It's as though you've dedicated your life to protect people you have no affection for, simply on principle rather than through any sense of fondness or loyalty."

"I'm a patriot."

"But are you really? Or are you just good at what you do? And you like that?"

"We don't have time for this."

I fit a Detroit Pistons cap over my head and pick my green khaki jacket off the bed, pulling it on as I approach the exit.

"Enough pockets in that thing?"

I look down and see there are indeed seven visible pockets – two at the breast, four lower at the hip, and one on the shoulder. This doesn't include the two pockets inside the lining of the jacket.

"If you need me to smuggle anything, I'm all set."

"I'll remember that." Rust throws his duffel bag on the back seat of the Corolla.

"It's probably a relic from your days when you needed a dozen tools and whatnot to get by. You know, before smartphone apps made them all redundant."

"You think?"

"Yeah, like the compass, address book, calendar, alarm clock. It's all there."

"I know about smartphones," Rust says, feeling condescended. "We were using that tech years before civilians."

"Oh really? Before it was cool? That's very hipster of you."

The sunlight outside energises me far more than the instant coffee. It sure doesn't feel like tornado weather in Wichita today. It's a lot smaller than my hometown but driving through the outer limits reminds me of Grand Rapids. I really should call my mother.

She'd flip out if she knew what I was doing, but I think she'd be proud too. She's always been supportive of my journalism career and the move into freelancing. Dad's been good too, but he's in his own little world most of the time. He's a retired engineer – an obsessive golfer and a total Civil War buff. He has plenty of time for reading and building, but little interest in modern politics. Dad would much rather be on the greens with his country club pals than reading about current affairs. He does enjoy my pop-culture podcasts, though, and even did a guest appearance last year when David Bowie died. I'm not sure he understands the route I took to get where I am, but he definitely recognises my success is beyond anything either of us could've imagined.

"What do you think Queen is going to do next?" I ask Rust as we hit the highway and start to pick up some speed.

"Probably smoke a bong."

"You really don't care about her? After all she's been through?"

"She knew what she was signing up for."

"It didn't seem like it."

Queen's story still doesn't sit well with me. As a journo, I've spent years telling stories that people don't already know. Journalism is about finding important issues and pushing them into the open until they're resolved. If there's a loose end, it must be covered until it's tied off. It took me a long time to realise that wasn't always possible and it's taken me even longer to see that life doesn't work that way either. The lack of closure with Queen is a prime example. I doubt I'll ever know what happened to her before and I'll probably never know what becomes of her.

I once viewed any goal, any need or longing or desire – be it success, relationships, career – as a loose end that needed tying off before I could be content. It's only constant failure in the face of success that has taught me some things are better left unsaid and some questions just have to remain unanswered. This is necessary to save our sanity, more than anything.

When it comes to Rust, Metric, Mars, Queen and Scarpino, it seems like everything I want to know is left unsaid. It's time to put on my journalist hat once again. I need answers.

"So, what's Mars like? As an agent.

"He's young. Brash." Rust pauses, probably considering whether or not to divulge more. "You could say we have a similar set of skills."

"Sure," I say, as if this was a given. "But here's the thing. Aside from watching you lay the smack down, I don't really know much about you to understand what you mean by your 'skills'. You know what I mean?"

"What do you want to know?"

"Where do we start? I have a lot of questions about you."

"I don't talk about myself," he fires back, almost as if the whole topic is overdue.

"I sense that. But I'm way out of my comfort zone here, so I think it's fair that you do the same – you know what I mean?" Rust seems to understand my point, but he doesn't look convinced. "Look. I've seen enough action movies to know we need to trust each other if we're going to be partners."

"We aren't."

"But we're working together. And you know, as a reporter, I build trust through communication. Ask me any question. Go ahead."

"I've seen your dossier. It's very comprehensive."

"Right." I'm not sure whether to be creeped out or flattered. But this at least saves us a lot of time. "That's kind of my point, Rust. You know everything about me and I know nothing about you. Let's change that."

The vibrating passenger window beside my head makes more noise than Rust. I take his silence as co-operation and proceed to ask if working as a Metric agent has robbed his life of normative experiences. Five seconds go by before Rust asks me to define "normative".

"Well, I imagine that even back to your teenage years you were primed for this career through some kind of military-based education."

"You make a lot of assumptions."

"Did you ever get to just hang out with your friends, play pinball, go on family vacation?"

"Of course."

I wait for more, but Rust seems to think he has sufficiently dismissed my curiosity.

This will take some work.

I used to interview touring bands for a Detroit newspaper and discovered a lot of the apathetic and sardonic musicians opened up after I asked them to talk about the specific craft of their music – amp settings, guitar pedals, drum tuning – whatever made them geek out. I need to try the same tactic here.

"That gun... You always use that pistol?"

"Always. That's a Custom M1911. And I know what you're thinking."

He really doesn't. I know literally nothing about guns.

"You're thinking 'Why not a newer lightweight .45?' I've tried the Glock 21, the SIG Sauer P220. But I always come back to the M1911."

"Yes, why is that?" There's nothing natural about my reaction, but feigning interest will keep him talking.

"I'm what the kids would call 'old-school'. My Custom was always standard-issue for US armed forces. The marines still use it. A lot of special ops agents find there's nothing better."

"Like a Fender Stratocaster. Can't beat a classic."

"I suppose."

"So, what does being old-school mean? Is that just an age thing?"

"I suppose."

"What does that mean for you? I'm curious where you've come from."

"You know what they say about curiosity..."

"Let's say you're in your twenties, you're at college and it's Friday night, so you're at the bar with your friends and you're shooting the breeze. What are you talking about?"

Rust's gaze remains locked on the road ahead. The rippled lines around his eyes reveal his age as much as his impressive physique masks it.

"Tell me," he says, ignoring my question. "Is this for your story? Or for the mission?"

"Honestly, I'm just intrigued," I admit. "You don't feel like being locked into this line of work since you were a foetus has meant you've missed out on the simple things in life?"

"Why don't you paint me a picture, kid? I know you want to."

I try to recall the highlights of my younger years and prepare to wax lyrical. I'm so nostalgic that sometimes it's depressing. It's not even that I get sad thinking of the memories and longing for the days of old – it's the fact that nothing here and now is enough for me to stop looking backwards. This is a problem I never expected to encounter. My life is almost literally exactly what I always wanted, but instead of being content with it, I have to accept that I cherish these old memories so much more than the blessings surrounding me now.

"Back in college, for example... I loved the way the laziness of afternoon morphed into the randomness of the evening. On any given night you could end up at a stranger's home, sitting on their roof, drinking shots of brandy or falling asleep on a beanbag with your hand inside a packet of corn chips. You could end up playing an impromptu game of lawn bowls on a highway median strip. Pretending to care about Gaelic football to pick up an Irish girl you just met. Setting things on fire."

I can't tell if Rust is shaking his head in disapproval or just checking the traffic as he merges from Interstate 135 to US Route 50 towards Manhattan. For as long as this trip takes, he's trapped with my questions.

"I suppose what I'm asking is this: is there anything trivial in your life at all?"

"I smoke cigars. And I cook. I enjoy it. But free time is hard to come by. I definitely don't occupy my mind with flirting and binge drinking."

"Well, me neither. Not anymore. These days my free time is more occupied with Netflix and stuff like reordering my CD collection... Trying to figure out why my cat hates me so much."

"I'm starting to see why."

I laugh – louder than I should. I didn't expect an attempt at witticism, but I also want to foster Rust's sense of humour.

"Look. I just think it's fascinating that you'd give up your chance for anything resembling a normal life to serve your country. No fun and games, no romance, no family."

Rust bites his lip, taking care to consider his next words. I can see he's swilling an idea around his head like the ice in his whisky yesterday.

"You can't use this for material..." He shoots me a fast look, his eyes burning mine like cigarette butts, just so I know he means business. "She was a Metric scientist."

The hint of sadness in his voice makes the implication clear. I nod in response, waiting and hoping for more details on a topic I never expected we would reach. Queen told me Rust had a soft spot for scientists – this must be what she meant.

"This woman... We were stationed together for months, often alone. Working in the clandestine arm of an overseas special operations task force. That's how it started."

Here we go. The onion layers are peeling back.

"All right, Rust. I get it. Forbidden love. That would've been hard to keep under wraps, even for a spy."

So far I'm having more luck getting answers by making assumptions that Rust feels compelled to correct.

"It's not forbidden. It's just... It's complicated."

"So how long did that last?"

"On and off. It's been twenty-nine years."

Again, there's a melancholy behind his voice that makes me wonder if I'm the first person to break down this wall. I don't want to pry – I mean, I do want to pry, but I don't want to ask the wrong question that ends the conversation. Rust's co-operation is like a teetering Jenga tower, ready to crash and tumble if the wrong piece is removed. I take a sip of water from my airline drink bottle and we sit in silence. This time I let it soak up until Rust breaks through.

"It didn't end well. And I won't discuss that any further."

"Sure," I nod. "But, twenty-nine years is a lifetime. Would've been hard, given your careers?"

"It wasn't exactly a normal relationship. Even I know that. We'd go months, sometimes years without contact. Not by choice." Rust has a sudden unease, realising how far out he is from his comfort zone. "I'm not sure why I'm telling you. But this line of work, it forces a lot of hard decisions. It never would have worked – it never would've lasted if there wasn't a common link."

"Uhuh. A link, like what?"

Now I'm racking my brain. A twenty-nine-year connection? An ongoing mission? They clearly worked in different fields and separate operations. His long drawn breath and tightened grip on the steering wheel gives the vibe that he's not ready to admit whatever it is that I'm dying to know. What could they have in common for almost thirty years?

"Rust, I'm going to take a stab here – are you saying you're a dad?"

"A dad..." He almost scoffs at the term. "I was barely there."

Holy atomic bombshell, Batman. I don't even have time to react before Rust continues.

"Her... she was amazing. She raised him. I tried to walk away, to be with them, but Metric... The work was too important. She understood."

I detect he's still convincing himself of those final two details, but now isn't the time to prod.

"And your son, he understood too?"

"Not so much. But as he got older..." His trailing voice indicates a sense of true sadness or regret that would be far too humbling to articulate. "The apple doesn't fall far from the tree. But I haven't seen him for fourteen months. No one has."

"You mean, like... he's missing?" Rust takes a deep breath and doesn't correct me. "And... what, so even Metric can't help find him?"

"That's why you're here, Maven. That's what we're doing. You're here to help me find my son."

Chapter 13

Assimilation

If my life were a movie, this would be the moment the needle lifts off the record player. You know what I mean – when someone enters a party or says something crazy, the music stops and every single person turns their head in disbelief. I'm not sure why there's always someone standing by to lift the needle at the perfect time, or who would even play a vinyl record at a party in 2017, but that isn't important. This is the moment when time stands still.

"Your *son?*"

"That's right."

"Agent Mars?"

"Yeah."

"He's your son."

I pause, waiting for some kind of explanation. As usual, Rust doesn't read the verbal cue, or he simply ignores it.

"Are you kidding me?"

"Do I look like I'm joking?"

He doesn't. Not even a little bit.

I think back, flipping through the mental notebook of my memories for any sign that points towards this being true.

Is it really possible?

"He looks like me, but younger. Twenty-eight years old. Fit."

"The apple doesn't fall far from the tree."

"We have a similar set of skills."

"So there's like an action gene. A stealth gene?"

"Heh... You'd be surprised."

Wow. Just, wow. All the signs were there. I feel stupid for not making sense of it sooner. But still.

"Why didn't you tell me?"

"Didn't seem important to the mission."

"Didn't seem important? Are you kidding me?"

Rust shoots me the same look as before, just to make sure I know he's not messing around.

"OK, I know you're not kidding, but you are sorely mistaken, Rust. This... This is... It's huge," I stutter, piecing it all together in my mind. "It all makes sense now. The secrecy about your personal life. Your determination to find Mars. The way you talk about him like a lost sheep. He's almost literally a prodigal son who's wandered away and just needs to return to his father."

"Please."

"I'm serious."

I flip open my notepad and dig back through my shorthand scribbling for anything that might have crystallised into a clearer picture with this new information.

"What about your wife?"

"My wife?"

"Well, Mars's mother. Where is she? What does she say about all this?"

"She went missing."

"And that's not relevant information?"

"It was two years ago. She left Metric for a civilian life. It wasn't long until Mars went off the grid. Mid-operation. It's only recently we started intercepting his attempts to reach people within Metric."

"About his Mom, or...?"

"No. The messages were nonsense. Conspiratorial nonsense.

We need to rein him in."

"So you don't think the two disappearances are connected? I'm no Sherlock Holmes, but it seems like an obvious theory."

"They've got to be connected. I don't know what happened to Alison..."

So her name is Alison.

"...But I think it triggered his defection. And I think he knows something about what happened to her."

"She hasn't... You haven't heard anything?"

"Nothing. My experience tells me she either doesn't want to be found, she's dead or she wants us to think she is."

This is the emotionless admission of a man who has come to terms with each of these possibilities over a long period. The family connection to Mars makes me eager and even excited at the idea of meeting him. Then I remember he's a rogue spy accused of plotting terrorism against America. The dread returns.

I scribble feverishly into my notepad, trying to remember as many details as possible. The missing mom. Alison. She's got to be the key here.

My next few questions seem to rub Rust the wrong way. He shuts them down with a firmness matching his handshake. I even bring up Moriarty's missing list, but Rust's care factor remains at zero.

"Quit asking about it. And quit interviewing me. It's too early in the morning for that."

"I don't quit."

"I noticed."

"I see things through. I watched every episode of *Lost*. You don't know what that means, so you'll have to trust me. It wasn't easy. I'm going to find out about that list."

~∞~

Manhattan, Kansas.

The Little Apple, as the locals call it. There's no way to confuse it with its namesake across the country. After wandering around New York for several days, I'm struck by the greenness of this smaller city. It boasts a population of around fifty-two thousand, including twenty-five thousand college kids at Kansas State University, plus some of the eighteen thousand soldiers and their families from the nearby Fort Riley military base.

"You know what?" I say to Rust as I peer out the window. "After seeing maybe a hundred and fifty miles of Kansas, I have to say it really isn't as flat as I've been led to believe."

He nods while navigating through downtown Manhattan's one-way streets. Most of the stores are old grey stone buildings. The nearby houses are made from weatherboard – tall and wide. I'm reminded of the neighbourhoods of *To Kill A Mockingbird* and the town square in *Back to the Future*. Throw in the odd Walmart and Olive Garden, you've got Manhattan, Kansas.

"There are probably twenty or thirty states flatter than Kansas," Rust says.

"Yeah. I'm seeing plenty of hills. It's a little disappointing."

We stop at a red light adjacent to a newsstand. There's quite a long queue out the door, thanks to the massive lottery jackpot this week. There must be dozens of hopeful citizens queued up, hoping to bypass hard work on their way to riches and happiness. We've all heard the concept that lottery is a tax on people who suck at math. These people queuing up now have decided the one hundred million-to-one odds of winning are still far greater than their chance of earning that much money in their lifetime. More than anything else, they're buying hope and a dream. It's sad, but I don't disparage that. It's just not for me. I put my hope in something bigger than I am, something even bigger than a $540 million jackpot.

There's also the fact that every lottery winner you hear about seems to rue the day they instantly became a multi-millionaire. It's unnatural and unhealthy to suddenly change every aspect of your lifestyle overnight. You often read about family feuds, depression, bankruptcy and even suicide from those "lucky" enough to win big. Some even call it a curse, like Hurley on *Lost*. I wasn't kidding before – I watched every episode of that show.

"So why do you think Mars is here, of all places?" I ask Rust, hoping he's ready to talk again. "What's here, if not Metric HQ?"

"If I had to guess, it's the Fort Riley US Army installation. Eighteen miles from Manhattan."

"You think he's spying on someone?"

"Not someone. *Something.* Riley's home to the Mechanised Infantry Division."

"Mechanised, what... What does that mean?"

"Tanks. Choppers."

"Oh. Good."

"Good?"

"I was thinking of bipedal mech units, you know? The mechanised tanks you see in anime and video games. Nerd stuff. Never mind."

"Right."

Fort Riley is best known for the 1st Infantry Division, the oldest constant-serving combined arms division in the US Regular Army. "The Big Red One" unit and thousands of other soldiers call Fort Riley home on a base that covers more than a hundred thousand acres, including restaurants, schools, houses, health services, stores and everything else a community needs to function.

We make our way through the city centre into suburbia, climbing around a tall green hill towards our destination. We only pass one or two homes behind long driveways as the Corolla sweeps up the road between the lush trees, arriving finally at a dirt clearing. The open space is about fifty yards wide. It almost resembles a parking lot, but there's no clear reason it exists. It's as if they cleared a space for some construction that never went ahead.

I slam my door closed and take a moment to stop and listen. Through the trees, the faint sound of traffic rises from the nearby highway. There's nothing but silence coming from our immediate environment.

This is Manhattan Hill.

I don't know what I expected to find. The distinct lack of anything notable gives no indication that this is the place we flew all the way from New York to investigate.

I thought maybe there'd be a nice panoramic view up here,

but the tall pines shielding the clearing have blocked any hope of a scenic landscape. A cylindrical water tower in the distance is the only thing higher than the tree tops.

I take a deep breath, skimming the area and wondering if this scavenger hunt will ever end. A vibration in my jacket pocket gives me a moment of promise. I usually ignore blocked phone numbers, but this is an unusual circumstance.

"Hello?"

"You're at Manhattan Hill." The voice on the other end is calm, quiet and knowing.

"Is this Mars?"

"Do you see a fire hydrant?"

I look around. "Just trees. A lot of trees. Are you here?"

"Look east from where you are, in line with the water tower. There's an address. Wait there at the bus stop at noon. We've got a lot to discuss."

"Sure, but hey... Will you be there? I'm kinda getting tired of playing *Where in the World Is Carmen Sandiego?*"

"Trust me - it's worth the trouble."

"So this *is* Mars?" I glance at the phone display to make sure we're still connected. We're not. I'm talking to myself now.

"What did he say?" Rust asks me over the Nano GEAR. This startles me, as I'd forgotten I was even wearing it. I look over and Rust hasn't left the car. He's out of clear view, slouched in the driver's seat with a hood covering most of his face.

"Just a second." I follow Mars' instructions, jog over to the fire hydrant and fumble underneath its protruding spout to find a piece of lined paper from the same notepad as the letter Mars left for Queen.

Relief washes over as it crystallises in my mind – this is it. This is the right place. This is "somewhere over the rainbow".

Sure, the coded message wasn't exactly written in hiero-glyphics. The solution was fairly obvious, but anyone who's done a crossword puzzle knows you can't always tell what someone is thinking when they leave a clue. It was still a risk to come here before we knew without a shadow of a doubt. I'm learning you have to celebrate the small victories, but the feeling won't last long. I'll soon be sitting opposite Agent Mars and trying to help Metric bring him down.

I explain the side of the conversation that Rust didn't hear, before reading him the note. I expected he would react with the same sense of relief, but he must have had more faith in our plan.

"He's going to meet with you. I'll find an opening to confront him."

"You think that's a good idea? What if he panics?"

"He doesn't panic. He's going to listen to me and I'm going to talk him out of this nonsense."

"OK, I guess you'd know. But hey. Mars was talking to me, on the phone before, like he could see me. It's a good thing you stayed in the car."

"This isn't my first rodeo."

As I return to the car, I punch the numerals and letters of the address into my phone's GPS. It's a toy store. Seriously. It's safe to say we're not going shopping for *Pokémon* cards. I suppose Mars wants me to jump on a bus, but I hope not. I've taken a timid approach to buses since a fellow passenger once poked me with a soggy baguette. And that's not a euphemism. It really happened.

It was weird.

He was one half of a bickering junkie couple. At first I thought "It's nice to know that ruining your life with drugs makes no change to a man's inability to listen and a woman's incessant need to nag". But the next thing I knew, the guy was jabbing me with his wet bread stick and asking me to weigh in on their dumb argument.

"Is the moon and the sun the same thing?" he asked.

"No. They're... very different," I explained.

Like I said, it was weird.

As I open the Corolla door, I see Rust, still hidden, talking to someone on a small device resembling a mobile tablet. I wonder if Apple could sue Metric the way they tried to sue Samsung over their alleged smartphone patent infringement.

"He's here," Rust says, facing the device.

"Who's this?" I close the door and buckle up. The woman on the screen is seated with straight-backed posture at a dark wooden desk. She's dressed in neat but bland office wear, staring down the camera like a presidential candidate preparing to speak in a debate.

"Andrew Hurrell Maven, it's a pleasure to meet you," she greets me, as Rust hands over the device. *"I'm the head of Metric operations. I personally selected you for this mission and I've been following your progress very closely. You can call me Scarpino."*

"Oh. Hello."

Honestly, I expected a man. Is that sexist? I feel like it's probably sexist. But either way, this is Scarpino and she's every bit as authoritative as I expected. She looks young, maybe late-thirties. Even more frightening than Queen. She's not the Bond villain first conjured in my mind when Mars emailed me, but my assumptions are my enemies these days.

"I've been pleased with your efforts so far, Maven, but rest assured, the gloves are off," she says. *"It's time to harden up and prepare for what could happen next. If Agent Rust asks you to carry a weapon, you will carry a weapon. Is that clear?"*

"Uh, well, yeah." Did Rust tell on me? I need to stand up for myself here. "I just want to say, I think we've done a pretty good job avoiding any fatalities up to now. I mean, there's been two bullets fired and they were at a fire extinguisher. So I think we could continue to get by without—"

"You need to wipe the milk moustache off your face and get real, Maven. You can't keep running around playing Clark Kent. Violence is part of the job description."

"Yeah, I didn't get one of those. And last I checked, I'm not even getting paid to be here."

"You need to understand - working this operation without a gun is like a dairy farmer trying to milk cows without getting dirty. One way or another, you're going to end up covered in crap. You either dress for the occasion or you're caught off-guard."

"Sure. While we're here, I've got a few questions... ma'am. Can you tell me what it is that Mars is supposedly threatening?"

"That's classified." Surprise, surprise.

"OK, and Moriarty mentioned a list of names the other day.

What do you suppose that would be referring to?"

"Without seeing it, I couldn't speculate. Bring Mars in and maybe we can find out."

"Could you hazard a guess? It must be something noteworthy for Mars to break into the hotel to steal it. You know what I mean? I just prefer to have as many facts, when I'm risking my life and everything... You know what I mean?"

"Mr Maven," she spits back at me in a condescending manner. *"I know what you mean. But you're here because you are necessary to complete the mission. This isn't a field trip. We're not here to get you the best news story possible. It's not a photo opportunity for your Instagram account and we're not obligated to answer your questions."*

"But don't you think—"

"Just follow the instructions from Agent Rust, help him secure the target, and then we can talk details. That will be all for now."

"Sheesh. OK... Rust." I look away and hold the device out towards him like a smelly sock, disappointed and a little disgusted with the way I've been treated. Scarpino's the Principal Skinner of Metric. She reminds me of a lecturer I had in college. I once described her as "passive-aggressive". My buddy Tresy was fast to correct me: "She's not passive-aggressive. She's straight-up aggressive-aggressive."

"Once you secure the target, you'll take him to a holding cell at Fort Riley. Agent Saluki has been working at the military base for the past few weeks. He'll be your back-up and you can make contact once the primary objective of the operation is complete."

"Got it. Speaking of back-up, I think we could really use the satellite surveillance team on this one."

"I'm afraid that's not going to work." Rust furrows his brow as Scarpino shuts down his request. *"We'll keep the NSA out of this,"* she explains. *"We don't want rumours of rogue spies and civilian partner-ships to get out of control. I'm sure you understand. Just keep to the plan and secure the target."*

Rust agrees, like a good little soldier, and attempts to end the transmission. It doesn't seem right to get this far and then risk let-ting Mars escape. Then again, he shouldn't be expecting anyone to show up other than a handsome, genius journalist.

"One last thing, Agent Rust." Scarpino leans in towards the camera, folding her hands on her spotless maple desk. *"Don't let your feelings towards the target change the outcome of the operation. Whatever happened to Alison is tragic, but that doesn't have to happen again."*

"I'm not sure you can compare th—"

"All we know is they both disappeared around the same time. We don't know if Mars had anything to do with her disappearance, but we certainly shouldn't rule that out."

I'd never considered that Mars was responsible for his mother going off the radar. It seems as if Rust has heard this theory before, but he's unsure of its validity. I figured it was the other way around, if anything.

Scarpino ends the conversation and Rust stashes the device into our glove box, the same way he's been packing away his true feelings about Mars for the past few days.

"She was friendly. Do you think she's on Facebook?" I ask Rust, my voice laced with sarcasm.

"No time for chit-chat if we're meeting at noon." He starts the engine and begins to exit the clearing towards the main road.

"I mean, she didn't even say 'thanks'... for all the hard work."

"Hard work? What hard work?" Rust isn't saying this as a slight or to be rude. It's clear he genuinely doesn't see the past two days as anything out of the ordinary. It never fails to surprise me how often people view their own unique and personal experiences as typical.

"It would be nice to be appreciated – you know what I mean? But I get it. I'm just the bait. The back-up singer. I'm Ringo. You're John, Paul *and* George."

"Mm."

"But right now I'm the only back-up you've got. Did you buy that, about the NSA? You don't think we need any of that surveillance satellite stuff?"

"You heard Scarpino. We need to trust her judgement."

"Yeah. I mean... I guess."

"Just focus on the task – you'll make direct contact with Mars. You'll hear him out, make him feel safe. Secure. Then I confront him and bring him in... with force, if necessary."

"You're willing to fight your own son?"

"He's a rogue," Rust reminds me.

"But he's your son."

"And an *enemy* of the *state*." He doesn't seem to get it.

"He's your *son*, Rust. Your offspring."

"Another reason to do whatever it takes."

I'm stranded on an island of silence as Rust stares at the road and fails to consider acknowledging my point, let alone the dozens of questions building up inside my brain. But I won't let this one go. I've had enough of being shut out.

"Why did she talk to you that way? No acknowledgement whatsoever that you're a father trying to save his son."

"Because I'm an agent first. Father second."

"It's really like that?"

Rust's head tilts ever so slightly, in a half or halted nod.

"So, Scarpino doesn't feel any fondness towards someone she presumably worked with, supervised for years, or whatever it is she does?"

"Mars has betrayed Metric. That's all she sees. She's taken that personally. He was an asset. Now he's a liability."

"Harsh."

"I'll make sure he comes in on the best terms possible. If he can show remorse for his actions, there's a good chance he'll be allowed to reform and possibly return to service. To this point, he hasn't caused any damage outside of talking like a maniac."

"Oh." This surprises me, based on what I've come to understand about Metric. They don't strike me as the forgiving types. "Reformation sounds like the ideal scenario."

"That's why I'm here. I'm not some heartless blue-blooded bastard. I need to stop him from doing anything stupid. I'm afraid the situation with his mother has pushed him over the edge."

We reach the bottom of the hill and Rust turns right on a road leading back to the highway, following Nano GEAR directions to our new address. It won't be long until it's just Mars and me.

"How did he join Metric? You recruited him?"

"Not a chance. I was against it. But they jumped at a shot to bring in 'the son of the Fox'. That was my name at the time."

"Right. Like a pair of jeans they loved so much, they went back to get another."

"Truth be told, he's a damn good agent. One of the best."

"Have you ever worked together?"

"We usually work alone. And he's not my biggest fan. But you need to stop with the emotional guilt trip, kid. I'm not part of Mars' life. He really doesn't want me as a father. If he weren't family, I'd haul his whiny ass to Metric without a word. I'm a professional. He *was* a professional. He's betrayed his country."

I glance at my watch. It's 11.40am and we're ten minutes from the destination bus stop. That leaves twenty minutes to talk this out.

"So what if he knows something?"

"You're not buying into his spin are you?" Rust seems borderline offended by my question. "I thought you were smarter than that."

"I haven't even heard his spin. What if he's not crazy? You haven't exactly been forthcoming about Metric..."

"You know what you need to know. If you can't trust your country, you—"

"Trust is a two-way street, Rust. And so is loyalty. There's a reason the only adjective used to describe loyalty is 'blind' – you know what I mean?"

"Kid, you've learnt more about me in three days than damn near anyone I've ever met," Rust says with conviction.

"And I appreciate that. But there's a lot of detail missing and I'm... you know. Kinda nervous. I know something is going down and I just want to make sure I'm on the right side of it. You know what I mean?"

"I *know* what you *mean*."

"Sorry. Bad habit."

"You just have to trust me."

It feels good to stand up to Rust, but it might be unfair. I know he's doing the best he can in a terrible situation. I'm not sure he even understands his own relationship with Mars. I have a better chance to figure it out when I finally meet the guy.

"Who was it Scarpino mentioned about Fort Riley?"

"Saluki?"

"Yeah. Who's that?"

"Metric scalphunter. He's been overseeing a trial for some R&D weapons projects."

"Good guy?"

"He's a Metric agent. But you don't need to worry about him. Look, we're almost there. Remember that I'll be listening on the Nano GEAR. Shout and I'll come running. Otherwise, I'll turn up when I need to. Just be yourself and don't mention me."

I peer out the window as we slow towards a stop sign, realising I really have no idea where I am. My only choice is to place absolute trust in Metric. I have to trust that Rust will have my back if something goes wrong. I have to trust that Metric will honour its word and allow me to come out of this with a publishable news story. I have to trust that helping them out won't put me on any list of names I really don't want to be on.

"Get as much detail from him as possible," Rust says, accelerating again.

"You want me to, like, extract information?"

"Scarpino wants to know everything he's saying, and he's not going to tell us a thing once we bring him in."

"What's my angle? Just go with it?"

"You're a sceptical reporter who followed a lead all the way to Kansas. You're interested, but you need to challenge him a little. He'll explain more that way, which gives us better intel."

"Gotcha. And you'll be where?"

"Can't say. For your own safety. I don't want to compromise your sense of innocence in there. Just know I'll be listening. You won't hear me, but I'll be monitoring everything, no matter where you end up. We'll track you there. Place your Nano GEAR in one of your three-dozen jacket pockets, out of Mars' view."

"Right. Why are we stopping?"

The Corolla creeps to a halt and Rust scans the sleepy neighbourhood around us. "You've gotta walk the rest of the way. Just to be safe. And try to avoid leaving this part of town. I'll be able to monitor the conversation and surroundings better in a quiet pocket."

"I'll stick to this pocket like lint."

"And one last thing," Rust stops me as I open the door. "Don't believe anything he says. He'll come up with all kinds of arguments to get you on his side. He wants you to shout his nonsense to the masses. Just try to stay somewhere accessible and quiet enough for us to follow along."

Rust leaves me promptly, feeling like a child on the first day of school. It's the only time I've been truly alone since I met him, right when I feel the most vulnerable.

I can't help feeling as if I'm the canary in the coal mine. If Mars flips out on me, Metric needs to proceed with lethal force. If he's reasonable to me, he might just come quietly when Rust arrives. The way things have gone this week, I wouldn't be surprised if there was a third unforeseen option altogether. I say a quick little prayer, take a deep breath, and step up to the bus stop of destiny.

Chapter 14

Locomotion

A blue Volkswagen Polo rolls up to the curb, stopping just a few feet from me. A tall, brown-skinned woman climbs out, dressed in baggy purple sports gear and tight jeans that fall short enough to reveal her bare ankles for the world to see. Another trend I don't understand. I must be wrong, but I always assumed no one would want to see an Achilles in public.

This young woman walks toward the bus stop and sits next to me. It's a little unusual, given there's plenty of space across the bench seat. As someone who only talks to strangers when there's a story to write, it's almost as intrusive as choosing a urinal beside another dude in a public men's room.

"Hey," she says, taking me by surprise again.

"Hey. Hi."

"You a reporter man?"

"Uh... Yeah."

"You're the New York man."

"Yeah, I am."

"Yeah, I thought so," she nods nonplussed. "You're pretty much famous on the internet."

As bizarre as this encounter is, it's nice to be recognised so far from home. This explains why she's so familiar, although it still feels unnaturally personal. She scratches a patch of acne on her otherwise smooth brown cheek.

"So, whatchu, uh... Whatchu doing in Kansas, reporter man?"

"I'm just visiting someone."

"Cool, cool. Well, I'm Sticky." She doesn't quite reach out to shake my hand, but she does nod her head back – the international gesture for 'what up?' She's either trying to act cool or maybe she just is that darn cool.

"I seen you on the... that YouTube show, the one with the talking funny guy. The talk show."

"Yeah, I'm Andrew. What-what are you... up to today?"

"You know, just hangin' out. Just... I'm goin' to Walmart to pick up some headphones. I had those Beats, you know? A pink set of Beats by Dre." Sticky has an adorable lisp that makes it hard to take her seriously, but I do my best. "I don't know how, but they're all busted up, you know, and I can't afford new Beats, so I'm gonna pick up some regular standardised earphones for the time being. Like, the Apple earphones, you know what I'm sayin'? But the cheap version."

"Sure. Sure." What a nice young woman. I'm equally charmed and freaked out by her candour and openness. As Sticky blows the hair out of her eyes, I realise how much she looks like a young Prince – if only Prince were a woman and a foot taller.

"You got a car?" she asks. "You headin' downtown?"

"Nah. I came on a plane. Hence, the bus stop." This is technically not a lie. It feels like Sticky is one or two questions away from Rust popping out of a nearby trash can like Oscar the Grouch and telling her to move on.

"Cool, cool, man. Wish I could take a plane, but I don't have the bread, you know what I'm sayin'?"

"Yeah."

"See, I really need to visit my Moms down in Florida. You been to Florida? Man, I love Florida."

I nod, wondering if she has two mothers or "Moms" is just slang, like "Pops".

"Yeah, she's got the shingles, man. You know what that means?"

"I do."

"We was just on the phone. You know, she thinks a baker's dozen is eleven? Because bakers are always ripping off their customers, she says."

"That's... interesting." It's actually funny, but I'm not sure if I'm meant to think it's funny.

"But Florida. It's a real shame, man. I would *love* to go to Disney World, man. I would *love* it." She wipes away a handful of fallen dark curls blocking her vision. "You been to Disney? Ain't been since I was thirteen years old. I'm twenty-two now, man! That's a *long* time. I need to get back there and pick up some of that exclusive Disney *merch*."

I know it's rude, but this time I don't even respond, choosing instead to look up and down the street for any sign of Mars. I imagine every slowing vehicle could be him, until they pass by and leave me here with Sticky. Maybe Mars will just call me. I look at my phone. It's a couple of minutes past the meeting time.

Nothing has ever stimulated my mind as much as this mystery. It seems as if all the knowledge lies with the people around me, but no one is willing to reveal any enlightening truth. As a journalist, this is incredibly frustrating, but as someone just trying to do the right thing, it's downright despairing. Perhaps meeting Mars will answer some questions. And maybe Rust will be more open once we have his rogue apprehended.

Maybe, maybe, maybe.

That's the common thread through this whole rigmarole. I'm hanging onto these "maybes", but sooner or later, I'm going to need some real answers. It's hard to make demands to a person like Rust, but he needs to understand the two-way street of trust and teamwork.

"You gotta look out for those gators in Florida," Sticky says, talking just to hear herself make noise. "You gotta realise it ain't just beaches and babes and Disney. You know what I'm sayin'? I don't want to hear about no one gettin' snapped up by a gator.

I used to mess around near the swamps and whatnot, but I don't play that no more. Nuh-uh. Too much to lose."

Is it racist to assume she's almost definitely here on an academic scholarship? Or is it just a Sherlock Holmesian deduction? Let's remove race from the equation. Sticky's college-aged, she's tall – at least six foot two – she's dressed in sports gear and she's a long way from home. I think a sports scholarship is a fair assumption.

Her diatribe is interrupted as a couple of youths approach the bus stop, talking unabashedly at high volume the way youths tend to do. Sticky doesn't appreciate their arrival at all. She sits straight up and looks visibly bothered by their mere presence. There's an uneasy tension as she interrupts their banter.

"Hey jackass," she barks. "Where'd you get that haircut – the thrift shop?"

The two teenagers look at each other sideways. One smirks at the question, but the other seems tentative about whether Sticky's a friend or foe.

"Hop it, jabronis. I know you got weed in that backpack." Sticky stands up, immediately intimidating the younger and smaller lads. "You want me to call the cops?"

"C'mon," the kid protests.

"Hey, I won't say nothin' to nobody, but you gotta haul ass outta here – now."

Regardless of whether they're carrying drugs, Sticky has freaked the kids out. They do as they're told and scatter.

"Sorry about that. This place is a college town." I laugh politely, but I'm uncertain of her point. "Millennials hate institutional structure. I should know – I am one. I ain't been to church since I was sixteen. I don't want no one tellin' me how to live. I get enough of that from my Moms, you know what I'm sayin'?"

I smile, but say nothing. I'm still deciding whether I want to be friends with Sticky.

"There's a lot of casual racism up here, too, man. I didn't like how those two kids was lookin' at me. Ain't a lot of brown people in Manhattan, you know?"

"That sucks, Sticky."

"It does. It really does. It's 2017 and nothin's changed. No one's born a racist. You gotta learn that from somewhere. Hey, you look nervous, man. You waitin' for somebody?"

I explain for the second time that I'm meeting a friend. Sticky asks if they're running late.

Since buying the engraved ring at the Hell's Kitchen Flea Market, I've caught myself toying with it whenever I'm nervous or deep in thought. It hangs just below my neck at a comfortable height to push my thumb through and twist it back and forth. I let it go and pull out my phone to check the time again.

The sudden weight of a slap down across the screen smacks my phone against the concrete. Before I can figure out what's going on, Sticky picks it off the ground and takes off.

"Hey! Come back here!"

"Come get it!"

Come get it? That's what it sounded like. Sticky swiped my phone!

I look over my shoulder frantically, searching for a secret agent to come to my rescue, but Rust is nowhere to be seen. If Sticky disappears, I'll have no way to communicate with Mars. If I leave, he could turn up and I won't be here. I do the maths for a couple of seconds until my gut instinct kicks in and my legs take off faster than I control them.

I regain my balance and pound the pavement in hot pursuit of this freakishly tall college kid. She has a twenty, maybe thirty-yard head start, but I think I'm gaining on her – at least until she notices me and picks up the pace.

"Stop... Sticky! Stop!"

She cuts from the sidewalk into a side-alley. Her strides are slower but far longer than mine. It's like chasing a sleepy ostrich. I pull my cap down over my head as it slips back in the commotion. We reach the end of the alley and Sticky bounds over a brick ledge to higher ground. As I pull myself up and take off in her direction, I realise we're entering in a park with multiple pathways. My view of Sticky is blocked by trees and foliage. Now I can't see her at all. I need to make a fast decision.

"Hey buddy," I call out to a nearby gentleman tying up his daughter's shoelaces. "You seen a crazy girl tearing through here?"

"Yeah, I have actually. This little ratbag here," he says, tussling his child's hair.

I wheeze in frustration before I take off in the most logical direction. No time to look for shoe prints. No time to listen for footsteps. I run hard, pushing my body and trying not to think about the possibility that everything will go up in smoke because of a random kid named Sticky. The ring around my neck bounces back and forth on its chain, smacking across my perspiring chest with the momentum of each stride.

I spot Sticky ahead as I round a corner into an open area. She's not as far away as I expected, but still too far to imagine catching. Even though I'm exhausted, I need to get that device back. Maybe it's fear pushing me to run. All the planning. All the research and travel. It can't be for nothing.

We'll find my phone.

I won't be able to stop Rust from choking Sticky to death, but we'll find my phone.

I call out again. Sticky doesn't care. She could be running all the way to Florida and I'd still never catch her without a gator interfering.

"Rust... If you can hear me... I'm just through a park. I don't know where. You'll have to track me. With Nano GEAR. Gonna need some help!"

There's no way Sticky heard me, but as soon as I'm done talking she stops right where the park meets the street.

"Please, God... Make this easy."

For no clear reason, Sticky lobs my phone underarm a dozen yards away. It tumbles through the long grass as she sprints away without an explanation.

Huh.

I rush over and pick it up. No damage. Still locked. How bizarre. I'm not taking any chances. I place the phone in the deepest depths of my jacket pockets, zipped up, hidden and staying there until Mars calls me.

I look up, but Sticky is nowhere to be seen. What a strange young woman.

"Are you serious?" I say out loud to myself, to Rust and even to God, who seems to have answered my brief but succinct prayer. Aside from all the cardio, this result really couldn't have come easier.

Before I can start retracing my steps to the bus stop or checking in with Rust, a blue hatchback pulls up at the curb.

"Get in, bro," a male voice shouts through the rolled down passenger window.

"Sorry?" I approach the car and crouch down to look inside.

"I said: get in," the shadowy figure demands. "We don't have time to chat, Maven. This is it. Get in."

It sounds like Rust, but this isn't his car. Either it's Mars himself, cruising around Manhattan in a Volkswagen Polo, or it's someone from Metric ready to drive me back to the meeting place. We speed off as soon as my jeans hit the passenger seat.

"Are you... You're Mars," I stammer. The young driver smirks and shoots me a sideways glance through his black Ray Bans.

"You found me. Took you long enough."

Wow. This is it.

Mars does indeed resemble a younger, more svelte version of Rust. He's more handsome, on account of his youth and the fact that he actually seems to care about his appearance. His hair could be straight from a GQ magazine – shaved back and sides, with a clean straight part, combed to the side.

"So tell me, Maven. I gotta know what brings you here?"

"Are you... Are you serious?"

"I know you came here for me. But what's in it for you? What's motivating you?"

I can't tell him I had no real choice. I can't tell him how intimidated I am.

"I believe you've got a story to tell," I say, before realising I've been staring at my hands. If Mars hadn't already researched my life story, I'd feel like I'm making a bad first impression. "It's just journalism. That's why I'm here."

"But to what end? Is it fortune and glory? Or are you here to seek the truth?"

This philosophical question forces me in an instant to evaluate my motivations from the first day he emailed me. Fortune and glory? That would be nice. But extrinsic motivations are rarely a journalist's incentives. The pursuit of a story is a search for unknown answers. Even though Mars is focusing on the road, I lock onto his eyes just to show I'm serious.

"Journalism is the search for facts – not truth. It's like archaeology. That's why I'm here. This is a fact-finding mission."

Mars stops the car and smiles from ear to ear with a satisfied sense of relief. "That's what I thought."

I know he's five years younger than me, but I can't look down on Mars in any way. He doesn't have that millennial naïvete or entitlement I sense with so many Americans living in the arrested development of their mid-twenties. I can tell he's seen some things. But I can't tell much else.

"Is this it?" I ask, looking outside to a strip of quiet stores and cafes.

"We have a lot to get through."

He pops open the locks and opens his car door. He couldn't be more incognito, wearing black chinos, a black duffle coat and a heather-grey T-shirt

"So, we should probably start by you explaining what you want from me?" I follow Mars into a diner where the scent of waffles, coffee, and bacon wafts through the air, almost making me forget about my week-long Taco Bell craving. "Your messages haven't exactly been informative – you know what I mean?"

"The tongue is like a rudder. It steers the whole ship." Mars sits down at a booth in the front corner of the building, as far away as possible from the majority of the customers. "There are powerful winds pushing it forward, but it's the rudder that takes it anywhere the pilot wants."

"I'm familiar with this metaphor."

"Of course."

"It's from the Bible."

"Right." Mars removes his sunglasses. To my surprise, he shares his father's scarred left eyebrow, but there's so much more energy in his eyes. For a brief second I consider whether scars are hereditary.

"It only takes one man saying the right thing to lead a group of people astray, stranded, shipwrecked. I've seen this before. But that same power of the word allows one spark to set an entire forest on fire." Mars leans forward, unable to hide his excitement. "I want you to be that spark, Maven. With the written word."

"That's very... Well, it's a romantic notion, really." The power of the written word? I'm not sure what he expects. I'm not here to write *The Great Gatsby*. "What's the forest in this metaphor?"

"We'll get to that. You're gonna bust this thing wide open." Mars certainly has a very un-Rust-like natural charm and charisma. Despite his reputation, he doesn't strike me as a terrorist. Then again, I've never met one. Maybe that's part of the deception. He is a spy after all.

"You have no idea how long I've been waiting for this," he says.

"Yeah?"

"I've been through a lot of crap lately. You wouldn't believe it. But I've got a good feeling about this. Things are just turning around."

As Mars signals to the waitress, I turn and look out the window for any glimpse of Rust or other back-up – not that I would recognise them. I gulp, trying to push down the pressure and expectations Mars is putting on me. He's sitting across the table and looking at me like I'm his saviour. Little does he know, he's about to buy coffee for his Judas.

Chapter 15

Revelation

I've never done any drugs. I don't drink a lot. I reserve junk food for special occasions. I smoked a cigarette once when I was fourteen, but Dad caught me in the act. He didn't make me smoke a whole packet like some parents would. He just made me confess to my mother. My poor mother. The look of pure disappointment and sadness in her dewy brown eyes was more than enough to stop me from smoking again. Several years later I was opinionated enough to decide that smoking is the single most pointless exercise a human could pay to partake in.

My point is that I don't have the typical addictions that plague so many Americans. Chai lattes are my only vice and my only window into the life of an addict. I'll never judge an alcoholic or druggie for failed attempts to kick their habit because I know if I found out tomorrow that cinnamon had lethal side effects, I'd be as good as dead. On so many occasions, especially during my office life, looking forward to that mid-afternoon chai latte was all that got me through the day.

A diner such as this one has been the home of many long writing sessions over the past couple of years. I often find comfort in the clamour of cafes, but right now as I stare into my porcelain mug, filled with the sweetest blend of milk, sugar, cinnamon and all those other mysterious Indian aromatic herbs and spices – I feel nothing. It offers no pleasure, no relief, no excitement. I'm too focused on the matter at hand.

"Are you afraid of me?"

"Hm?" I've been staring into my drink, forcing my glasses to slip down my nose. I push the frames back and ask Mars what he means.

"You look nervous," he says with a wry smile that's either sinister or just amused. I can't tell. It's hard to get a read on him. "Do you think I want to hurt you?"

"No. I don't know..." I respond, before stopping to consider the question. "I don't think you do."

"If I did, you would know."

Mars shares his father's strong jaw, but he's free from the constant look of sourness. Rust is out there somewhere listening through the layers of my jacket's fabric to hear his son's voice for the first time in who knows how long. Without the NSA's satellite surveillance crew, I have no idea how long it could take him to track me down. I must've veered half a mile off-course chasing after Sticky. We drove another mile or two before arriving at the diner, so it could still be a few minutes before Rust finds me. It could be ten minutes. It could be half an hour. I have no experience with this.

"Did you pay Sticky to swipe my phone? That was your car I saw her climb out of, wasn't it?"

Mars smirks, which I take as an affirmative response. He's had a sparkle of excitement in his eye since I started taking notes.

"We have a lot to get through."

"OK. Let's hear it. Tell me all about the evil doctor rocket science monsters planning to destroy the entire universe."

Mars looks a little bothered by this joke, but not for long. He chuckles like a bad poker player dealt a full house. "I expected some of that patented Andrew Maven sarcasm, but you'll be taking this seriously soon." Mars looks sideways, ensuring there are no ears nearby, but he can barely contain what he's about to unleash on me. "You've come a long way. I can only assume you've crossed paths with Moriarty. You've met Queen. You've learnt about Metric. You know this group isn't America's sweethearts."

"Yeah." I'm a little uneasy lying to Mars, but I've been working this angle for the past couple days and I'm getting used to it. My former colleague Tim Tomlinson once observed I often advised people to stretch the truth in situations in which I'd never actually do it myself. Timmy Tommy is a known liar and nobody really cares what he thinks, but this was an astute observation.

"I mean, I know bits and pieces. Nobody's been forthcoming. I really want to know – what's on Moriarty's list?"

Mars grins at the mention of the single item he stole from the Manhattan Commonwealth Club Hotel. "I'll get to that. To put it simply, you need to know that there's a small group of people pulling a lot of strings. And they want to control *everything*."

"I've heard this fairytale before, Mars. Hail Hydra. I'm gonna need some details."

"They're influencing major corporations, government spending, social engineering – even wars. But it's not enough – they want complete control. They want a new world order."

"Can you go into specifics?"

Mars explains his information is the result of months of investigations into classified dossiers and reports. He's reluctant to spell it out, but insists he can't ignore so many examples of things that don't add up.

"If you don't believe me by the end of this, I'll drive you back to Long Island myself."

"I think I'd prefer to fly, but go ahead."

"OK. It started in my work with Metric. I came across a sizeable tranche of documents recovered from a national compound. The release was meant to be classified, after a rigorous interagency review. This would've been consistent with national security prerogatives, *but*—"

"I'm going to need you to speak English here."

"Right... Forget that. It doesn't matter. The short version... OK. Just, imagine there was a group that had control over every significant corporate and government power. Worldwide. The Vatican, Wall Street, the Commonwealth. Even the President."

"Uhuh."

Mars senses my early scepticism. "How do you think we ended up with Clinton and Trump to pick from last year?"

"Is it that simple?"

"It is. You think the US government self-appointed world police cares about Syria all of a sudden, but will ban their refugees seeking asylum? Where were we with the Rwandan genocide? I'll tell you – I was there, on my own, carrying out Metric orders that came down from this dark force pulling strings. We're not dropping bombs in Syria because of sarin gas, I can tell you that much."

"We're not?"

"I've got evidence that a new world order is acting as the power behind the throne. They've been shifting chess pieces around, meeting in smoke-filled rooms for *six decades*."

"That's... quite an accusation," I say, scribbling feverishly in my notepad. Truth be told, this is the type of conspiracy theory I expected. "On a scale from one to ten, how confident are you about this?"

"This is a definite ten, bro."

I can't tell if Mars speaks the way he does because he's trying to "come down" to my civilian level, if it's part of his training to blend in, or if it's simply who he is. Maybe he spent time in a regular college fraternity before he joined the CIA or whatever group led him to Metric. He's no doubt intelligent and cerebral, but I wonder if an emotional state of mind reveals something in his speech that his training couldn't remove.

"I know. It sounds crazy. But by the time we're done here, your world is going to be shattered. I'm almost sorry to have to break it to you."

I genuinely believe Mars means this. Whether he's insane or not, it's too soon to judge. I look around the diner, concerned that there could be trouble if the wrong person overhears our conversation. Like many establishments of this sort, it's filled with geriatrics. I can see an old man with his granddaughter at the counter

and a couple of women playing cards in a booth. It's an ideal setting to sit and do a crossword or consume copious amounts of coffee and scones. There doesn't seem to be anyone who appears to
care or even notice us. Everything about this place is ordinary. The
fittings, the colour scheme, the chairs and floors, the posters on
the wall – they're everything you'd expect to find in a Kansan
diner. The waitresses are exactly who you'd expect to find in stereotypical Middle America. The chef... I guess he just looks like a
chef. Maybe the descriptive side of my brain is flat. I'm trying so
hard to decipher every single word and action from Mars that my
analytical perception is shot.

"This is a lot to take in," I say, trying to formulate the right
question to verify Mars' theory. "How... When did you..." I stop
and exhale a slow breath. There's so much to unpack and corrob-
orate. "I'm sorry. I need you to tell me *what* you know and then
you can explain *how* you know it. I need facts. No theories."

"Sure. Let's go back to the beginning. There's a lot of history
of secret organisations pulling strings in the US, but when it
crosses with Metric, that's where it gets interesting. You know,
Metric isn't even at the top of this chain."

"What, are we talking about an illuminati or something?"

"Even stranger. There was a secret cult developed in Ger-
many in the late 19th-century – Ordo Templi Orientis. Order of the
Temple of the East. It's not-so-secret now; you can read all about it
online. But at the time, they were into some freaky stuff. Triads,
rituals, Hermetic science and sex magick."

"Sex magick?" I look up from my notes to check if he's messing with me.

"Yeah. It's called 'sex magick'. It's as weird as it sounds. But
it's a legit thing. Trust me. The less you know about it the better."

"Right."

Mars explains the OTO moved to the US after World War I
broke out. One of its members had written a book of law they
called Liber AL vel Legis – a bunch of gobbledygook about humanity's spiritual evolution through New Age hedonist philosophy.

"Total nonsense," he says. "I've read an exegesis of some of the qabalistic symbolism and I can tell you – that's four hours of my life I'll never get back."

"I have *no* idea what you just said... but please continue."

"Right. I might be getting off track. I spent *months* researching these guys and you're the first person who's actually listened to me, so forgive the rambling. I uncovered a link from Metric back to the OTO forefathers and since then I've been following the trail forward through everything in between their origin to present day Metric."

"And Metric is involved how? That seems to me like a big jump."

Without even pausing to think, Mars begins to recite the unknown history of how the OTO cult splintered off into two subgroups during the 1950s. Each formed their own organisations with their own philosophies, while keeping the secretive structure of the OTO and introducing new ideologies. One group erased its entire history of religious symbolism, all humanist philosophy and almost everything that linked back to the occult.

"So if they started clean as a new group," I begin to ask; "what relevance do they have now?"

"Let me answer your question with another question. Have you ever heard of a 'shadow government'?"

"Only in video games."

Mars shifts his eyes up at me without lifting his lowered head. "*Metal Gear?*"

Cutlery rattles as I drop my hand on the table in shock. "You play video games?"

"Hell no. I'm a rogue Metric agent. I don't have time for games. I'm not even on Facebook."

"Oh. You should get a PlayStation Vita. Portable. Great library of games. Awesome for long plane rides, waiting at airports."

"I was a kid in the '90s, just like you, with a dad who was never around and a mother who wanted to spoil me. My old man was a Metric agent too. I used to play *Metal Gear Solid* and imagine it was him. Little did I know..."

"That's awesome. You basically became Solid Snake," I say,

referencing the video game action hero, while steering the topic away from Rust. I hope this isn't too obvious of a deflection.

"Life's not a video game, Maven. There are no restarts or checkpoints on the battlefield."

This actually sounds like something Solid Snake would say, but now is not the time to nerd out. I can see we've digressed enough.

"So, does this shadow government have a name?"

"Too many to keep track of. It changes all the time. That's one of the ways they remain secretive. At various points they've been The Atlanteans, The Ex-Patriots, The CLIQ Administration, Technion... but one name has always been used interchangeably: The New. World. Order."

"The NWO." I'll have a hard time not picturing Hollywood Hulk Hogan's heel faction, existing only to wreak havoc and vandalise World Championship Wrestling in the 1990s.

"I'm certain that the Order's secular conspirators came together in the late '50s. I've discovered that as they've become more powerful, the hierarchy has whittled down to just a dozen people at the top."

I have to stop Mars here. "How's this possible without a whisper of it at any point throughout history? There's got to be sources for these claims – you know what I mean?"

Mars lowers his voice even more, to the point that I wonder if Rust would be able to hear.

"There have been investigations. They never *end*. The reports never make it to where they would make any difference at all. The Order destroys all the evidence. They're too careful. Even digital footprints are wiped."

Mars is as engaging as Rust is impersonal. It's unsettling how much eye contact he's giving me. He doesn't fiddle, he doesn't look out the window. He just stares into my soul, as if humanity's existence depends on me believing his diatribe.

"The Order is so hidden that their existence is known only to each other and their immediate instruments. Think about it. A week ago you didn't even know Metric existed."

"Right. I mean, it sounds possible. It would definitely explain... some things. But how does it actually work? What do they do? And how? Why?" I realise I've been so caught up in the conversation that I haven't taken any notes for several minutes.

"They've got people, sometimes individuals, sometimes multiple moles working in tandem, operating inside these influential groups. They each have positions of power – not complete control, but enough prominence that they can point these groups towards a single direction for an ultimate prize."

"Which is what?" I ask, pausing briefly from my shorthand annotations.

"From what I can gather, to destroy western sovereignty and institute a one-world socialist government. It sounds crazy, but it's not just a US operation anymore. This thing is worldwide."

He's right. It does sound crazy. I don't want to tell him it sounds crazy, but it is.

"What about nationalism?" I ask. "How could this type of movement surpass even one man's determination to see his countrymen prosper? I only have a civilian's political education, but I was always taught that global governance was impossible. Like, we can barely manage to govern our own country – you know what I mean?"

"I'm not sure it could ever be explained without sounding like a conspiracy nut. But I know it. And there's so much that people don't know, and they don't want to know."

I nod and adjust my Pistons hat, thinking about whether people would even believe what I've seen in the past two days.

"Yeah, I can see that."

It's very important to acknowledge the merit of someone's argument when you're trying to get along, no matter how batty it might sound.

"I mean, as a reporter I've noticed some unusual things and even the experts aren't able to explain them with certainty. I just always assumed there was an undercurrent of activity behind the things we don't understand – nothing as sinister as this. But, like, I never met anyone who understood how Bitcoin works."

"Bro." Mars' eyes bug out as if he's about to burst, such is the magnitude of what he wants to shout at me. "Take this with a grain of salt. Nothing but a theory, but it's an educated theory."

"Right."

"The Order funded the invention of Bitcoin as a way to control the banks."

"You're serious."

"Serious as cancer."

"This isn't a joke?"

"Bro. If I'm lyin', I'm dyin'. Just hear me out. The Bitcoin concept was formed in October 2008, just a few months after the global financial crisis. The Order used the instability of the GFC to place even more of its people in power and help develop Bitcoin as a decentralised virtual currency. The reason it never took off was because the Order gained enough influence inside Wall Street to do their dirty work, so they pulled the pin and let Bitcoin fade into the background. My theory is that it's there now as a perpetual threat for any time the banks threaten to shun the New World Order."

"But is there any proof?"

"It's a matter of public record that the NSA created the open source program Bitcoin uses to secure transactions. All these cryptocurrencies are masterminded by our intelligence agencies to finance terrorism and revolutions. Now, I can only speak of what the Order does in the US. That's been my experience, through Metric."

"You still haven't explained how they're connected."

"I've seen it, bro!"

"Seen what, though?"

"A ton of shady stuff. When I was with Metric it became obvious that a shrouded organisation was controlling America's economy, information, and material distribution. Something bigger than even the US government. Did you ever watch *The X-Files*?"

"If you're here to tell me about aliens..."

"Remember the bad guys on that show, The Syndicate? It was an intangible entity, but it was a massive menace to the world."

"Sure." I never actually watched the show, but I think I get the picture. Mars' detailed knowledge of *The X-Files* could be the strangest part of this very odd conversation.

"Well, the things we know about US operations are a drop in the ocean. Everything I've done with Metric, whether it's been for the good of humanity or for the good of this country, has ultimately served to further the cause of the New World Order. Metric is like 'the black hand' of the Order. Good and evil, their existence only serves to take out anything that threatens the Order's position and progress. I've infiltrated enemy lines to assassinate powers developing nuclear technology that I know was never intended for military use. I've learned those '*evil*' organisations fighting hidden wars with Metric were no more corrupt than the US government. I'm not some sympathiser. I'm someone who's looked in the eyes of good and evil. I can tell the difference."

This here is the part of Mars' argument that strikes me as irrefutable. It's difficult to argue with someone's personal experience. Time after time, he was sent on operations with scarce details, only to have Metric retroactively justify his need to infiltrate and assassinate. Sounds somewhat familiar.

After dealing with Mr Bald and Ms Ponytail, Rust, Moriarty and Queen, I was starting to feel starved for real information. It's refreshing to speak with someone who is not only willing to answer questions, but actually wants to tell me everything they know.

"Can I get y'all another drink?" a young waitress asks in a southern drawl, reminding me how close we are to Oklahoma and Texas. We shake our heads and she scoots away. Mars takes a second to recall where he was going before the interruption.

"So my Mom... she's a former Metric scientist. Lo and behold, she disappears a few weeks after retiring. This is two years ago."

"Yeah, right," I say, feigning concern. It's not that I don't care about his mom, but it's hard to be genuinely shocked by such a revelation when Rust was telling me about it only several hours ago.

"Once that happened, I started asking questions about

everything that didn't add up. Suddenly I'm thrown into the middle of an operation that backfires and portrays me as the bad guy."

"You were set up?"

"By someone in Metric. I know it. Did you study Scarpino?"

"That's how I ended up here."

Mars smiles. "I knew it. See, that's why I'm here in Manhattan, investigating. Between the military base and contacts at Metric HQ, I've only got theories."

"This is starting to make more sense. The only thing that's missing is proof."

"I understand that." Mars reaches into his pocket. I wait for a flash drive, CD, photograph or some kind of evidence to appear, but he produces nothing. Instead his hand just rests inside his jeans. "Everything I've said up to now has been deliberate. This is the conjecture, the loose ends and the historical background. I'm trying to show you these ideas are out there – that things don't add up. This is how I got started down this road. You think I would go *rogue* from the government's most covert espionage agency if I didn't have a good reason?"

I have to admit – this doesn't sound like the motivation of a terrorist, nor does it sound like a threat to national security. I hope Rust is listening closely.

"Look. Maven. When a government can benefit, things happen that shouldn't be allowed to happen. Permits get approved. Budgets get ignored. And when anyone brings it up, it's too late. The wheels are in motion. They move on. You're in this now because I trust you."

"Why?"

This question slipped out. Thankfully, Mars seems distracted by his own side of the conversation and may not have heard it. It's not wise to ask someone why they trust you when there are plenty of reasons they shouldn't. The very reason I'm here is so that Metric can put him behind bars. So why does he trust me? Is it because of my reputation? Shame washes over me in an instant. What if – just, what if – Mars is telling the truth?

Was I manipulated to come here? I absolutely was, but it was through no fault of my own.

Does this mean I believe him? I actually don't know. I need to buy some time to figure it out. If Rust were to turn up now, I wouldn't want to see Mars go without hearing the rest of what he has to say. But I can't give up my cover.

"Time's up. We're movin' on."

"Where are we going?" I ask.

"I've got this plan. I call it Operation Snowden."

"Like Edward?"

"Yeah. I told you, we're gonna bust this thing wide open, bro."

My pal Jay Rosen in New York came up with this concept called "The Snowden Effect". The public gained an incredible amount of knowledge in the fallout of reporting over Edward Snowden's CIA leaks. All this classified information about America's surveillance state was released and a thirst for secret knowledge swept the US, sparking debate over national security versus individual privacy. It's not the right time to talk about it, but I suspect that's been an inspiration for Mars. It's opened the door, in many ways, to prepare the world for a conspiracy of this magnitude. But I still need to establish some facts. I ask Mars again to drop some hard evidence. He shakes his head and stands up, looking down at me as I turn a page of my notepad.

"We have to go. Now."

"Wh... why the urgency?"

"I think you know why."

"What do you mean?"

Mars is being very assertive, in an uncomfortable way. I don't like it, but leaving here will at least buy me that extra time I need before Rust arrives.

Wait. Is that what Mars is talking about?

Does he know?

Chapter 16

Agitation

With each turn we make, Mars drives faster. With every car we overtake, his grip on the steering wheel becomes tighter. He doesn't say a word. I'm too nervous to speak and too afraid that he knows I brought his father with me to Kansas. I have no idea where we are or where we're going, but it's starting to become obvious that this was Mars' plan.

"Give me your Nano GEAR."

"What?"

Mars flies around a sharp corner, making a startled pedestrian leap in fright.

"You've got one. I know it."

"Mars, I – I didn't have a choice. They came to my house—"

"Bro. I know. It's OK. It's all part of Operation Snowden."

We make a hasty U-turn and spin around another sharp corner.

"You wouldn't have found me without him. I planned the whole thing. You hear that?"

I realise he's not talking to me anymore. Holding the Nano GEAR right to his chin he taunts his father.

"You're a bit rusty, Rust!"

Oh no.

"I hope you've been listening close, old man. I don't want to repeat myself."

"Mars, if you just—"

"This is probably the most attention he's ever given me, Maven. Did he tell you that?"

"Can you pull over? I think we can talk this out."

"That's the problem with you, normies. You think talking can fix everything."

"Normie?"

"That's what I call you normal people. Civilians. The non-spies. Don't interrupt me, please."

Mars puts his foot down, pushing the VW Polo to its absolute limit. We're nearing the outskirts of Manhattan's suburbia and I'm amazed there isn't a squad of police cars following us. I crane my neck to look in the passenger side mirror and, of course, Rust is trailing behind in the Corolla. He's likely been on our heels the whole time.

"Back off, old man. You need to let this happen."

"He thinks you're insane. He's not going to back off."

"For a smart guy, you're pretty dumb."

I still don't know which side I'm on. Mars is acting more than a little crazy here, but I never fully trusted Metric since my harsh introduction to Mr Bald and Ms Ponytail back on Long Island. I peer out the window and briefly consider jumping from the car. The moving bitumen doesn't look the least bit inviting.

We hoon past a farmer's market and swerve around a truck backing up across our lane of the road. Rust closes the gap, nudging our rear fender and jolting the whole car.

"That's enough." Mars silences the Nano GEAR's microphone and drops it to the floor.

Approaching a roundabout, I start to wonder if I'm really going to die in a car crash after all I've been through this week. Instead of slowing to give way to oncoming traffic, Mars drives straight through, hitting the middle of the roundabout at high speed. The car launches into the air for what's probably no more than two seconds, but it feels like forever. The suspension takes a hit as we land and Rust follows behind, ramming us again. We spin slightly, but Mars corrects the steering and slides back onto the road, taking the closest exit. The Polo is making sounds no hatchback should make.

The chase continues for a few more turns, with the occasional nudge from Rust's car to ours. I don't say a word.

What am I supposed to do? Convince Mars to pull over and hand himself in? We're well and truly outside the city now, with industrial warehouses and businesses taking the place of the residential homes and shopping malls. Mars crosses into the left lane, overtaking a truck at seventy-five miles an hour. My heart jumps as a motorcyclist approaches, but he freaks out and stacks his bike to avoid a collision, sliding off the roadside in his protective gear.

"Dude!"

"It's OK, he'll be fine" Mars assures me. I wonder if he's just trying to convince himself. Rust's immunity to panic must be hereditary. Before I can reach for my hidden phone to call an ambulance, the sound of gunfire and shattering glass pierces through the roar of the Polo's engine.

"Wha-whoa!"

"Relax, bro. He's just trying to scare us."

"That's your *dad*, bro!" I shout, reciprocating Mars' choice of affection. He weaves in and out through a series of vehicles, daring Rust to follow or be left behind. As we pass a 4x4, Mars gives it a slight nudge in the side and accelerates to leave it behind us. The 4x4 oversteers and clips an overtaking Rust, sending his car hard into a roadside barrier.

I turn to watch the fallout in time to see the Corolla scrape across the concrete wall and brake to avoid oncoming traffic. As Rust shrinks away in the rear-view mirror, I can see hope fade from his eyes. He does his best to maintain his course, but with no clear path he's forced to either reverse or wait for traffic to clear. Mars chuckles maniacally, watching his father disappear as we round a bend. He keeps his foot on the gas and speeds through a series of corners and back roads, eventually pulling over into a car dealership to hide out of view and turn the trail ice cold.

This is where the NSA's satellite support would have helped. Rust must be fuming. I can't help feeling bad for him, given the journey we've taken together and his noble motivation. Then again, he's as stubborn as they come, like a jar of salsa that just won't budge. He won't give up.

Right now, I'm Natalie Imbruglia. *I'm torn.*

"So, am I a hostage or what?"

My pulse slows as I accept we're free from danger – at least, for now.

"You're not a hostage," Mars barks back. "I'm on your side. You get that right?"

"Yeah, but—"

"You said you were looking for facts. Do you want to find them or do you want to become another puppet of the Order?"

"Well... The first one."

"But you still don't believe me."

"I don't *not* believe you. I just need some kind of... I dunno. Where's the hard evidence you were talking about? Or is it up to me to figure that out?"

Mars takes off his Ray Bans and sips some water from a plastic bottle.

"I've been digging around in state libraries and checking them with some data I took from Metric dossier servers. They don't match."

"They don't match?"

"It's like an alternate timeline of history. Small details. As if they know a whole lot more than anyone else."

"That's to be expected, right?"

"Sure, but the context changes everything and points towards even bigger discrepancies."

"Could they just be errors? Mistakes?"

"That's what I thought too, but I kept pushing it and peeling it back, layer by layer. I managed to access Scarpino's safe deposit box at a private club, recovered some enlightening digital and hard-copy materials."

"Saying what?"

"Maven, I'm gonna tell you a lot of things here. But there are some things you'll just have to take my word on. Honestly, it would take too long to fully explain and you still wouldn't understand. That's not a shot at you. It's just that you're a normie."

"I might be a normie, but you chose me to expose this conspiracy, so you need to trust that I'm capable of comprehending what you can tell me. I need at least a general sense of what you found."

"Ongoing plots, identities and locations, among other things. But let me get to *the list*."

At last.

"First, I should point out, a lot of the puppets of the Order don't even realise what's happening. If they knew enough to have a legitimate suspicion, it would throw chaos into the Order and disrupt the entire way they operate. That's going to make our job a lot easier."

"Sure. And by the way, you could've said that from the start without all the hoops to jump through. Not that it hasn't been interesting to meet Rust and Queen and everyone else..."

"I needed to test you." Mars turns the ignition and drives out of the car yard, satisfied that we're free from pursuit. "I needed to make sure you could handle yourself, that you could track me down. No one else has been able to do it. But I also wanted you to piece some of the story together."

We seem to be driving even further out of town into the countryside. I want to ask where this road leads, but that could derail the conversation.

"See, Moriarty told you about the list. He probably told you he was in Metric's bad books. I'll tell you why."

"Please do."

"The Order used to meet at one of his clubs. He's another of their puppets, controlled through the arm of Metric. He doesn't know about the Order, but he started asking questions. He was demanding answers. You know what he's like, with that pompous attitude."

"Right."

"Scarpino wouldn't play ball so Moriarty barred them from using his club. He knew too much for anyone to take him to task, but not enough to get close to uncovering the Order's purpose or true identity. They left him to his own devices for the past few years... until a month ago. I got word Metric was working to secure this list of names, records of their meetings at Moriarty's club, if nothing else. So I went in ahead and retrieved it for myself. The data was encrypted, but I managed to get one name."

"Scarpino."

"That's right. That was the tie back to Metric that I needed. Whether she was the liaison or an active member of the Order, there was scope for investigation."

"How do you know all this?"

"Like I said, I got word."

"Mars. I need to know how."

He sighs, realising I deserve to know, despite his clear desire to keep it to himself.

"Every time they went after me, they'd send someone to fight off. They started with CIA mules and worked their way up to Metric agents until they were dumb enough to send someone close to the Order."

"And meanwhile, you're killing all these people?"

"Hardly." Mars is so nonchalant about his work that I can't tell if his response means murder wasn't necessary or he didn't kill *all* of them. "They're not exactly innocent, by the way. Metric would only send dirty agents to take care of a rogue. Someone who they think can't be 'corrupted' by the truth, which is why I had to give them no choice, but to bring in a normie like you. That was the only way I'd get the ear of someone who would actually listen."

"So you think Rust is a 'dirty' agent?"

"No. There just aren't many left who are capable enough to confront me – and I knew he wouldn't be able to sit back any longer. And so I left a trail of bodies, from the bottom to the top, until I had the information I needed."

"You got Scarpino?"

"I got someone who knew enough. They told me everything. All of this – about the Order, the cover-ups, the hierarchy."

"And how do you know it's true?"

"Truth serum rarely lets me down. I made it myself. I'm actually quite proud of that."

"Kudos, Walter White."

Mars turns on the windscreen wipers as a light pitter-patter of rain turns to a heavier downpour. I hope this isn't how tornadoes begin.

"You're sure Rust can be trusted with this? He doesn't seem very open-minded."

"He's so loyal to Metric that it'd be hard for them to imagine him going against protocol. But he'll have to listen. I'll make him, if I need to."

"Right."

"So do you believe me yet?"

"I don't know," I respond thoughtfully. "I mean, I have an open mind. I wouldn't come this far without believing in something."

"That's what I like about you, Maven. Character. You'll probably find this creepy, but I know a lot about you."

"That is creepy. But not shocking. And now I have to ask, what do you know? What details of my life are deemed important enough to make it into a government dossier?"

Mars flicks his right indicator and veers off towards a less busy road.

"You did four years at Cornerstone University. You could've gone interstate to some Ivy League school, but you picked a private Christian college in your hometown, and you still speak at their graduation ceremonies. This tells me you're loyal, ethical, faithful, grounded. You're a hard worker. You felt enough conviction to leave your job in New York, your health care, the steady wage, to go solo because you wanted to cover that city hall investigation."

I fold my hands and turn my head intently as Mars continues.

"That tells me you're a man of principle, willing to take a risk for a cause. I've read all your news features since then. Those experiences tell me you've seen how the system can cover its tracks. You're all about truth and transparency. As far as I can tell, none of your sources have ever surfaced. That means I can trust you. And that's what I need right now."

I can't help but smile. It's not every day you hear all of your best features listed off by a total stranger. Whether his summation is one hundred per cent accurate or not, I'm flattered.

"You weren't worried I'd be too much of a wuss?"

"You're already brave. We just need to translate that bravery to physicality. But enough of that." Mars starts speaking slightly louder to compensate for the heavy rain. "Are you ready to take down Scarpino or what?"

I nod, which seems like the least committal way to agree. "She's the scapegoat, I take it?"

"It's more than that. Some people would say she's pure evil. I wouldn't say pure, but... she's not far off."

"She's certainly not very friendly. I was—"

Without warning, I'm cut off mid-sentence as our car implodes with a thunderous boom.

That's how it feels. But I don't understand what's happening.

I hear a loud crash. I feel the sensation of incredible movement, so fast that it sucks the air out of my lungs. I gasp for breath and try to focus my eyes on something – anything – but it's all a blurred mess. My lungs scream for oxygen. I feel a sudden whip. My head hurts. And then I see black.

Chapter 17

Dissension

The very real throbbing of my head enters my consciousness before I can tangibly recognise I am awake.

I'm alive.

Help me, I'm alive.

I open my eyes and panic. My fear of sudden blindness subsides as I realise the spider-web in front of my face is a broken window and not my own distorted vision. I can't describe the feeling in my hand because there is none. It's numb.

Dear God, my hand is numb.

What's wrong with me? I shake my wrist with frantic urgency. OK. I'm sure it's fine. I woke up lying on top of my arm so maybe the circulation was cut off.

The last thing I remember was talking to Mars and then...

I look over to the driver's seat where he should be, but he's gone. A deflated airbag has taken his place.

My head.

I reach up and touch my pounding temple, expecting the worst. Instead of a giant hole, I find a wet gash is the source of my pain. The red liquid trickles down my finger and stops in my palm. I'm no doctor, but I know red is a bad colour.

The sun hits me like a punch in the face, or maybe that's just the wound giving me a headache I can't ignore. The car itself is upright but mangled. Inches from my bleeding head rests the caved windscreen. The rain makes a constant drone and hiss as it hits the smoking heap of steel and mangled aluminium. My instinct says to leap from the wreck before an impending explosion, but my limp body and cloudy head says I should just chill here for the time being

As I turn my neck, endeavouring to survey my surroundings, I faintly hear the muffled sound of commotion outside.

"What did you do?"

"Is he OK?"

"Well, he's alive. No thanks to you."

Am I hallucinating? I'm not dreaming. This is different. It's Rust and Mars. Father and son, having it out. My eyes have adjusted to the light and I can clearly see the two agents standing up to each other in the roadside clearing, pistols drawn. Rust's car is somehow in far better condition than ours. I try my hardest to leave this metal box surrounding me, but I haven't built up the strength. For now I'm in no position to do anything more than sit and watch Rust and Mars sort their differences.

"This has to end, Mars. There's no conspiracy. This is crazy."

"You're the one who's crazy. You can't see it. The inmates are running the asylum."

"C'mon."

"You're part of the problem, Rust! You turn a blind eye to anything that doesn't add up. Just think about it!"

"Put the gun down."

"You don't know what I know."

"Why don't you sit down and let me tell you all the things *you* don't know? You think you're the first one to question Metric?"

"I've got something here. It's time for an awakening!"

Neither agent appears to really want to use their weapon. The loaded guns are both empty threats, necessary only to save face in this stand-off.

"This isn't what she would've wanted, Mars. Your mother, she—"

"Don't even talk about her. Either join me or turn around."

"That's not going to happen." Rust is creeping closer to Mars as he shouts through the rain.

"So what, are you going to shoot me, old man?"

"Your angst has a body count, kid. It's time to end this game."

"It's not a game!" Mars bellows back, escalating the tension with an anger that's so real. "You heard *everything* I told Maven, so you have to know it's true. You have to know it's worth questioning. The anaesthetic has to wear off eventually, Rust!"

They're now only five feet away from each other, guns still pointed in a meaningless gesture.

"You're not right, kid... I know what it did to you, losing your mother."

"I *told* you!" Mars thrusts his gun for emphasis, his words punctuated by the hot spit flying from his tongue. "Don't. Talk. About her."

"It was hard for me too." Rust has been steadily lowering his gun in a subtle effort to reduce the tension.

"You should've been there, Rust. She needed you."

"Son..."

"Don't start with that. Don't you dare."

"I want to find her too. But she's gone. And you need help. *I* can help you. *Away* from Metric. They don't need to know."

"I don't believe you. Your whole life is Metric and it's *all* a lie – can't you see that? Scarpino's put you here to *manipulate* me. And I'm not gonna let that happen. I'm sorry."

I'm starting to worry Mars is letting his guard down. He's emphasising his words by gesturing with his gun, as if it's any meaningless handheld object, like a dinner fork or a TV remote.

"I'm not saying you're bad – but they are. And Scarpino will keep using you until you don't know what's right and wrong anymore. Look what they've done to you."

Standing face to face, Rust and Mars look square into each other's eyes, the way NBA ballers threaten to throw-down as they wait for teammates to hold them back. Are they about to brawl? Are they going to hug it out? I can't tell. All I can see is that they're close enough to see inside each other's nostrils. I need to get out of this car.

"I'm sorry it has to be this way," Rust says.

"It doesn't." Mars looks more emotional than I've seen him in our dramatic short time together.

"It does."

Rust cracks his gun across Mars' hand, knocking his weapon to the ground, then takes a swing at his head. Mars ducks the swipe and throws two punches into Rust's side. I wish they could've just hugged it out.

Rust tries using his elbow to gain some space, but Mars steps back, giving his father enough room to raise his gun. Mars is swift enough to wrestle it away, forcing it to fire in the air and tumble to the ground. A fast kick to the calf trips Rust, but he pulls Mars down with him. Like young lions, they start rolling around in the rain, each trying to gain the upper hand.

Rust leers at Mars, fighting to pin his arms until he's thrown clear. The more athletic younger agent springs up and beats his father to his feet. Mars grabs him by the wrist and whips him along the ground. Rust slides across the asphalt through shards of broken glass and lands right front of me. He stands up and we briefly make eye contact.

"Hey." I clear the huskiness from my throat. "Hi."

Rust huffs a grunt and brushes the glass fragments from his clothes. Gathering all my strength, I slide across to the opposite side of the car and drop out through the open driver's door. The wreck supports my weight as I catch my breath and watch Mars approach Rust with his fists raised like a young, insane Mike Tyson. He squares up and weaves around his opponent.

"C'mon, old man!"

Rust dodges a series of quick punches, alternating left to right.

"You're faster than I remember!"

Mars jumps and spins with a textbook roundhouse kick, but

Rust again ducks out of the way and catches a follow-up punch in mid-air, just inches from his face. He twists Mars' arm, putting him down on one knee, then drops a hard elbow into his shoulder.

"Speed kills, kid."

Mars shrieks in pain as he absorbs the contact. Rust throws him face first into the muddy roadside surface and puts him into an awkward grapple. Holding each arm from behind, Rust pulls Mars' limbs upward and thrusts his knee into Mars' spine, pushing and pushing until they're both crying out in anguish. I'm not sure who it hurts more.

"This ends... now!" Rust shouts through the strain.

"Guys..." I call out. "Stop!" Rust barely flinches. I stumble over my own feet, then regain my composure. "You don't need to do this, Rust. Let's just talk this out, the three of us."

"The time... for talking... is over, Maven," Rust groans with gritted teeth. "Just stand back – or you'll be next."

Writhing in excruciating pain, Mars moves his legs through a wicked angle to free them from underneath Rust's weight. He jolts his arms free and jumps to his feet, taking Rust by surprise with a low kick followed by a backhand across the throat that would make Andre Agassi proud. Three quick hits to his midsection and a smack across the face send a splatter of blood flying from his father's mouth.

"That's gross," I say to myself, pushing back the mounting terror.

With Rust down and dazed, Mars reaches for his gun and walks a few feet to find the second pistol. Breathing heavily and soaked in the rain, he looks down at Rust with fury. He's defeated, in no position to fight back. Mars raises both guns, pointing them directly at Rust's chest.

"You see? *This* is what they wanted. *This* is what we can't do anymore."

Rust says nothing.

"Because we're *better* than this. We can do it. You just have to trust me."

"I don't know what to believe." Rust is calm. Exhausted, but calm.

"Just give me a chance." I hear a click come from each gun, as two magazines drop to the ground. In a dramatic gesture, Mars tosses both weapons into the nearby bushes. A perplexed Rust looks into the wind-shaken foliage, then locks eyes with his only son. After a few moments of heavy breathing, he reaches up his hand. Mars smirks, and helps Rust to his feet.

"You and me, old man. Metric's not gonna know what hit 'em."

"I'm sorry, kid."

"Rus—"

A single punch to Mars' jaw drops him to his knees. A second one sends him to the ground, turning a shocked expression into a blank face of unconsciousness. Mars' bleeding face bounces in a shallow pool of water. I watch it turn red as the rage builds inside. Unbelievable.

Tripping over my feet again, I run towards Rust, regain balance and shove him hard in the chest. He doesn't budge.

"What is wrong with you?" I scream, expecting to hear an explanation and some level of regret over his actions.

But instead of delivering such a statement, Rust frowns with an enraged look of devastation that shows no semblance of self-control.

"Rust... You're not yourself."

My suspicion is correct – confirmed by a hard punch in the face.

Chapter 18

Incarceration

I wake up in a cell. That's what it looks like to me. I've never been imprisoned, but this sure feels like a cell.

There's a single bunk, a toilet in the corner, and the lights are way too bright. There are no windows. Metal bars stand between me and an empty room occupied only by a desk, chair and single filing cabinet. A low groan alerts me to the presence of another human. Mars is slumped in the corner behind me with his eyes closed.

He doesn't look good.

My head is pounding like an AC/DC kick drum. I reach up to feel my crash wound, but it's been bandaged. At least Rust made sure I wasn't thrown into prison with a bleeding head. I'm no neurologist, but I feel fortunate to be alive and functioning after blacking out twice in the space of twenty minutes.

This feels like a fever dream. It's crazy and it's starting to sink in. A government agent punched me in the face. A *government agent* saw me as a threat. A *government agent* threw me in a prison cell!

"I've made a huge mistake."

A spluttering cough responds from the corner.

"You picked the right team, bro."

"We're in a prison cell, *bro*."

"Fort Riley."

"The military base? Fantastic."

"Don't worry."

"I am not supposed to be here. This isn't... what was meant to happen."

"Sure, it was."

"Come again?" I look at Mars like he's crazy, which he is, and I am too for trusting him. Then again, I can't even trust Metric to feed my cat, so what's left in this crazy world?

"If you think about it, this was probably the third or fourth most likely scenario. There are plenty of variables and a hundred ways it could've gone down, but once you look back at it... this doesn't seem *that* crazy."

"I can't... I don't really follow. You expected this?"

"I've got to expect anything."

"Does that mean there's still a plan? Operation Snowden?"

"I always have a plan, bro. Sometimes you gotta make a bad situation worse before you can make it right."

That's reassuring. My Nano GEAR is gone. My *notebook* is gone. I'm in big trouble here. My clothes are damp and my sleeve is blood-stained. I shudder as I picture Rust stuffing Mars and me into the back of his damaged Corolla – tied up and limp.

"That was cold-hearted... what Rust did to you. I'm sorry."

Mars shrugs. "It was a risk. Things got a little heated."

"A little heated? A cup of coffee is a little heated. That was a volcano. He knocked me out!"

"He did?"

"I mean, it wasn't him. He had this look on his face. He was flustered. I haven't seem him flustered."

"I was hoping he had a heart inside that barrel chest." Mars leans forward, pauses, and spits a gob of blood on the floor beside him. It's disgusting. "You've spent more time alone with him than probably anyone I know, aside from my mom. What do you think? Am I crazy for trying? Or is there good left in him?"

"He's not Darth Vader. He's just confused - you know what I mean? He doesn't believe you. He feels like trash about your mom disappearing and I think he's probably scared that – I mean, this is my interpretation - but I think he's got this fear of losing you too. Whatever your relationship is, you're his last connection to her. And I know that means something to him."

"Strange way of showing it."

"He has a decent intention. But I can't justify what he did to you... or me." I touch my jaw, which still hurts from his brutal punch. "So you assumed Rust would be the one to bring me here. That part of your plan too?"

"It was. I knew you wouldn't find Queen without him, and I knew he wouldn't get to Kansas without your help."

"He wanted to go to Hong Kong."

"*Ha.*"

I take a deep breath, hoping it will help me relax. The cell's odour is a combination of concrete, dust, damp clothes and blood.

"You guys really beat the hell out of each other. How's the..." I gesture around my face. "You know."

"I feel like crap." The cut under Mars' swollen eyebrow and the dry blood around his nose concur with his statement. "But it's OK. Nothing broken. Just some cuts. Maybe a fracture."

"Fractures are the worst," I say, as if I have any inkling of what he's feeling. "All the pain with none of the sympathy."

I stop and think for a second about how I ended up here and what could be coming up next. I really need to catch a break, but after all this, I'm not sure I'd even know what to do with it.

The creak of a door opening around the corner diverts our attention outside the cell. Several sets of footsteps echo around the other side of the L-shaped room. A tall man in military fatigues emerges with two soldiers close behind. The clear leader of the troupe approaches the cell and stands in front of us with his arms crossed and his mouth curled into a self-satisfied smirk.

"So you're the one the boss keeps talking about."

Mars' first response to the long-haired blonde Rambo is to spit half a mouthful of blood and saliva against the floor in front of him. "Saluki. Nice place you've got here. Could we get a deck of cards or something?"

Blonde Rambo laughs, but I don't think he's really amused. I remember now. Rust said Saluki was a Metric scalphunter – some kind of assassin.

"How have we *never* met?" he asks Mars with genuine astonishment. "Metric's next big thing, reduced to a pile of bloody, wet laundry. Stand up, Agent Mars."

"But the concrete floor is so comfortable."

"What is it they call you? *'The Red Revolver of Rwanda'*. I've heard all about your African escapades. I don't know how you did it. You *must* be good."

"I am."

"But you're not the best."

"I'm in the top two. And my father's getting pretty old."

"OK. So you're good. But I'm pretty good too."

"There's *nothing* pretty about you."

I can't help but scoff at Mars' nerve. This unfortunately shifts Saluki's attention to me with an annoyed glare.

"And you." He folds his arms again, with even more contempt in his face. "I hope you know what you've got yourself into."

"I really don't. Maybe you can fill me in?"

"I thought you were meant to be smart. Sorry, I've forgotten your name already."

"Never said it. How do you know me?"

"I read your file," Saluki says dismissively. His accent is neutral and regal, almost sounding British compared to the Midwestern twang I've heard from some Kansans.

"Man. Is there anyone who hasn't read my file? It's like they're handing them out on street corners."

"Metric agents like to know what they're getting into."

"Saluki... Sounds like a Pokémon."

"He's named himself after a dog," Mars adds. "Middle-Eastern sighthound."

"Yeah? My ex-girlfriend's roommate had something like that. Cute."

"Silent hunters." Saluki reaches into his pants pocket, pulling out a small can of tuna and a plastic fold-out fork. "Just like me."

"For a silent hunter, he talks a lot." I look back for Mars to validate my quip, but he gives me no such satisfaction. He's too focused on standing and hobbling across the cell like a newborn deer trying to walk for the first time.

"Metric agents pick their own codenames ever since—"

"Hey. Mars." Saluki interrupts, forgetting that it's both rude and disgusting to speak with a mouthful of tuna. "How about we keep those things in-house?"

"He knows a lot more about us than how we name ourselves, Sal."

"OK. That's enough. Private Daxter." Saluki turns to the two soldiers behind him. I hadn't considered that they wouldn't know anything about Metric.

"Yes, sir."

"Take Private Jack outside. Keep an ear out."

"Yes, sir."

Once the two soldiers close the door behind them, Saluki points his fishy fork at Mars in a threatening manner.

"Listen here. We're not just protecting this country anymore. We're creating an entire world."

"What are you talking about?" I ask.

Saluki rattles the fork between the steel jail bars, taunting us in the most condescending manner possible. I watch the fork shake in front of my eyes, trying to telekinetically force it from his hands. I'm fully confident Mars could escape a prison cell with just a plastic fork. Unfortunately, the cutlery stays firmly in Saluki's grip.

"It's a new empire, boys. It's the *Order*... The New! World! Order! I know all about it. Do I know as much as you? I'm not sure. But bottom line – it's something I want to be part of."

Hearing Saluki acknowledge the NWO is the final nail in the coffin of my innocence. This means what Mars said was true. All of it. I'm horrified. I think I might be in shock. This is the adult ver-sion of finding out there's no Santa Claus, Easter Bunny or Tooth

Fairy, on the same day you learn where babies really come from. I wish I could just wake up back home in my bed, with my dumb cat shedding hair all over my apartment. I want to control-alt-delete out of this week and start over.

"Listen, Sal. I know you've been doing this as long as I have." Mars' attempt to sway Saluki seems futile, but he continues regardless. "You've seen just as much. Maybe more. You've gotta know Metric's on the wrong side of history here."

"That's where you're wrong, Mars! You think you're a model citizen or something? Good for you. Take a handshake and a kick in the ass. You want to be a good person? Join the Salvation Army. Go build some schools in Africa. Peace and love aren't the status quo anymore. That nonsense ended fifty years ago. Bottom line – you gotta do what it takes in this work. And you don't have it anymore, Mars. You just don't have it. You'll be buried for this. Literally. Even if we let you go, there are paid assassins who would kill you for free. Believe me."

"You might think you know about the Order, but let me—"

"Ba ba ba ba." Saluki interrupts, holding his hand up to the cell bars, still holding his plastic fork. "Nothing you say is going to beat the offer I've got from Scarpino. She's lined me up. I'm her right-hand man. Bottom line – I'll be running this agency one day, and you'll be six feet in the ground. It's the truth!"

"I'll be walking free in forty-five minutes."

"Oh, you make me *laugh!*" Saluki says, without laughing. "What could have been... I suppose I should thank you for making way for me. You were the *golden boy*. Is it true that you pulled the trigger on Bin Laden? I'd give *anything* to be there when that psychopath ate lead."

I gasp louder than I care to admit and twist around to see Mars' reaction to this revelation. His grimace tells me he's either fed up with hearing such rumours or he's unhappy the story is being shared.

"Do you realise what this will cost you? Selling your soul to the Order?"

"To build a mountain, you've got to dig some holes."

"That's a little cliché," I interject.

"I've forgotten your name again."

"I never said."

Saluki snaps his fingers into a pointing gesture. "Maven! Andrew Maven. The news reporter. The pride of Long Island."

"That's Billy Joel. And I'm from Grand Rapids."

"I remember you now." He grips the prison bars with two hands, leaning in to look me in the eyes. "You certainly found more than you bargained for. What a scoop! Too bad you'll never write it."

"Your breath, man... Smells like my cat's ass."

Mars' anti-authority attitude must be contagious. Nonplussed, Saluki tosses his empty tuna can at a trash bin in the corner, missing by several inches.

"It's ironic. The same fire that thrust Metric into such a position of power momentarily had our agency hanging in the balance. And it's all because of the Fox boys."

It makes sense now. Queen told me something about the Foxes yesterday. I never considered it was more than a codename.

"I guess it could've gone either way," Saluki continues. "But Rust made the right call. He almost looked sad when he left. I've never seen so much near-emotion on his face. Your father has an important role in this regime we're building. And, bottom line, now that the NWO is out in the open, we're only going to push deeper into the system. Metric will take this empire from strength to strength."

"Today's empires are tomorrow's ashes," Mars says.

"Spoken like a true proletariat. I'll be sure to pass that on to Scarpino when she arrives."

"We'll be gone by then."

A moment of silence passes as Saluki stares into the ground, his hair hanging over his still face. His body breaks into silent laughter, jerking back and forth.

"I once felt the same way as you, Mars. On my way up through Metric I saw so much that rubbed me in all the wrong ways. But I realise now, this is the way it has to be because this is the way it's always been."

"That doesn't make sense."

"Oh, come on," Saluki purrs, dripping with patronising familiarity. "You honestly believe humans aren't wired to seek domination? There is always an alpha dog. You're looking at the next one." Saluki gestures across his trim body, making me question if he missed his calling as an obnoxious pro-wrestler. "The Order is going to thrust me straight to the head of the table. Think about how far ahead you could've been if you knew that Metric was merely a front to serve their purpose. The chance to be on the right side of history is all this is!"

"You're insane."

"I'm really not, Agent Mars. We're not that different. You picked your side, I've picked mine."

Saluki reaches into his pants pocket again and produces an orange high-visibility vest. He threads it around his army camouflage sleeves, leaving me to wonder if he wants to be seen or not.

"Now, I've got some work to do. It's been a pleasure to meet the two of you. I'm afraid this will likely be our last encounter."

"Don't count on it," Mars says.

"I *will* count on it."

"Well, don't."

"Hey, Saluki. Before you go," I say, halting his exit. "I was wearing a Pistons hat when you brought me here. Like a baseball cap. Do you know where it is? Maybe a lost and found?"

Saluki looks disappointed in himself for even stopping to hear me out.

"I only got it a few weeks ago."

"You know, the problem with you journalists..."

Oh, here we go.

"...is that you think you have power over the masses because you control the message. You think you control what people care about. But you're wrong. *We* control it. We control you. And you don't even know it."

"That might be true. I'm not sure anymore."

"Well, you haven't got long to figure it out, Mr Maven! All the answers will soon be lost to the sands of time, as the shocking gravity of life and death brings you down to earth in utter, hopelessly gasping vitality."

Honestly, I've never been so intimidated by something so corny.

Chapter 19

Conversation

Saluki hollers a maniacal laugh and disappears around the corner, telling Privates Jack and Daxter to keep a close watch on us. Their interpretation of this instruction is to sit and play cards while we chill in the cell with nowhere to go and nothing to do.

I think back to Moriarty's insistence that Metric was up to more than meets the eye. He didn't know what it was, but he had a suspicion about what the NWO was doing, enough to lock up a list of their names. Kenton was right.

"What are you thinking?" Mars asks.

"I'm trying to figure out a couple things."

"For example?"

"One, will I ever eat Taco Bell again? That's the burning question."

"I'll make sure you do," he promises. "What else?"

"Two, does Saluki have a perm and is he naturally blonde? And thirdly, I'm trying to decide: is this the best thing I've ever done or the worst?"

Mars spits again, mostly blood. It's disgusting.

"I know what you mean. I've done a lot of bad. I think that qualifies me to tell you – this is a good thing. That pit you're feeling in your stomach is just fear."

"It's new to me. How do you deal with it? What you said, about your past. The bad things."

Mars exhales a long sputtering breath before breaking it down for me. "In the moment, you tell yourself it's necessary... that the guilt is a burden you have to carry to keep your country safe. I thought this was my sacrifice. That part was true. Now that I know better, my actions are something I just have to live with."

"Hey! You two, shut up in there." Apparently Private Daxter doesn't want to hear our life stories. Or maybe he's Private Jack. I walk over to the corner of the cell where Mars has been camping out. I sit on the floor beside him and we resume talking with hushed voices.

"What's the worst thing you've ever done?" he asks me. "Ever."

"I dunno. Public urination, maybe." I take off my glasses and try to clean the rain spot stains using my damp T-shirt. "I actually downloaded a ton of albums when Napster first came out. I don't know if you were old enough, but it was quite the big deal at the time. We must've spent three years not paying for any music. But I eventually went back and bought everything I downloaded. Except that Smash Mouth album. I couldn't bring myself to go that far."

"Yeah. So, I've killed people," Mar tells me with a straight face. "A lot of people. And most of them deserved it. That was obvious."

"I guess that's a good thing? They were bad people, right?"

"Yeah. Just depends where you fall on murder. I'm not saying I'm proud of it."

I can sense he's a *little* proud of it.

"But the rest of them? I don't know. I actually... genuinely *don't know*. Were they bad guys? I don't know. Were they moral people standing in the way of the Order? I've realised I don't know anything. And that's what I've been questioning since I went rogue."

"That's heavy."

We sit in silence for about a minute and I try to think of anything I've seen or heard over the past few days that could help us out of here. Mars must be able to see distress in my eyes because he asks what's wrong. I try to explain I'm still coming to terms with accepting everything he told me as fact.

"It feels like real life is a lie – you know what I mean? We have no freedom. We have no privacy, no influence."

Mars lightly taps the back of his head against the blank wall and stares up at the ceiling, perhaps feeling guilty for exposing me to this reality. "It's a hard pill to swallow. But people need to know."

"Will they even believe it? I know I wouldn't if I wasn't sitting here, if I was just reading the news, sitting on the toilet and looking at my phone like most people. *Fake news,* and all that stuff."

"People know there's something off. There's so much that doesn't add up in this country."

"Yeah, but... see, I'm not sure. I mean, yeah, I always assumed there were dark forces at play. But I thought they would be just twisting things here and there, more like reality TV producers or the NBA commissioner working with referees. I assumed there were tastemakers and billionaires with influence. Drug companies, people nudging politicians... but not this. There's a difference."

"Try discovering all this and figuring out you were the bad guy all along." Mars slides his back to the wall and hugs his knees, staring through his toes.

"I don't envy that."

"But that's done with. I'm no one's puppet."

"Can you explain to me – how did the Order go from a secret cult to a powerful group embedded in every major governmental organisation? It seems unlikely."

"It actually started with the Five Eyes."

"Which one is that again?"

Mars explains the Five Eyes is an intelligence alliance between the US, the UK, Canada, Australia, and New Zealand, which formed in the 1940s after the Atlantic Charter was issued. It's pretty much a union between the English speaking Commonwealth and good old America. As the Five Eyes, each country is bound by the multilateral UKUSA Agreement.

"Right. I know about this," I tell Mars. "The treaty for joint co-operation in signals intelligence. It's like the grand slam of espionage, basically."

"That's right. The Order's most influential figure started as one of the founders of the Five Eyes alliance and found like-minded delegates to serve under each of the five powers. From there, it just spread. Corporations, banks, international collectives, governments. You name it. They started trading secrets back and forth, like currency, and now their network extends across the world. They're not all members of the Order, but people of influence have formed a hierarchy below. Everyone has their own agenda and thinks it's a symbiotic relationship, but it all comes down from the Order. No one is immune from the power of suggestibility and manipulation."

"Even Metric, huh?"

"They're quite high in the pyramid, from what I can tell."

"Is there anything else you want to tell me, while you're revealing secrets? Did Rust kill JFK?"

"He would've been running around in diapers at the time."

"Right. There's got to be something you can tell me."

"9/11 was an inside job."

"Stop it. Are you kidding me right now?"

Mars tries to keep a straight face but breaks into a quiet chuckle.

"Don't do that... I'm vulnerable."

"Sorry. That would've made quite the tweet."

It dawns on me that after chasing down the thieving Sticky, I placed my phone deep inside my jacket's hidden chest pocket – one that Rust didn't even know about. With an eye on the soldiers responsible for watching us, I reach over my chest, giving my jacket a gentle pat.

There it is. I have my cell phone.

Maybe Rust thought I'd lost it in the car wreck. Maybe he searched my other seven pockets and found nothing. Either way, it's not as if I can call up a friend in New York and ask them to break me out of a Kansan military base. I need to keep this to myself on the off chance that Metric has bugged the prison cell.

"What did Saluki call you? 'Red Dead Rwanda' or something?"

"The Red Revolver of Rwanda." Mars can see I'm waiting for an explanation. "I killed a lot of bad guys there."

"I guess that falls under the 'not evil' category?"

"That's right. But it still served to meet the Order's purpose, like always."

"So is that true what he said, about Bin Laden? Were you in SEAL Team Six?"

Mars shakes his head, but I still can't tell if his denial is genuine. I thought the shooter had already identified himself, but something in Mars' eyes leaves me wondering.

"Tell me something crazy. Like, what's the damnedest thing you've ever seen?"

"Man. I've seen a lot." Mars pauses for only a few seconds. "This isn't the craziest thing, but it's the first that comes to mind."

"OK."

"So, I was in Uganda a few years back on a counter-insurgency op. I spent weeks tracking the Lord's Resistance Army. You know much about the LRA?"

"Joseph Kony?"

"That's it. But it's not him anymore. I had one of the leaders there. A total dirt bag. Child soldiers, prostitution, drugs, gun trade – you name it and he was behind it. For as much as I've seen, it still makes me sick thinking about it."

"Huh. And you're with this guy?"

"Yeah, I had a gun on him. Everyone else had fled or been taken out in the chaos. So he's three, maybe four feet away from me and I'm screaming at him to put his hands up, get on the ground, whatever. I'm yelling at him in English, French, Bantu, Swahili – anything I can think of to give him a chance to surrender. This guy, we wanted to know what he knew. But he was pathological, *obsessed*, doing these unbelievable things and trying to justify it with spiritual delusions that he was a god and he could do whatever the hell he wanted."

"Wow. So, then what?"

"I had my gun on him, right in his face. I'm ready to pistol whip his ugly mug and he says to me, with no fear at all, he says: 'Don't you know I'm a god? Bow before me and I shall let you go free.' At this point he's defenceless, mind you."

"Crazy."

"Yeah. I'm thinking 'Is this guy for real?' He's so used to mis-treating people, acting as judge, jury and executioner, that he's lost all sense of reality... He's entered another world."

"Sounds intense."

"It was. So I cock my pistol, you know – ch-chk – just for intimidation, to show him I'm not hearing anything he has to say. I'm not messing around. I'm ready to put a bullet through his mouth if he so much as cracks his knuckles in my direction. The dude turns around and reaches for his rifle – the same rifle he's used to manipulate and kill families and escaping kids in the LRA for literally years and years. I didn't hesitate. I pull the trigger – bam! Straight through the back of his neck. He hits the ground like that Saddam Hussein statue in Iraq – right down, face first."

"Holy smokes."

"Yeah. But even with his last breath, spluttering his own spit and blood all over himself, he tells me: 'I am your god. I am god.' I'm there, I'm standing over him, but he says this over and over, as if he's thinking 'This can't be happening to me. A god among men.' I look down and say: 'God – I don't believe in you.' I walk away, he bleeds out, dies alone, I free the kids and take them back to their families."

"Wow. That's... wow."

Mars inhales a self-entitled sniff. "Yeah. I mean, I'm more of an agnostic anyway, so you know. Whatever. But it was a moment."

"Shut it down, you two! I won't tell you again."

"Bite me," is Mars' response to the supervising soldiers. Tricking Jack and Daxter into opening the cell to beat us up could be our best chance to get out of here. Both guards stand up, offen-ded by Mars' candour. One of them nears the front corner of the cell until something startles him.

"Did you hear that?"

"Saluki, sir?"

All I can see is a hand reaching to pull Daxter out of our view, before he's sent hurtling back again into the room's lone filing cabinet. Rust is back, baby!

"What the...?"

Jack hoists his rifle but Rust pulls it in close and reverses the momentum, thrusting the butt into the soldier's face. Two seconds later he has dismantled three parts of the gun. One drops to the floor, but he uses the bolt cover in his left hand to crack Jack in the skull. With his right hand he tosses the dislodged ammo clip across the room, smacking a stirring Daxter right in the face. Rust knees Private Jack in the groin, which is enough to put him on the floor just a few feet away from Daxter's limp body.

"Ouch. You know you probably ruptured something down there?"

"He'll get over it," Rust tells me while looking over his latest carnage. With both soldiers indisposed, he continues staring at the ground, far longer than necessary. It strikes me that perhaps he's just not sure how to look us in the eye after what he did to us only a couple of hours ago. Rust finally packs his emotion into its usual hidden storage and starts fumbling around with the cell's lock.

"What are you doing here, Rust?" Mars asks accusingly, hiding any semblance of being impressed or thankful to see him.

"We don't have a lot of time. We can talk later. But just know that... that I'm sorry. To both of you. I should've listened to you... I believe everything you said."

"You do?" Mars scoffs.

"I just... couldn't accept it. Until now."

"Well. What changed?"

"Hm. Something Maven said."

Mars shoots me a glance, folding his arms and grinning with a sense of vindication before responding to his father.

"I knew I got that guy involved for a reason."

Chapter 20

Liberation

The prodigal father has returned, but there's no time to throw a celebratory banquet. We need to get out of this musty prison before Scarpino arrives, and before the unconscious guards wake up to raise an alarm. Our issue is Mars being slow to trust his traitorous father. Rust assures us that a jailbreak with two enemies of the state will do nothing for his reputation. The new problem is getting out of here unnoticed.

"We're in the middle of an army base," Mars says. "Surrounded by eighteen thousand service members, a first infantry division, a garrison command and an air support operations squadron. How in the blue hell are we getting out of here in one piece?"

"That's not exactly true," Rust says. "The north-east side of the base is bare. Houses evacuated. All we have is the explosive ordnance disposal team to get past."

"You called in a bomb threat?"

"Not a bomb threat. An unexploded ordnance. It happens all the time at these installations. People find old shells, mines and grenades that sit dormant for decades. Plus, most of the Big Red One has been deployed to Afghanistan and Iraq."

"That's right," Mars' voice picks up as he forms a thought.

"Plus, there'd be thousands of soldiers spread across Kansas and neighbouring states because of the tornadoes. Recovery aid and preparation."

"The rest are probably bunkered down with family and civilians."

"This might be our lucky day."

"How convenient," I point out, hoping someone will speak up if it really is too good to be true. "I guess we had to catch a break eventually." I mention the threat of Metric, but Rust assures me we need to act quick to get out before Scarpino arrives with a ton of backup. "This is what you're trained for, right? You've got the stealth gene."

"Hm." Rust grunts, taking me back to a simpler time when all I wanted to do was extract personal details. "Except we've gotta babysit you too."

"That's the old curmudgeonly charm I was missing. Glad to have you back, Rust."

The door to our only exit flies open and three armed soldiers burst through, shouting as soon as they see Privates Jack and Daxter on the floor. I instinctively throw my hands in the air. Without warning, Mars leaps across the room like a game-saving goalkeeper. To my surprise, he tucks his body into a roll and rises up to springboard off the wall with his right foot. Before anyone has time to act, he uses his momentum to deliver a swift kick to the first guard's unsuspecting face. He falls hard to the floor and Mars follows the kick with another flawless forward roll towards the second and third guards. I hit the deck and look over to see Rust merely spectating. The soldiers' attempts to spray bullets at Mars are futile as he moves about the room with the speed and precision of a hyperactive breakdancer. From his rolling position, Mars grabs hold around the taller guard's heels and trips him as he rises to his feet. He then sweeps his leg to send the last remaining guard to the floor. With a foe on either side, he drops to the floor and delivers an elbow to each of their throats. In one swift motion, he locks in a hard sleeper hold on one soldier, while using his legs to squeeze the air out of the other.

It's safe to say he's recovered.

The room is clear after no more than ten seconds of Mars' impersonating a violent hybrid of Spider-Man and Stone Cold Steve Austin. Mars hasn't even raised a sweat. I look over to Rust, wondering why he never stepped in to help. His bewildered expression tells me he's as stunned as I am.

"What the hell was that?" he asks.

"That? I learnt it from you. Tanzania campaign, 1996. Comms Tower VR simulation."

"Virtual reality training?" I ask, seeking clarification like a good journalist always should. Rust looks at me with just a hint of nostalgic sadness.

"Times have changed."

Despite his acrobatics, or possibly because of them, Mars is walking with a slight limp. He feels one of the soldiers up and down, presumably looking for any keys, information, weapons or other useful loot.

"Can we leave now?" I ask. "I feel like we just cheated death and I don't want to roll the dice again. There's going to be dozens more of those guys, right?"

"Rule number one. Know your enemy." Mars takes the dog tags from each soldier and places them in the pocket of his jacket. "Metric agents handle their own business. Saluki is arrogant. I'd be surprised to see him raise the alarm and have to explain how he let two rogue agents and a news reporter run free in the depths of a US military base. Scarpino on the other hand, she's got resources."

"That's right," Rust nods. "There's a pool of Metric agents she can call on."

"Except they're not just Metric, Rust. You need to adjust to that concept."

"NWO." I fill in the obvious blank, reminding Rust that the New World Order is the inevitable boss battle ahead of us. It's at this point I realise the Fox boys have addressed each other by their Metric codenames, rather than anything more personal. No "Dad". No "son". I still don't know their real names. Maybe it's a sense of professionalism, but it creates a distance between them that fails to foster any sense of a family connection.

As we step outside the room, I discover it was actually an underground bunker, which explains the lack of windows and the concrete walls. We rush up the stairs to the surface – Rust first, then me and Mars following behind. The sky has changed colour since I last saw daylight, reminding me it's now several hours after the car crash.

The vast emptiness of the army base is the second detail I notice. Rust wasn't kidding about the bomb warning. I walk with soft strides, treading as lightly as possible to dampen my footsteps.

"Maven. What are you doing?" Mars asks, looking at me as if I have three heads.

"I'm sneaking. Stealthily."

"You look like Elmer Fudd. We're not hunting rabbits. Just... hurry up a little."

"Where are we going?"

"I know a place."

"How long is this going to take?"

"How long is a piece of string? We can't know until we get there. There's too many variables."

As much as it looks like everybody's gone or been raptured, leaving the immediate vicinity of the bunker takes us into more populated territory. Our escape to the north-east outskirts of Fort Riley is slow, with a varied approach over more than an hour of sneaking. The strategy switches back and forth – sometimes we sprint between cover, sometimes we bide our time to avoid detection. Soldiers are running around everywhere, going about their business and generally ignoring or not noticing us. The further north we get, the fewer we see. The Fox boys are maestros at work, using every tool at their disposal as we slip past the soldiers and occasional surveillance cameras. Sometimes we hide in plain sight. At one point we even pull the old "captive Wookiee" trick from *Return of the Jedi*. That's what I call it in my head, as Rust orders us to march past a security patrol with our hands behind our backs in imaginary cuffs.

I spot Fort Riley's very own golf course in the distance. Under normal circumstances, my heart would sink with the realisation that I don't have time to stop and check it out. My total lack of interest confirms that these are anything but normal circumstances.

With the sun starting to set, we approach a large sign casting a shadow over a wide cemented area surrounding an odd-shaped structure: "Central Issue Facility (CIF)". The building appears hexagonal, maybe even octagonal, with several wings extending in different directions from the centre. From above, I imagine it resembles a giant asterisk. The sparse concrete space around it reminds me of an abandoned airport runway, scattered with shipping containers, a lot of stationary vehicles and what appear to be storage sheds.

"This way." Rust motions toward the CIF building where we can take cover from the wide open space. We've been spotted a few times, but fortunately the soldiers are busy enough to go about their business without much convincing. There's still no sign of Saluki, Scarpino or any other Metric agents, even though their search has to be under way by now.

A large roller door on the side of the CIF building seems to suck in the Fox boys like a gravitational tractor beam. There's something they see that I clearly don't. The combination lock keeping us out could suggest there's something worth hiding, as Mars begins twisting its dial ever so carefully.

"How does that work?" I ask, assuming he knows what he's doing. "Do you hear it click or something?"

"Nope... You have to feel for the tumblers. As you hit each one, there's extra tension on the dial. You... manipulate the wheel until the... Boom." He slides off the lock and lets it drop to the ground. "I got it faster than I could explain it to you. Look it up on YouTube if you really want to know."

"You made that look easy."

"I've just got a knack for it."

"A knack. Right."

Rust lifts and holds the door until Mars and I can crawl

underneath. As it drops down behind us, I hit a light switch to reveal an armoury loaded to the roof with shelves of gadgets, gear, weaponry, and ammunition.

"Jackpot."

"Let's gear up."

Mars and Rust waste no time exploring the room like two kids in a toy store. I feel a little out of my depth.

"Advanced grenade launcher?" Mars asks Rust, inspecting a shelf of goodies.

"That's the XM25 weapon system. I'll take it. Along with my 1911, I'm sorted."

"You didn't happen to pick up my Mark 23? You know, after you knocked me out."

Rust grunts no, recalling their confrontation earlier today, as Mars wanders into the far back corner where the light is dim and the dust tickles my sinuses.

"This one." He bangs his fist against a metal locker. "There's gotta be some good loot in here. There's another damn lock."

"Can you rig it?"

"It's just a latch. Pass me one of those grenades in that box."

"You're not gonna blow it up, are you?"

Mars laughs as I gently scoop my fingers around a single grenade. The explosive is heavier than I expected. I handle it with the utmost respect, nursing it with two hands like a newborn child. Mars doesn't show the same reverence. He grabs the grenade, yanks out its pin, and hands it back to me as casually as you'd pass a bottle of ketchup.

"Just hold that clip down, bro. Real tight. Don't let it go, or we're all dead. One flash and you're ash."

"Wh... What? Really?"

My palm and fingers immediately start sweating, increasing my fear of dropping the handheld bomb.

Dear God.

Please don't let me die in this dusty armoury because my fingers are too sweaty to hold this clip.

Please God.

"Done. Six seconds flat. Damn, I'm good."

Six seconds? It felt like an entire minute. My nerves kept me from watching Mars use the grenade's pin to pick the lock. He slides it back in place and I return the grenade to the carry case where it belongs. Phew.

Mars flings open the locker and pulls out a large gun, measuring somewhere between a shotgun and an RPG launcher. A hook protrudes from its barrel and a cardboard tag hangs at the grip, like any product you'd find on a Kmart shelf.

It says "P-TAIL – Pocket Tactical Air Initiated Launch."

I think I've heard of these. It's far too big to store in your pocket literally, but it's far smaller than the regular model I've read about online. A prototype, maybe?

Mars holds up the P-TAIL and looks down its sights.

"Grappling gun. Cool, ain't it? Doubt I'll get a chance to use it though."

"I'm sure you'll find an excuse. It's cool that you even know how to shoot one of those things."

"Shoot? Yes. Grapple without falling to my death? Hopefully it's as easy as it looks."

"Are there any, you know... bulletproof vests in here? You guys are grabbing a lot of guns for people who try to stay unnoticed."

"Be prepared. Rule number one."

"Hey, Batman and Robin," Rust interjects with an uncharacteristic pop-culture reference. "If you're done playing dress-ups..."

Mars shrugs off the insult and reaches across to the shelf behind me. "Think you can handle a pistol, Maven?"

He holds out an ominous semi-automatic handgun. I'm reluctant, but I'm wise enough to recognise at this point it could be necessary for our survival. I ask for a dummies' guide to guns, just in case Mars doesn't realise I'm a total noob.

"Treat it like it's loaded at all times," he tells me. "Keep your finger off the trigger until you're ready to fire. Know your target." He places the pistol in my right hand and adjusts my hold. "This is a Glock 19 – you want to grip it tight with your finger along the slide and wrap your support hand around your other fingers. Thumbs on top. There's the safety. And that's about it."

"I've got a bad feeling about this."

"You'll be fine. Just don't use it unless you have to."

Rust is already at the exit, squatting low and scoping the area outside. He lets the door roll to the floor and emits a seething breath.

"Saluki."

"He's... out there?" I ask, knowing the answer.

"Yep. And he's got a chopper. I hate choppers."

As soon as the words leave his mouth, I realise I can hear the approaching aircraft.

"How d'ya know it's him?"

"You can spot that blonde mop a mile away."

Rust lifts the door again and motions for us to leave. We make a run for a shipping container some thirty yards away, hoping Saluki doesn't spot us from above. Staying in the armoury any longer would only increase our chances of being caught.

The nearby chopper is so loud that Rust hands us two Nano GEARs from his rear pocket to communicate. Over the sound of the whirring blades, the digital signal lets us clearly hear him identify the helicopter as a Piasecki SpeedHawk. It has two wings, two engines and, like many military helicopters, wheels instead of the usual landing gear.

"I thought they were still in development," Mars says, impressing me with what could be rudimentary military knowledge, as far as I'm aware.

"They have to test these machines somewhere."

I look up at the sky above, which is starting to dim as the sun sets across from us. The bright glare could play into our favour as Saluki searches the area below.

"You better pray to your God they don't find us here," Mars tells me.

"You better... just do whatever agnostics do, I guess."

"We hope for the best. It's fairly futile."

"Well. Do that, then."

There are a number of conveniently large objects to hide behind, so we'll attempt to stay behind cover until Saluki moves on. I can see a large power transformer, like a substation, a few more shipping containers, some vehicles, and other ambiguous boxes – the type I pass every day on the street without thinking about what's inside. They could be internet nodes or switchboards. Maybe it's powering some of the military equipment nearby. Whatever it is, it's a giant square covered in sheet metal.

"At least it's just a compound chopper," Mars says.

"What's that mean?" I ask. "No guns?"

"It means we're safe – for now."

"Not exactly. Stay down!"

Rust yanks me back as I peek around the corner, squinting into the sun. One second later, a fury of bullets shreds through the metal-cased transformer nearby, creating a cacophony of noises my ears have never experienced in person. I duck for cover and instinctively shield my face as one of the Foxes pulls me into a more secure position. My masculine shriek is muted by the terrible combination of roaring chopper blades and machine gun fire, along with the hiss of the malfunctioning power equipment falling to pieces inside the destroyed sheet metal container.

We're still safely behind cover, but Saluki has discovered our general location. Maybe the NSA's satellite support team has joined the search.

"I really hate choppers," Rust grumbles.

"I thought you said it was a SpeedHawk," Mars shouts over the audio obstacles. "I've never heard of one being armed!"

"It's a prototype – DARPA must have issued a combat model."

"DARPA?" Mars seems incredulous at Rust's naïvete, doubting the Defense Advanced Research Projects Agency would be responsible for developing such a weapon. "You still don't get it, do you? This is the *New World Order*. The DARPA chief is just another one of their pawns."

Rust interrupts Mars before he starts a soapbox speech, explaining the SpeedHawk's fuel tanks are self-sealed up to at least 25mm, fitted with couplings and multi-point fire suppression.

Whatever that means.

"You know those Kevlar rotor blades can withstand a hit from a grenade. It'll take a lot more power to bring him down."

"RPG!" the Fox boys yell in unison.

Rust will backtrack to the armoury while Mars keeps Saluki busy. That's the plan. I ask what I can do to help, hoping dearly that the answer is "nothing".

"Just stay out of the way, kid."

"I can do that." With the gunfire on pause, Mars and I swing open the shipping container door to hold up inside its solid walls. If worst comes to worst, I could always hide in one of the empty cardboard boxes stacked in the corner.

Rust waits on the other side of the steel as his son finds a moment to strike. Holding the grenade launcher up next to his face, Mars takes a deep breath and sprints to the closest cover – the remains of the hissing and sparking transformer.

"Got any tips, Rust?" I ask over the Nano GEAR.

"Stay in there. Don't move. Remember to breathe."

"Got it."

Peering through a ventilation grate, I watch Mars prepare for combat. Like a meerkat popping out of its hole, he rises, turns and fires a grenade into the sky. It misses the moving chopper, causing a loud explosion to the CIF building behind. A second shot hits square on the tail of the SpeedHawk's sleek, black design. It shakes and wobbles in the sky after absorbing the contact, but it does not fall.

"There you are!"

To my surprise, we can hear Saluki clear as day. This must be the open Metric channel Rust told me about when he introduced me to the Nano GEAR two days ago.

"I don't know how you escaped, but I have to say I'm impressed. Even for you!"

"Catch me if ya can," Mars replies, still squatting in cover. It sounds as if Saluki hasn't arrived to the seemingly obvious conclusion that Rust aided our escape. Maybe he's as arrogant as Mars suggested.

"*It's funny. I heard so much about you. But now that I can see you? Ha-ha! There's no mystery anymore!*" Saluki keeps the SpeedHawk hovering in place as he delivers his over-indulgent soliloquy, oblivious to our plan to bring him down. "*I feel like you took every assignment that would've advanced my standing with Metric. It's your fault it's taken me so long to rise to the top. But those days are gone! You won't hold me back another day.*"

"*You sound like a jealous high-schooler, Saluki. Did I steal your girlfriend too?*"

"*It's funny. We've been to Mars. The red planet is a mere barren wasteland with no hope for life. Death is all that awaits anyone foolish enough to fight against the system. There's no hope in your primitive plan for survival.*" The chopper begins a steady elevation. It rises to a high position that brings Mars into view with nowhere to hide from whatever Saluki has planned next. "*Your archaic ideals will be the death of you and anyone you manage to string along. I'm sure we'll be sorry to lose such a talented member of our team... but something tells me even your father wouldn't mourn you, Mars.*"

"*I guess we'll see about that.*"

"*Enough talking. You're in my sights. Now – die!*"

Chapter 21

Affliction

Mars dives away from the sparking transformer as bullets cut through its remains like a chainsaw. His leap to safety covers a distance that would make Super Mario proud.

Now hidden from the hovering chopper, the next couple of minutes become a game of cat and mouse. Mars jumps around, hiding in cover while the SpeedHawk pans around, tearing up anything in its way. Mars fires shot after shot from his grenade launcher, some making impact and others missing altogether. He has to be careful to pick his spots. Each time he steps out, he risks giving up his position. Saluki can always elevate to find Mars, but at that angle he has no way to attack.

"Have at you!" Saluki shouts, catching sight of his enemy and unloading a barrage of ammunition.

Out of breath, but somehow still inside his comfort zone, Mars finds his way to new cover and launches a high-arching grenade past the chopper to a small radio tower on the CIF building. The explosion blasts its foundation, toppling the structure over the edge. Its steel poles land across the SpeedHawk's blades and abruptly shoot out of my view.

"Nice shot!"

The powerful chopper takes the hit, shaking back and forth before stabilising in the sky.

"That was inventive, Mars! You're as good as they say. Maybe I can learn something from this experience."

"How very interesting," he responds with a lack of enthusiasm. *"Now, shut up and come get some."*

The hits from Mars' grenade launcher are taking a toll on the SpeedHawk's manoeuvrability. Its fast movements seem less precise and effective. There's a thin trail of smoke rising from its rear, but I wouldn't know the difference between exhaust fumes and something more serious. It just doesn't look right.

I peek my head out of the shipping container, searching for any sign of military backup. Nothing. You'd think all of this commotion would draw a crowd, but either the Fort Riley soldiers are more distracted than we predicted, or they've learnt to ignore the sound of gunfire, helicopters and explosions coming from inside the military training base. I also can't rule out the chance they've wisely decided to keep their distance from this chaos.

Aside from giving Mars some third-person perspective from afar, there's little I can do to change our situation.

"Rust, where the heck are you?" I shout.

"Hold tight. I've got an RPG, but there's no ammo."

"C'mon, Rust," Mars says. *"There's only so much I can do with this peashooter."*

I look around the shipping container at the stash of weapons left behind. "There's always the grappling gun."

"Great idea. Get ready to throw it to me."

"That... I was... OK, sure." There's no use arguing. I pick the prototype P-TAIL from the floor and prepare to toss it. Mars takes cover once again behind the shredded transformer and catches his new toy with a wry smile.

Mars braces himself and fires the grappling gun. Compressed air pops from the pneumatic cannon's barrel and the metal claw sails through the air with a loud whistle. The SpeedHawk has no landing skids or crossbar to latch onto, but against all odds, the hook latches firmly onto the base of a small wheel to the right of the chopper's cabin. It's a thousand to one shot, but Mars has nailed it.

"Heck yes!" I shout.

"Watch me." Mars runs out of his cover and towards the SpeedHawk. He jumps in the air and slowly ascends along the Kevlar line. It's not the instant reel-in we've seen Batman use so many times on the rooftops of Gotham City, but Mars is moving closer every second. Saluki has deciphered the tactic and begins swaying the chopper from side to side, bringing Mars higher with increasing momentum.

"I should end this..." Saluki screams maniacally. *"But I'm just having too much fun!"*

He's clearly aiming to swing Mars against the CIF building, but the timing works in Mars' favour. At the last second, he lifts his legs to avoid colliding with the roof.

"Rust..."

"I found ammo. I'm just... Give me a minute. I'm not as fast as Mars with the locks."

I have a mental image of Rust throwing an ammo crate against the wall when it doesn't behave the way he feels it should.

Mars has reached the SpeedHawk's wheel, right where the hook has attached, and anything he does from here will surprise me. Pulling a handgun from his holster, he begins firing into the base of the helicopter, aiming with intent at particular spots.

"Nice try, Mars! Ever heard of bulletproof casing? You'll need more than a SOCOM Mark 23 to hit the fuel tank."

Mars doesn't appreciate the taunt, judging by the way he takes hold of the hanging grappling gun and lowers himself enough to swing up, firing a rapid volley of bullets into the cabin window. After three or four swings, each allowing space for several shots, Saluki has had enough. He spins the chopper, faster and faster, until Mars loses control and begins to fall.

As I squint, I realise he's not quite falling – he's been wise enough to lower himself using the grappling gun, avoiding a sudden forty-foot descent. The Kevlar line extends far quicker than it reels in, which catches Mars off-guard. He loses his grip through the spinning momentum and falls the final eight to ten feet onto the hard concrete.

It's brutal. His body lands hard and goes limp as his head hits the ground. I'm losing count of today's concussion tally.

"Mars! Get up! Dammit. Can you get up?" I can barely see him through the vent, but there are no signs of movement. "Rust, hurry! I don't know if Mars can hold out any longer."

"For Pete's sake... I'm going as fast as I can. One minute."

A minute. Sixty seconds. It's too long if Mars doesn't move. He's a sitting duck and I couldn't possibly drag him to safety without the SpeedHawk's machine gun turning me to mincemeat.

"Oh, did that hurt, Mars?" Saluki cackles, descending towards his motionless body. The SpeedHawk tilts backwards to line up a deathblow. *"It's a shame this has to end with a stationary target. I wish I could keep killing you forever!"*

I have to do something.

I reach for my gun and it doesn't feel any more comfortable in my grip than when I first handled it. I'm shaking before it even leaves my jacket. Can I do this?

I lift the Glock to eye level.

C'mon. I can do this. Of course, I can.

Why am I so nervous?

I can see the hovering SpeedHawk through the vent. If I step out, I'll have a perfect profile view on the chopper's cabin. I make my move into the open, gun raised, using every technique I can remember from Mars' tutorial. I grit my teeth and squeeze the trigger over and over again.

The Glock vibrates through my entire body as I fight the recoil, sending a stream of ammunition towards the chopper. I'm not sure whether to be thrilled or horrified, like a young teenager being kissed for the very first time. I fire shot after shot, with no idea if they're hitting or missing. The unfamiliar smell of burnt gunpowder fills my nostrils.

I keep shooting until my clip is empty. It must be fifteen or twenty bullets.

I don't know.

It's kind of a giant blur. I hear a faint, tinny symphony of brass shell casings bouncing and rolling across the concrete as the SpeedHawk rotates away from Mars to face my direction.

"There you are! The mouse has come out to play."

The thrill of realising at least one of my bullets connected with the cabin disappears once it dawns on me that I'm the new target.

"Like a lamb to the slaughter. I hope you've thanked Agent Mars for bringing you into this."

"Not yet," I say, too frightened to talk trash.

"Maybe I could leave you unharmed if you tell me where Rust is."

Two thoughts enter my mind. The first is that I must look as scared as I feel. Saluki's offering me a chance for survival if only I'll betray my allies. He wouldn't be foolish enough to make this proposition if I appeared in any way confident in my own ability. The second thought is that my occasional checking-in with Rust has tipped Saluki off and he knows we're working together. I still don't understand how these Nano GEAR private and open channels function. I know I should've tuned into Rust's frequency, but in the confusion it didn't seem like a priority.

"So what'll it be, Mr Maven?"

"You remembered my name."

"Rust is as clueless as his son. No one can stand up to the Order! You need to ask yourself whether you're willing to go down with Rust, just like his boy here."

"You're the one who's going down."

I admit - this isn't the greatest comeback. But something I see in the corner of my eye motivates me to just hold Saluki's attention.

"Me? Ha! I'm going down, sure - down in history. See you in hell!"

"Take this with you," Rust shouts, dramatically emerging out of cover with an RPG launcher resting over his shoulder.. He fires a single rocket-propelled grenade, which strikes the SpeedHawk's cabin and explodes on impact.

Saluki curses in confusion as he whirls out of control into a freewheeling spin. He's a flower in the wind, a passenger of his own momentum.

I wonder if he remembered to wear a seatbelt.

Chapter 22

Disassociation

The undefeated force of gravity tips the chopper sideways after it connects with the ground. The rotor blades fight to spin as they are designed, but the concrete challenges them to a volatile battle of physics they just can't win. Each blade reaches a point of fragmenting and flying away. One part hurtles only a few feet from me, ricocheting off the shipping container into the dusk sky.

My urge to check on Mars is superseded by my instinct to hide from the gears and fuselage flying through the air, not to mention the soaring chips of shredded concrete. Rust isn't afraid at all. He ducks in low and drags Mars towards the cover of the shipping container, just before the SpeedHawk explodes. Even though I'm fully protected behind four walls of steel, I can feel the incredible heat of the rising fireball through the ventilation grate.

"Get up, boy." I rush over to see Rust shaking Mars by the shoulder until he opens his eyes, looking at each of us in shock, as if he's woken from a bad dream.

"What? I'm OK. What happened?"

"Rust found the RPG."

"Damn."

"It's over. We need to go," Rust commands, giving Mars no time to recover.

"Age hasn't slowed you down one bit."

Mars sits up, observing the flaming wreck of the SpeedHawk nearby. I feared the fall could have paralysed him, but here he is, ready to roll again.

A whirring siren breaks out across the area, which we take as a sign that we should leg it. The base's boundary is now only a few hundred yards away. If Mars has any serious injuries from our car crash, his fight with Rust, his brawl at the prison bunker or falling from the grappling gun, he's doing a stellar job of hiding it. There has to be an explanation for his incredible durability and I make a mental note to bring it up later.

~∞~

With the sun setting and crickets starting to chirp, a successful escape now feels more likely than our capture. We come up against a mesh fence topped in barbed wire, but a quick shot from the grenade launcher clears space to pass through. The Fox boys ditch their bulky weapons and conceal their pistols as we run through a corn field as tall as I am.

The stench of fuel and fire from the SpeedHawk's explosion is still polluting the air. I'm trying not to think about Saluki. He was evil and he was unmistakeably trying to murder us, but it's still weird to think that someone I just had a conversation with is *dead*. I expect Mars and Rust would have experienced a lot of cognitive dissonance reduction as a way to justify their work with Metric. They'd tell themselves their targets deserved to die, that it was for a greater good. I'm not sure one man should ever get to decide if another deserves death, but I know they'll sleep easy about putting Saluki in the ground. His death was self-defence at the very least.

After another hundred yards we reach a dusty, dirt thoroughfare. Instead of crossing into the adjacent field, Mars turns to walk along the road like a hitch-hiker. I hope he's not planning to carjack some poor, hapless farmer. Life is tough enough on the land without three outlaws taking off with your tractor.

No more than a minute later, a red pickup truck slows from behind us, unnecessarily flashing its headlights to gain our attention. The occupants are two men. The passenger is just a kid, college-aged with tanned skin and dark hair. You don't see a lot of Asian-Americans in Kansas. The driver is a bit older and clearly a farmer, unless he's the only non-farmer I've ever met with a penchant for John Deere baseball caps and flannelette shirts. He winds down his window and flashes us a sporadically toothy grin, like a jack-o'-lantern that's survived a bar room brawl.

"What are you soldier boys doin' all the way out here? Sneakin' off base?"

Mars steps up to the window and improvises a tall tale. "Between you and me and the pine trees, we're just a couple of military folk trying to catch some R&R after a long week. That's 'rest and relaxation', if you didn't know."

"Oh yeah," Jack O'Lantern nods. "I hear ya. Just like me and this young blood over here. It's gonna be a big night, I can tell you." Young Blood waves nervously as Jack O'Lantern goes on. "We're wrappin' up a long day of work and headed for Manhattan, if you want a ride. Plenty of room in the back."

The bed of the truck is scattered with loose tools, some hay band and plastic crates full of water or gasoline.

"That would be fantastic," Mars responds.

"You look like you've been in the wars."

"CQC training today, sir. Close quarters combat can get a little out of hand."

"Oh, don't I know it. Well, we can scoot off. But, uh..." Jack O'Lantern looks over Mars' shoulder and lowers his voice. "Who's the old fella? Sergeant Slaughter over there."

"He's... actually our drill sergeant. A real loose cannon. Would you believe they banned whiskey in Fort Riley? Not a drop. It's like we woke up and we're not in America anymore."

"Good golly, Miss Molly. That just ain't right. Like this guy here - can ya believe the boy has never tried Kentucky bourbon? I call him 'the pure one'. Just look at that face."

"Is that so?"

"Jump on in and we'll get you boys into town."

"Ogden will be fine."

"Alrighty."

The three of us pile into the pickup's tray, sitting with our backs against the cabin. Mars grins at me before sliding into an exhausted heap, spread out across the cold steel.

"We need to ditch our Nano GEARs," Rust says once the truck is moving. "They'll track them."

I hand him the tiny gadget, feeling a little sad that I have to part ways with such a cool toy. I expect him to crush it in his palm like a corn chip, but instead he holds it for a good two minutes. As a rickety old truck approaches with a trailer full of livestock, the wily old man tosses the Nano GEARs. The passing vehicle takes our tracking signal in the opposite direction. The devices will eventually be trampled, covered in manure and destroyed, giving us a clear headstart on our escape as Metric searches in all the wrong places. Rust does the same with Mars' Nano GEAR on a separate truck just a few moments later. With any luck, the two vehicles will end up in opposite ends of Kansas by the morning.

"That's why you're the spy."

Rust presses his eyes closed, breathing slowly and deeply.

I don't think he heard me.

Chapter 23

Consolation

The farmers pull into the Ogden gas station and I start praying that folk around here think it's normal for three grown men to chill out in the back of a pickup truck. Ogden is a small, quiet town. One convenience store, one bar, one gas station, one post office, and so on. Mars seems to have a nearby place in mind where we can take refuge.

As the engine stops, I realise how riveting the conversation is between Young Blood and Jack O'Lantern.

"I'm not racist – I just hate all Mexicans and Asians. No offence."

Yep. This is an actual sentence.

"It's OK," Young Blood replies. "I mean, I don't even like Asians that much, and my old man's a full Vietnamese."

"You know exactly what I mean then."

"I got an unrelated story," Young Blood says, as he pumps gas into the truck. "Ya know how my uncle's all about experimental irrigation and such? Last Tuesday, I'm down at the Ace Hardware with Gary – you remember, Gary Hughes?"

"The 'Superman' guy?"

"Yeah, Hughesy. We ask the clerk for directions to find some plastic tubing, ya know? Just that regular plastic tubing. The guy looks me up and down, he looks at Hughesy, and he tells me the beer bongs are in aisle seven."

"Ha!"

"I said 'Beer bong? I'm twenty years old, man. I can't even buy alcohol.' You know what he says?"

"Yeah?"

"He says 'This is Kansas, dude.' Like some California hippie. And I'm like, 'What's that supposed to mean?' I still don't get it."

"What'd he say?"

"Oh, I didn't say it out loud. We were already on our way."

"I kid you not. One time, me and my cousin Fozzy made a beer bong out of one of them plastic flamingo lawn ornaments."

"For real?"

"I kid you not. Fozz called it a flabongo."

"You boys have too much time."

"Say there, lads," Mars interrupts, putting on the slightest of Southern drawls. "There's a bar up the road, you know the one? I think we'll jump off there, if you don't mind."

After saying goodbye to our hitch-hiking heroes, we march into the darkness along several long, quiet roads. Everything in Ogden is so far apart. In the space of a New York City block, there's about ten Ogden houses on one side of the street. The neighbourhood's silence stands out the most. Aside from a ringing in my ears, all I can hear is our footsteps across damp asphalt and the swaying of the tall trees standing in every single yard. There's very little light illuminating our path, but I can read "Thirteenth Street" on a nearby road sign. I'm surprised there are even thirteen streets in Ogden.

"Are we hiding out at an old folk's home?" I ask, looking at the facilities ahead of us.

"Better," Mars says. "It's a trailer park."

We trudge past a dozen or so mobile homes and the occasional barking dog before we arrive at a lone caravan in the back, opposite a picnic area surrounded by trees.

"This is home. Or it has been for the past couple weeks." Mars collapses into a padded chair outside his trailer. He gestures towards a pair of deck chairs and a fold-out card table. Unless he has trailer park friends I don't know about, the whole exterior is arranged to look lived-in. Empty beer cans. A dead pot plant. An ash tray. A dart board with Hilary Clinton's photo pinned to the centre. Just the usual trailer park stuff. It's even darker here than on the street. It seems appropriate, given our circumstances.

We're alive – hooray. We're free – technically. But what is waiting for us next? Today I discovered the whole world is a lie and the US government is a mere cog in an evil machine. The ringing in my ear is the living proof, either from the SpeedHawk's buzzsaw machine gun, the numerous grenades or the explosion that allowed us to escape the clutches of the Order.

"I'm guessing this place is secure," Rust grumbles to Mars. "No nearby CCTV?"

"The closest ATM is half a mile away. Trees give a pretty good cover from satellite surveillance."

"But you know Metric knows that too. Now they have your general location, it's only a matter of time before they come knocking."

"I know that," Mars snaps. "If you've got a better idea, I'm all ears, Rust."

"Hm."

"That's what I thought."

Now that we're well and truly out of harm's way, it's time to debrief and figure out the plan of attack. Rust asks if we have any allies and Mars makes it clear that we're on our own. They take the conversation to another level, talking about people within Metric. I struggle to keep up as they discuss the NWO and how it functions, each citing examples of evidence from their years of espionage.

As the two rogue agents go back and forth, their secrets fill and overflow my ears – the type of secrets I used to crave. I know journalists who would sell their souls to be a fly on the wall for this conversation, but it's too much for me right now. Each revelation I hear adds to the avalanche of self-awareness that's crushing me with the simple realisation that I'm helpless. Each word adds to my understanding that things in this world are just really messed up, beyond any of our educated inclinations.

The conspiracy nuts are actually right. They've got the details wrong, but in principle they are totally correct. The crazy, outlandish theories are justified.

"It's like a puzzle," Mars says, referring to Metric's relationship with the NWO. "Once you know what it is, the pieces start to make sense and fit together."

"Guys, I hate to interrupt, but this place is... I mean, it feels like we're still at Fort Riley."

"Exactly," Mars says. "I guarantee they're out sweeping Junction City or Manhattan. Hiding in plain sight is the way to go."

I wheeze out a long and slow breath, trying not to consider all the ways I may have messed up my life.

"Try not to worry, bro. Tomorrow's another day."

"Yeah. Sure," I say unconvincingly, as Rust leaves for the trailer, closing the door behind him. "Hakuna matata. It's just the end of the world as I know it."

"C'mon," Mars says optimistically.

"How are you OK with this?"

"I'm not. I've just had a long time to process it."

There's a genuine sincerity in Mars' voice that makes me consider all of this from his perspective. He probably grew up wanting to be Luke Skywalker, wanting to save the world. He signed up for the job and performed with the best of intentions, only to discover he was no more than a stormtrooper serving the evil Empire. I let my mind wander, looking up to the dark sky. A glowing halo of misty light surrounds tonight's full moon.

"Pretty amazing, huh?" Mars says, also staring skyward. "It's like... it's a portal. Or something."

The moonlight searches out the silence in between our attempts at conversation. Even though there's a scientific explanation to this moon ring, it feels like an unearthly phenomenon that would disappear as soon as we told anyone else about it. Even though mankind has explored the moon, I still look at it as an inherently mystical and inaccessible object. The same way people stare at crashing ocean waves, I often watch the starry sky and wonder where my life will lead next, visualising what it means to be alive and awake to reality. Often the adventure of life seems like a journey that's perpetually leading to something more. It's always around the corner. But then one day it becomes clear the adventure has been going for years.

My belief in purpose and providence makes me look back at every decision I've made over recent weeks, months and years to find retroactive meaning. Now it's crystallising in my mind – everything has led me here.

I don't know if I believe in predestination. Those discussions always led to arguments, so I preferred to chalk it up as a mystery rather than waste my time debating the theory. But I believe right now, this has been what I've been working towards. My experiences have prepared me for this, as much as any civilian experience could. This gives me some comfort that things will work out. But I can't shake the anxious feeling that comes from being a fish out of water. I want to look over at Mars beside me, but I just can't bring myself to break my wide-eyed gaze. I'm so comfortable ignoring all imminent concerns in this moment.

"I think I just realised... I'm not who I thought I was." I turn to see Mars listening intently, showing concern with solemn eyes. "But I'm OK with it."

He slaps a hand on my shoulder and squeezes gently as an offer of support. "I think I've been there before, Andrew. It's a..." He pauses, considering his words. "Life is a weird thing."

I nod and smile to show my appreciation. I'm not sure he understands what I'm feeling, but he's connected with something I've said. That's enough.

"Near death changes you, bro. I worked with a guy who'd say 'You don't know who you are until you've stared down the barrel of a gun.' There's some truth to it, I think."

"I wish I didn't have to face that. I'm not made for this."

"You're doing pretty well, if you ask me."

"By the grace of God."

"Sure. Why don't you ask that God to get us out of all this?"

I shake my head, even if Mars is half-kidding. "I don't think God's, like, some genie granting wishes – you know what I mean? You don't encounter God like a gorilla at the zoo. It's more of a relationship you have to seek out and experience."

"How's that meant to work when you can't see or hear anything?"

"I'm not the best person to explain it... but you pray, you tell Him what's grinding your gears, what you're thankful for, what you want in life. You spend time doing these things like you would with any person you value. You acknowledge there's a greater power."

"Like in Alcoholics Anonymous."

"Yeah. I mean, I surrender everything to 'His will', even when I don't understand it. That's the idea, in theory. I'm not the best at doing it. But that's what I believe. It's not easy, but when you can commit to that... it's very liberating."

"You know what? I respect that."

Mars says this as if I should be surprised by his tolerance. Sometimes it feels as if Christianity is the only common religion that "open-minded" people will openly mock without fear of being offensive. The statistics will tell you eighty-three per cent of Americans identify as Christian, but I think less than a quarter of those people actually make an effort to follow Christ. I'm no Apostle myself. I get caught up in the grind of work, the ways of the world, and the distractions of Netflix, but my faith is always the cornerstone that keeps me centred. It's my anchor.

"Your respect is much appreciated, Mars."

"I'll tell you why," he continues. "All those Richard Dawkins atheists are like... 'ha ha, what a fool. You're in church on your knees, you're praying there. You think you're talking to Jesus and God.' But you know what? Even if God and the angels and all of it doesn't exist, you're still flushing things out of yourself by doing it. You're finding happiness and purpose and... that's a good enough reason to be a nutbag into Kabbalah and seances and prayer and believing in angels."

I can't help laughing at Mars' generalised understanding of faith. "I wouldn't put it that way... but sure. There's a lot to be gained from giving your life over to a higher power. Even still, I'm struggling right now. I probably just need some time."

"Everyone's different. I channel it. Even before I was in Metric – any anger or fear, I'd just push it into my work."

I nod, trying to process what Mars' life would have been like before the government recruited him. "It must've been tough, growing up without your old man."

Mars looks at me, as if he's entertaining the idea of disagreeing. "It was. I guess I have what you people would call 'daddy issues', but... I'm OK with it."

It's not clear what he means by "you people", but I can only assume he's talking about anyone with an analytical mind.

"It's pretty amazing, what you've accomplished, though, after that childhood. I don't mean to assume anything, but from what you've told me you have a father you're so disconnected from that you don't even call him 'Dad'. And yet, apart from the crazy secret agent side of things, you're fairly well-adjusted. Your mom must've been pretty awesome."

"Thanks. She was... is." Mars looks to his feet after correcting himself. "I still don't know where she is, if she's alive or dead. But I know she would be right here beside us if she could."

When Rust talks about Alison, it's clear he has nothing but admiration for the way she raised his son. This is the first time I've thought about her absence impacting Mars on an emotional level.

"That's rough, man. But I guess you must get used to uncertainty in this work, with the whole 'need to know' management style keeping you in the dark."

"Nah, bro. You never do get used to uncertainty. You just have to live with it. Try not to think about it, unless you're able to channel it into something positive."

"Rust says she probably wants us to think she's dead... if she's still alive. What do you think?"

"I don't know. But I'll find out. I'd give my life to save her."

"Yeah. With my mom and dad... I mean, sorry, you probably don't..." I trail off, feeling insensitive to bring up my nuclear family in these circumstances.

"It's cool," Mars assures me. "You're worried about them?"

"I just don't know if I'm ever gonna *see* them again. They'll never know why or what happened... It's a strange feeling."

"Hey, they'll know. The word will get out and you'll be a hero and everything."

"But would they be safe until then?"

Mars realises he has no words to offer – at least nothing that will put me at ease. "Can't answer that. Metric means business. They'll use your family, your friends, anything to get what they need. We really have to cut the head off the dragon and end them for good."

I pull out my phone, no longer able to just think about my parents. There's no signal. I'm unsure if it's a momentary issue or if Ogden is a black hole for cell service.

Mars points me to a pay phone beside the picnic area, a dozen yards from where we're sitting. This will be my first contact with the outside world since this all started. I've been ignoring emails and texts from my friends and collaborators. It's only been a few days since everything started, but I feel like a different person when I consider the trivial concerns and thoughts occupying my head back then. I fired off one tweet this morning, hoping to curb the amount of messages I was getting about my online inactivity.

"Working on something pretty big right now. Stay tuned."

That's all it said, but it reached about two hundred retweets in a few hours. In retrospect, that might help the news spread if we can find a way to get it out there.

I haven't used a pay phone in years. This one doesn't even take coins. In fact, I can't recall the last time I initiated a phone call that wasn't setting up an interview. I text, instant message, tweet, snap and email, but rarely call. If anyone besides my parents pops up on my caller ID I naturally assume I've done something terrible or someone's in trouble.

I swipe my bank card on the pay phone and try to remember the area code for Michigan. It rings three times before a familiar voice talks to me.

"Hello, Diane speaking."

"Hey. Mom. How's it going?"

"Oh, hello Andrew! I'm good, thanks. What's this number?"

"I'm calling from a pay phone in Kansas, so I probably can't talk for too long."

"A pay phone? In Kansas?" She sounds shocked, as she should be.

"Can you do me a quick favour and Google if there's any phone service issues here?"

"Sure... Dad's telling me there have been tornadoes all around that area. Is everything OK? Give us a second. He's turning on the computer."

"OK. I'm fine. Just wanted to call..."

"Your father wants to know if you've seen the new Star Wars advertisement."

"Yeah, tell him I have." I can only sigh. They're so innocent. They have no idea what is happening. Worse still, Dad's question reminds me that a month ago I was podcasting my predictions for *Episode VIII: The Last Jedi*, and now I'm fighting my very own evil empire.

"That trailer came out a while ago. Tell him we'll go together when I'm home for Christmas."

"Sounds great. He says it wasn't as good as the one that came out for the Star Wars *movie before this."*

"Uhuh."

"Did you hear him just then? He says 'How are the Kansans?'"

"Tell him they're great."

She delivers the message and I hear familiar chuckles at the other end of the line.

"He says the Michiganders are doing pretty great on this end too."

"Cool. So, what's the news say?"

Clearly reading off a monitor, Mom tells me damage to a tele-communications exchange in Topeka has cut off several service providers in Kansas and Missouri. No internet, no cell coverage, no

EFT transactions. Sounds like chaos.

"Where are you reading that? Which newspaper is it?"

"*Scroll up, honey... It's called:* The Mercury.*"*

"Right. Their internet is obviously still working."

"*Is the storm why you're there, is it?*"

"There's been tornado alerts, but no. It's safe. That's not the reason. There's actually something pretty big going on that I can't say much about."

"*Oh. I could tell... There was something in your voice. Is it OK?*"

"Well, I don't know. I think it'll be OK, but it's a little risky."

Do understatements count as lies?

"*Uhuh.*" Mom sounds reservedly concerned, but I have to give her some kind of warning.

"I don't want you to worry about me, OK, but I'm just saying, there are people involved with this who can't be trusted. Not good people, Mom."

"*Oh dear.*"

"I don't know what's going to happen with it, so please don't answer your door to anyone you don't know."

"*Oh, Andrew. What's wrong?*" The maternal angst in her voice makes it hard for me to respond without my voice breaking. "*That doesn't sound good at all.*"

"It's not. But I'm working on it. I'm gonna try to fix it. And I think it'll be OK. I just... Yeah. I don't know how it's going to happen. But I need to do this."

After all the cryptic conversations I've had this week, it feels weird to be the one speaking in vague and abstract terms to someone I trust. Hearing Mom's voice and being so far away makes me feel incredibly isolated. There she is, talking on the other line, but there's a distance through the receiver that weighs on my heart.

"*I'm sure you know what you're doing,*" she assures me.

"I hope so."

"*You'll be careful though, won't you?*"

"I will. I'm going to run out of time on the call, so I'll check in with you tomorrow."

This isn't a lie, but it's not the reason I want to end the call. I mostly just can't bear to talk any longer. I don't want to mislead my own mother and I don't want her to hear me choking up either.

"*I'll be praying for you, Andrew. You always do what's right.*"

"Thanks, Mom."

"*OK. I love you. Bye now.*"

"Love you too. Say hi to Dad."

"*Will do. Bye now.*"

I'm a wreck. My mouth is dry and there's a lump in my throat the size of Kansas. It takes me a minute to calm down before I can even move on. As I turn around, I catch Rust, cigar in hand, leaning at the caravan entrance.

"Sorry," he says as I approach. "Couldn't help overhearing some parts there."

"It's all good," I say, scratching my nose and attempting to mask the emotion in my voice.

"They'll be proud of you, kid. What you're doing... This is a big thing. And you saw it from the word 'go'. You get credit for that."

"Yeah. Thanks. I just want them to be safe – you know what I mean?"

Rust runs the cigar right under his nose and stares into the surrounding trees. I wonder if this is how he relaxes.

"Maven, there are people I know. They've got no Metric allegiance to speak of. Once we're out of this, I'll talk to them. I'll find someone who understands the situation and they'll look out for your family."

"Really?"

"Of course. Grand Rapids, right?"

"That's it. Thank you. Agent Rust: the man with the golden heart."

"Don't push your luck, kid. And definitely don't go crying on me."

"You know, I fired my gun at Saluki, right before you showed up. Think you would've been proud."

"How did that feel?"

"Honestly, like a teenager wearing his old man's business shirt, three sizes too big. Let's hope I don't have to do it again."

"Trust me, kid. I'll do everything I can to make sure the future of our nation doesn't depend on your aptitude with a firearm."

Chapter 24

Preparation

I wake up early. For the second morning in a row, cheap curtains have ruined my precious slumber. Even though they're taped closed, the light finds a way through. Maybe I'm just restless. Maybe I'm anxious from everything that's happened. There's been several times I feared I'd never see the light of day ever again.

Mars' trailer reeks of photo film solution and take-out Chinese. It's an odd combination. Looking up from my makeshift bed, I see a string of developed photos showing licence plates on military vehicles beside other images connected to Fort Riley. Either Mars prefers the aesthetic of working with film or he has no access to a digital camera. It's a mystery to me – it bothers me – but it's not something I need to explore at the moment.

I stand up, careful not to lose my balance, and peer outside through a gap in the curtains for a sign of anything meaningful. The sky is cloudy. The grass is green. There's certainly nothing pointing towards the risk of tornadoes. Nothing stands out as extraordinary and nothing suggests today will be anything but a typical day in Kansas. I really, *really* wish this was true. I know too much. Today is the day that everything changes. It could be my last day on earth. It could be the day the world stands still.

We'll see soon enough.

"Go outside."

Mars caught me peeking. Through a mouthful of cereal, he insists it's safe to venture out.

"This place is an afterthought... They won't even consider looking outside the cities until tomorrow."

I step into the light and savour the fresh air. Opposite our trailer is a picnic barbecue in a small courtyard, surrounded by a set of caravans. A boy sits right in the middle beside a stack of comic books and a pile of pistachio shells. With one hand he rubs the belly of his sleeping dog and with the other he messes around on his phone.

"*What's up, everybody!*" A booming voice, dripping with ego and confidence, blasts from his phone's muffled speakers. "*Welcome to the* Kinda Funny Morning Show!" The video's sound cuts out, probably struggling to buffer through the crappy Kansan 3G phone coverage, which is still better than what my phone provider is offering. The kid doesn't seem to care. A pretty girl has arrived, all dressed in black and smiling as if she just found $50 in an old pair of jeans. She hugs her friend with violent energy, to the point that he stumbles and grimaces underneath her smothering enthusiasm. The dog wakes up startled, but wags its tail once it picks up the friendly vibe.

It's kinda cute.

Their carefree happiness is infectious and takes me back to a simpler time. I'm floored with envy as I realise it's not my joy, but theirs, I'm experiencing. The things they don't yet know about the world are an anchor around my neck, weighing me down with a crushing force.

"Those two..." Mars says from the trailer's doorway. "Their homes were destroyed by a tornado a couple years ago. Their families have been here since then. Sad story."

An alarm goes off in my head, one that I've trained in my years as a reporter. In normal circumstances, this would make for a fascinating news story. But I'm not here for a scoop anymore. There's something bigger.

"You've talked to them?"

"Barely. I mean, I've overheard bits and pieces. You ever seen one of those things?"

"A tornado? No. Nothing like that."

"This one time, I was in Argentina... An EF5 twister sounds like a freight train, does twice as much damage. If you're not underground, you won't live. These guys..." Mars nods to the playful pair outside, still laughing and bouncing around. "This time they've got nothing to lose but their lives."

It's a selfish yet natural response, but I have to ask about our own safety. Mars tells me there's no plan. He thinks Manhattan will escape mother nature this time.

"We'll know if there's a tornado watch. That usually gives you at least four or five hours to clear out."

"To where?"

"We'll think of something. Don't worry. We have enough on our plate."

A long spluttering cough resonates from inside our trailer. Rust emerges and takes a seat, looking more relaxed than a teenage lifeguard on summer break.

"Morning."

"Good morning," I respond, surprised by Rust's newfound peace. "You're... cheery."

"I'm embracing the day. It could be my last."

"And that's refreshing, is it?"

Rust lights up a cigar and leans back, propping his feet up on the card table.

"I'm free from Metric's puppet strings. It's terrifying, but liberating."

"I agree with the terrifying part."

Rust coughs again, deep from the lungs. It's a familiar sound from my days in the newsroom.

"You still smoke cigarettes?"

"Not anymore. Just these bad boys."

Rust holds up his brown Montecrisco cigar pack, admiring it like a framed cancer certificate.

"Should we talk business?" Mars asks. "We've got a shadow government to expose and a journalist with hopefully a ton of ideas about how to do it."

Rust raises his scarred eyebrow, seemingly unwilling to submit control to me of all people. "It's his decision? Do you think that's wise?"

"Do you think it's wise to suck back those cigars like the Cubans are going out of business?"

Without shame, Rust turns his face away and exhales a cloud of white smoke. "You want one?"

"Heck no," I respond.

Mars appears to stop himself from firing back with his natural negative response. Instead, he shrugs and reaches over to his father. "What the hell? Seems like the closest thing to a regular father-son experience I'll ever get."

This is where I confess my semi-bigoted views toward smokers.

"Don't you think it's impressive how cigarette companies have no trouble successfully marketing what's essentially a poison to the masses, without being allowed to advertise in any traditional format?"

"I guess," Mars shrugs, unimpressed by my pointed question. "It's just instilled into culture by now."

"The damage is done," Rust says. "Years of evil bastards telling us to suck it back."

"It's basically self-prescribed euthanasia at this point," I say. Rust closes his eyes and takes a long drag on his cigar before puffing out a ring of smoke.

"Well, if you ask me – poison never tasted so good."

Free will is fantastic. But there are dangerous things we make illegal simply because they are dangerous. If I concocted a delicious soda that caused cancer, it wouldn't even make it to the shelves. Cigarettes have evolved over the course of several centuries, so for some reason – that is, freedom – they've never been banned for public consumption. Medical drugs like Immunokine WF10 that can dramatically aid cancer recovery can't even get approved in the western world, yet our sense of self-preservation can't beat our desire to poke burning toxic sticks out of our mouths, despite causing about four hundred and eighty thousand deaths every year. Even if you argue there's a conspiracy around these numbers and only half of these deaths are caused by smoking, that's still two hundred and forty thousand fatalities – forty times more than the number of people who died in car crashes without wearing a seatbelt. We have laws about buckling up in the front seat, but I can walk into a deli, gas station, corner store or supermarket and buy human poison off the shelf. This is the world we live in and most people have no problem with it.

"Don't people typically smoke cigars to celebrate?" I ask.

"People smoke cigars because they're excellent," Rust says.

"Right. You know, I think even the 1950s surgeon general said smokers were morons."

Rust doesn't take kindly to my judgemental tone.

"Listen, kid, you didn't hear me questioning whether you needed to choke back that monstrosity of a hamburger at the airport. Or the bag of candy. Or those arancini balls. I haven't seen you touch a vegetable the whole time we've been together."

"First of all – I smashed down some broccoli and cheddar cheese on Friday night. That stuff is nature's candy. And secondly, I compromised. You *know* I wanted Taco Bell. Still do. And the third thing – are you really throwing attitude at me, after all this? After what you've done to me?"

Rust could crush me like an ant, but right now I don't care.

"It's not my fault you're here," he says as a matter of fact. "You got your invitation from the boy."

Mars drops the cigarette lighter back on the table and motions back to his father, with his own cigar burning between his fingers. "If I knew I could count on you, I wouldn't have had to bring in a normie."

"How long are you going to hold this against me, kid?"

"I'm not holding it against you. I never expected anything more from you."

"Here we go."

"Here we go? You're still an asshole. Mom was right."

I'm surprised to see Rust has no response, which tells me he can't even disagree with Mars. He coughs quietly and we each sit in silence. It's awkward, like a homeschool sex-ed lesson. No one wants to look anyone else in the eye.

"Even if you went straight to Rust, what would be the next step?" I ask, breaking the tension. "All of a sudden I'm the back-up option. You weren't saying that before."

"Bro, you know that's not what I mean."

"Quit acting like a punk," Rust snaps. "You're not the one who's going to live with the world's best headhunters on your tail."

"Oh what, so I'll just have to put up with the second or third tier of the world's best headhunters? That's comforting."

"Yeah, he's right," Mars says in my defence. "This isn't his world."

"He's a quick learner."

"Rust, since I've been dragged into this mess I've been lied to, shot at, and smacked with a golf club. I've lied to *cops* and I've flown across the country only to survive a car crash and get punched in the face. I've been thrown into a cell, and damn near hit by exploding helicopter blades. Now I've got the New World Order after me and I don't even know what my life *is* anymore. This job didn't come with a spy manual. There's no *Espionage for Dummies*. So show me some empathy and consider that, you know, this is hard for me... and I'm doing the best I can."

Mid-rant, it dawns on me that I've been so focused on what's happening in my life that I haven't stopped to think about what I'm leaving behind by default. At least, I haven't considered it for long enough to sink in.

"For Pete's sake," Rust spits out, disgusted by my diatribe, but clearly embarrassed over his own wrongdoing. "I know you're a reporter, but you can't keep a running sheet of every time something goes sideways."

I push back my slipping glasses and defiantly fold my arms across my chest. This guy has some nerve. He's no longer my protector, my guardian angel who can do no wrong. Now I can see him for the flawed mortal human he really is.

"Are you even going to apologise for punching me in the face?"

"I said I was sorry," Rust exhales, almost passive-aggressively blowing smoke in my direction. "Back at the cell."

"You apologised for not *trusting* us."

"OK then. I probably shouldn't have done that. I'm sorry I did."

"Wow. It takes a big man to admit he was *probably* in the wrong. You know I *probably* had a concussion from that car crash. You could've killed me."

"I was emotional. Wasn't thinking."

"You couldn't have put me in cuffs?"

"Wasn't the time. I'm sorry."

"I can't deal with this."

"Come on, Maven. Grow up."

"Really?"

I stare at Rust, my heart pounding, waiting for a response. He looks up from the ground for a second before gazing off into the distance. I hear his silence loud and clear. That's enough.

Like a petulant teenager, I leave the Foxes, rushing down a path towards a cluster of trees. My body language as I perch on a wide stump would justify Rust questioning my maturity level – at least in his mind. But they don't realise that my complaints aren't a reflection of how I really feel. I'm mostly just afraid and I don't want to talk about what that means. The slightest disrespect is setting me off and giving me a reason to consider bailing out of the mission.

The truth is I can't stop thinking about Edward Snowden and how much I *don't* want to be him. Almost four years ago, after leaking thousands of CIA documents to the international media, Snowden was charged for violating the Espionage Act and stealing US government property. I don't want to flee America to live in an Ecuadorian embassy or take asylum in Russia while people talk about whether or not I'm a traitor or a hero. I don't want to live in a windowless room, hiding from my own people like a prisoner. But I assume Snowden didn't want that either. As much as he changed society, it wasn't what he set out to do. He wanted society to become self-aware and decide for itself whether it needed to change.

"I get it, Maven."

I turn around and see Mars standing nearby, trying to empathise as best he can. He joins me on the tree stump and we throw rocks into the woods like a couple of bored adolescents. I briefly explain my Snowden dilemma and he seems to under-stand.

After a long pause followed by a reluctant stutter, he broaches a subject he's clearly less than comfortable discussing.

"I don't know how to explain this," he says. "But I had a really vivid dream after Rust knocked me out."

"I just woke up with a headache." I rub the sleep from my eye, nudging my spectacles down the bridge of my nose. The pain from yesterday is gone. My head wound still hurts if I touch it, but that's about it. I need to count my blessings.

"You have to promise not to make fun of me, OK?"

"You might've noticed, I'm not really in the mood for fun, Mars."

"OK." He huffs out a short breath and stands up, staring at his feet as he tries to recollect his memory of the dream. "I was high above the ground looking down in the dark. It was out on the street, but so cold and so empty. Really, just a vast darkness every-where. Then this small light appeared, like a match stick or a candle. But it got bigger and bigger, and I could tell it was, you know, a lantern... hanging along the street."

"Yeah, right," I nod along, curious at where this going.

"And at first it was just one lantern, but then there was another and another, and soon there were dozens of lanterns lighting up the street. Each one was closer and closer to where I was standing, and it started to shine so bright that it burnt my eyes. I got really mad and I could hear murmurs, like people weren't happy. They were blinded by the light too. But then as our eyes slowly adjusted, the brightness lit up the scene as much as daylight and we could see perfectly. There was a stunning landscape beyond the street."

"That's pretty cool."

"Yeah, it was the most incredible sight. The most amazing nature. But here's the strangest part. There was this one guy walking around and lighting the lanterns. I could see it was all because of him. He was bringing light into the world, into the darkness, you know? And Maven, I'm pretty sure it was you."

"Me?"

"Yeah."

"Huh. That's interesting."

"It's weird, is what it is. But I think it could mean something."

"I think you might be right."

"People might not be ready to hear what you're going to tell them. They might hate you for it. But eventually they're going to see that you're right. They'll see you're bringing light to the darkness, and maybe that will lead to something that makes the world a better place to live."

"Are you sure you're not a prophet, Mars? You might be my new favourite theologian."

He laughs.

"Thank you, seriously. That really helps my mindset – you know what I mean?"

I explain to Mars how this ties into the epiphany I had last night, about my true purpose and my identity, how everything has led to this. I suppose I'm what some people would call a "bad Christian". I don't read my Bible enough. I can go months without attending church. I struggle my way through life with the same stumbling blocks and pitfalls that plague any thirty-three year old bachelor. The only difference is that now I can remember why. I've remembered what I always believed but occasionally lost sight of. I'm forgiven for all my shortcomings, my doubts, and my irrational lack of trust. I don't need to convince anyone I'm more than a mere mortal, a screw-up and a simple man. I'm not running from it anymore or trying to achieve so much in my work that I can sit back and marvel at my accomplishments.

I don't need to.

I believe – *I know* – that I have a greater purpose than what the world would tell me and I've been put in a unique position to fulfil that purpose.

Over the years, a lot of my friends and colleagues have questioned my faith and argued against my conservative views, but you can only live your life according to the truth that makes sense to you. For me, it's simple and I have an irrefutable argument. Before I found my purpose in God, I was blind. Now, I can see. My own experience is undeniable. The world makes sense. Sure, sometimes it's blurry, but that's my own fault. I can see. And I've been waiting a long time to become something that can't be defined.

Now I realise that's been the case all along. A person can be explained in just a few words, but they can never be fully described in a way that's true to their identity. Sometimes I struggle with my purpose and I try to place meaning on things that maybe just don't have any. But if you can be inspired or encouraged by something small and seemingly random, who's to say it doesn't exist for that reason?

"The great thing about the future is that it's unwritten," Mars says as Rust joins us among the trees. "Rule number one. Know your enemy. The Order has an arrogant belief that they can control and manipulate the universe. But this leads them to overlook important details. They got a journalist involved. But they're the ones who are getting more than they bargained for."

"You're preaching to me, Mars. Keep going."

"It's time to shine the light on them. We're busting this wide open, just like I promised. Operation Snowden. I say we go in there ready to fight. It's win or lose. If we go down, we go down in a blaze of glory."

"I've never been a big fan of blazes... glorious or otherwise."

Mars chuckles but tries to wear a serious face before he continues speaking.

"I have to be honest. Even if we succeed today, you can't go up against the world's most powerful intelligence agencies and just walk away unscathed. The only way we leave this behind us is if we make such an impact that the Order is disbanded and altogether destroyed. Once the wine has been uncorked and poured, you can't get it back in the bottle without changing it's essence. So let's get it out there. Now's the time – dazzle us with your media wizardry."

Rust and Mars look at me expectantly as I consider the accuracy of this wine analogy. There's an idea I've had ticking over in my brain since we left Fort Riley. It might take some convincing, but I think it's the best shot we have. I pull out my phone, the same phone Rust should've confiscated, but somehow overlooked.

"I want to make you two YouTube sensations."

Mars raises an eyebrow of intrigue. Rust looks like he's never heard of YouTube.

"I want to sit you down, both of you. And just talk. You tell me everything. About you, about Metric, about the Order. We get it out there and put your faces to it."

"I like how you think," Mars says. "But... you're the voice with a following. This is your investigation."

"Yeah. I just think it should be heard straight from the horse's mouth. They can say that it came from me, or it can go to my YouTube channel."

"But—"

"You know espionage. I know the media. I'm the James Bond of the internet."

"Hey, I've seen that movie," Rust says, finally understanding one of my movie references. I don't have the heart to tell him there are twenty-three Bond films.

Chapter 25

Identification

I've gone into full producer/seducer mode. Rust and Mars must think I'm crazy as I move around the trailer, setting up a clear backdrop, adjusting the curtains and flicking switches to experiment with different combinations of lights and lamps. If you're making a video watched by millions of people, you've got to at least aim for decent lighting.

"Do you have *anything* that identifies you as Metric or government? Military?" I ask. "Badges, ID, documents, photos?"

A gravelly grunt is Rust's non-committal response. He pulls out his wallet and hands me a weathered photograph. Sure enough, there's Rust with medals and distinguished crosses covering his chest like sparkling sequins. There are too many to number without losing count. Beside him is an evidently younger Mars and an older woman – presumably his mother.

"Can I see that?" Mars snatches the photo. "That's... the end of my fifty-six-day Criminal Investigation Training Program."

"You look like a proud father, Rust."

"I was. As much as I tried to talk him out of it."

Mars studies the image, which he appears to have never seen. He's more surprised than I am to learn Rust carries around a family photo.

"I guess it only took becoming a CIA Agent in Clandestine Services for you to pay attention to me."

Rust lets out a wincing groan. I'm not sure what it means, but I can only assume he regrets his lack of a relationship with Mars over the years. I'm really starting to understand Rust if I can interpret an array of emotions from his grunts and curmudgeonly mumbling.

"So are those Metric medals or what?" I ask, taking the photo back from Mars.

"Some."

"He was military before Metric."

"1st Special Forces Operational Detachment-Delta," Rust states.

"Is that the Delta Force?"

"It is."

I turn to Mars, who's now studying his reflection in a small mirror near his bed.

"And how did you end up in the CIA?"

"They basically recruited me straight out of college," he says, combing his hair with his hands. I'd want to look good too if I was about to become a household name.

"What was your major – espionage? A minor in computer hacking?"

"International relations. But I guess the family name caught their attention and the US government had different plans."

I can't really imagine Mars as a college frat bro, but it would go some way to explaining the way he speaks.

"The son of Rust, hey?"

"It was still 'Son of the Fox' at that point."

"Enough reminiscing," Rust says, taking the photo back. "How are we going to do this?"

"Just spill your guts," I say. "Let everything out. But be sure of what you're saying. Don't hold back. We need it to be clear – Metric are the bad guys. The NWO is badder. The baddest, even."

Mars and Rust sit side by side, with a black rug pinned up behind them to set a clear contrasted backdrop. They're outside their comfort zone, about to bare their souls, but I think I could be even more nervous. I sit opposite them, holding my phone up with my elbows pressed against my body, locked into a sturdy grip. Even with our lack of cell phone reception, the handset is switched to flight mode to prevent any phone calls interrupting the most important recording of my lifetime. Forty-four per cent battery should be plenty enough to film the video and get it uploaded. Rust swallows loudly, clears his throat and begins to speak as soon as I give him a slow nodding go-ahead.

"My name... is Brian Fox. I'm currently an agent for a classified government special operations group known to few as *Metric*."

"My name is David Fox," Mars states. "Like my father here, I too have worked for Metric as a field agent, carrying out black ops in the US and across the globe. What you're about to hear will shock you, but please understand, what we're revealing in this video will do nothing for our personal gain. Our only goal is to expose the US government for what it really is and to shine a light on the dark forces that influence our world leaders."

Rust clears his throat again when it's clear Mars has concluded his opening input. "For the better part of three decades I've spent my life serving Metric in clandestine operations, both home and abroad. For too long, I've felt an obligation to conceal our nation's worst secrets. But it's become clear now that the leaders I've followed and operations I've undertaken are no more noble than many of the enemies I've been ordered to infiltrate, apprehend and assassinate."

Rust's delivery reminds me of a military general testifying in court. His speech is stilted but authoritative as he outlines his career in espionage and his recruitment to Metric. He holds up the photo from Mars' graduation and a second picture of former president George Bush Sr, with a young Rust clearly present in the background. Speaking about the objectives of several past special operations, he spills the beans on numerous ways Metric has broken US and international laws for "a twisted perception of the greater good".

"Today I sacrifice my status as one of the US government's

most trusted and experienced special agents to lift the veil on Metric's secret history of corruption. We will likely become fugitives and will likely be forced to flee the country we love. But the truth can't stay hidden any longer."

Rust speaks of his past in general terms, as if he's talking about somebody he'll never be again. This self-eulogy is his way of closing a door on that life, while opening another to a completely unknown state of existence. Rust's revelation about Metric's atrocities would be enough to create headlines, and yet that's nothing compared to the bomb Mars is about to drop.

"Metric is responsible for both acts of good and evil," he says, tapping his knee as an active tick. "But even Metric is a mere puppet of a *shadow government* pulling strings behind the scenes. It did not begin this way. My father here, and my mother, once a Metric scientist, carried out some of the most important special operations in American history. The influence of a secret society has slowly twisted this once honourable group, this country, and many other world powers, into tools of destruction and manipulation, in order to carry out its bidding for global order."

Mars pauses, gulps and takes a deep breath. It's a moment of weakness perhaps, but to me it only adds to his sincerity.

"This group is known to Metric's head, Clara Scarpino, as the *New World Order*. Their influence, through planted moles, extends to the following groups..."

Mars spends the next minute naming and shaming a long list of international government organisations, multinationals, worldwide committees, corporations, banks and other influential bodies known to millions across the world. The Foxes speak without compromise as they reveal everything they know about Metric and the NWO. Even with everything I've learnt, it gives me chills to hear it described all at once. I can just imagine the reactions when this hits social media. We'll break the internet – at least, more than Kim Kardashian ever did.

"Let me reiterate that these revelations are not being shared to make a name for ourselves or to spread distrust for the everyday Americans who serve our authorities, most of whom do their utmost to protect the nation's best interests. It is with heavy hearts that we bear this news. But it is *imperative* that independent reviews are held to disband the covert government agency known as Metric, and to *remove* those holding office under the influence of the New World Order." Mars adjusts his volume as the wind increases and rain starts to hit the roof of the trailer. I hope the phone doesn't detect it, but I know it will. "Soon we will identify each member of the Order and see them stand trial to answer for the atrocities they have committed over several decades. Citizens will soon know the facts and it is the public's responsibility to demand change and transparency from the government officials, public servants, multinationals and powerful groups that profit from their hard work. Once again, I'm Agent Mars. He's Agent Rust. And this... This is just the beginning."

After a few seconds of staring into the camera, I end the recording and Mars looks up to me.

I'm speechless.

I have the same feeling I get when the cinema lights fade in at the end of an amazing movie experience. I don't want to be the first one to talk about it. I just want to bask in it for a second and try to understand what I've witnessed.

"How was that?" Mars asks.

"Illuminating," is the word that I come back with.

"Did I look nervous?"

I shake my head. "Not really. I'd say you nailed it. Both of you. That was seven minutes, almost eight minutes."

"That long? Wow. So, what next?"

"Well," I start, flicking around my phone's screen. "It's going to take a while to upload. Especially if the phone signal doesn't improve."

"What do you mean?" Rust asks.

"I've got no signal. Wait. Nope. It's still gone."

"You're trying to connect?"

"There's no signal?"

"You didn't shut off the GPS?" Each of Rust's questions is more hostile than the last, and now I realise why.

"Crap. No. Can they... How would that work? It's OK. They can't track it. Can they?"

Rust sighs the angriest, most elongated sigh possible. "Of course, they can track it, dumbass. You need to shut that thing off. Now."

"What? No. How?" I stammer back, holding up my phone like an ancient artefact that maybe I don't understand as well as I thought.

"I told you, those things are too easy to hack. You don't think Metric can't find someone to wipe your phone for them?"

"Why didn't you say something?"

"I thought you were broadcasting live."

"No, there's no *signal*. It's gotta be uploaded. I said that, I thought."

"Shut it down. We need to get that thing off the grid. Once the signal is back up, they could even use it to track us."

"How come no one said anything until now?"

Mars tries to mediate between our back and forth. "There's a lot going on, bro. Remember what I told you. We need to be patient."

We begin discussing our options for distribution. Do we send the video to a contact at the White House? Do we trust anyone in the CIA? Are there any high up sources who can guarantee this thing sees the light of day? Does it need to get out there at a grass-roots level?

"WikiLeaks," I say, feeling as though I've found the solution. "I'm sure Julian Assange would love to know all about this."

"That won't work," Mars says.

"There's got to be a Snowden type out there."

"That would be you, in this instance."

"Snowden fled to Hong Kong to leak his information to the media. You want to just throw it out there?"

Rust has been quiet, sitting to the side, leaning back on his chair and puffing on another cigar. "So *now* you want to go to Hong Kong?"

"Very funny."

"We wouldn't make it out of Kansas by air."

"Come on, what happened to the stealth gene?"

"There's three of us. That's a lot harder to disguise through security checkpoints."

"Plus," Mars interjects. "Metric, or the Order, whoever, isn't going to keep this quiet too long. Another day without finding us and we've got a nationwide manhunt."

"I don't know what's left then." I throw my hands up in the air, frustrated by the absence of a clear solution. "You want to walk into a Best Buy and ask for a laptop with a broadband connection? Be my guest."

"Most, if not all, of the phone lines are out," Mars reminds us. If the slight shaking of the trailer is any indication, the weather is starting to turn outside. "The question isn't the messenger, but the channel. We could be on the run for days before this gets out, if we don't think of a way to get this online."

There are apparently no internet cafes in Ogden, and even if there were, there's no working internet. A tidbit of information tumbles through my brain – something I wish I'd forgotten. It's a small detail that could save us all, while putting me in incredible danger. This genius of mine is a curse.

"There's a newspaper in Manhattan," I mutter. "They seem to be online still. They'll be able to help. Publish this video, maybe take ownership of the story."

"C'mon, this is *your* story. It's your *Serial.*"

"I don't know if I want my name on this anymore."

"This is exactly what you wanted."

"Is that a joke? This is *not* what I wanted. You get that right?"

"Then why did you find me?"

"OK. In principle, you're right. I want to tell the truth regardless of who gets mad about it. But this will be considered *treason* until the Order gets overthrown or whatever. I don't want to spend however long that takes inside a padded cell. Or dead."

"That's the point of this. It's the first step. A giant step."

"Saluki was right. I got more than I bargained for."

"Do you think *we* signed up for *any* of this, just because—"

"Let me explain..."

"–just because we were recruited by Metric?"

"Let me explain. Look. It's different."

"It's not."

"But *you knew* what you were getting me into, Mars. You found out, and you found out some more. And you still roped me into it."

He has no comeback. He looks at Rust and then back to me with a scornful sorrow, remembering that feeling he had in the cell when he realised what he had done to my idea of a life.

"OK. I can't argue with that. But we're here now. We're in this together. You've got to look at setbacks as set-ups. What's next? What opportunity does this open? If we pull this off, you can walk away and we can wipe any trace of your involvement. Or you can take the credit you deserve. But to do that, we need to take this into town."

"We? I keep hearing this 'we', as if I have a say."

"You can't stay here. You speak these people's language. They might even recognise you."

"You're the spies. Can't you fake it? Better yet, tell them the truth. They'll love it. Every journo loves a scoop."

"They won't be able to handle the truth."

I fight back my urge to bust out the appropriate Jack Nicholson impersonation. This isn't the time. And Mars is right.

"OK. Let's just say I have to go with you..."

"You have to go with us."

"Right. How's it going to work? We jump on a bus? Call an Uber?"

"I like that bus idea," Rust says, gesturing with his cigar.

"You're serious."

"They certainly wouldn't expect it."

I give up. Right when I think I understand these guys, they surprise me all over again.

"I never saw Jason Bourne ride the bus. Can't we hijack a chopper from Fort Riley?"

A menacing look from Rust forces me to declare that last quip was a joke. "You think this is about adrenaline, fast cars, gadgets and big guns." I sense from Rust's tone that he's put on his invisible professor hat. "The thrill of battle, the suspense and the glory. Submarines and helicopters. But it's not a video game, kid. It's not like those movies. Sometimes we take the bus."

"It is a little bit like the movies," Mars admits to me quietly.

"Only a little bit?"

"Yeah. He just really hates choppers."

Chapter 26

Formulation

"Can we make those *Mission Impossible* masks, with the latex?"

"We don't have the materials."

"Can we hack all the traffic lights to get us a clear path into town?"

"Not unless you know how to do it."

"C'mon, Mars. Do some spy stuff."

"This is the spy stuff." Mars is getting changed behind a curtain, so all I can do is sit at the table and ask annoying questions in our final stage of preparation. "We need to stay under the radar."

"What about stealth camouflage?"

We're at the tail end of planning our mission logistics, which means Rust is gathering together all the nearby ammunition and cleaning his handgun. For Mars, it's meant a few hundred push-ups and putting my concerns to rest.

"Did you hear me?" I ask. "I know there's something you can tell me about stealth camo that will just blow my mind."

Mars steps out from behind the curtain and folds his arms, demonstrating his new dark grey skin-tight outfit. From a distance it would appear to be a full-length wetsuit, but up close I see it's a thinner material. There are lightweight pouches and holsters, as well as padding to the elbow, knee and chest areas. The best comparison I can think of is Christian Bale's version of Batman, without the cowl, cape and utility belt. I wonder if it comes in black.

"This is the Spectral Suit."

"*That* is cool."

"It was designed as an early prototype for a metamaterial cloak – a device that directs the flow of light smoothly around an object."

"Stealth *camo?*"

"In theory. Like the way water flows past a rock in a stream. The tech never quite got all the way there, but when it's activated, the base suit's design is as close to invisibility that we have."

"Nice." I unwrap one of the protein bars that Mars has presumably been living on for who knows how long. He has a commercial-sized box of these things on display. There are wrappers scattered around the trailer and stuffed inside empty Chinese takeout boxes. If I were Mars, I'd be motivated to clear my name just so I could eat some real food.

"Tell me more."

"Well." Mars looks down at his outfit, turning over his arms. "There are components of active camouflage, but it's lightweight, durable and mostly passive. A couple years ago, DARPA added a fitted musculoskeletal fibre that helps with fatigue, reduces injury risk and physical stress. There's even actuators that detect and stabilise shaky movement and improve balance."

"You're like Captain America."

"But with stealth. It's awesome. And it feels great."

"What's it like, being invisible?"

Mars inspects his gun and fits it to one of the suit's holsters. "Sometimes it makes me feel alone. That's good. It gives me confidence to do whatever I need to do. Other times I act as though it makes no difference. You know. I can't afford to risk being seen."

"So you were wearing this the other day? Underneath your regular clothes?"

"Correct. Just without the holsters." Mars starts to throw yesterday's clothes on top of the Spectral Suit. Even the best camouflage known to man isn't designed to hide someone riding the town bus.

"I was wondering how you took such a beating. The crash, the chopper, all of that."

"Yeah. I'm human. Sorry to ruin the illusion. But Rust wears it too."

"You're kidding. I assumed you guys lived on CrossFit and P90X workouts. I can't imagine seeing Rust in anything that tight."

"Don't get any ideas, kid," Rust bellows across the room, without looking up. The dismantled pistol in front of him demands most of his attention.

Mars practices whipping out his handgun from the Spectral Suit's holster before placing it back at his hip. His preference is the Mark 23 handgun, while Rust uses the older 1911 semi-automatic. I've gathered through their conversations that the Mark 23 was designed to be familiar to shooters intimate with the 1911 design, given the similarities in layout and control scheme. I'm no gun expert, but the weapons seem to be an appropriate metaphor for the Foxes' differing personalities. One is classic, sturdy and reliable. The other is sleeker, modern, approachable, more accurate.

I tell Mars and Rust I'm planning to leave my gun behind, but they don't seem to care. At this point, our success won't hinge on whether I wield a pistol or not. This phone is my weapon and its battery charge is my ammunition.

Everything is ready. The Foxes have all their gear. I've got thirty-seven per cent battery on my phone. But there's one last thing I want to do.

"Before we get out there, is there anything anyone needs to say to each other?"

"What is this, *Dr Phil*? C'mon, bro. Let's move it."

"This is serious." I stand firm, forcing the others to stop and turn back. "This could be, you know... This could be it. C'mon. You'll feel good about it. It's therapeutic. Better to say it now than maybe as your last words."

"For Pete's sake, kid, can you shut him up?"

Mars turns his wrists to show his palms in an apathetic shrug, admitting my behaviour is out of his hands.

"I'll go first, if you two are just going to stare at me." I clear my throat and go straight into my spiel, trying to reduce the awkwardness and emphasise that it's not a big deal to communicate honestly. It's what grown ups do. "I just want to say, first of all, I'm not mad at either of you for what's happened to me. I realise this is what needs to go down. And everything before now has led up to this point. So I forgive you, you know what I mean? For everything cruddy that you did to me... which I won't mention again, because I think we covered that already. OK? Cool. That's all. I'm glad we're all here together."

Mars nods with a look of regard for what I've said. "Thanks. And bro, I'm sorry about that cruddy stuff, as you put it. You know, I'm a very 'big picture' guy, so I didn't consider at all what it would do to you, putting you in this predicament."

"It's cool. But thanks for saying."

"It's like *The Hunger Games* or something... and you didn't volunteer as tribute. I just threw you in there. And it wasn't very decent of me to not think about what that would mean to you. And I really want to be decent."

"Given your line of work and past experiences, I think decency is a great ambition."

I look over to Rust, expecting to see the old dog shaking his head and muttering under his breath about these over-sensitive sissies getting all emotional when there's a job to do. Nothing I've learnt about Rust has prepared me for anything less than that.

But instead, he's disconnected completely. His eyes are locked into an empty stare, his lips shut tight. I follow his sight line and realise he's watching a woodpecker in a nearby tree. It's moving across several branches, searching for a spot to extract food. Is Rust listening at all? I know therapeutic admissions aren't part of his typical pre-mission briefing, but nothing about today has been typical.

"I used to paint."

I look to Mars for clarification, but we're equally bewildered by Rust's confession.

"Landscapes. Still life," Rust says, still staring at the woodpecker and beyond. "I used oil paints, mostly. Tried water colours, but I liked the time and commitment it took to finish an oil on canvas piece."

"What are you saying?" I ask.

"Yesterday morning, in the car... you asked if I had any hobbies. If there was anything trivial in my life."

"Yeah."

"I used to paint. Started in school. Gave it up once I joined the military... but your mother," Rust turns to Mars, finally breaking his empty gaze. "She pulled me back into it. I was a different person with her. I wish I could've spent more time with her. With you. But this damn agency swallowed my entire life. And I let them. I thought she... and you... were better off with me at a distance. That way I couldn't mess things up."

"You realise that's insane," his son responds, as a matter of fact. "She needed you."

I can tell from his voice that Mars needed him too. But of course, he won't admit that here and now.

"It made sense at the time. There are things I can't get into..."

"Look. I get it. I don't know if I'll ever let it go. But I get it now. And Mom certainly seemed to understand."

"She did. I could tell it hurt her... but she never tried to stop me. Said it was my choice. That doesn't mean it was right though."

I can't believe what I'm hearing. Rust's voice is as soft as butter, dripping with authenticity and more gentle than his persona would ordinarily allow.

"I'm sorry she disappeared. I'm sorry I let Scarpino manipulate me into thinking you could've had something to do with it. I should know better. I do now."

Mars looks away, momentarily unsure how to proceed. "Where do you think she is?" he asks, his voice breaking slightly.

Rust opens his mouth, but pauses to pick his words with great care. "I think *they* know. I think... maybe they took her out."

"Then maybe she's still alive. Is it possible?" Mars asks full of hope, but Rust's lack of a reaction tells him his hope is in vain.

"I'm sorry. If you think she knew something and that's why she left... Metric's secrets don't stay secret by accident. If she isn't dead, she's as good as gone."

Mars nods and admits he feared as much. He's been trying to convince himself otherwise. "Part of all this for me... I was trying to find out what she knew and make sure it wasn't all for nothing."

"You can always hope," I say. "Stranger things have happened. Maybe she ran away. She could be on the run, the same as you."

Rust's head jerks in firm denial. "That's not her. She was a scientist."

"She wouldn't have stood a chance," Mars says. "Not against a scalphunter like Saluki. But that's enough chatting. Let's channel all this into the work at hand."

We pick up our stride again and let the conversation return to normal as if nothing heartfelt was ever said. Grief is truly one of the most difficult emotions to process. Very few people ever get to blame their sorrow and angst on an evil organisation or secret society and actually be justified. I wouldn't want to be anyone from the NWO if Rust or Mars cross their path.

~∞~

We step onto the mostly empty bus as a trio, ready to take on anything. Choppers, tornadoes, billionaires, drug lords, cops, soldiers – it's all in a day's work for the Foxes. If there's a crossword that needs solving, that's my area. I feel powerful standing between Metric's two rogue agents. The sensation will fade, but I've psyched myself into a mental zone where I believe I can do anything with my new partners. Rust is the old shark who knows the waters and has lived to see them change. Mars is a young cheetah, capable and cocky. He has believed he owns the savanna for so long that's it become true. And me, I'm a Jack Russell terrier, yapping at passing cars and hoping it makes a difference.

I double-check with the bus driver, making sure we're heading towards Manhattan and not Fort Riley. That would be a disaster. She asks if we're taking a one-way trip or if we want a return ticket. Mars boldly declares we'll "definitely" be coming back. I'm not sure we have any reason to return to Ogden, but his message is clear.

This isn't the end.

Mars is planning to walk out of this with an empty gun clip, victoriously pumping his fist in the air like John Bender at the end of *The Breakfast Club*.

Chapter 27

Transportation

Mars and I take aisle seats opposite each other, five or six rows back, and Rust eases himself down behind us. I notice a Hawaiian hula doll dancing on the bus dashboard to a soundtrack of *Hello! Ma Baby*. I recognise the 1899 Pan Alley song from the Warner Brothers cartoon *One Froggy Evening* that first aired at least twenty-five years before I was born. There's something about the upbeat old timey music that just chills me in this context. Together with the wind and rain, I'm getting an "end of the world" vibe. It could be prophetic or maybe it's a Pavlovian response from hundreds of hours spent playing dystopian *Fallout* video games with a similar soundtrack.

I let my mind race back over everything I've learnt in the past two days. I've lost my handwritten notes, but our video has all the essential details and I'm sure Mars would be happy to sit down and record a sequel. Maybe I will end up writing a feature on this. A book even. A podcast would be the simplest way to get the message across. I could get a million downloads, easily – if we get out of this.

Every time I try to think about the positive outcomes of our messed up situation, it's closely followed by that qualifier – "if we get out of this". My confidence is out of control. It's bi-polar, vacillating from positive to negative, trying to balance optimism with realism.

As Ogden fades into the horizon behind us, Mars leans toward me with a crazy grin. "This is exciting, isn't it? Are you pumped?"

"Mostly just terrified."

"You're not excited?"

"No!"

"C'mon, bro. I'm sure it'll work out."

"Let's bring it down a notch. Talk about something else."

"Like what?"

"Like... I just learnt your names this morning. I've got a David and Brian in my family too."

"Yeah. Right. I haven't heard those two names together in a while."

"Where did Rust and Mars come from?"

Mars looks around to see if any passengers could be eavesdropping, but I can read in his face that his caution is more out of habit than anything else. We're about to reveal a whole lot more when this video hits.

"Some years back they introduced the codename system to increase anonymity. They let agents choose any title they liked. Changed them over whenever necessary."

"So, God of war? Or are you maybe a big *Veronica Mars* fan?"

"Believe it or not, it was a nod to the old man."

"I'm flattered," Rust says.

Mars gives me a science lesson, explaining how the red planet's iron oxide is transported in dust clouds, covering everything in a layer of rust and creating its blood-like appearance.

"Hence, Mars."

"And what about Rust? You got a codename origin story?"

"I just liked it."

Mars comments on how little traffic is sharing the road as we approach the Manhattan Regional Airport. I gaze out the window, watching the weather turn even bleaker. The cloudy sky is dark and ominous enough to freak me out, making me wish we could postpone the mission.

"Should we maybe come back tomorrow morning? I've just got a bad feeling about this."

"You're not serious, after all those speeches and everything? That's just your nerves," Mars assures me. "It's now or never."

I imagine Tiger Woods waiting for me at home. That poor cat. I rescued him from a shelter and gave him a home. He's been through too much for me to never come back again.

Who am I kidding – he's probably found a new family already. I bet he forgot about me as soon as I stopped feeding him a few days ago. Cats really are jerks.

"What's that? Look, look," a teenage boy shouts to his parents at the front of the bus. "That's a damn tornado!"

"Babe, I told you we were due for a twister here. It's been too damn long!"

"What, I can't see it? And don't say 'damn', you two."

"Mom, it was right there!"

I'm with her. I can't see anything unusual. Rust and Mars don't seem concerned by the alarming conversation. As I start to raise the subject, Mars holds up a finger to shush me. He leans forward, eavesdropping on the bus radio while the vehicle slows to a stop.

"Seriously?" The driver sounds annoyed talking back. "Oh, if it's anything like last time, I'm done. We've only got a handful on here. They aren't gonna wanna stay out here in all this right now."

"That doesn't sound good, guys."

The driver turns into the airport and parks at a deserted bus shelter. She stands up and raises her voice for everyone to hear.

"OK, people. Everybody needs to get off the bus right now. There is a tornado warning and we need to hold up right now inside the airport where there's plenty of shelter, OK? Once it's over, we'll get you anywhere you need to be. Don't worry about that. But we need to get out of this for our own safety – right now."

The half a dozen passengers in front of us waste no time

clearing out, murmuring about the menacing weather and trying to make phone calls to loved ones.

"I'm not about to argue with that," one woman tells her friend. "I was at K-State in 2008 and that was enough for me."

Rust nods knowingly at Mars and moves to the front of the bus once the aisle is empty. He flashes a badge to the waiting driver, but she doesn't seem to notice it at first.

"You need to get your friends up outta here, sir. What's this?" She inspects his identification with a raised eyebrow.

"CIA, madam. I'm going to need your vehicle."

"CIA? Are you playin' games right now, sir?"

"Certainly not, madam."

"You don't need to call me madam. I'm not some brothel queen. I'm a bus driver."

"Apologies, ma'am. But you need to get inside to safety, and we need to get out of here."

"And what am I supposed to tell my boss? This ain't my bus to give away."

"You're a government employee, right? We have the same boss. But mine's a lot scarier than yours. Trust me."

"OK, sir. But if you don't survive this storm, I'm playin' dumb on this one."

"Works for me."

She hands over the keys as Rust assures he's more than capable of driving this thing.

"CIA?" I ask Mars.

"It's the easiest thing for normies to understand. It never fails. Plus, if we screw up, it's the CIA's problem to deal with."

Using an offline map on my phone, I find the newspaper office location and hand the GPS display to Mars as we start picking up speed. Water is pooling up at the road sides as the rain and wind become a more powerful presence.

"Is that... Is that what I think it is?"

The wheel of a windmill tumbles across the highway in front of our bus, reminding us how close we are to the countryside. I imagine most motorists have bunkered down or are on their way to safety. You'd have to be crazy to stay out here. Crazy like a Fox.

"You can stay on this freeway the entire time."

"I'm taking the back roads. Just in case."

"I think the Kansas River is over that way," I state nervously. "Are you sure you want to mess around there?"

I quietly point out there's been at least three inches of rain, but if I defer to Rust's best judgement, I'll at least have someone to blame if I drown.

"Mars!"

Rust sounds alarmed.

"We've got a Shadow comin'. Right on our tail."

I watch the excitement drain from Mars' face. "Son of a..."

"What's that?"

"You sure, Rust?"

"Take a look back there and see for yourself."

Mars puts his hands to the side window for a clearer view behind us. He curses, throws his black coat to the floor and tears away his chinos to reveal the Spectral Suit in all its glory.

"This just got dangerous."

Feeling very left out of the excitement, I ask again for an explanation. Mars points out a black 4x4 behind the bus. "You see it?"

"Kinda. I mean, not really." I'd usually lie in this instance, for simplicity's sake, but I don't want to take any chances. "I can't see much unless I move out of my seat. But I'm willing to take your word for it."

"Well, that's a Metric Shadow – a specially trained driver. Not so great in combat, but they're most likely transporting Metric agents who we definitely *don't* want to mess around with."

"Oh."

"Yeah. So, this is about to get real. Get the wheels on the bus, Rust!"

"What?"

"I don't know - just drive faster!"

Rust hits the pedal, ensuring we put some space between the bus and the Shadow following behind. We overtake a slow pickup truck and gain some more distance, but it seems the Shadow is quick to replicate our move. The road is a blur to me as the wind-screen wipers do their best to fight the pounding rain. The rhythmic squeak of the blades against the glass adds to the cacophony, accompanying the hum of the bus, the roaring wind and the directions Mars is shouting as he tries to keep an eye on the Shadow.

Rust drives with an urgency usually reserved for a man transporting his pregnant wife to hospital in the late stages of labour. In any other circumstance, I'd ask the driver to slow down, but Rust is locked in, ignoring every call that comes across the radio. Desperate commuters trying to wave over the bus for a ride are rewarded with a giant splash of water at every stop.

The Fox boys go back and forth, discussing the tactics of the Shadow as I try to keep up. Rust is convinced they'll stay behind and try to take us out, rather than risk coming up beside the bus and getting run off the road. Mars points out a Shadow typically avoids being spotted, which means they're in uncharted territory right now and anything is possible.

"Hey guys," I interrupt, pointing forward to the stalled traffic waiting for us in a couple of blocks. "Should we find another road?"

"This is still the best way," Mars says.

"But... Traffic."

Rust veers onto the wrong side of the road without a second to spare, bypassing the stationary traffic. This move forces us to take on a panicked line of oncoming motorists. Rust swerves off-road to dodge the first two cars, and swings back just in time to avoid a roadside bus stop by a foot or two.

An approaching motorcycle veers hard to our left, but Rust mirrors its movement in hasty confusion. He corrects the bus as the biker turns into the roadside. We push as far right as possible, taking out a row of side mirrors from the oncoming stationary vehicles. The light collisions make a rapid series of loud clicking sounds, like a spinning Wheel of Fortune. I glimpse back at the Shadow trailing our path, manoeuvring through the road blocks with far more ease than the bus.

The road's inadequate drainage struggles to funnel the flooding rainwater coming down in Biblical proportions. We approach a long line of cars in our way, banked up by the dozen.

"We can't stop," Mars says.

"Don't need to."

"What?"

Rust takes the bus off-road across an elevated train railway, running parallel to the flooded street.

"Buses aren't made for this!" I shout as we bump along the uneven surface. I'm holding on for dear life, but Mars finds it hilarious.

"You'd be surprised."

After only a hundred yards or so, Rust slows slightly to roll back down to the roadside and accelerate into the flooded street. The bus ploughs through the storm water with fierce momentum, pushing the massive pool of water aside like Moses crossing the Red Sea. I turn back to see the Shadow following across the railway line, but they won't get very far. Rust keeps his foot hard on the gas, maintaining the speed for an entire block as he passes several stranded cars, creating long rolling waves on each side. The bus's rear radiator and engine allow driving that would be foolish for any other motorist facing flooded roads. As a result, the Shadow is stranded back on the train tracks and now reversing to retrace its path.

We can't afford to drop the pace. There could be Metric agents stationed all around the city and there's no doubt they're tracking us from above, like Will Smith in *Enemy of the State*. I can just picture it.

"I need real time imagery coverage at latitude 75.3, long 115.3. max resolution, confirm visual. Roger that. Air one, target is on the move. Go, go, move, move!"

The traffic is far more sparse as we leave the main road for the city to avoid the obvious route Metric might expect us to take. Large megastore and mall parking lots on either side of the street are filled with motorists taking refuge, reducing our road obstacles.

Approaching a low roundabout, Mars calls out to his father: "Just up that hill and across the other side."

Rust takes the directions to heart and literally drives through the upcoming circular intersection, treating the bus as if it has the suspension of a dune buggy. We cross over and reach a steep slope, slowing enough that Rust has to take it down a gear.

"Here we go. Another damned Shadow," Rust fumes. "Those bastards are all here. Must be spread over town."

I look around but I can't see any cars. I guess that's why they're called "Shadows".

"Should we be concerned?" I ask.

My question is answered in an instant as the window behind me shatters in a blast of gunfire.

I throw my head between my ankles for a second, then I scramble to the floor, lying as flat as possible to avoid subsequent bullet sprays. Rust swerves hard and attempts to ram the car to our side, but I don't feel any impact. Our slower speed makes us an easy target. After reaching the top of the steep road, Rust wastes no time accelerating across the plateau and heading downhill. We're moving so fast that I can't even focus on the street lights through the wet weather.

"Take that left, Rust!"

I crawl back to my seat and grip it tight as the bus drifts across the foot of the hill, sliding around the corner and spraying a ten-foot wave across the sidewalk. We approach two parked cars resting in twenty inches of water – a shiny red sports car and a '90s hatchback. A group of people, possibly the cars' owners and occupants, are huddled nearby, taking cover in a large walled bus shelter. The road isn't wide enough for the three of us. Something's got to give.

Rust puts his foot down and tears right through the middle, clipping the sports car from behind and sending it off-road into a streetlight. Maybe he felt some fondness toward the hatchback after his adventures with the Corolla and Golf yesterday.

Mars leans towards me, his eyes still locked on the road

ahead. "If you have a choice, always take out the expensive cars. It's more fun. And the owners are always insured."

At last, some practical advice I can maybe use someday. Mars is a real circus of values.

More gunfire takes out the rear window and several others along the bus wall, allowing the heavy rain and wind to form puddles across the hard floor.

"Manhattan isn't that big. We must be near the newspaper office."

"Where are you going?" Rust shouts as Mars hands me the phone and steps down the bus aisle.

"I'm sick of these Metric jabronis. They need to respect the Fox and the Maven."

Crouching between two seats at the rear of the bus, Mars wipes his saturated face. The rain is pouring through the window, blurring his view of the road behind us. Water beads and runs off the Spectral Suit without soaking in.

"Where are we, kid?"

"Uh, the next right!" I tell Rust, fumbling my phone as I try to watch Mars. "Just take the signs towards the highway."

Clutching his pistol, the younger Fox waits for our next turn, which changes the direction of rain across his face. With clear eyes, Mars rises, smashes the broken window with the butt of his gun, and points it into the street below. He fires three rapid shots. Even with a silencer attached, the noise bounces off the bus walls and rocks my eardrums. I peek across to see the Shadow slide out of control, clipping the rear of our vehicle. The impact coincides with the bus hitting a puddle or pothole, forcing us into an hydro-planing spin.

"Hold on!"

"Geeze, bro!"

Mars trips back as the bus grinds to a stop, sliding down the wet aisle face first and out of control. Steadying myself, I lunge to grab his leg, halting his slide just an inch from the broken glass collected in a pool of water.

"Whoa," Mars says, staring into the pile of shards before him.

"Nice save."

I grin as he rolls over and gives me a thumbs up. Even the Spectral Suit wouldn't have protected his face from getting torn up like grated cheese.

"Out of the bus," Rust yells, making no sense at all. "Quick. Before the next Shadow. You can make it on foot. I'll try to run them off."

I look to the open door and see a huge tree branch hanging over the top of the bus, swaying in the wild wind. We could step outside and try to go unseen as Rust leads Metric astray. In theory, the satellite surveillance crew would follow him instead of us, meaning we'd be free to enter the newspaper office without being followed.

I ask if he's certain, given the newspaper is only a few more blocks.

"Even more reason to throw off the trail."

This is it. We're parting ways.

"Thanks. For coming back yesterday. For... keeping me alive. For everything. Except the punch in the face. That really hurt."

"Get outta here, kid. It's go time." I should've known Rust would have no time for such sentiment. "I'll find you again. Just don't screw this up."

Mars is raring to go. He simply gives Rust a knowing nod and exhales a long breath before facing the howling wind outside.

"OK. Let's get outta here."

"You've got this." Rust nods.

"Yeah, I got this."

Mars dives from the bus into the stormy weather, performing a flawless somersault to the ground. Rust furrows his brow, displeased by his son's showmanship and natural flair.

"Show off."

Chapter 28

Production

I pull my hood over my head and jump outside, passing over a rippling puddle. I land awkwardly on the nature strip, smearing mud across my Nikes. This graceless exit from the bus bears no resemblance to the poetry in motion that was Mars' dismount.

The cold wind is ice against my face. Rust accelerates away, but I can barely hear the bus over the sound of rain pouring into the sewers and trees blowing in the storm. I follow Mars' lead, crouching and waddling right over to the nearby tree base to rest beneath its heaviest foliage.

If our exit went unseen, the tree will help shield us from any Metric satellite surveillance. I can see how Mars would be almost invisible from a distance, hidden by his adaptive camouflage and the current low visibility. The breeze pushes the rain sideways, so the tree offers no shelter from the wet. My glasses are covered in water droplets, but I can still tell there is not a soul to be seen nearby. The wreck of the last pursuing Shadow isn't even visible, having disappeared over the opposite roadside slope after spinning out.

My engraved ring and chain are cold against my chest. Its spiritual relevance reminds me to say a quick prayer as we sit and wait.

Please God.

Don't let me be shot.

Don't let Mars die. Thank You for keeping me alive until now. You put me here for this moment. I know that.

I'm the sheep, you're the shepherd. Guide me safe. I'm just a vessel. But please keep the tornadoes outside Manhattan or maybe even lose them altogether. That would be awesome.

Give me strength. But let Your will be done, as always.

OK. I'm ready. What now?

I ask Mars if we should move on, but he shakes his head and tells me to wait. He points down the road towards our previous location. Another black 4x4 with tinted windows arrives, speeding across the shreds of rubber and skid marks left by the previous Shadow. It passes us without slowing, likely in hot pursuit of the unseen bus.

"Hell yeah," Mars says to himself, motioning that we can leave. We dart through the nearby bushes to a sidewalk and pick up some pace towards our destination. I hold my phone up, wipe away the rain drops and point Mars in the right direction. We may have given the Metric Shadows the slip, but we won't feel secure until we've reached the newspaper office.

"Down the end of this street. Keep going!"

I struggle to keep up with Mars' stride, but I'm glad he's ahead of me to keep an eye out for hazards. There are a lot of residential homes in the neighbourhood, built from quaint weatherboard that won't stand a chance against a tornado. I glance sideways at the buildings we pass – a dentistry, a bank, an insurance agent, a real estate business. They all appear empty. A loose deck chair appears to have smashed a window, blowing in from who knows where. Those "end of the world" vibes aren't going anywhere.

As we pass an old office building, a reflection in the tall windows catches my eye. I try to look back without stopping, but I see nothing. My eyes lift up and I freeze.

"Mars! What is *that*?"

A clap of thunder in the distance ensures he doesn't hear me.

"Mars!"

He stops and turns around, at first appearing annoyed that I'm no longer following. Before he can tell me to hurry up, his eyes open wide like saucers and his mouth briefly forms a gasping mask of horror.

"Get down!"

In just tenths of a second, Mars draws his gun and fires.

I drop to the ground, grazing my palms and smashing my right elbow across the asphalt while trying to protect my phone. The sharp pain sinks in as I count five rounds blasting over my head. I look up just in time to see a circular mechanical device collide with the pavement, bouncing with a dull thud.

"Is that an aerial drone?" I shout, squinting at the sparking mess of metal and wires beside me.

"Get up. We need to go." Mars reloads and cranes his neck to point in the opposite direction. "Now!"

I don't need to be told twice. We sprint away from the broken surveillance robot, rounding a corner until we see our finish line. The newspaper office looks like it was designed by a prison architect. High brick walls extend at the edge of the property's parking lot, matching the bland brick facade of the building itself. *The Mercury* is clearly a surviving dinosaur of the old days when newspapers printed their broadsheets on an in-house press. A large satellite dish perched on the roof reminds me why I'm here and gives me hope for the potential of the technology waiting inside.

We're only a few buildings away when a roaring engine pulls my attention to the next street corner. A black 4x4 flies around, spraying water across its path until it slides to a halt in front of us.

"Hit the bricks, bro!"

I look around for anything to hide behind, deciding a two-foot high fence is the closest thing resembling protection. I duck and brace myself for gunshots, but instead hear the slam of car doors followed by shouts.

"Where is he?"

"Freeze, agent!"

"I can't see him!"

"He was just there!"

I don't dare move until I hear the clear audible signifier that Mars is cracking skulls and taking names. I peer over the brick wall to see a shadowy figure throwing around three agents dressed in black. I can only assume they're not Metric, the way Mars is handling them with his stealth camo activated. To my surprise, he keeps his weapon holstered and instead detonates his fists in an explosion of punches across their helpless bodies. The first of them to fall resembles an exclamation mark as his skull bounces across the turf. Each of Mars' systematic strikes lead to hard take-downs until the three agents are lying motionless across the pavement in shallow puddles of water.

"Let's go, Maven!"

I run to catch up with Mars, interrogating him about whatever just happened.

"I don't know who they are. Probably CIA. Maybe feds. But they're not Metric."

Scarpino must have called on every possible resource to apprehend us. For a minute, I forgot Metric is a small organisation and its agents are typically stationed around the world in one-man operations. Those available are likely hot on Rust's heels, leaving the NSA and CIA to follow surveillance tips around Manhattan.

We rush through *The Mercury's* wide parking lot before any other agents arrive. I stare at the door handle for a brief second, as if it's a portal that will transport me to a place free from all this mess, just as soon as I touch it.

This is my terminus.

I push into the empty lobby. The lights are still on, but the reception desk is unattended, leaving us stuck behind a glass security door with no handle. I rap my knuckles across the window until a head pokes out from down the carpeted hallway.

Yes.

I clench my fingers into a reserved fist pump as the middle-aged reporter fronts up to inspect the commotion. In one hand he grasps a notepad and pen, in the other hand a coffee mug. I imagine he's here for the long haul, ready to cover this storm for as long as it takes. After sizing me up, he hits a button that slides the door open.

"Everything OK?" He scrunches up his nose, contorting his ginger moustache into a wavy caterpillar.

"I've got something for you."

He looks me up and down with a straight face. I'm soaking wet and out of breath.

"Oh geeze, pal!" I follow his gaze behind me. "Put that thing away. What the hell are you wearing?"

Mars is standing watch at the entrance, with his pistol drawn and his eyes on the car park. The reporter's relatively cool reaction takes me aback. The weapon and Spectral Suit would be enough to frighten anyone unsuspecting. Mars' strangeness could be my most compelling argument for legitimacy.

"You're a crime reporter, right?"

"Yeah," the man says with a suspicious tone. "What's going on?"

"I've got something you're gonna wanna see."

The intrigued journalist stares at Mars for a few seconds, before motioning inside.

"How'd you know I'm on the crime desk?" he asks, leading us through a corridor to a small interview room.

"I'm a journo. This is a small city. I'm guessing anyone who isn't a cub reporter straight outta college has a senior role. Plus, the world's ending out there, you're still here and you didn't freak out that he has a *gun*."

We take opposite seats at an old wooden desk, lit by a blinking fluorescent bulb. I can't help but think back to the last time I was taken to a small room with a single desk, way back on Long Island with good old Mr Bald and Ms Ponytail.

Shaking my hand with uncertainty, the reporter introduces himself as Ross Kinney. He seems comfortable enough around me, but it's clear he's never seen anyone like Mars in his storied life.

"So you're a journo? Kansas City?"

"New York."

"New York?" Ross's eyes dart between me and Mars, who's now lingering in the doorway with his hand resting at his holster.

"Which paper?"

"I'm a freelance. Used to work at *The Times*."

"What in the Sam Hill are you doing chasing Kansan tornadoes? Did you see it?"

"Just the flooding. That's not why we're here, Ross."

"Pal, can you take a seat over here? You're making me nervous." Mars ignores Ross's request. Flipping open his notepad, the senior reporter asks what we've seen outside. He's evidently trying to piece together as much as he can about the storm for an online update, but he's barking up the wrong tree.

"We're not here about the storm," I state emphatically.

"What is it then? Can you get your friend to sit down? This storm is the story of the year, so it better be good."

I slide my phone across the table, with the damning video ready to play. Ross studies it until he recognises one of the faces on the screen. Rightly confused, he looks up at Mars.

"Who the hell *are* you?"

"Just watch it."

~∞~

Eight minutes later, after several gasps and curses, the video ends. Ross blinks.

He blinks again, this time more slowly and purposely, as if he's attempting to process what has just taken place.

"How do I know this isn't some prank?" His question is answered as he looks up to see Mars' Spectral Suit change colour, blending with the wall behind him. Ross looks at me briefly and presses the phone's touch screen to play the video once more.

"No, c'mon," I interrupt, taking the phone back and sounding more rude than I'd normally allow. I've come too far to let Metric catch me soaking wet and hanging out in this room. "We've got to get this online. Like, *right now*."

Ross cocks his head to the side, staring at Mars in the doorway until he notices the bruising and cuts across his face. I can see the weight of the situation hit him like a damp football in the nose.

"They're after you *now*?"

"*Right* now! They've got eyes everywhere. They're probably tracking us or using our phones to listen in - we don't even know. But these guys are legit, Ross. It's super spy stuff. You gotta believe me and get this out there. Now."

This grizzled reporter is stuck in the moment, glitching out and unable to speak.

"Listen, I have been through *a lot*," I explain, trying to snap him out of his stupor. "We're risking *everything* to be here and if we don't get this online as soon as possible, it could all be for nothing. Just get me to a computer."

Ross blinks a few more times, taking in everything I'm saying and connecting it to everything he heard in the video. I understand a news outlet has to be responsible for its content, but this is America and it's almost impossible to sue a newspaper.

"C'mon!"

"OK! Sorry. I'll take you to our online guru."

Mars nods and stays camped right where he is, keeping watch on the front entrance as I follow Ross into the newsroom. Despite never visiting this office, it's an incredibly familiar setting. The accounts and sales desks are deserted by staff who have no reason to be here today. The office layout is spacious – likely a result of downsizing. The convergence of modern newsrooms means less staff are given more tasks, while customer service and production work is often carried out at interstate or even international hubs.

We reach the editorial department, occupied by just three journalists spread out across the room. Each of them is transfixed by their phone and computer. None of them seem as senior as Ross, which would make him the acting editor on a day like today.

"Tim! Andrew." This is his version of an introduction. "He's got a video we need to get online. You're not gonna—"

"Holy crap! Andrew Maven!"

"Uh, hello," I stammer, not expecting to encounter a follower of my work. Tim jumps out of his chair to shake my hand with a beaming grin, completely dismissing whatever he was working on before I arrived.

"This guy," he says, looking back to Ross, "is pretty much famous on the internet."

The older journalist nods, almost paying no attention at all. "In half an hour he's gonna be a lot more than that, Tim. Do whatever he asks."

"I saw your tweet yesterday." Tim slumps into his chair, still brimming with positivity. "What are you doing in *Kansas*?"

I ignore his question and hold up my phone. "You got a cable for this?"

"Hell yeah. You got a video? This is big, isn't it? Man, I can't believe you're actually here."

Tim assists me with unbridled enthusiasm while Ross pulls up a chair and sits, watching the upload process with a look of vacancy. Tim clearly knows what he's doing as he navigates to a video hosting platform with quick clicks across his monitor. I ask him to host the video on a multitude of servers. I want it to spread so far that it doesn't matter if Metric gets it pulled down.

"Put it on your site, sure, but we need this on YouTube, Twitter, Facebook. Even Vimeo, Dailymotion, and all of whatever you kids are into these days. We need it to spread fast."

"Right on."

I take a deep breath and allow relief to wash over my entire body. It feels good. For just a few seconds I bask in the glow of my achievement. My sense of self-satisfaction is interrupted by the shattering sound of breaking glass piercing through my soul.

"What was that?" Tim stammers.

"That's your friend out the front." Ross is up and moving, rounding up his colleagues like a Border Collie. "Everybody get down. Under your desks. Now!"

They don't waste any time following his instructions and it makes sense, given the storm and the crashing sound of interior damage. I'm unsure if I should follow their lead or check on Mars, but I decide to take a big picture approach to my desire for self-preservation. With apprehension, I creep up to the corridor at the end of the newsroom. I can hear the crashing flutter of violence and a testosterone-induced scream. I really wish I still had my Nano GEAR. Rust would know exactly what to do.

I poke my head around the corner to inspect the damage. Mars and a man dressed in black are rolling around on the floor, wrestling and taking in turns punching each other. Glass is scattered across the floor like masses of sharp hailstones. Puffs of plasterboard are dissipating in the air as the two agents smash and bash their own path through the hallway.

"Upload... the video!" Mars yells between strikes.

I can't just leave him here. I look around. There's a fire extinguisher beside me, but I don't have a gun to shoot it. That stunt wouldn't work twice in a week.

The man-in-black's hulking inverted pyramid of a frame towers above Mars by at least six inches. Mars uses his momentum to throw him down the hallway into the empty sales department. He pushes an office chair into the recovering agent, trying to solve his problems with a boot stomp. The man-in-black manages to pull him down, jump to his feet and show his brute strength by scooping Mars and tossing him into a desk with one swift motion. His back thumps across the wooden surface, covered in computer accessories and other office stationary.

Reaching for any object within grasp, Mars thrusts a pointed metal paper spike through the man-in-black's hand. He recoils with a gruesome shriek and removes the metal spike from his metacarpals, sending dozens of bloodstained memos and receipts floating to the carpeted floor. Mars takes the opportunity to throw stiff punches at the man-in-black, but they appear to do nothing. The man-in-black catches Mars' final punch and rolls him to the ground, pinning him by sitting across his chest. He raises a clenched fist, grasping the bloody metal spike in the air and I realise he's just half a second away from puncturing my friend's brain.

My friend.

He's attacking my *friend*.

Fuelled with a heated rage and sense of injustice, I throw myself at the man-in-black, tackling the unsuspecting behemoth to the ground. Even caught off-guard, he's able to toss me away effortlessly like an outdated TV guide. But that's OK. I've created the only opening Mars needs to lock a choke hold onto the giant. With a scream worthy of an Olympic javelin gold medallist, Mars applies pressure to his neck. After a few moments, I watch the life vanish from his eyes, right in front of me, in an instant. One second it was there, the next gone.

"Is he... Is he done?"

I can't bring myself to say "dead". Mars nods, out of breath as he admires his handiwork, the way a carpenter relishes a canoe crafted after hundreds of hours in a workshop.

"Don't feel bad for him. That guy was Metric, bro. A real bad egg."

"Metric?"

"Nice work." Mars holds up his hand for a high-five and I timidly oblige.

"You snapped his neck like a farmhouse chicken."

"Yeah."

"And I tackled that dude."

"Yeah, you did!"

"I don't know what came over me. I was just... psyched up."

Mars bends to retrieve his gun from underneath a desk, likely lost in the initial glass-breaking scuffle.

"Pat yourself on the back when that video is up."

"It's on its way."

We return to the newsroom and inform the frightened journalists that they're safe for now, but they might want to hang out in the break room until we're done. They don't argue. One look at Mars in his Spectral Suit and they know he's no one to trifle with.

"Should we call the cops?" Tim asks.

"I've got a guy." Knowing what he does, Ross insists he has a personal contact at the police department who he can call on to help out.

"Don't you dare," Mars tells him. "Not until that video is up and we're out of here."

"You want to just leave us with a corpse over there?"

"You've got cameras outside, right?" I ask rhetorically. "It's all part of the story. Metric tried to stop you from telling it. Now you guys have an angle no one else does."

Laptops and phones in hand, the journos trudge across the newsroom to the kitchenette, down a second corridor opposite the lifeless Metric man-in-black. I feel it's better if I don't learn his name. The sight of living consciousness being sucked out of his body will haunt me enough without any humanising.

With my heart still racing, I take a seat at Tim's computer and shake the mouse. A chill runs along my spine, partly from being drenched in rain, but also due to the levity of what I'm here to accomplish. This is it. Finally.

I name the copied file and drag it to the uploading tool, praying to God that our internet connection survives for the next five or ten minutes.

"There it goes. Now we wait. We did it, man. We did it!"

Mars pumps his fist and starts to congratulate me before a familiar voice booms across the room.

"Hold up!"

Rust emerges from the hallway of death, hobbling like a sickly raccoon. Blood covers his ear and neck. A separate wound has him holding his left arm, dripping red from his sleeve.

"God, are you OK?" Mars says, rushing over to help his father walk.

"I'm fine. I took a couple shots. Is the video up?"

"A couple shots?"

"Sit down," Mars says. "Lemme look at you."

Rust refuses. I can sense true pain in his eyes as he masks his vulnerability, like a brave, old wolf returning to its den after surviving a quiver of hunters' arrows.

"Rust, you're bleeding everywhere," I state as a matter of fact. "Can I at least get you a towel? If not for you, then for the carpet."

"It's fine. I'm not sitting down... And you're not uploading that video."

I try to read his face again, this time observing an emotional anguish that's equal to the pain he's experiencing from the gun-shot wounds.

"Yeah... It's going. What are you saying?" I ask, my voice wavering.

"Just stop the upload. You need to stop it."

"*What* – are you talking about?"

Rust pulls out his gun and points it at my chest.

"I won't ask again. Kill the video, kid."

Chapter 29

Conclusion

Just minutes away from our goal. Mere moments from achieving everything thought impossible. This is where we are right now, having defeated every obstacle. I thought maybe I would screw up and ruin our chances, but I never thought Rust would be the one to keep us from success.

"What the hell are you doing?"

Mars is furious. He can't believe what he's seeing. It's as if every repressed fear about his father has triggered and become a reality at the least opportune time.

"You have to trust me."

"Trust you?" Mars screams. "Like the last time you pulled a gun on me?"

"This is different."

"Different how?"

"Rust, what happened out there?"

Mars curses and whips out his own gun, pointing it at his father with a burning anger.

"Whoa, whoa, guys! Let's chill on this."

"He's gone back to Metric, Maven. Can't you see? He's a total coward."

"That's not it. I just—"

"Shut up! Drop the gun."

"Just let me explain."

"Maybe you should've explained it *before* you pulled the gun on us."

"Mars."

"Don't talk! Just drop it. Can't believe I actually thought—"

"David," Rust calls gently. "It's your *mother*."

At the sound of his given name, a stirred Mars lowers his weapon in disbelief.

"What about her?"

"She's alive."

"She..."

"She's alive and working with Metric."

"No." Mars shakes his head vehemently. "She wouldn't."

"It's true."

"I don't believe you," Mars spits back, raising his gun again.

In the corner of my eye I see the video is almost halfway uploaded. Another few minutes and we're there, but there's no guarantee that we'll get out of here alive. Of all the secret agent duos, I had to get attached to the father and son with more family issues than the Skywalkers.

"She's working against her will, deep undercover. International."

"How do you know this?"

"Please, just trust me," Rust says, far too calmly for someone pointing a firearm at my abdomen. "*Stop* the upload."

"How can I trust you?"

"*You don't have a choice, Agent Mars.*"

A self-assured feminine voice cuts through the tension. As if by teleportation, a woman has appeared in the hallway, leaning casually against the wall.

"Or should that be 'former Agent Mars'?"

"Scarpino," he utters in response.

Metric's boss is dressed neck to toe in luminous black material in a variant of the Spectral Suit. A padded vest and sleeves offer physical protection, along with knee pads and combat-ready boots. Her fingerless gloves grip a handgun in her right hand, though she brandishes it with a lackadaisical informality.

I can't help being surprised that *this* is the head of Metric. It's not that she's a woman. I misjudged that at first, but I'm over it now. Our single conversation was enough to tell she's not someone you want to cross. But even still, she looked far less intimidating and striking on the screen of Rust's tablet device yesterday. In normal situations, I'd be taken back by her imposing figure. But right now, Scarpino could pull off her face to reveal she's a Reptilian alien overlord and it would barely raise an eyebrow.

"Surprised to see me?"

"I'm more surprised that neither of us has killed you yet."

Scarpino feigns offence and wags her finger. I despise any physical gesture that makes me feel as if I'm back in high school.

"That's no way to speak to your commander."

"I'm done with you. The rest of the world will be too, when the truth gets out."

Part of me is screaming for her blood, willing Mars into shooting her right here in the newsroom, but I still have a genuine desire to see this conflict end as peacefully as possible.

"So you know about the New World Order. Is it really that bad? Sure, Metric is a cog in a larger unit. I'm sure you always knew that much. Is there really any difference between your view of the United States government and what you've learnt so far about the Order?"

Rust wears a face of shame as he stands still, gun pointed at me, avoiding eye contact and listening to his son argue with Scarpino.

"I'm not even going to argue with you," Mars scolds. "You've lied to us, to your country. You've killed without compromise and you've done it in the guise of freedom, security and democracy. You're a phony and a traitor, Scarpino. And you'll pay for it all."

"Me?" she scoffs, pointing her gun at her chest. I try to telekinetically will it into misfiring, but I have no such luck. "I'm holding up a mirror, Agent Mars, and you don't like what you see.

You did those things – and you were all too happy about it, might I add. You're one of the best assassins we've ever had."

Mars turns his attention to his father. If there ever was a time to make a connection, this is it.

"Are you serious, right now? Whatever she told you, Rust, you can't believe her."

"She says..." Rust chokes back his words and Scarpino takes over.

"Your only chance of seeing your mother again is to listen to what I have to say."

"Speak fast." Mars doesn't allow his face to react to her announcement. "I'm listening."

The video's reached almost eighty per cent of the upload and I'm just glad no one is talking directly to me.

Scarpino explains everything about Alison's disappearance two years ago, suggesting she's alive and well, but she'll only stay that way with full co-operation from the Fox boys.

"I'm supposed to believe she's OK, just take your word for it?"

Scarpino stares into Mars' eyes from across the room, considering her options.

"Yes." Her confidence is unwavering.

"And why would I do that?"

"Because you don't have any other choice. Your feeble attempt to put an end to Metric today won't make a difference to the work of the Order. Your mother is working hard to co-ordinate field training for Metric's next generation of R&D engineers, medical staff and chemists." Scarpino starts to strut across the room, closing the gap between her and the Foxes. "Alison's in a hostile, foreign land, supported only by Metric's deep pockets and security resources. You want to send that balance into turmoil and risk the consequences?"

"What's the alternative?"

This question worries me. "You're not buying this are you, Mars?"

"This doesn't concern you, Mr Maven. Just do as you're told, stop the upload and let the grown-ups talk in peace."

"I'm not stopping anything," I mumble to myself. I'm surprised Scarpino hasn't shot me herself by now. She's testing the Fox boys' loyalty – clearly arrogant enough to think they'd side with her over me, after all we've been through. Maybe she knows something I don't.

"I have to admit – you've exceeded my expectations. Who would think a Long Island news reporter would make it this far?"

"Thank you?"

"I just thought you'd go along for the ride and be happy to walk away with a heavily redacted news story. Instead... you've become a stain on the curtains that won't come clean."

"Boiling water and salt. Works on *any* stain, guaranteed." Even in mortal danger, I can't help myself.

"Agent Mars." Scarpino holsters her gun, clearly done talking to me. "You can go this alone if you want to. Try to take me out. Try, and fail, to bring down Metric. Never see your mother again. Or we can contain this. Maybe we can have a conversation about some of our tactics and come to an agreeable position on some of your... issues with the way we do things right now."

"But, the Order—"

"The Order is nothing without Metric. As much influence as they have, they're all but defenceless without their muscle. That's us. Come back and together we can shape the New World Order into a force that benefits the citizens of the United States like never before."

Mars' ever-steady hand appears to tremble slightly with the gravity of Scarpino's proposal. Whether he's exhausted or emotionally shaken is unclear.

"Rust. Is this..." He turns back to Scarpino as he realises Rust's mind is made up. "You'd really ask a man to choose between his family and his country?"

"What is a man?" she responds. "Without the things he holds most dear, he's just a miserable pile of flesh, bones and dirty little secrets."

Scarpino's taking her words straight from the *Guide to Villainy 101*. It's unbelievable, really. I hold my tongue and inhale through my nose, confident that Mars, and even Rust, will see through her lies and flimsy facade.

"Sorry, bro."

"For what?" I ask, refusing to accept that any of this is our fault. My eyes bulge like an expanding balloon as Mars rotates his body, turning his pistol's sights from Scarpino to me.

"Mars. C'mon."

I was almost getting used to staring down the barrel of a gun... but two guns? I'm not made for this.

"I said I'm sorry. Just..."

"Bro... *Bro.*" Mars doesn't falter and the two guns remain transfixed on my chest. "*Bro!*"

"I'm sorry. I just... I need this. This is my family. You know I'd do anything—"

"What about *my* family?"

"They'll be fine. Stop the video."

"You think I'm gonna be able to walk out of here and go back to my old life?"

"Shut it down."

"No. I'm not gonna do it."

Mars thrusts his gun towards me in desperation, his bulging eyes threatening to pull the trigger. "Do it! Or I will."

I ignore all logic and follow the stubborn instinct telling me Mars won't go through with this. I shake my head and turn my body to block any foreseeable lunge towards the computer.

"I thought we were bros," I say, stalling for time as I glance down. The video upload has reached one hundred per cent. It's still far too soon to celebrate. I need to click an "approve" button before it will finalise and go live.

Mars doesn't respond with words. He takes another step toward me and shifts his gun from my beating chest to my red face.

This is it. Rust and Mars, side by side against me. I should be sweating blood, but the fear and anxiety I've battled for the past few days has left my body, replaced with a willingness to finish the job. It's not out of bravery – it's pure stubbornness. I simply *cannot* allow all this to be for nothing. I refuse for this to end so close to our goal.

I recognise there's some clear cognitive dissonance telling Mars that his connection to his mother is worth sacrificing everything he's worked for. I don't even know if there's any sense in arguing.

In a brief moment of panic, I allow myself to contemplate the future wife I'll never marry, the children I'll never conceive, the exotic locations I'll never visit, and the Marvel Cinematic Universe crossover movies I'll never experience. Dad will have to see the new *Star Wars* movie alone.

Somehow it still feels worth it.

Yet again, I catch myself playing with the ring hanging over my chest. Against all good sense, I take my eyes off Mars and hold the ring up, studying the German inscription.

"You know what this says, Mars?"

"Can someone shoot this guy already?" Scarpino bemoans.

In an overly dramatic gesture, I yank the chain and tear the ring loose from my neck. The rain has stopped outside, allowing my words to pierce through the tension with ease.

"You speak Pashto, Sudanese, Arabic – how's your German?"

Mars' eyes dart up and down, vacillating between looking at the ring and ignoring it, as he gives the slightest shake of the head.

"It's small writing, so I'll give you a hand. It says 'Peace if possible... but truth at any cost'. I'm not asking you to sacrifice your mother. I'm asking you to think about this and make the right choice. Think about what is under *your control.*"

"I... Maven—"

"Truth. At any cost."

"Enough," Scarpino bellows. "Shoot this clown, already, or move out the way. I've been waiting for a chance to get my hands dirty."

"Dammit, he's right." Mars alternates his pistol back onto Rust. "We need to do this. We need to get this out there. Then we can tackle the next part of this – together."

Rust's mouth stays shut and he shakes his head with a slow,

sorrowful twist. He's a man who's achieved incredible success in his service to this country. But the pain of his personal life, an entire generation of emotional disappointment, haunts him with a shadow of regret. I can only imagine he sees this as a way to make things right.

"I can't risk that," he says. "I let her down. I let you down. But I'll keep working for Metric. You can get out of here. You can save her. *You* can do it. Go now... Don't turn back."

"That doesn't make any *sense*," I say, before reading Mars' reaction telling me to butt out.

"It's not your fault, whatever happened to her." Mars takes a small step towards his father, gun still drawn but clearly meaningless in this conversation. "*Scarpino's* the one to blame, and she's going to keep using Mom to manipulate us until we *stop* them. Lower the gun."

"Agent Mars, you don't know *what the hell* you're talking about! If it weren't for your father, you'd be on the carpet by now." Scarpino has dropped the buddy act and is now gesturing violently at Mars with her own pistol. So, just to recap:

Rust is aiming at me.

Mars is aiming at Rust.

Scarpino is aiming at Mars.

I'm wishing I went to the bathroom when I had the chance.

"This feels like a family matter, Scarpino, maybe you should leave," I suggest.

"You're nothing but gum on my shoe, Maven. I'm sure—"

"Enough!" Rust shouts, cutting her off as his eyes lock with Mars. "I wasn't there for you, son. I'm sorry. But I need to do this for her."

"*Dad,*" Mars pleads, gently pushing his gun into his father's chest. He loosens his grip until the pistol falls to the floor with a thud. "She wouldn't want this. *Please.*"

Oh no. I *cannot* believe Mars has done this again. The first time he dropped his gun, we both got knocked out and dragged to a military prison cell. Did the concussion wipe that from his memory?

"Enough of the family drama," Scarpino shouts. "You want her alive, you co-operate."

"No." Mars defiantly snaps back. "We're not your puppets."

"Fine. I'll end this myself."

Scarpino moves her pistol from Mars to my head, with a penetrating stare. I instinctively duck.

Covering my head, I hold my breath until the echo of two gunshots fades from my buzzing eardrums.

Chapter 30

Resolution

Am I dead?

It would almost be poetic if I survived so long, terrified of the unknown, only to overcome my fear and meet my demise so close to the end.

So am I dead?

No, I'm not dead. I'm very much alive. I can smell Ross's coffee going cold in a porcelain mug nearby.

The dead don't appreciate coffee.

My heavy breathing is all I can hear over the ringing in my ears. But Scarpino's gun had a silencer.

I look up to see Rust towering over the head of Metric, his gun raised with smoke escaping from the barrel.

Scarpino is spread across the floor, coughing up blood and ruining her make-up.

"You... messed up," she splutters. "You don't see it... The Order is everywhere. You're finished."

"That's so cliché," I say to no one in particular, wondering if we should call an ambulance.

"You want to see Alison again – you'll see her real soon."

"Is that a threat?"

"She's dead. And so are you."

I look from Rust to Mars and both of their faces are stoic, refusing to give Scarpino any satisfaction of a reaction to her parting words.

"Anything you're planning..." she says, wheezing between her painful attempts at breathing. "People aren't ready... This is one more inconvenient truth. Sw–swept under the rug."

"Save your breath, Scarpino," Rust says. "You're done."

"Why, Rust? Through it all... you were—"

"I'm done being manipulated. I'm not a vessel for your agenda."

"You're a killing machine, Rust. Always were... That's what this country needed, and you got it done."

Scarpino's words are a flaming farewell arrow, shot into the air with a hopeful prayer of hitting an unlucky target. Nothing she says will save her. She only wants to cast doubt and bring us down, to rain on our divine idea of a solution in this messed up situation. As if he's woken from her spell, Rust sees right through the venom this time.

"Humanity doesn't thrive under manipulation. We're not tools of the government or any other force that aims to control and profit from fear and influence." Rust's tongue appears to be doing more damage than his bullets, as Scarpino sinks deeper into the ground with every self-affirming statement. "We're not here to make a difference just by forcing people to change. That's where dictators and bureaucrats get it wrong. Real progress doesn't come through fear and puppetry. People need to see the evidence before they can accept the world needs to change."

"But that's not what this is about," Mars says, half talking down to Scarpino, and half aiming to complete the thought that Rust started. "We're not here to change the world. We just want to show people enough facts and truth that they have a chance to make that decision for themselves."

I adjust my glasses and hit the button that sends our video to the World Wide Web.

At last.

Trembling silence fills the air as Scarpino stops speaking and I realise my task is complete.

I find the hiding journalists and explain that they're safe.

Ross takes my business card and I ask him not to call for two days. Tim will use *The Mercury's* social media accounts to push our video out to the masses. I'll do the same from my Twitter, then I'll turn off my phone. I'm afraid the flurry of notifications in response will melt its circuits and burn a whole through my pocket.

Mars follows me to the parking lot outside where the sun has broken through the clouds. Our trusty bus is taking up almost half the space, looking like it's seen better days. The side panels are riddled with bullet holes and more scrapes than a *Mad Max* battle car. Our bus driver won't be happy.

The sound of water running through downpipes and flushing into the streets eases me into a pacified state. I close my eyes and imagine I'm standing in a forest. Peaceful and tranquil. Only the lightest wisp of rain is dropping from the sky now, but it's enough to wash the diluted saltiness of sweat across my face and over my top lip. It's bitter, and as much as I try to think differently, so am I.

We won, if there's such a thing as winning in this situation, but it hasn't changed our grim reality. Now there's no goal to chase. There's just a new world waiting for us. I don't know how to process that.

"We survived the storm," Mars tells me, shielding his eyes from the sun that's showing up half an hour after the party ended. I'm not sure if he's referring to the tornadofest or our battle against evil, but we have indeed survived. I nod and look up to the parting clouds.

"We did."

I can't imagine what he's feeling right now. We don't know whether Scarpino was lying about his mother being alive or lying about her being dead. That can't be easy. But if anyone can figure it out, it's Rust and Mars.

As we shuffle away at a snail's pace, the muffled sound of a single mercy gunshot echoes across the neighbourhood and forces my eyes shut again. I close them so tight, clenching my fists and just hoping, praying that I'll wake up from this nightmare. There's nothing I can do to unlearn what I know.

We're safe today. But for how long?

I don't even care why Rust decided he had to put Scarpino out of her misery. It's harsh and it's vindictive, but I feel good about it. And then I feel guilty for admitting it to myself. It weighs on me and I think it will for some time. I don't know. I'm still new to this whole life-changing violent trauma thing.

Mars' hand on my shoulder shakes me out of my thought process, startling me so much that he apologises.

"No, it's fine. I'm just a bit jumpy."

"I would be too," he nods. "That was intense. Even for me, bro. I got so caught up in everything. I'm sorry, you know? I caved in. I was ready to throw it all away for a chance to find my mom again. In that moment, it just seemed pointless. But you were strong. You're a hero, bro."

Mars smiles and I recite something Rust told me in Hell's Kitchen only a few days ago.

"I've heard it said there are no heroes. Just old dogs with pockets full of stories that no one would believe."

Mars smirks as if he's heard this line before, but remains silent, staring into the heavens.

"I feel like we know too much. But then again, everybody will soon."

"That's the way it should be," Mars says. "That's why we're here."

"I'm not disagreeing. I just feel regret that it's become this way. I wonder if the NWO would've become so powerful if people cared enough to pay attention."

"What do you mean? You can't blame yourself for that. It's a bunch of evil, greedy people doing evil and greedy things. Even Rust didn't see it... and he was right in the middle. For decades."

"You're right. That's fair. I'm just feeling nostalgic for a time before apathy was the way to be. It feels like nothing short of a global tragedy could bring the world together."

"Well, maybe there's another positive that'll come out of this," Mars laughs softly, despite feeling as sombre as I do.

"When my parents were kids they watched in awe as man landed on the moon. No one knew what would happen. Heck – no one knew if it was even possible. But we haven't been to the moon for forty-five years. What have we accomplished as a society in the past decade? Faster internet? Self-driving cars? We put cameras and rovers on another planet, but people hardly even blinked. It was just another news story on their Facebook feed. Disaster is the bread that... nourishes the masses."

"I can't argue. Terrorist attacks, earthquakes, school shootings... Ebola virus. It's like—"

"The bedtime stories of the millennials."

"Yeah, pretty much. The normies won't know what hit 'em."

Rust emerges from the door behind us, limping and holding his chest.

"Oh, dang." I'd totally forgotten that he'd taken a couple of bullets before he turned up. He insists he's capable of patching himself up. I'm in no place to disagree, but I do have to ask what we missed after we left the bus.

"We went for a bit of a ride," Rust says, delivering the understatement of the day.

"A bit of a *ride*? Splash Mountain is a ride," I say. "Looks like you took a fleet of Metric agents to the Smackdown Hotel."

"Hm. That's funny, kid. I'd laugh... but I think my ribs might shatter into a thousand pieces and puncture my lungs."

"Hey. Rust. That was an actual, not just sarcastic, legitimate joke. Am I rubbing off on you?"

"For Pete's sake," he says, reaching into a pocket for a cigar, careful not to push his body too far. He lights up. This time it is undoubtedly a victory cigar. "Maybe leave that part out of your story."

"My story. I forgot about that. Would you believe I'm actually looking forward to sitting down at a keyboard and figuring all of this out? I think it'll be very cathartic."

"I would absolutely believe that," Mars says, rotating his stiff

shoulder one hundred and eighty degrees, backwards then for-
wards. "But before any of that we still need to clear out of here
and I don't like the look of that bus. We need a vehicle or we need
to lay low."

"Do you think Taco Bell would be open?"

"Look around, bro. I don't think anything is open."

Rust hobbles from the stoop into the parking lot and exhales
a long satisfied breath of dirty cigar smoke. It forms a constant
stream, dissipating like a mist into the spitting rain. I didn't realise
that much smoke could physically occupy one man's mouth and
throat.

"I need to get going," he says.

"You mean 'we'?"

"Metric HQ. You're not coming."

Mars doesn't like this at all. He insists on either joining to
help or making his father wait a few days until his wounds have
healed. Rust swings his head back and forth in strong objection.

"That place is going to be in shambles. It's not long before the
feds show up and seize everything, either try to wipe their hands
of it or turn it into a witch hunt. I need to find some answers
before that."

"What are we supposed to do?" For the first time since we've
met, Mars is requesting some fatherly advice. When you chase
something for so long, it can be daunting to reach the destination
and have no clear goal to follow. Bringing down the Order from
here on isn't something a couple of Metric agents can accomplish.
The Foxes will have to work with government officials, FBI and
CIA field agents they can trust, to eradicate the influence of the
NWO for good. There's certainly piling evidence to prove their
story, but going about that task is now a whole new ball game.
There will no doubt be critics and detractors, threats of lawsuits
from the deep-pocketed companies and groups cited in our video.
It would be safer to leave the country until the smoke clears. But
the Fox boys aren't necessarily enticed by safer options.

Rust ponders Mars' question, cigar between his teeth and
arms folded. It's not often he has a chance to give his son advice.

"If I were young, I'd run without stopping."

"You would?"

"Yeah. Get away from all this. Seek a normal life."

"If I were old, I'd do the same thing. Cherish my days. But neither of us are going to do that, are we?"

Rust grunts in realisation that his son is wired exactly the same way. There's not a hope of either of them settling down to a life of simplicity.

"Seriously. You guys have nothing to prove," I say, looking each of them in the eye. I have their attention. "After all this, you don't owe anyone a single thing."

"There's too much left to do. This is just the start." Rust shakes his head yet again. "I need to go."

"Stick with me and we'll do it together. The Fox boys. We'll find Mom, we'll save her. If she's out there, if it's true."

"No."

Mars' face sinks and he turns away, feeling the frustrated sting of another rejection from his father. Rust realises exactly how it looks and raises his unwounded arm to comfort Mars. With his hand only inches away from his son's shoulder, he hesitates, then pulls it back. He's not ready to show that level of affection, or maybe he doesn't believe it's what Mars needs right now.

"It's... something I need to do alone. It's not you, trust me. There's people I need to chase down. David – are you hearing me?"

Mars turns, biting his bottom lip, but he remains silent.

"What we've done today is huge, son. I don't know if it was just Scarpino's ploy to get us to turn on each other. But if she's really alive... if your mother is out there, it's not as easy as finding her and saving her. I need to focus everything on that. The NWO is your fight. You and Maven. You can help where the system fails. Someone needs to tidy this up and be the face of the movement."

Rolling his eyes, Mars swears under his breath and flashes an uneasy smile, shielding his sadness and his desire to finally spend time with his father – even if it is in tactical espionage. He knows Rust is right. It won't look good if they both disappear right after dropping this truth bomb. I'd assumed my role would be more or less over after this, aside from documenting the process, but I'm starting to realise I'll have to testify about what I've learnt and overheard this week from Scarpino, Mars, Rust, Saluki – even Queen and Moriarty.

It's surprising how much I know just from observing, but the biggest surprise is that I'm not afraid anymore. It's daunting. It's unsettling. But I'm not afraid. To be vindicated in such spectacular fashion is a huge confidence boost. The odds were always against us, but I had the strong belief that this was where I was meant to be and this is what I was made to do – regardless of whether I felt prepared or ready. I remember hearing as a teenager that God doesn't call on the equipped – he equips the called. I think I always believed that, but now I understand it.

Mars claps his hands together, driving the conversation into the next stage.

"I guess this is it, then."

Rust grimaces and nods, then points his cigar towards the bus. "I can give you a ride to the airport. I know a guy who'll fly down in a jiffy and get you across any border."

"That would've been good information to have – *two hours ago*," I howl, feigning crazed anger.

"I just remembered. Sorry, kid. But hey. You got a chance to be brave. That was impressive. And sorry, about the whole threatening you with a gun thing. Not my best moment."

"Would you believe I'm getting used to it?"

We laugh together, like we never have before. Not at each other, but with each other. It feels good – really good. It's a moment I'll hold onto as one that proves joy is never more than a second away, even in times of confusion and mourning. Maybe I'll call Dad later and tell him to pre-order those tickets to *Star Wars*.

And we *will* find a Taco Bell tonight, whether it's here or somewhere on foreign soil. Taco Bell *is* happening. I'm sure they have Taco Bell in Panama.

Despite everything we've endured, at least for today, I have to let myself enjoy the fact that I survived. We won. Today is a day for the good guys. We really have a lot to celebrate, so when that divine moment arrives, I'll savour this victory as I bite into a delicious, mouth-watering beef and rice burrito with beans. That melted nacho cheese, fiery hot chilli sauce, that tasty guacamole. All washed down with a Coke. Not a Diet Coke. A real Coke.

In that moment, peace will reign. For five to ten minutes, nothing else in the world will matter. It'll be the best meal I've ever tasted.

www.ingramcontent.com/pod-product-compliance
Lightning Source LLC
Chambersburg PA
CBHW020400110726
47899CB00006B/1790